PRAISE FOR THE NOVELS OF
NANCY GEARY

"Fascinating . . . a taut plot, complex characters, and smooth dialogue that make for a great read."
—Linda Fairstein

"Strong scenic detail and a winning heroine."
—*Kirkus Reviews*

"Highly recommended."
—TheRomanceReadersConnection.com

"Few writers succeed in describing the world of the American aristocracy or how they truly live. But Nancy Geary has an authentic voice. She knows this world."
—Olivia Goldsmith

"Geary is a wonderfully mordant observer of the rich gone awry. Her books are sharp and stylishly written."
—Sally Bissell

"Geary has a refined talent for exposing the dark edges of all too human characters and the ripple of violence in their lives."
—Lynn Hightower

Also by Nancy Geary:

Misfortune
Redemption
Being Mrs. Alcott

REGRETS ONLY

NANCY GEARY

WARNER BOOKS

NEW YORK   BOSTON

Copyright © 2004 by Nancy Whitman Geary
Excerpt from *Being Mrs. Alcott* copyright © 2004 by Nancy Whitman Geary
All rights reserved. No part of this book may be reproduced in any form or by any electronic or mechanical means, including information storage and retrieval systems, without permission in writing from the publisher, except by a reviewer who may quote brief passages in a review.

Cover design and photograph by Shasti O'Leary Soudant

Warner Books

Time Warner Book Group
1271 Avenue of the Americas, New York, NY 10020
Visit our Web site at www.twbookmark.com

Printed in the United States of America

First Warner Books Printing: July 2004
First Paperback Printing: June 2005

10 9 8 7 6 5 4 3 2 1

In loving memory of John W. Geary, II, and
G. Willing Pepper

Acknowledgments

Jane Pepper made this book possible. She shared her endless knowledge of Philadelphia. For her help, energy, encouragement, and hospitality I am deeply in her debt. I thank Lieutenant Joseph Maum of the Philadelphia Police Department Homicide Unit for generously giving of his time and expertise. He made Lucy's world come alive. I am forever grateful for his patience and guidance.

I thank Jamie Raab and everyone at Warner Books for their commitment to my novel. Many thanks to Jamie and to Frances Jalet-Miller for all their editorial insights, thoughtful questions, and hard work on shaping and reshaping this manuscript. Thank you to Leni Grossman for her careful copyedits, and to Ben Greenberg for his help on every detail. As always, thanks to Tina Andreadis and Miriam Parker for all their publicity efforts on my behalf.

Thank you to Pamela Nelson and Levy Home Entertainment for believing in my work.

I thank Jennifer Cayea, Abigail Koons, Katherine Flynn, and Katherine Merrill, for their hard work, dedication, and kindness. Thanks to everyone at Nicholas Ellison, Inc., and Sanford J. Greenburger for their patience and commitment. Words cannot adequately express my appreciation to Nick Ellison, the one-man rescue unit, for all that he does and all that he is.

I am deeply grateful to my dear friends, who bolster my spirits, provide much-needed advice, and show me again and again the true meaning of loyalty. I thank Missy Smith, Amy Kellogg, and Aliki Nichogiannopoulou for listening, caring, celebrating and commiserating. For help and much-needed words of support, especially while I have been on the road, thanks to Virginia Nivola, Jane Broce, Juliana Hallowell, and Sally Witty.

For including me in her inspired community, providing me with a spiritual anchor, and offering me her invaluable guidance, I thank The Reverend Lynn Harrington. Thanks to Anne Testa for her enthusiasm and encouragement, and Susan and Craig Hupper for their friendship and thoughtfulness. I am blessed to be part of St. John's Parish.

Finally, I am forever indebted to my extraordinary family. I thank Natalie Geary for showing me what it is to have true courage and for her constant help, love, and pediatric services. I thank my mother, Diana Michener, for her advice and understanding, and I thank her and Jim Dine for their love, encouragement, and inspiration. I thank Daphne Geary, Ted Geary, Jack and Dolly Geary, and Wing and Evan Pepper for all their support. And I thank Harris Walker for making life meaningful. That I am his mother is my greatest joy.

REGRETS ONLY

1

Friday, December 20th
7:35 p.m.

*T*he muddy slush and melted snow on the hardwood floor appeared to bother no one. Men and women pressed elbow-to-elbow by the bar and shared seats at the twenty or so mismatched iron tables. Oversize pewter hooks that hung at various spots around the room couldn't accommodate the population of overcoats and many lay crumpled in a heap in the corner. The air was filled with noise from dozens of lively conversations and the smell of beer, smoke, and wet wool. Body warmth and the heat from several loud radiators had fogged the windows, obscuring any view onto Rittenhouse Square. It was Friday and the weekend at The Arch was well under way.

From where Lucy sat she could watch Sapphire behind the bar, pouring, mixing, stirring, embellishing, and rinsing, all the while keeping up the lively banter for which she was famous. Her multiringed fingers seemed to dance between glasses, bottles, lemon wedges, and maraschino cherries as she created colorful potions to inebriate her fans. Sapphire specials, the ingredients mixed so fast that no one could tell what exactly had been included. Tonight she'd dyed her hair bright orange and wore colored contact lenses that made her eyes appear emerald green. Every few moments she'd turn away from her audience and ring up a sale at the old register. Although the crowd's conversation muffled the sound, Lucy could imagine the "ka-ching" as the drawer popped open to receive cash. Sapphire placed the change directly into each patron's hand, perhaps hoping the physical contact would bring a larger tip.

"How'd you ever end up at this place?" Jack Harper asked, taking a sip of his draft beer.

At the sound of his voice, Lucy turned her attention to her companion, who looked off balance as he perched awkwardly on a garden chair. He had to be the oldest person in the room; the gray at his temples highlighted his forty-eight years. Medium height and medium build, he'd recently started to complain about his growing waistline. "Too much bloody paperwork," he'd commented to her just the day before. "Not like when I started around here, when the Captain realized we were better off out on the street. No crime gets solved from behind a desk, but the bureaucrats in Internal seem to have forgotten that fact. We'll all end up fat, or at least those of us who aren't already." Although he'd removed his tie before they left the precinct, his white shirt and camel overcoat stood out in the predominantly black-clad crowd.

Lucy now followed his gaze to an oval table opposite the bar where a group of seven pale, thin men and women huddled together smoking and drinking a blue concoction out of martini glasses. One man had a series of small gold hoops piercing his eyebrow. A woman wore a top that more closely resembled a bra. One or another in the group periodically looked up at the series of charcoal drawings that hung on the walls, pointed at something with considerable animation, and then returned to the conversation.

"You fooled me, Detective O'Malley," Jack continued. "Here you are mingling with creatures who retreat to their coffins at daylight, and I had you pegged for the paper-shamrock-on-the-wall-and-glass-of-Guinness-dark type, being a direct descendant of a Boston police commissioner after all."

Lucy laughed. "My forebears, esteemed though I'm sure they were, were more likely models for jolly old Michael, the cop who stops traffic for the baby ducks crossing Beacon Street," she replied, remembering the classic children's book *Make Way for Ducklings*. "But I've spent my fair share of hours in pubs, if that's your question. Nothing like the smell of stout on your clothes and wood shavings on your shoes in the morning."

"You can take the girl out of Ireland but you can't take the Irish out of the girl."

"Something like that."

They both laughed. Despite their age difference of nearly two decades, Lucy had the sneaking suspicion that this partnership would work. She liked Jack's easy demeanor.

"Seriously, though, how did you find this place? You don't live around here, do you?"

"Maybe I shouldn't admit it but I'm not too far away—an apartment above the health food store on the corner of Walnut. I've thought about moving out to join the rest of you in Torresdale or Fox Chase, but the rent here is okay." She took a sip of her drink. "I guess that makes me the only homicide detective to live in Center City."

"Can't beat the convenience, though," he said. "Although I'm not sure about your local hangout." He looked around the room with obvious skepticism.

"This place is a recent discovery even though I'd passed it a million times. This fall there was a sign in the window for a reading—some author with a book on being in a harem. The sign caught my eye."

"Harem?"

"She was a Moroccan woman who shared her husband with eight or nine other wives. He fathered children with all of them, and the women jointly raised the whole brood. Anyway, I thought it sounded interesting—intriguing may be a better word—and I came back to hear her speak. She talked about the difficulties of mothering the children who weren't her own, but who were the children of the man she loved. The jealousies, the rivalries, she was very candid about her emotions. Since then you might call me a regular here, especially on nights when the literary stuff happens because you never know what you're going to learn. Then there are also art openings," she said, gesturing to the drawings on the wall. "They're usually on Thursdays, so tonight must be something special. The displays change every week or so. I think there's some connection to the Creative Artists Network, but I'm not positive. Anyway, the place just feels cozy to me."

Jack raised his eyebrows. "Cozy as a cattle car."

"It's not usually this crowded." She glanced around and shrugged. "Maybe the artist has a lot of friends."

"With art like this, he'll need them," Jack said as he passed her a red paper flyer. *"The Twelve Faces of Suicide": Self-portraits by Foster Herbert. For a complete price list, please inquire at the bar.*

Lucy shuddered involuntarily. The series of sad, charcoal faces that stared out with empty gazes was haunting. She didn't need to read the title of the collection to know that the artist had to suffer from interior demons, that he was—like so many—a young man in pain. Just as Aidan, her brother, had been.

Although nearly ten years had passed, she could still recall the last conversation they'd had. "Ever heard of Dubuffet, the French painter?" he'd asked her. She had. "I read this interview where he explained that he was able to journey into madness and return. His art, his visions, grew out of those trips. And I keep thinking to myself, How did he do it? How did he return? I'm there in that horrible place but I can't get back." Those fateful words still echoed in her mind.

"I take it you won't be purchasing a painting for your living room." Jack's voice interrupted her musing.

She wiped her eyes quickly and diverted her gaze, hoping he wouldn't notice the welled tears. If he did, he was polite enough not to comment. Instead he rested his hand on her forearm. "On a brighter note," he said, raising his glass to clink with hers, "here's to you. Congratulations on making it through your first week, Detective."

Lucy smiled in appreciation and gulped her beer, feeling the cold, frothy liquid soothe her throat. She'd survived her first five days of life in the Homicide Unit of the Philadelphia Police Department. After two years in the Narcotics Bureau, she'd made Detective and then spent the next three in the South Division before being promoted, if a unit where the victims never survived could be called that. Partnered with the most experienced detective on the force, she'd managed to crack her first case—a contract hit on the owner of a gaming operation—within twenty-four hours of the crime. Jack had been patient and careful in his explanations; in return, he'd seemed mildly amused by her enthusiasm.

Although in her years at the police department she rarely fraternized with her colleagues and passed on the drunken festivities held annually at the Ukrainian-American Club, she'd agreed to her new partner's suggestion that they have a drink to celebrate the quick resolution of her first "job," as each murder investigation was called. She'd heard that unlike past partners, he was happily married and the proud father of two teenage boys; a beer after work was simply a way to start off on a friendly footing. Plus he'd agreed to let her pick the bar and been perfectly content to wander beyond the two watering holes within shooting distance of the Roundhouse, as the police headquarters located on Eighth and Race Streets was called.

"That must be the painter," Jack said, nodding in the direction of the door. "Sad part is he looks just like his pictures."

Through the crowd, Lucy could see a tall boy wearing a navy blue T-shirt that hung loose around his thin frame and blue jeans speckled with paint. His face was pallid and drawn; dark circles surrounded his black eyes. Leaning against the wall, he cast a vacant stare around the room. His face could easily have been the thirteenth portrait.

As she watched, another man with thick, curly brown hair and wire-rimmed round glasses approached the boy, said something, laughed, then swung his arm around the boy's neck, pulled him close, and kissed the top of his head. The boy spoke; the man smiled a flash of white teeth and knocked his knuckles quickly but gently on the boy's skull. The boy grabbed at the man's baggy oxford shirt, the two stumbled backward slightly, and the man tickled his side, making the boy smile, too. The man looked familiar—perhaps she'd seen him here before— and the exchange had a fraternal sweetness to it, a playfulness that made her miss Aidan even more. How many times had she roughhoused with her Irish twin? He was bigger and stronger by far; she could still feel his grip on her wrists as he inevitably managed to pin her to the floor and tickle her until she begged for mercy.

Jack picked up the flyer and appeared to reread it. "All the peer pressure and drugs, it's gotten really hard for kids. I feel sorry for this guy's parents. I've always wondered what I'd do if one of my sons had mental troubles. Probably wouldn't handle it too well," he said, seemingly to himself. He finished his beer and licked the foam from his top lip.

"Want another?" she asked. "My treat."

He glanced at his watch. "No thanks. Sarah's waiting dinner for me." He stood up, reached into his wallet, and dropped a ten-dollar bill on the table. "Maybe we'll get you out to the house one of these nights. Beers are cheaper, and my boys would love to meet a cop with great legs." He winked. "Have a good weekend, O'Malley."

"Yeah. You too. See you Monday."

Lucy watched him weave his way through the crowd and disappear out the front door just as a couple in fur Cossack hats pushed their way inside. She sighed and leaned back in her chair. Her glass was empty but there was no particular reason to leave. She'd canceled her date several days before. Who wanted to spend another evening in forced getting-to-know-each-other conversation filled with painful pauses and muscle-aching smiles? She preferred to get home, change into flannel pajamas, put a log in the wood-burning stove that heated her one-bedroom apartment, and read with her pet rabbit, Cyclops, asleep in her lap. But whether her routine began at seven or eight or nine hardly mattered. The only thing affected by delay would be the number of chapters she could get through before fatigue hit.

There were moments, especially on winter nights such as this, when she missed the Somerville community she'd left behind in Massachusetts when she'd decided to stay in Philadelphia after graduation. While she was growing up in the house in which her father had been born, there was never a moment without company—a relative, a friend, or a neighbor passing by for a few minutes of socializing, which included the exchange of gossip for a cup of tea and a piece of cake. Even when she'd first started dating, there was little awkwardness with two brothers around to help break the ice, and few moments alone given the constant stream of teenagers both male and female parading through the house. The blessing before supper in which her father thanked the Lord for all the goodness He had bestowed on the O'Malley family was the only quiet minute in the day that Lucy could remember. With that upbringing, she'd thrived in a college dormitory; unlike some of her peers, she was never bothered by the lack of privacy. It had taken her years to realize that she often preferred to be alone, to do things on her own rather than suffer through idle chatter or boring conversation. Still she wondered whether the right person might change her relatively recent, self-imposed isolation.

She grabbed her coat, moved to the bar, and rested her elbows on the mahogany counter.

"Hey there," Sapphire said in a voice that was low and breathy. "What can I get you?"

"Just a beer. Draft, please." Next to her, a woman got up from her stool and she quickly slid onto it.

Sapphire placed a glass in front of her with a bit of foam making its way slowly down the side. "You should gamble tonight lady 'cause you must be lucky. A place to rest one's ass has been virtually impossible to find."

"I'll buy a lottery ticket on the way home."

"Pick one up for me, too," Sapphire said, moving on to serve the next customer.

The beer was cool but not chilled and Lucy pushed it aside. Obviously consumption was up this evening and the new batch hadn't had ample refrigeration. She inhaled deeply, cherishing the secondary smoke as yet another reminder of Aidan in a night that seemed filled with his memory. The Christmas season highlighted his absence.

"May I introduce myself?"

His voice had the resonance of a radio announcer. She

turned to see the curly-haired man with glasses whom she'd noticed earlier with the artist. He had a rectangular face, deep blue eyes, and prominent cheekbones. "Archer. I'm Archer Haverill," he said, extending a hand.

She shook it as she introduced herself. His palm was large and warm, and her small fingers seemed to disappear in its grasp.

"My pleasure." He bowed his head slightly. "I won't ask if you come here often since I know you do. I've seen you at several of the readings recently."

She nodded. "I enjoy them."

"I'm glad. Truly. Because I constantly wonder when I'm reading work and picking someone to come speak whether anyone who listens will share my excitement. It's so hard to gauge reactions."

"You choose?"

He gave her a quizzical look and then commented, "This is my bar. Archer. The Arch. Get it?"

Lucy felt herself blush. "Sorry. I didn't put two and two together."

"So I guess that means even though I'm here virtually every night, I haven't made much of an impression." He clasped his hands together. "Maybe I should dye my hair, too. I obviously need a gimmick."

"Or work the bar. That helps," she said, wondering whether she should confess that he did look familiar or that she'd been watching him earlier. No, she decided it wasn't worth mentioning. She couldn't tell whether his humility was entirely genuine, and she didn't feel like fanning the fire of male arrogance if it wasn't. But there was something besides his good looks, something in his manner that was appealing, and she didn't want the conversation to end. "Do you pick the art, too?" she asked.

"Yeah. What do you think of these self-portraits?"

"Painful. They'll stay with me," she responded. "I'm not much of an art critic but I think they're good. It's amazing what someone can do with a piece of charcoal."

"He'd sent me slides but they didn't do it justice. My impression changed completely when he brought the drawings in. He's a great kid with a lot of talent though I wonder about him. The title was his idea. Of course I'd already agreed to hang the show before I realized I might have problems because he's underage—only sixteen if you can believe it—but he's practically lived here the last couple of days and so far not had a drop of alcohol. I think I'm safe."

"I won't report you."

Archer smiled. "I appreciate that." He paused, looked at her as if to gauge her reaction, and then asked in a voice that actually sounded timid, "Can I offer you a drink?"

Lucy was about to respond when she felt a vibration in her pocket. Her beeper. She must have forgotten to turn it off when she'd left the precinct. Her shift had ended, but her squad was short-staffed around the holidays. Lieutenant Sage must have decided to call back some of his off-duty detectives. Although she wished she could ignore it, she pulled the BlackBerry from her pocket and checked the text file. *Nineteen-year-old black male. Multiple stab wounds. Gang related? DOA at Thomas Jefferson Hospital.*

"I'm sorry. I can't. Perhaps another time," she added before she could stop herself. *Lucy O'Malley*, she heard her mother chastise. *How dare you be suggestive?* She could still envision Mrs. O'Malley with a checkered apron tied tight around her waist, shaking a finger in her face. *A proper girl waits for a proper invitation.* Even at a ninth-grade Sadie Hawkins, her mother had drilled it into her brain that she couldn't be the one to ask a boy to dance.

"A patient calls?" Archer said.

"No. I'm not a doctor."

"What do you do?" He sounded disappointed.

"I'm a cop. Homicide Unit." Her new assignment sounded strange. The novelty was still hard to believe.

"You?" He laughed. "Now that's a first. With looks like yours, why in the world would you ever do that?"

"What's that supposed to mean?" She felt a surge of rage. How many times had she heard derogatory comments about being a police officer? The litany of insults—the suggestion that she was a public servant punching the clock as she waited for a retirement pension, the constant innuendos of corruption, as if she couldn't own a cashmere sweater on a law enforcement salary, the snide remarks that she simply was trying to meet some hunk for a husband—made her see red. Her thighs didn't rub together from too many doughnuts; her only criminal activity was jaywalking; and she logged longer, more intense hours than almost everyone she'd ever met. That she came from a legacy of honest, good cops was a source of tremendous pride. What did this yuppie bar owner know anyway?

"You just . . . you don't strike me . . ." Archer stammered. He eyed her up and down. "You just don't look like the type."

She was about to explain that being five-three and ninety-nine pounds had nothing to do with her ability to investigate and apprehend drug dealers, rapists, and now killers, but stopped. Any explanation sounded defensive, something she certainly was not. "Apparently for the same reason a person like you is drawn to the hospitality industry," she said instead, relieved that she hadn't confessed to anything remotely suggestive of attraction. "Going against character."

With that she hopped off the stool, shoved the Black-Berry back in her pocket, and buttoned her overcoat. As she walked away, she thought she heard him call out, "There's a wonderful poet coming Tuesday night. Eight o'clock. Maybe you'd take the drink then."

But she wasn't really listening.

2

Saturday, January 11th
9:17 p.m.

*F*oster hated the putrid smell of his own sweat. It was one thing to perspire from physical performance—he'd been on the lacrosse team and still occasionally lifted weights. There was a cleansing sensation to that, a purging by osmosis. But he felt entirely different tonight as he sat behind the barn. Despite the freezing wind, his shirt stuck to the clammy skin of his underarms and back. Beads of moisture congregated on his forehead, his upper lip, and behind his knees. Even his toes slipped in his Adidas sneakers. Anxiety and fear made his synapses fire too rapidly, leaving him drenched in sweat. He needed to peel off his damp flesh and escape, abandoning the body that tortured him and the soul that tormented him. Fortunately that was exactly what he was about to do.

He adjusted his position and felt a jagged rock dig into his coccyx, causing a shooting pain up his spine. Quick shallow breaths helped dissipate his agony, but he still felt a throbbing sensation. He crossed his legs in front of him and leaned back against the red-painted building.

Inside he could hear the horses, Fern and Jumpstart, as they snorted, stomped, and rearranged themselves in their stalls, settling down for the night. The dressage horse was black with white socks; the other—a chestnut brown—had retired years ago but remained a family pet. They were majestic, loyal animals that had eaten carrots from his hand for as long as he could remember. Although never an equestrian himself, he'd always liked the feeling of their soft lips flapping against his extended palm. He hoped his shot wouldn't startle them.

He stared up at the waning crescent moon, illuminating a scattering of cirrus clouds in the dark sky. Aside from the stir of the horses, and the rustle of small animals, the night was still. He ran his fingers along the chamber of the .38 caliber gun, then cupped its steel snub nose in one palm while he gripped the wooden handle in the other. He'd gone to great lengths to procure this $500 weapon for which he'd paid more than a thousand. It had taken considerable coaxing and a substantial bribe, but eventually the bearded shop owner in his Orvis fishing vest had acquiesced, overlooking the birth date on his license and falsifying the age on the permit application. For an envelope of cash, he'd gone from sixteen to twenty-six with the flick of a ballpoint pen. So much for gun control in the commonwealth of Pennsylvania.

He squeezed the trigger, hearing nothing but a loud snap in the empty chamber. He'd yet to load his bullet of choice, the 158-grain lead semiwadcutter, which, according to the article he'd read, was designed to ensure maximum penetration. Given the location of his shot, he could sacrifice expansion. He shivered and then squeezed again. Snap.

Closing his eyes, he listened to the sound of his breathing and felt his heart pounding in his chest. For the first time he wondered who would find him. At least it wouldn't be Avery, his twin sister. Protecting her was the only thing that mattered to him, but he needn't worry. She'd returned to boarding school the day before. Her Christmas break was over and he and his mother had driven her back to Garrison Forest last Sunday in time to make the 7:00 P.M. check-in.

So the discovery of his body would undoubtedly be made by one of his parents, if he could call them that, and that might not happen until the light of morning. They'd left shortly before seven for a dinner party in the neighboring town of Villanova. His mother had worn a gray gabardine pantsuit and a fur jacket, a Christmas gift from her husband. From his bedroom window, he'd watched his father open the passenger-side door for her, lighting the leather interior of the Lexus. Before settling in her seat and affixing her seat belt, she pulled down the visor to check herself in the mirror and apply just a touch more Garnet Shimmer to her thin lips. Foster had stared at the car lights until the dark green sedan disappeared around the bend in the long driveway.

By now they would be embroiled in the festivities at the home of Bonnie and Hugh Pepper, their close friends. Although he'd never been to one of what his mother termed their "casual" dinners, he imagined that Mrs. Pepper didn't really know the meaning of that word. Just look at the Christmas party she'd thrown less than a month before for the best that Main Line society had to offer and their teenage offspring. The big stone house had bowed wreaths hanging in every lighted window. An enormous blue spruce adorned with electric candles and Victorian ornaments filled the entryway. His family—yes, he could say that now, now that the relationship was about to end—had wandered through room after welcoming room, engaging in snippets of jovial conversation, admiring the many roaring fireplaces, eating scallops wrapped in bacon and celery with foie gras. In front of the ebony Steinway his mother had stood arm in arm with his father singing Christmas carols. *Oh come, oh come, Emmanuel, and ransom captive Israel.* Standing back from the crowd, Avery had put her arm around his shoulder. "It's Christmas. I'm home for three whole weeks. Your opening is next week. Can't you be happy?"

"Can't you?" he'd asked instead of answering.

"My problems are nothing compared to yours." She'd smiled, playfully tousled his hair, and then returned to the song just in time for the "Rejoice" chorus.

The Peppers' dinner party tonight was certain to be seated, to go late into the evening, and to include several different bottles of wine, plus champagne with dessert. Nonetheless, when his parents returned home, his father would insist on a nightcap. They wouldn't think to check his room, wouldn't realize he wasn't asleep in bed or watching television in the den. They'd wake up the next morning, stumble into the kitchen for coffee and buttered toast, and begin their search only when he didn't appear dressed and ready for church by ten o'clock.

He reached into his pocket and removed the bullets.

Foster fingered the metal casings, imagining the potential damage. The bullets were cool in his hand, and he rolled them over one another as if they were lucky dice. His big gamble would be a success.

It seemed as though he'd planned for this moment his entire life. Each morning that he'd spent with the covers drawn over his head and his mind thick with images of long steel blades slicing his face or ripping the flesh of his belly, each day that he could barely concentrate, each afternoon spent paralyzed in his room wondering if he could get his body to cooperate enough to stumble to the bathroom, each evening he'd thrashed on his mattress knowing it was still hours before the gift of sleep might be his, had led inexorably to now. His fifty-minute, three-times-per-week sessions with Dr. Ellery made matters worse. And the antidepressants prescribed for him made life worse still. Tricyclic antidepressants, selective serotonin reuptake inhibitors, norepinephrine reuptake blockers, benzodiazepines—he'd tried everything in varying dosages and combinations only to add dry mouth, jitteriness, and impotence to the list of tortures that plagued him. His parents had spent thousands of dollars on unreimbursable experiments that left him feeling more freakish and isolated than he had before. What sixteen-year-old American male didn't at least get the joy, the release, of masturbating?

The thought made him laugh again, louder this time. But he didn't have to worry. Aside from the housekeeper, he was alone on more than six acres of countryside. And she was no doubt watching television, still wishing Jay Leno were Johnny Carson. That and a blue moon were at least some things to hope for.

He loaded three bullets and stared at the open chamber now half full. A three-eyed Titan, who today would forge the thunderbolt for him instead of Zeus, looked back at him. He spun the chamber and clicked it shut. He might fail once, but three bullets had to be enough.

"Do you remember when you first began to experience depression?" He'd been asked that question so many times he'd lost track. He'd never had an answer. There wasn't a time, a life, before or without.

"Is there any activity that gives you any respite? Anything that can even distract you?" Dr. Ellery had asked during his initial interview. He'd thought lacrosse might save him, but he'd had to quit the team after only three weeks. He was too unreliable; he missed games altogether or suited up but found himself unable to play, to follow the rules, even to recognize his teammates. That left only painting. And he'd demonstrated his lack of success in that field. His only show came down at the end of December. The one sale—no doubt a pity purchase by the affluent bar owner—generated $400, hardly enough to cover the framing costs.

He gripped the .38 in his right hand and raised it to his chest. Because of its size, his wrist was at an odd angle and he hoped the kick of firing wouldn't throw off the bullet's trajectory. If so, he'd have to shoot again, a prospect he didn't relish. He knew he had the strength and the ammunition but doubted he had the skill to get off a clean shot if he were already injured.

"Avery." He said his sister's name aloud, as he pictured her the week before—her tall, thin body in tight blue jeans, a bright red turtleneck sweater, and a green down vest, her long hair loose about her shoulders. Why had she ever decided to go to boarding school? Why hadn't she stayed home with him? He'd been unable to stop crying at the thought of her pending departure. Although he'd been desperate to talk to her, to tell her everything he was thinking and feeling, he couldn't speak. Sensing this, she'd linked her fingers in his and led him out into this field, their boots cracking the frozen twigs and small patches of ice. She'd stopped to pry open a dried milkweed pod with her fingernail, peeling back the rough skin and exposing what was left of the soft white down inside. "We'll pretend it's spring in January," she'd said. Then she'd blown gently, launching the shrunken cluster of seeds into the air. "Make a wish!"

He'd wished she wouldn't leave. And since that was an impossible dream, he'd wished that where he was going, there would be no capacity to feel loss. She would be the only thing he missed.

With the strength and power of a spiritual mantra, he believed firmly in the special bond of twins. Their entire lives they'd had the rare capacity to experience each other's emotions, to feel connected in a way that required no explanation. He'd known when Avery had her period for the first time before she'd ever mentioned it. She didn't need to blush at the mention of Andrew Witherspoon's name for him to sense she had a crush on the captain of the debate team. He alone could anticipate her rages. And she'd asked him about his drowning nightmares before he'd admitted to anyone that he had them.

Now he wondered about how she would survive without him. He couldn't have gone on without her. But then again, he couldn't go on. Period. Would she be his mythological Pollux, willing to sacrifice her life in order to have the two of them remain together? He would gladly pay the price that Pollux had in order to stay with his dead twin brother Castor forever—to spend half of each year in Hades. Six months in Hell seemed worth it to be united for eternity. But at the same time, he wanted Avery to go on, to be happy, to make a life, to make a real family of her own.

He shook his head. Better not to think of her right now. It was too painful, too distracting. He'd written down everything he needed to say and posted the letter earlier in the day. She'd receive it Monday, Tuesday at the latest. By then she'd know of his death. And when she read his words, she'd know why.

As he tightened his grasp on his gun, he realized that his hand trembled. With his left wrist he wiped the moisture from his forehead. His skin felt clammy. The muscles in his face tensed as he squinted in anticipation. It seemed appropriate to recite the Lord's Prayer, something simultaneously formalistic and spiritual, but the words he'd been forced to memorize in Sunday school and had recited every week since then as part of the Episcopal service suddenly escaped him.

Why had his parents kept him in the dark about his identity? Why hadn't they told him all along he was adopted? Maybe then he would have understood why his life, his family didn't feel right. Maybe he could have accepted himself. Maybe he would have taken comfort in Dr. Ellery's explanation that depression was genetic, chemical, that he was plagued by traits beyond his control. But how could he understand when the Herbert family seemed the bastion of mental health? How could he not feel like a freak when he spent days unable to leave his room? His father never missed an hour at the office, let alone a business trip or client conference, because he wasn't up for it. His mother never declined a tennis match, never forgot a garden club meeting, and never slept through a parent–teacher conference or a school play. She'd been at the bus stop at precisely the right time to meet him every single day of his entire childhood. That was stability.

"Your best interests were put first and foremost. Don't think the decisions weren't difficult," Dr. Ellery had suggested. "Faith and Bill love you. They wanted to give you and your sister the best possible life, to make you both feel secure"—a prospect that had about a-thousand-to-one odds, and they hadn't been in his favor.

He lifted the gun and pushed the nose into his chest. Just the hard metal pressing against his skin hurt. He waited. The pounding inside him increased. Perhaps he could will himself to have a massive cardiac explosion so that he'd die of seemingly natural causes. But his heart kept up a ferocious beat, unwilling to quit. If he wanted to end his life he would have to pull the trigger.

Throughout his last night he'd contemplated his options—the body part to target: head, mouth, chest. As the first light of the sun came through his window he'd decided on his chest. One bullet straight to the heart. It was a somewhat impulsive selection, but at some point he had to make a decision. The heart seemed the most lethal. He wouldn't want to end up in a persistent vegetative state from a misfire to the brain. Sucking on the end of a gun seemed a particularly pathetic last gesture.

Having made his decision, he'd survived the day without changing his mind.

He inhaled deeply, then blew the breath out in a noisy exhale. He wished he had a cigarette. Having never been a smoker, he craved what he imagined was the taste of nicotine, the calming effect of an unfiltered Camel.

He positioned his index finger on the trigger and wiggled it slightly. Come on, Foster. Do this. End this. You've said your good-byes.

Then he applied pressure.

The explosion blew out his eardrum. He felt warm liquid run down his neck even before he experienced the excruciating pain, the intense sensation of heat, and the smell of his own charred flesh. The force of the shot had toppled him sideways onto the grass. With his left arm pinned under his body, he couldn't move. Blood spurted from his chest in a crimson arch. He coughed but no sound came from his throat. He sensed a slight breeze as he struggled unsuccessfully to breathe, but the chill inside him had nothing to do with the frigid temperature.

Don't fight it, he said to himself. This is what you've wanted. This is what you want. And it's too late to change course anyway.

Jumpstart whinnied, but the familiar sound seemed miles away. He stared up at the night, now a blur of gray and gold. He'd dropped his gun somewhere, and his right hand twitched. He fingered what remained of the front of his shirt, now saturated with blood. There was no longer any air in his lungs.

He scanned the northern sky, hoping to catch a last glimpse of Gemini, his favorite constellation, but the stars twirled, eluding his gaze. The stellar twins—the rectangular arrangement of Almeisan, Mekbuda, Wasat, Pollux, Castor, and Gemini Mebsuta—stayed hidden. Please, he begged, although to whom he didn't know. Let me see you. Let me know you're there. Show me that you're real.

He gasped. His body convulsed involuntarily. Then everything went black.

3

Monday, January 13th
4:12 p.m.

David Ellery shut the door to his office, closed the Levelor blinds, sat in his ergonomic chair, and pounded his fists into the forest green blotter on his desk. Part of him wanted to cry, but he hadn't done that in fifty years and wasn't about to start now. Half a century before, his mother had accidentally run over his dachshund in her Cadillac convertible. He'd been only eight, but he still remembered holding the limp creature in his arms and realizing it was no longer breathing. That day his emotions had gotten away from him and he'd vowed it would never happen again. He'd survived medical school, his father's death, a psychiatric residency, and a divorce, all without shedding a single tear. Now he would have to add having lost his first patient in thirty years of private practice to the list of adversities he'd faced and overcome in his personal and professional life.

"How could this happen? How come you didn't stop him?" Faith Herbert had screamed over the telephone, her voice hysterical. "You should have saved him. That was your job. You told us you could help him. We trusted you!"

He'd tried to talk to her, tried to find out what happened, but her words had been incomprehensible. Tears, gasps, and coughs swallowed whatever explanations or details she'd offered. All he'd understood was that Foster was dead, and the Herbert family thought he was to blame.

After what seemed an interminable time, Bill finally had taken the receiver from his wife. His voice was low and controlled, although David had thought he noticed a tremor in the cadence. No surprise. From the several times they'd met, and from what Foster had told him of William F. Herbert, Jr., the man was unlikely to expose his vulnerability. Any sorrow, anger, or other extreme emotion that he was experiencing would be carefully hidden behind the Pennsylvania fieldstone of his mansion.

"We wanted to apprise you of Foster's death," Bill had said. "He died of a self-inflicted gunshot wound. The police tell us that the time of death was approximately nine o'clock on Saturday night. We didn't find him until late afternoon yesterday."

"Is there anything I can do?" David had asked.

"No. We'll handle this ourselves," Bill had replied.

"Maybe you'd want to come in. We could talk," he'd persisted. Foster had been his patient for nearly two years. They'd spent fifty minutes together three times a week, plus endless nights on the telephone when Foster, experiencing anxiety, depression, or irrational fears, called without an appointment. He'd met him on Saturdays when he needed an extra session. He'd consulted with Foster's pediatrician and several different psychopharmacologists as he'd struggled to find the right mix of antidepressants. He'd agonized over ways in which to deal with an adolescent who he recognized early on was in trouble. There wasn't anything he hadn't done, and he didn't appreciate the insinuations to the contrary.

"The police may try to contact you," Bill had reported, ignoring David's suggestion. "Faith and I ask that you say nothing. We want our privacy. We want to protect Foster's memory. This is absolutely painful enough without having his difficulties made public."

"Would you like me to meet with his sister? This must be exceedingly difficult for her." Even though he'd never met Foster's twin, David had heard enough about her and the nature of their relationship to know that the news of his death would be an enormous trauma. Sibling loss was difficult; twin loss could be devastating. At least one study in identical twins showed that, if one committed suicide, there was a 40 percent likelihood that the other would at least attempt it, too.

And from what Foster had said, his sister wasn't without her share of issues to begin with. He'd spoken numerous times about a particularly troubling incident when his sister had flown into an uncontrolled rage at their father, who had failed to remember and honor Mother's Day. Her screaming, crying, and carrying on had lasted for more than an hour. She'd even thrown his golf clubs out the window before her tirade ended. Maybe such acting out was typical of any adolescent but, given her genetic connection to Foster, maybe not.

There had been a pause, and then Bill had cleared his

throat. "Avery was at school when it happened. She hasn't been told. Faith and I are driving up there tonight."

"I'd urge you to at least consider the possibility of professional help. I could—"

"Dr. Ellery," he'd interrupted. "I don't want you to speak to anyone in my family ever again, least of all my daughter. Please send any outstanding bill to my office. My secretary will make sure you are paid promptly. Now I have to excuse myself. Good-bye." The line had gone dead.

David stared at the certificates and diplomas that hung in bird's-eye maple frames on the walls of his office, then at the comfortable leather couch and club chair where he sat day in and day out, helping people who suffered from all sorts of emotional problems—bipolar I and II, major depression, anxiety, personality and mood disorders, even sexual dysfunction. He'd treated dozens of men and women in his career, many of whom stopped therapy because they felt—and from a clinical point of view were—better. He'd achieved success; his former patients, his honorary degrees, the substantial grant money awarded to him, and the Jaguar parked outside were testaments to that. And yet a suicide meant he'd failed, failed in the most fundamental way.

What had he missed? Although Foster had discussed killing himself, it had never seemed to be a true threat. The references were sporadic; there was no plan. *You should have saved him.*

He put his face in his hands. The pressure in his head was intense. He should never ever have taken the referral of this boy who'd been to three different therapists before the Herberts came to him and implored him to get involved. But he'd been lured by the challenge of trying to succeed where no one else had, and by Bill's offer to pay one and a half times his regular hourly rate. His own arrogance and $225 an hour even if Foster failed to show for his appointment had convinced him.

His thoughts were interrupted by a knock. Looking up, he realized he had no idea of how much time had passed since Faith's fateful call. Dusk was beginning to fall. Who was still around? His office was part of a suite of three that shared a secretarial station, although the sole support staff—Betty Graham—had called in sick again with a claim of seasonal allergies. He'd heard her excuses and alleged ailments so many times that the lies bored him, but she was too competent when she did show up to dismiss her. Nancy Moore, a psychiatric social worker, had given up her Monday hours to have more time to spend with her family. That meant it had to be Morgan Reese, working late as usual.

"David," she called through the door, as she knocked again, louder this time. Her concern and apprehension masked the normally melodic quality of her voice. "David, may I come in?"

He quickly pulled a tissue from the box he kept for his patients and blew his nose just as the door opened. He swiveled his chair and saw Morgan standing on the threshold. She had sandy brown hair that she wore pulled back from her face in a thick braid, blue eyes, and smooth, pale skin, except for the dark circles that seemed her trademark. He'd never known anyone who kept the professional schedule that she did—patients, primarily children and adolescents, ten hours a day, often six days a week, a full-time research grant to study some sort of reactive attachment disorder in early childhood, plus full faculty responsibilities at the Medical School of the University of Pennsylvania. Despite what must have been chronic exhaustion, she never seemed to lack either energy or concentration.

"I heard about the Herbert boy. I'm so sorry."

"I can't believe it, honestly," he said. Then he registered the import of her comment. "You heard? How?"

"It was just on the news."

But she didn't have a television in her office. And he'd never shared the names of his patients.

His confusion must have shown on his face because she offered, "The radio commentator reported that he'd been under psychiatric care, and . . . and identified you as his therapist." Then she walked over and laid her hand on his shoulder. "I can only imagine what you're going through. Do you want to talk?" The physical contact felt odd; they'd been colleagues for nearly ten years and had a professional friendship but nothing more. Even after his marriage ended he'd never asked her out. Although attractive, she'd struck him as unapproachable.

"What else did the reporter say?" He felt an emotion akin to panic and clamminess in his palms. How could his name have been mentioned publicly? How dare some radio station broadcast that information? What if his patients had heard the same program?

"Very little. Neither of his parents would comment on his death."

"So who disclosed my name, my involvement?"

She shrugged. "You know how it is. Medical records that are supposed to be confidential never are. God only knows what the police had access to."

"And the media wants someone to blame. Even his parents blame me, and they of all people know how hard I tried to help," David said, feeling anger creep into his conscience. He needed to get hold of himself.

"I'm sure you did the best you could. There are limits to what any psychiatrist can do. You don't need me to tell you that."

He forced a smile. "I appreciate the vote of confidence."

Morgan took a step closer to him. "We all second-guess our decisions, personal and professional, but you have to compartmentalize. I'm the first to admit I struggle with issues of distance and boundaries, as if going to medical school somehow taught us not to feel. But when the worst happens, you've got no choice but to remember your training. Otherwise the boy's suicide will destroy you, too."

He closed his eyes, listening to the sound of her voice but ignoring her words. He knew she was trying to comfort him and he also knew his focus should be on Foster, the tragedy of a life interrupted, but he found himself preoccupied with the scarlet letter that was being publicly affixed to his name, his reputation. He needed to formulate a defensive response to the accusations that were sure to be leveled against him. He needed to gather his supporters, who included Morgan, so that his career would not be tarnished by circumstances beyond his control. Short of locking Foster away in an isolation unit and having him disappear into the hidden world of private psychiatric hospitals, nobody could have done more to keep him alive.

"I'm not sure what steps to take next. I offered to help

the family. They don't want to speak to me. Do I notify my malpractice carrier?"

She cocked her head slightly to one side, considering his question. "What do you think happened?"

He thought for a moment, choosing his words carefully. "Foster suffered from recurrent major depressive disorder and had very little coping mechanism. Textbook 296.3x," he said, referencing the *Diagnostic and Statistical Manual of Mental Disorders*. Clinical shorthand—his professional code—reminded him that he got paid to know best. And he did. He'd dedicated his life to understanding the workings of the mind. "He was noncompliant with his medication. We'd tried a number of combinations, plus we adjusted dosages constantly, but he often refused to take them as prescribed, so short of daily blood tests it was impossible to know whether we'd achieved therapeutic levels."

"Had he gone off his meds recently?"

"I don't know. He canceled both appointments last week. His voice sounded good on the telephone, and I didn't push because his explanation seemed plausible given his history. His twin sister was home for the holiday break, and he said he wanted the time to spend with her. I knew they were very close."

"A twin?"

"Yes. Based on what was described to me, their connection was more comparable to what the literature says about identical twins: an uncanny attachment, an almost sixth sense about each other. The eerie part was that, according to Foster, they even both had pits under their left ears. He was obsessed with that physical similarity."

"Really," she remarked, furrowing her brow.

"I can't say I know much about a pit, but it did seem odd."

"Pits are small indentations, common dermatological phenomena in the population at large, but most doctors would tell you they are statistically very improbable in fraternal twins. So your instinct was right. It is very unusual."

Morgan never ceased to amaze him. Were there any medical minutiae that she didn't know? No wonder she had virtually the entire psychiatric faculty, as well as a sizable percentage of the regular faculty at the Medical School, thinking she walked on water.

"In any event, when his sister went to boarding school last fall, Foster fell into a downward spiral," David continued. "He felt abandoned. In my view, his parents simply did not provide the support they should have known he would need when his sister left."

Morgan sat in a high-back chair opposite his desk. She was smaller than he'd realized, more delicate. She clasped her bony fingers together in her lap. "Are you concerned for the girl?"

"I've never met her, so from a professional point of view I suppose I can't say one way or the other. But if I were her father, I would be. You're familiar with all the twin studies."

"I am, but there's a big difference psychologically between identical and fraternal. As far as I can recall, nobody's suggested there's an elevated risk of suicide or attempted suicide in nonidentical twins," Morgan replied.

Leave it to Morgan to remember the clinical details better than he.

She paused for a moment and then cocked her head to one side. "Why would you be concerned for the sister?"

He shrugged. "The girl just sounded volatile, that's all. Probably nothing. She's sixteen, off to boarding school, asserting her independence. No doubt some defiance is part of any healthy detachment process. My concerns— to the extent they're justified—should be more generalized. It's a terrible trauma for the whole family."

"And the parents are undoubtedly lashing out right now," Morgan interrupted. "Imagine what they are going through. But that doesn't mean when the smoke clears they are truly going to hold you accountable. Anyone who knows you could vouch for your dedication and commitment to your patients."

"From your lips to God's ears," David said, rising from his chair. He moved to the window, opened the blind, and glanced out at the alley behind his building. An old man bundled in layers of blankets, the same poor sot who showed up virtually every evening making rounds in search of recyclables, pushed his grocery cart filled with empty cans. The rattle of the wheels echoed.

"Were you surprised?" Morgan asked after a moment.

"Absolutely. If I hadn't been, I would have done something to try to stop it."

"Do either of the parents have depression?"

"I wasn't told anything to lead me to think the Herberts do. But the kids were adopted. So as far as biological predisposition, it's impossible to know."

When he looked over, Morgan had turned away. She seemed suddenly interested in the collection of books in the shelf to her right. He stared at her for a few minutes before she realized.

"I've actually wondered whether the adoption played a role," he continued. "The parents had just decided to tell him and his sister—after sixteen years, and over the Christmas holiday to boot. Foster took it very badly."

She stood up abruptly. "Is there anything I can do?" she asked, still distracted.

"No. I appreciate your coming in, though."

"You and I don't know each other well, but if you want to talk, or there's anything you need, please, don't hesitate. The service can page me—as you well know—but feel free to call me at home." She nodded and bowed slightly with an almost Oriental formality before turning to leave. "It's a horrible tragedy, but not your fault," she mumbled more to herself than to him as she closed the door behind her.

David checked his schedule for Tuesday and then stuffed a pile of paperwork into his briefcase. Foster's suicide wasn't his responsibility. He felt more confident of that having spoken to Morgan. If there was blame to be hurled, it should be thrown at the Herberts.

Perhaps he should call the media and make a comment to offset whatever damage might have been done. For a moment, he allowed himself to imagine such a tactic, one that he couldn't resort to because of ethical restrictions but one that had a certain appeal at the moment. He'd wear a red tie, which resonated credibility, and a dark suit. As he stood before the reporters and television cameras, he'd give his own sound bite. "It's a sad commentary that the parents of today do not take responsibility for the emotional health of their children. Simply writing a check to a professional isn't enough. A child deserves support, love, and guidance during the twenty-three hours of each day that he or she is not in the care of a trained therapist. Only a family—only parents—can fulfill that role."

Maybe then Bill and Faith wouldn't be quite so quick to attack him.

4

Tuesday, January 14th
2:18 a.m.

$\mathcal{M}$organ tossed and turned, unable to sleep and unable to concentrate on any of a stack of books by her bed. Her flannel nightshirt itched, and she pulled it off only to put it back on moments later when the cool breeze through the open window sent a chill down her spine. She opened the drapes but the black night sky beyond her window offered no solace so she drew them again. Suddenly a cold sweat overcame her and she shivered, feeling her hair stick to her neck and face. All she could think about was that fateful hour sixteen years, three months, and two days ago, when she had walked out of Our Lady of Grace Hospital knowing she would never see her twin babies again.

Baby John Doe and Baby Jane Doe. Four pounds two ounces and four pounds four ounces. She'd had a few moments to hold them together in her arms in the delivery room, the boy on her right side, the girl on her left. Their red faces grew redder and they'd both shrieked with the unique power of infant lungs. Restless, their arms and legs flailing, they'd fought off any attempts to wrap them in striped hospital blankets until Morgan had moved over in the bed and put the two babies together side by side. As they'd lain with their shoulders and arms touching, they'd quieted. Who knew what transpired between them, but they'd seemed instantly serene, completely peaceful.

Nobody in the primitive delivery room had made the normal effusive comments. Instead the doctor, a general practitioner who had driven more than fifty miles for the delivery, had conducted two Apgar tests and dictated brief comments to a nurse for the file. He'd missed the dermatological pits behind the twins' left ears, and it had been Morgan who noticed the tiny, pin-size indentations that were almost invisible to the untrained eye. The nuns in attendance seemed to execute their duties in a perfunctory way, throwing cold stares her way when they passed by the bed. They knew she had decided long before this moment to give up her children and the silent disapproval was palpable. A wealthy couple from Main Line Philadelphia, a couple who had never been identified to her, waited in the wings, out of sight, ready to name the babies, take them home, and no doubt baptize them. The paperwork had been signed a month before. The discretion promised by her attorney had failed in the remote hospital setting she'd chosen outside Los Alamos, New Mexico, but would be preserved back in Philadelphia. He'd assured her of that.

Could it possibly be true? Were the Herbert twins her children?

Morgan got out of bed and walked barefoot, following the trellis-patterned wool runner down the winding stairs.

For the past twelve years she'd lived in this house—it had been a source of tremendous comfort to her—and yet it suddenly felt overwhelming, huge and vacant and echoing in the night. Four bedrooms, a finished basement, it was a home meant for a family with children and pets, yet she'd somehow convinced herself that it was perfect for one person who rarely if ever had guests. What had she been thinking? What form of self-deception had she mastered?

Morgan tiptoed across the foyer and opened the double doors that led to her library. In the dark, she made her way to her desk and nearly collapsed into the upholstered armchair beside it. She flicked on the desk lamp and then removed a blue leather photo album from the bottom drawer. Holding the large book in her lap, she opened the cover. *Mr. and Mrs. Walter Wallingford Reese announce with pleasure the engagement of their daughter, Morgan Adele, to Rodman Carlisle Haverill.* The newspaper clipping had yellowed and its corners were torn. Above the text was a photograph of a pretty nineteen-year-old girl, the ends of her hair curled up. *Morgan was presented at The Assembly last winter.* The next page held the engraved wedding invitation and a small card announcing the reception immediately following at the Union League.

Flipping through the pages, she saw image after image of a bride in a dress covered with delicate beading. In each, her smile seemed careful, reserved. She cut cake, danced, mingled with guests, but never stared directly at the camera. But in every photograph a pronounced spot appeared on the front of her bridal dress—the black mark she would never forget. "What on earth have you done?"

her mother had screamed in near hysterics. As she'd waited to be escorted down the aisle, the plate of cherry cordials in the ladies' room had tempted her. One, just one, she'd thought, but as she bit, the liquid center had oozed out unexpectedly, dripping from her mouth to her chest. "How could you be such an idiot? All this effort and expense and we'll be staring at your stain for the rest of our lives." Those were the last words her mother had uttered to her before she became a wife.

To love and to cherish until parted by death. She'd taken that solemn vow but had been unable to keep it. The expectations were too high. All she remembered of that time was the sensation that there wasn't enough air in the house; each day was a battle not to suffocate. After five years of marriage, she'd walked out, leaving behind a baffled, heartbroken man and their toddler son, who would never know his mother. It was the first—but far from the last—completely selfish thing she'd done. More than a decade later, while she was in the final year of a psychiatric residency, the twins had resulted from an affair with a man who'd failed to mention that he was married. At that point, what choice did she have?

She shut the album and hugged her knees to her chest. How could she ever have thought that she could forget the past? How could she have expected not to suffer with her choices? She could construct a reasonable argument that her past decisions were ordered, rational, some part of a grand plan. She'd had ambitions beyond maintaining an exquisite estate, serving on the boards of prominent charities, and living out the preordained mission of the daughter of Walter Reese and the wife of Rodman Haverill, and she'd acted in accordance with that design. But if she allowed herself to feel—to really feel—she realized that her policy in life had been more closely akin to one grounded in scorched earth. To what had she been reacting? From whom had she been running away? For a psychiatrist, an expert schooled in the contours of emotions, she found herself now without a single answer or explanation for her own behavior. She'd left three children behind and one of them was dead. No words, no logic could begin to explain that. The only sensation was a feeling of pain that was beyond anything imaginable.

Perched atop the mantel was a white marble bust of one of her ancestors. In the gray light of early morning, the carved eyes stared at her. Harsh. Accusatory.

The album fell to the floor. She dug through the clutter on her desktop until she found the newspaper with a story on Foster's suicide. Although she'd stared at his face a thousand times since she'd bought it that evening, she needed to look again at the long face, full lips, thin nose, and big eyes, features that so closely resembled her own. "My son," she whispered into the empty room. "My child." Her voice trembled as she repeated the words. Who would he have been? Who might he have become? Could she have saved him?

Suddenly, her stomach convulsed and she lurched forward to grab the wastebasket under her desk. Her mouth filled with water and she struggled to swallow what didn't want to stay inside her. Every joint ached and the muscles in her lower back cramped, as her intestines felt ready to explode. Her fingers and toes tingled. Her eyes throbbed.

She eased herself down onto the rug and curled up in a fetal position, hugging her knees. Lying on the floor, she listened to the tick of the ogee wall clock, the scratch of a branch against the mullioned window, the creak of an upstairs floorboard. The sounds of her house seemed magnified into a deafening cacophony. She wished she could pray for guidance, but as a scientist, she knew no mystical help would come her way. She had to decide her fate for herself, which left her with only one answer. Despite the passage of time, despite the rage she had no doubt caused, she had to talk to her children, or at least to the two that remained. Maybe, just maybe, she could salvage something from this emotional wreckage. And if not, failure would be her ultimate punishment. If that happened, if her children rejected her, she knew she would lack the courage and energy to continue. That she'd accomplished what she set out to do thirty years earlier meant nothing now.

5

Thursday, March 6th
6:45 p.m.

"*Y*ou look truly lovely," Archer said as he helped Lucy out of her overcoat.

"Thank you," she replied, feeling a mixture of modesty and excitement no doubt brought on by the novelty of this evening. That she was at the Philadelphia Flower Show—a social event she'd only read about in the papers—was odd enough. A fund-raiser to her meant a chowder supper at the Somerville VFW or a raffle at the local library. One that required advance ticket sales, let alone formal dress, was a novelty. But that she was attending this gala as the date of Archer Haverill was odder still. Had he simply worn her down? Or had his persistence made him more appealing? she'd wondered as she stared at the pile of pink message slips on her desk with the box marked "Please call" checked on each one. "Why don't you just see what he wants? And if you're not interested in the answer, give him my name," Janet, the administrative assistant for the Homicide Unit, had offered. In an effort to ignore Archer, she'd stayed away from his bar, missing several good readings and a poetry contest in early February. But when the dozen white roses in a cobalt blue vase arrived on her desk, even Jack had suggested a response was warranted. "Give the guy a break, O'Malley. Maybe your finely honed detective instincts aren't right. What have you got to lose?"

She hadn't answered that question, but she'd agreed to meet Archer for a drink on a Tuesday, a day that held no significance in the dating world. And, as they stayed until closing, sharing a reserve Cabernet from his private stock, he hadn't seemed half-bad: polite, interested in her work, clever, and undeniably handsome. She'd laughed as he related stories of the many crazy submissions he'd screened for his literary series—an essay on a rodent colony that lived under the author's sink, a 900-page memoir by a failed ballerina who couldn't do a split, a so-called collection of poetry that turned out to be all the same poem except for single word changes. His appeal rose further when he drove her the short distance home in his brown BMW that had to date from President Reagan's administration. "I just can't part with it," he'd said, somewhat apologetically, as he'd held open the passenger-side door. She'd admired the lack of pretension, as well as the apparent loyalty. Only by reciting her mother's admonishments in her head had she been able to resist the urge to invite him up to her apartment.

She'd barely arrived at her desk the next morning when he called to invite her to the preview dinner for the Flower Show. "I have to admit I usually go with my father," he'd said, "so I've never paid much attention to the band. But we can try to make the best of it."

Black tie. The invitation had precipitated a fashion crisis of proportions she was unwilling to admit even to herself. Only after trying on virtually everything in her closet had she settled for a navy blue ankle-length maid-of-honor dress that she'd worn in her elder brother's wedding. "Be sure to iron the bow in the back," her mother advised when she'd called for reassurance. "Men like a nice, round fanny," she whispered as if the telephone could report her blasphemy directly to the Pope. "The bow makes it look as if you've got at least a bit of one."

Archer now handed their overcoats to the woman running the coat check at the Pennsylvania Convention Center, took the claim stubs, and put a five-dollar tip in the glass jar on the counter. He adjusted his cummerbund and stuffed a handkerchief in his pocket. Turning to Lucy, he offered her his arm. "It's a Latin-inspired theme this year—*fiesta de las flores*. Perhaps I can borrow a guitar from a troubadour and serenade you."

Inside the main hall, they found themselves standing in a village, a reproduction of Loiza, Puerto Rico, facing a yellow-painted church with ornate trim. A warm glow reflected from the mock street lamps onto a rectangular pool, which was surrounded by daffodils, tulips, hyacinths, and heuchella. Samia rose topiaries made an outline of a couple dancing. The air smelled sweet. Incredibly romantic, she thought as she walked past well-dressed men and women strolling through the displays or standing in small groups.

"This is amazing," Lucy exclaimed, unable to contain her enthusiasm. "If I'd known you were offering this kind of beauty, I'd have accepted an invitation sooner."

Archer smiled and squeezed her arm. "There's more. Lots more. The place is huge." He removed a crumpled diagram of the convention hall from his pocket, unfolded it, and consulted it briefly. "Can I get you a sangria?"

She nodded, and let herself be led to a bar that had been set up next to a series of smaller flower arrangements. As Archer got drinks, she scanned the entries submitted by various area garden clubs and several Center City florists. A blue ribbon dangled from a moss-covered urn filled with bird-of-paradise.

"The judging takes place in the afternoon before the preview dinner," Archer explained as he handed her a goblet. "I always thought there was as much politics in the decisions as merit, but I suppose that makes the Flower Show no different from any other institution."

"Spoken like a true cynic." She reached for the ribbon and turned it over to see if it offered more information on the back. It was blank. "Who decides the winners?"

"I'm not really sure. But it couldn't be only people who are involved with flowers because one year my father was a judge. And he couldn't grow a cactus in the desert. In the show's defense, he wasn't invited to do it again."

She laughed and took a sip of the sweet wine. Remembering she was there on Mr. Haverill's ticket, she asked, "Why didn't your father want to come tonight?" Then she added quickly, "Not that I'm not happy to be here in his place."

Archer paused for a moment and seemed to stare at something between her eyes. "Today is the anniversary of the day my mother left him. He tends not to leave the house."

Her attempt at polite chatter had failed miserably. "I'm so sorry. I had no idea."

"Thanks. But it was nearly thirty years ago. I don't have memories of her or of life with her so there's not too much to miss."

"You haven't seen her at all? Is she alive?"

"No, and very much so I think is the sequence of answers to your questions." He took an awkward step backward, as if startled by the sudden realization that he was standing too close to her. Apparently he needed to respect an imaginary line, the appropriate physical distance for a second date in a public setting. "My mother, if you can call her that under the circumstances, is quite a prominent psychiatrist over at the U Penn Medical School. You'd probably recognize her name. She's been in the paper a lot recently because she's under consideration to run that new psychiatric hospital."

Lucy nodded. "King shrink. Or should I say queen." News of the Wilder Center had filled the business and health sections of the *Inquirer* for months. Huge amounts of money, primarily from a large pharmaceutical company nearby, had been poured into lavish accommodations for the discreet, state-of-the-art medical facility. With an electroshock therapy room directly above the health club and professionals providing everything from urinalysis to complete spa services, the hospital seemed to be something out of science fiction.

"An Arab sultan has already reserved a bed and the place won't open until early summer. Apparently whatever ails him is interfering with his diplomatic obligations," Archer continued, chuckling.

"We read the same article," Lucy said, recalling that several noteworthy people had signed up at a cost of more than $2,500 per day: In addition to the sultan, there was a

Hapsburg dynasty descendant who suffered from schizophrenia, the chief financial officer of a Fortune 500 company whose fits of mania were causing legal problems, and a soprano with the Metropolitan Opera who hadn't been able to leave her apartment in seven weeks. Lucy couldn't imagine having that much money, let alone having the luxury to spend it on an attempt at self-understanding. But she didn't need to imagine the nightmare of mental illness.

Could proper treatment have saved her brother? *An accident, a horrible accident*—her parents had clung to that explanation, refusing to see any other interpretation. Aidan had driven his Jeep at fifty miles per hour into a parked utility truck. "It was late. It was raining. Who expected the electric company to leave their truck on the road after the close of business? Why in God's name wasn't the thing parked in ComElectric's lot for the night?" her father had said, but she'd always wondered.

"I guess the esteemed Dr. Reese will have her hands full if she gets the job," Archer said with obvious sarcasm. "Although from what I read, her specialty is children and the Center can't be expecting too many of those. Doesn't it take at least a decade or two to get totally screwed up?"

"I don't know about that. I think it happened to the three of us in the O'Malley clan at about six months," she retorted, willing to play along with his attempt at humor. It had to be agony to know his mother was just miles away yet had no interest in him. That she became a pediatric psychiatrist only added to the painful irony. "You don't see her at all?" She reached for his hand and gave him a wink. "You have to realize it's my instinct to pry. It's also my profession."

"In that case, Miss Detective, I'll give you the short answer. I saw her here and there for a while, but it was very sporadic. We'd go six months. Then I'd see her standing on the side of a soccer field during my game, but she'd be gone before I had a chance to talk to her at the end." He paused for a moment and then added, "You'll get the longer version when I know you better. I don't want to drive you away with boring details."

"I doubt that would happen," Lucy said as images of her own mother flashed into her mind: Mary O'Malley in a stained apron, scrubbing Lucy's back with oatmeal when she had chicken pox; hand-stitching lace on her First Communion dress and pearls on her white gloves; driving her out to the Chestnut Hill Mall to buy her a push-up bra at Bloomingdale's; making her hot tea with lemon and honey when her high school boyfriend stood her up for the senior prom. Since she'd moved out of the house on Washington Street, they spoke nearly every day. A motherless life seemed inconceivable.

"Anyway, suffice it to say that she broke Dad's heart," Archer said, obviously wanting to close the subject. "The sixth of March is the one day he still allows himself to mourn his loss."

"Astounding," she mumbled. "I couldn't control my emotions that well."

"You're not my father. Thank God, I might add. He seems to be able to control how quickly the lawn grows. Chaos theory is his greatest nightmare." Archer lifted his drink to his lips and drained his glass. "Let's look around. Although I may not find it in this tropical paradise, I'm on a quest for mistletoe."

Lucy gave him a quizzical look.

"I've been waiting since long before Christmas to kiss you." He smiled and took her hand. "If I can find the perfect sprig, or even a close relative, maybe I'll have an excuse to plant one on the finest of Philadelphia's finest."

9:12 p.m.

"I don't think this is an appropriate conversation. Not here. Not now," Tripp Nichols whispered as he glanced over Morgan Reese's shoulder, scanning the crowd for his wife. In the distance he thought he saw the bright turquoise of her floor-length dress. Although he could safely assume she was absorbed in conversation with one of the many patrons she knew at the preview dinner, the last thing he needed was for her to notice him alone in a corner with a beautiful woman, especially one whose professional accomplishments had recently filled the media.

"If you had returned one of my calls, I wouldn't have to hunt you down at a charity event," Morgan said.

Tripp said nothing. He couldn't deny that his secretary had faithfully handed him nearly a dozen messages in the last week, or that he'd heard her voice on his voice mail and felt a mixture of emotion and fear. Morgan had been out of his life for almost seventeen years, and he'd done his absolute best to forget her. Even if he'd failed at the latter, he'd kept his thoughts—and fantasies—to himself.

"I'm here with my *wife*," he said, although Morgan would hardly need reminding. He'd been the adulterer. He'd removed his thick gold wedding ring and never once mentioned his wife of five years, their toddler, or their second baby who was due in a few months. She'd been a resident who, because of her relatively older age, no doubt had difficulty making friends among her peers. But her fabulous figure was impossible to overlook and he hadn't cared if she was fifteen or fifty. He'd done everything in his power to seduce her. "If it's that important, I'll call you next week."

He started to walk away when he felt the firm grip of her slender fingers on his forearm.

"Please don't make this more difficult than it is. I . . . I don't know quite how to phrase this other than to be blunt. But I need you to listen." She loosened her hold.

He took a gulp of his drink and felt the vodka burn in his throat. Given the intensity of her stare and the tremble in her voice, he had the creeping suspicion he'd need several more before this conversation ended.

"I know it's been a long time," she began.

Yes, he thought. And as the four months he'd shared with Morgan receded into his distant past, he'd realized how very lucky he was to have survived an affair with his marriage intact. Little escaped the notice of Sherrill Bishop Nichols, but he'd managed for that brief season to pull it off. Perhaps she'd been too absorbed with her daughter or her pregnancy with their son to question his late nights at work or his weekend travel. But such distractions had been an aberration. He couldn't do it again.

And he didn't want to jeopardize his current situation. Sherrill had been the winning lottery ticket for this son of a Baltimore Realtor. His father had supported a decidedly middle-class existence selling ranch-style homes and center-entrance Colonials in subdivisions with names like "Rolling Acres" and "Windy Hill." Now Tripp lived in an eighteen-room mansion in Haverford with a full-time housekeeper and gardener. He and his wife shared a trainer twice a week. A personal assistant paid the insurance on his Infiniti, dropped off his dry cleaning, reminded him of his anniversary, and arranged for weekly floral deliveries to his wife, including larger bouquets for special occasions. He liked the comforts that came from marrying a woman with a substantial family fortune, a woman who asked for little by way of intimacy and wanted no part of intellectually or emotionally charged conversations. As long as he dressed appropriately and accompanied her to myriad social and charitable events, as long as his name appeared after hers on the photo-ready Crane's Christmas card of their smiling children, as long as he didn't embarrass her in any way, his life was easy.

"I never terminated my pregnancy." Morgan now stumbled, as if the weight of her words made her lose her balance.

"What?" Instinctively, he looked around again, scanning the crowd for the telltale turquoise. *Please, Sherrill, stay away*, he thought, feeling sweat break out on his forehead.

"I'd told you I was pregnant. I told you at the time it was your child."

"But . . . but . . ." he stammered, although he knew she was right. He couldn't argue that point.

He could still picture her sitting across the Formica table at Eddie's Diner with a cup of lukewarm peppermint tea. She'd worn a pale blue sweater and gray flannel skirt. Psychiatric journals, papers, and patient folders were piled on the banquette next to her. She'd made her announcement with what he thought was dismay. She'd spoken of how much she wanted to finish her residency, to begin her practice, that she wasn't sure she was prepared to revisit that plan. She'd given up her domesticity once because she'd believed in what she was doing. "You told me you'd had a vasectomy," she'd said.

And then he'd had to confess to the greatest lie of all. He'd never had surgery of any kind. She'd been so apprehensive about sleeping with him, about even the remotest possibility of getting pregnant, that he'd said that to reassure her while making himself sound more liberated, more egalitarian than he'd ever dreamed of being. He'd never expected the relationship to last past that first night, or ever to see her again. And the lay was worth the lie. "I have a family," he'd said. "I can't leave my wife. I can't abandon my children." Those words had sounded more pitiful than he'd intended.

That look on her face—her mouth slightly agape, her head tilted, her nostrils flared—he'd never forget that. Had it been shock? Anger? Disbelief? It had taken her a moment but then her eyes had welled with tears. "I'm sorry," he'd said, but he didn't have to articulate anything more. They both knew instinctively that it ultimately didn't matter what she decided because his mind was made up.

She hadn't said a word. She'd just stood, gathered her papers and journals into a bundle in her arms, and walked out. Two days later, he'd received a small ivory card upon which she'd written simply: *How could you think I wouldn't find out? Or did you just not care?* He'd had no answers. He hadn't spoken to her again and hadn't given the baby another thought. Of course it had been aborted.

"I thought about having the twins, of raising them on my own." Her voice pulled him back into the present. "I debated so long that by the time I decided I couldn't do it, that I couldn't be a single mother, it was too late. I was well into my second trimester. I'd seen their hearts beating on a sonogram. I'd seen an ultrasound image where they almost appeared to be holding hands. Placing them up for adoption seemed the best course for them and for me."

Blood rushed to his head. What was she saying? She'd given birth to twins who were his? There were now two adolescents in the world who were his offspring? What was going on? He felt completely disoriented. Ten minutes before he'd stood with a vice president of PNC Bank debating the degree of flex for a custom fairway driver. "Depends on swing speed," he'd said. "That's why you pay for quality. They test your swing in a wind tunnel. State-of-the-art stuff." Next to him, Sherrill had discussed with the man's wife, a decorator, a cranberry Brunswig & Fils pattern with coordinated two-tone cording she was considering for the armchairs in the library. All around him, permutations of similar conversations were occurring, the types of conversations he liked, conversations that didn't alter the universe. Now he'd just learned information that changed everything.

"Our daughter lives right in Gladwyne. Her name is Avery Herbert. But . . . but . . . but her brother is dead."

What was going on? None of this made sense. Out of the corner of his eye, he saw a glimpse of turquoise. Was another woman in the same couture color or was Sherrill approaching? The pinks, reds, oranges, yellows, blues, and purples of dresses and scarves and accents and flowers assaulted him. His heart raced. He needed to get out of here. Despite the enormity of the convention hall, he felt claustrophobic.

"What happened to the boy?"

She bit her lip. "Suicide," she said, so softly he thought he'd misheard. But she repeated, "He killed himself."

"This is insanity," he blurted out.

"If you'd just returned my calls, we could have talked about this in a calmer way," he heard Morgan saying. "I'm not trying to disrupt you or your life. But I've felt desperate to find Avery. To tell her about me, about us, to tell her she has biological parents, too."

Parents. *Parents!* His daughter, Beth, was a senior at Pine Manor. She'd accepted a job as an intern at the Barnes Foundation. He'd provided the first and last months' rent for her two-bedroom apartment. The lease started June 1. Tripp Jr. was at the Naval Academy, learning discipline and playing rugby. He'd be home for Easter in a few weeks. They were going together to the Volkswagen dealer to buy his first car. Those were his children. They were the two who each got $11,000 a year deposited free of gift tax into a money market account. They appeared on either side of him and his wife in the biannual family portraits. Beth and Tripp Jr.; there was no room for anyone else.

"Does the girl know who I am?" he managed to ask.

"No. She doesn't know anything yet. There are still a few legalities to work out. I don't want to approach her until everything is in order. But it won't take much longer now. I feel that she has a right to know who we are."

"Why? If you were so concerned, what's taken you so long?"

Morgan's face was flushed. Despite the elegance of her understated taupe gown, the long line of her neck adorned only with a small gold locket, her neatly styled hair, she looked as anxious and earnest as she'd looked that day at the diner. For a moment he felt compassion, the urge to embrace her or to make some sort of reassuring gesture, but that was out of the question. This woman is about to ruin your life, he reminded himself.

"I've made mistakes, many horrible mistakes. But now there's a person, a young woman. She's lost her brother. Maybe she'll want nothing to do with me or you but I have to take that chance."

Think, Tripp. But his mind couldn't focus. He needed time, time to make a plan, time to protect himself and his assets. Having a nearly full-grown child emerge as the product of his affair, his only marital aberration in twenty years, was out of the question. Sherrill wouldn't understand. He might as well have his bags packed before he ever uttered a word. The scandal, even more than the betrayal, would close off any possibility of reconciliation.

Out of the corner of his eye, he saw his wife. It was definitely she, not a figment of his imagination, and her stride was quickening. A few more seconds and he'd be faced with his ultimate nightmare: introducing his paramour to his wife. Morgan gave him a quizzical look, but he had neither the skill nor the inclination to interpret her expression. All he wanted was for her to quietly disappear.

"My, my, the famous Dr. Reese," Sherrill cooed as she

joined them. "I had no idea my husband's company would appeal to such an esteemed psychiatrist."

Tripp knew this act: The stalking tigress who makes her prey feel comfortable just before she's ready to go in for the kill. He could recognize her fake smile anywhere, her squinted eyes, curled lips, and big teeth protruding from pink gums. He held his breath.

"Please call me Morgan," she said, graciously extending her hand. "It's been my pleasure."

Was she going to betray him right here and now?

"Morgan's been kind enough to update me on the comings and goings of a mutual friend," he offered before she could say anything further. Did he sound adequately dismissive, uninterested? "Hard to believe we know someone in common. The only doctors I know are my own, and I do everything possible to avoid them." He forced a laugh. Tripp as the witty master of small talk; it was a role he knew well.

"Six degrees of separation, isn't that how the expression goes?" Sherrill asked rhetorically as she linked her arm through Tripp's, establishing her territory.

"And so much can happen to all of us," Morgan added, clasping her hands.

He watched Sherrill's eyes dart to Morgan's bare fingers, immediately registering the lack of either an engagement ring or a wedding band. She could home in on marital status within seconds. Thinking back, he'd been lucky it wasn't a skill Morgan shared.

The three of them stood without saying a word.

After what seemed an eternity, Sherrill finally broke the silence. "I certainly didn't mean to interrupt whatever catching up you were doing on your *friend*." She lingered over the last word, as if suspicious of such a person's existence.

Tripp felt sick. This triangle had to end. He put his arm around his wife's waist, feeling the thickness of her middle, the roll underneath her body-contouring control-top pantyhose. "Have you looked around?" he offered meekly. "It's a wonderful show this year. The best I can remember."

Morgan took the hint. With a slight bow in Tripp's direction, she excused herself. "We'll have a chance to talk again soon."

Not if I can possibly help it, Tripp thought as he watched her walk away into the crowd. He removed his handkerchief and wiped his forehead. He felt as if he'd awoken from a nightmare and now faced the task of coming to terms with whatever demons had emerged from his subconscious. Revealing his identity, making his daughter aware of his existence, was out of the question. But his brief encounter with Morgan had been enough to convince him that her mind was set. No amount of arguing or even begging would persuade her otherwise. Could anything? How could he keep his past at bay and protect his cherished existence? He needed an answer. And he needed it fast.

10:44 p.m.

"We've been friends a long time, is that fair to say?" Dixon Burlingame asked in a deep, slightly hoarse voice.

They sat together on three steps leading to the peach-colored facade of a set-designed Puerto Rican home.

Dixon, a heavyset man in his late fifties with a head of thick salt-and-pepper hair, had loosened his tie. He'd lost one of his shirt studs during the course of the long evening, and David could see his white undershirt protruding through the opening. In the background, salsa music still pulsed although many of the patrons had left.

"Indeed we have. I dare say, I've known you longer than anyone," David replied. They'd been friends since the fifth form at St. Mark's and then roommates at Haverford College. As bachelors, they'd shared an apartment on South 37th. David had been the best man at Dixon's wedding, then a godparent to Dixon's eldest son, and, since his divorce, he had been going to the Burlingame home for Thanksgiving dinner.

"Do you remember that redhead freshman year? Ramsey Whitmore."

"The one who wore shorts so short her derriere was ever-so-teasingly visible?" David laughed, remembering.

"That's the one," Dixon said, smiling. "Do you remember the advice you gave me about her? I'll never forget what you said. You told me not to ask her out. That she was too hot for a pudgy guy from Pennsylvania who hadn't made the cut for even a club sport. You told me that it was better to preserve my ego and not put myself in the position of being turned down. That it was better in the long run to focus on the girls who might say yes. Some of the best advice you've ever given me."

David smiled, remembering the conversation. Since then, he'd offered professional advice and medical consultations on subjects far more important than how to deal with the most popular girl in the class. Dixon was chairman of AmeriMed, one of the three largest pharmaceutical companies in North America, and he'd relied heavily on David's expertise and guidance over the years. David had helped Dixon survive numerous mergers and acquisitions by providing information about the status of FDA approvals, translating into layman's English the medical terminology in patent licenses, and keeping him abreast of potential areas of research to exploit. All the while, Dixon had grown his company into a monolith and amassed a fortune in stock options.

But now, finally, payback time had come. Because of Dixon's power and prestige in both the medical and business communities, and because of AmeriMed's role in the development of the facility, he'd been named head of the search committee for the director of the Wilder Center, a position that virtually guaranteed David's appointment.

"So now it's my turn to be blunt." The reminiscence about Ramsey wasn't just the drunken reverie of a middle-aged man. There was a point.

"When have you been anything *but* that?" David asked good-naturedly.

"Well, what I've got to say kills me but I'm in a bind." He coughed. Phlegm rattled in his throat. "I need you to withdraw your application for the directorship."

"What?" David must have misunderstood. His reputation in the medical community was well established. He had strong ties to the University faculty, as well as to the FDA and NIMH. Navigating through various governmental agencies would be key to operating a brand-new psychiatric hospital. Dixon had capitalized fully on that experience when it served his purpose. Plus David had a proven track record of fund-raising capabilities. Sometimes he wondered whether he should have been a salesman because he was so good at getting others to part with their money in support of his causes. But most important, he had extensive experience with pharmacological advances in the treatment of mental illness. "Why would I do that?"

"For your own good. You're not going to get the appointment. So I'd rather have you withdraw than lose out."

This couldn't be true. He was the front-runner. All the newspaper articles had given him that label. The selection process had to be perceived as fair, and the committee had initially included an African American and two Jews in its list of nominees. But he'd survived the initial cuts. Now the contest was between him and Morgan. She might be the token woman, but she couldn't get the position over him. He was by far the more qualified.

"Look." Dixon leaned toward him and spoke in a conspiratorial tone. "You and I both know that what happened with the Herbert kid wasn't your fault. It was a horrible tragedy. But the press . . . public opinion . . . The Center and its investors simply can't endorse you. The last thing a psychiatric hospital needs is a high-profile suicide to open its doors."

"You've got to be kidding."

Dixon stood up. "Follow my advice. Make it your own choice. Down the road, things may open up. The air will have cleared. No one will remember the Herbert death. You don't have to be the first director."

"You're giving Morgan the job?"

He nodded. "There's one other candidate publicly in the running, but she's got it locked up. Although it won't be public for another couple of months—the end of May if everything goes according to schedule. We want the announcement to coincide with the opening and we're still doing some finishing construction work, finalizing some administrative details, that sort of thing."

"She treats children!" His voice sounded shrill, bordering on hysterical.

"Not exclusively. She's got experience almost as varied as your own. And she's got impeccable credentials, dozens of publications, research experience. Most important, everybody respects her. She wowed the pants off the committee. That woman knows her stuff. She has unbelievable contacts. Between her personal background and her medical experience, she has access to everyone, including a hell of a lot of people with money. And we need that. You know as well as I do that the director is primarily a political position. She's not going to be seeing any patients."

"Let me come in and talk to the committee. Give me one more chance." He hated begging and hated Dixon for making him beg.

Dixon shrugged his shoulders, leaned on one knee, and pushed himself upright. "It's too late for that. The decision's been made. Unless Morgan doesn't accept the position, she's got it. I'm giving you an out. If you don't want to take it, that's your business. But as your friend, I'm advising you to pull yourself out of the running."

As David slumped forward, he felt Dixon's hand on his shoulder. "Give me a call next week. Let's have lunch. Maybe the Union League."

David looked up. He wanted to shout. To discuss what? Your betrayal? That I'm being punished for something over which I had no control? That the committee is too filled with cowards to give the job to the most qualified applicant? That my own friend is swayed by media pressure? It would take all his self-control not to throw an order of turtle soup in Dixon's fat face. But he said nothing.

"I'm sorry, buddy," Dixon remarked.

Not as sorry as I am, he thought. He thought of Morgan in his office just after Foster's death, her apparent concern and her apparent sympathy over the adverse publicity. Had she known then that this tragedy would be a windfall to her? How had the media learned that Foster was his patient? Apparently not from the Herberts, who hadn't given a single comment to any newspaper that he'd seen. *You know how it is. Medical records that are supposed to be confidential never are.* He remembered her words. Could she have gone through his files? Would she have done something so unethical? Had he been betrayed first by a colleague and then by a friend, or was this disappointment making him paranoid?

He rubbed his eyes. It was late, and he was tired. Ultimately the truth didn't matter. The job was hers instead of his. The only way to avoid the inevitable was to convince her not to take the position. And short of having her drop dead, David could think of no possible strategy that could achieve that end.

6

Sunday, April 13th
4:15 p.m.

L ucy, can you bring the mint jelly in for me? It's on the pantry sideboard," Mrs. O'Malley called out in brogue as she navigated around a boisterous game of jacks and placed a steaming bowl of mashed potatoes on the buffet. She rested her hands on her hips and surveyed her Easter table. She'd been starching and ironing linens for days in anticipation of the family gathering. The cut-glass goblets had all been washed by hand, and her mother-in-law's china unpacked from the attic for the annual celebration. She'd even Pledged the cherrywood chairs, although she'd had to add some metal folding ones from the basement to accommodate several extra guests. Home magazines might put a premium on the visual beauty of the table arrangement, but hospitality had always been her concern. She wasn't about to turn anyone away on a holiday.

"Could one of you smokers come get these candles lit?" she called out. Although she could hear voices and laughter in the adjacent room, no one responded. "You'd think I was the only one here for all the work I'm doing," she muttered.

Meghan, her eight-year-old granddaughter, threw a red Super Ball up in the air and scrambled to collect the metal jacks, but she was too slow. The ball bounced off the back of her hand and rolled under the table. On all fours, she followed it, bumping her head as her sister, Tara, giggled uncontrollably.

"You two have exactly thirty-seven seconds to pick up those jacks," Mrs. O'Malley warned, shaking her finger at both girls, "or I'll tan your hides—Easter or no Easter."

"Give it up, Mum," Lucy said as she entered the dining room holding a crystal dish filled with mint jelly. "Your threats have never been taken seriously." She smiled. "Anyway, it's my fault. The jacks were a present from me."

"I dusted your championship trophy in that game not long ago," her mother remarked, and then paused as if lost in thought. "Speaking of which, we'll have to clean out your room one of these days. If you're really planning to stay in that Southern state after all, your father wants your room for an office."

"Dad's retired. And Pennsylvania isn't the South."

"Whatever," Mrs. O'Malley said, waving her hand dismissively. "It's too far, that much I know. No good can come of leaving your family. At the end of the day, that's all anyone's got. But you've wanted an adventure since the day you were born." Turning her attention back to her granddaughters, she said in a louder voice, "Girls, did you hear me about those jacks?"

"Do you remember how much Aidan and I loved to play?"

Mrs. O'Malley crossed herself at the mention of her deceased son, but said nothing.

For Lucy, being home meant being with Aidan. It wasn't just the visible reminders—the formal studio portrait that sat in a silver frame on the mantelpiece or his racing bicycle that gathered dust in the garage. It was that each room held memories of games, stories, and the daily events that marked the passage of life with a sibling. She could still hear his voice from upstairs accusing no one in particular but everyone in general of taking his Dire Straits tape. She could visualize the anxiety on his face when he left for his algebra exam in the seventh grade. How many nights had they lain side by side on a giant beanbag in the basement, watching reruns of *The Mod Squad* and dreaming of being undercover cops? "Hippies," Mrs. O'Malley had muttered accusingly whenever she saw Linc, Pete, and Julie on the television screen, but to Lucy and Aidan the threesome were heroes.

Now she closed her eyes, momentarily picturing the face of her brother as he lay in the morgue. Aidan had cuts over one eye and minor external bruising, nothing compared to the massive swelling that the coroner had found within his skull. Her brother had called her just that afternoon and asked her to call back as soon as possible, but the piece of paper with the message taken by her college roommate had blown off her bureau and under the bed. A breeze from an open window kept her ignorant of what might have been his final plea for help. More than a decade later, she still couldn't look at the notation "ASAP" without feeling overwhelming numbness.

Lying on the metallic table was his lean, eighteen-year-old body covered by a blue tarp. She'd reached over and embraced him, begging for a response, a squeeze, a tickle, a tiny finger wiggle. But by the time she'd traveled from her college dormitory to Massachusetts General Hospital nearly ten hours had passed, a lifetime since the automobile accident, and she felt nothing but cold, hard, unresponsive flesh beneath her hand.

The clatter of serving utensils on a platter snapped Lucy out of her nightmarish fog. "I see you took the plastic off the sofas," she teased, wanting to distract herself with the gaiety of the gathering rather than morbid times she couldn't forget. "This must be a very special occasion indeed."

As a child, she'd been mortified that her mother kept protective covering over the two couches and three armchairs in the first-floor parlor. But Mrs. O'Malley's own childhood in Ireland had been frugal; even though her husband had provided well for his family and they now enjoyed a more than comfortable retirement, waste and carelessness simply weren't in her lexicon.

"Mind your tongue," Mrs. O'Malley replied, only half-amused. "You never did understand that luxuries have to last. This is quality upholstery fabric. One day when you have a home of your own, you'll see."

"Everything looks beautiful. Truly. You've outdone yourself." She extended the dish. "Where do you want this?"

"Find a spot on the table if you can." Opening a drawer in the buffet, Mrs. O'Malley pushed aside assorted napkin rings, half-melted tapers, and a stack of doilies in a hopeless search for matches. "You'd think I was mad all the talking I do to nobody but myself. Did anyone hear me about the candles?"

Lucy laughed. "Not likely." There were a dozen people packed into the square kitchen and spilling out onto the back porch, not to mention the array of small children who seemed to weave in and out of feet, through legs, and over and under furniture. Her father presided over the crowd that included her brother, Michael, and his wife, Mary, plus her brother's in-laws, a recently widowed cousin, the neighbors with their ninety-three-year-old grandmother, an aunt and her husband. And in the middle of it all, she'd left Archer Haverill with a perplexed expression on his face and a glass of sherry in his hand.

Who would have thought? They'd hardly spent a night apart since the Flower Show. "Love at second sight," he liked to remind her.

But bringing a boyfriend home was something new. She hadn't introduced a single male companion since she'd moved to Pennsylvania, and each year that passed added to her parents' anxiety that she'd end up a spinster. Once she'd mentioned Archer's existence, her mother wasn't about to let him slip away. Even her father had insisted. "Give your mother a day of peace and bring the lad home for her to welcome," he'd said on the telephone a week before. "She talks of nothing else."

"But we haven't been dating that long," she'd responded.

"Your mother told me he answered your telephone at eight o'clock in the morning. That means you've been dating long enough."

Archer had accepted her invitation without hesitation. "What about your father?" she'd asked. He spoke little of Mr. Haverill but she pictured an older man in a cardigan sweater alone with a TV dinner. Did Stouffer's even make an Easter version with traditional fixings? That he would be alone on a holiday seemed too sad.

"He'll go to his club for lunch," Archer said. "Don't worry. My dad was raised a Quaker. Althoug'. I don't think he's been to a meeting in forty years, the doctrine about no special celebrations seems to have stuck. We hardly celebrate Christmas. Easter's a nonevent."

Lucy moved the salt and pepper shakers to make room for the mint jelly and returned to the kitchen just as Mrs. O'Malley removed the roasted leg of lamb in a massive cast-iron pan from the oven. The smell of garlic and rosemary and the exclamations of the hungry observers filled the air, even as the cook elbowed her way to the sideboard. "Tell your father the party's over if he doesn't get inside right now to make himself useful." She held up a large carving knife.

Lucy stepped out onto the porch, inadvertently letting the screen door slam shut behind her. Mary's baby spit out his pacifier and started to cry. Archer and her father turned in her direction.

"A ladylike entrance as usual," Mr. O'Malley remarked.

"Oh blarney," Lucy said, imitating her father's cousin who used the phrase as often as he could. She'd never understood what it meant but liked the sound of it. Walking over to her father, she hugged him. "I hope you're not scaring him off."

"To the contrary," Archer replied quickly. "I can't remember when I've had such a nice holiday."

"Was it the traffic through the Sumner tunnel, the two-hour Mass in Latin, or the eye-burning incense? I want to keep track of what you love best." Seeing Archer happy made her feel the same.

"I'm hearing from this young gentleman what a pesky bugger you are." Her father pinched her cheek.

"Archer, what have you told him?"

"How hard it was to get you on a date. How I had to beg, plead, and cajole, and make promises of all kinds of riches before you'd agree to be seen in my company." Archer winked, knowing his description wasn't too far from the truth.

"You'll fit right in around here if you keep fabricating stories," Lucy replied. Turning to her father she instructed, "You're needed to carve the lamb. Mum's got the knife out already."

"Very well then." He took a step toward the door but turned back to face Archer. "My one piece of advice on the women in this family is that it's best not to disobey when they're brandishing a weapon." With that he disappeared inside.

8:23 p.m.

Most of the dishes had been cleared and the visitors had departed, leaving the O'Malley family still at the table too full and too content to get up. Mr. O'Malley produced a new bottle of Baileys and even Lucy, who'd never been a fan of Irish cream, enjoyed a few sips.

On her lap, Tara had fallen asleep. Her head hung back and her mouth was slightly open, just enough to let drool run out onto her aunt's shoulder. Despite offers to assist in moving her to a bed, Lucy had resisted. The

chubby body and hot breath felt warm, comforting. As
Tara sighed in a dream, Lucy hugged her closer. Next to
her, she watched her sister-in-law feed little Aidan, as he
lay cradled in her arms. He sucked vigorously, his jaw
moving rhythmically back and forth. She could see the
perfect fingernails as his tiny hands gripped the bottle
and could smell the wonderful mixture of baby oil and
talcum powder.

"She's made for motherhood," Michael remarked to no
one in particular. "If I get sent to the Market Basket at
four in the morning for another bottle of Similac, I'll lose
my mind. But Mary's patience is endless."

"No surprise there. She married you," Mr. O'Malley
chimed in.

"I'm glad to see you finally recognize your wife's
many gifts," Mrs. O'Malley said as she came in from the
kitchen and settled next to her husband. She took off her
shoes, exposing the reinforced toes of her pantyhose, put
her feet up on the empty chair beside her, and sighed in
relief. "Now, you must tell me, how does one get a name
like Archer?" She reached for her husband's glass of Baileys and took a generous sip.

"If you let Ma grill him, Lucy, you may never see the
guy again," Michael teased.

"He can take the Fifth if he needs to," she replied.

"It'll take more than a curious mother to keep me
away," Archer said, as he rested his hand on Lucy's thigh
and gave her a squeeze.

"You make a grown girl blush," Lucy said. "Not that
modesty has been one of my particular virtues."

"Lucy O'Malley, I'd send you to your room if you

weren't old enough to resist," her mother said, only partly in jest.

"I'm named for my father, Rodman. But it seemed so pompous. 'Famous man' it means in German. Do you think that's me?" he asked, smiling at Mrs. O'Malley. "Anyway, I started calling myself Archer. Sort of a pun, or at least I thought so at the time. I was about ten and into bows and arrows, cowboys and Indians stuff. It stuck."

"I see." Mrs. O'Malley looked a bit confused. Name variation within the several-block radius of the O'Malleys' Somerville network was limited. And nobody was named after someone in the family who was still alive. That honor came with death. "You have an interest in garden ornaments, I hear. How interesting," she said, obviously struggling to change the subject.

"It started when I was trying to find furniture for my bar. I wanted small tables—bistro, but sturdier—and I looked at a lot of old wrought-iron stuff, most of which had been used outside. It was beautiful. The patinas, the mosses, the age, each piece was so different that I thought it would make my bar unusual. So I started buying it up. Then I got into stone birdbaths, statuary, and fountains. I'm quite sure I violated the fire code, although I guess I'm not supposed to admit that in this company."

"Violating an ordinance is fine. What you're not supposed to admit is that you like decorating—or shopping for that matter." Mr. O'Malley laughed. "Now I'm going to have to excuse myself from this scintillating conversation. My wife has declared an end to my cigar smoking indoors. I say something's got to get you, but to show my gratitude for the exquisite meal she produced, I'll head outside." He leaned over and kissed the top of his wife's head. "If anyone cares to join me . . ."

Archer rose quickly. "I'd love to. I've a couple of Macanudos in my coat. I wasn't sure I'd have any takers."

Mr. O'Malley patted Archer on the back and grinned back at the group as they walked outside. Lucy watched with a mixture of delight and apprehension. How could it be that Archer was this comfortable? "Just relax," she could imagine Aidan's voice as if he were sitting beside her. "He's a hit."

9:15 p.m.

Lucy leaned against the butcher block, waiting with a dishrag. Mrs. O'Malley, wearing yellow rubber gloves, stood at the sink, slathering her platters, bowls, and crystal with soapsuds, scrubbing them vigorously with a bristle brush, and then rinsing them under fresh water before passing them off to her daughter. It was a familiar scene. Despite the pride her parents took in their daughter's accomplishments on the police force, women still did the dishes in the O'Malley household.

Lucy didn't mind. She enjoyed listening to the sound of Archer and her father talking outside on the porch, and smelling the cigar smoke that wafted in through the screen door. Her brother and his family had left, and she welcomed the few minutes alone with her mother.

"Aidan would've liked your gentleman friend," Mrs. O'Malley remarked, as if reading her mind.

"Did the police ever question the circumstances surrounding Aidan's death?"

She heard a clatter as her mother dropped a handful of flatware she was holding. "What are you talking about?" she asked, burrowing beneath the suds to retrieve the forks, knives, and spoons that still needed washing.

"Was there ever any doubt about the accident?" Perhaps it was the several glasses of wine and the bit of Baileys she'd drunk, perhaps it was the birth of her nephew, his namesake, perhaps it was her own sorrow that Aidan wasn't outside with her father and Archer, or, perhaps, it was her recent promotion to the Homicide Unit that spurred her to ask what she'd wondered for years.

"I don't know what you mean. Your father looked at the report. Go ask him if you need to be raising skeletons. It could have been written in French for all I remember."

"I spend a lot of time thinking about it, about what happened, about what might have happened. It never made sense to me," Lucy replied. "And I truly wish I understood."

"It was a long time ago. May he rest in peace," her mother said, crossing herself. Water from her gloves left dark spots on her chest and shoulders. "But it would make sense to you if you'd recognize that God has a plan for all of us. We don't need to understand the particulars of why. It just is."

Lucy wasn't about to challenge her mother's Catholicism. One of the most vivid and constant images she had was of her mother kneeling before the crucifix mumbling a litany of daily prayers. Mary O'Malley had tried to impart her deeply held faith to all of her children. There had been grace before each meal, prayers at bedtime, adherence to the Love Thy Neighbor commandment, Sunday school where the nuns instructed Lucy on how to make a rosary by stringing Froot Loops cereal on garden twine, monthly confessions to Father MacGregor. Lucy had been allocated penance and given absolution for sins ranging from kissing Rory Pearson on the lips just before he scrambled down the school bus steps, to lying about her schedule to avoid a date with Monty Ernsberger, the fifteen-year-old math genius, who had orange fingertips from his subsistence diet of Cheez Doodles. When she came home to visit, she accompanied her parents to church to maintain family harmony, but the rituals held little meaning.

"Aidan drove into a parked car. Parked right—"

"It was a truck. It was an electrical company truck. And it could've happened to any of us. That truck had no business being left out on the street. There weren't any orange cones or flares or anything." Her voice cracked.

"But still," Lucy persisted. "It was after dawn. He would have seen it. The autopsy showed no signs that he was under the influence."

"Aidan didn't do drugs. He was a good boy, a responsible boy. You know that. It had been raining that night. His accident was a tragedy, a horrible, horrible tragedy. But there's nothing to be gained from revisiting old sorrows. Why don't you go join your father on the porch?"

"Wouldn't you want to know if the truth were something else entirely?"

Mrs. O'Malley turned to face her daughter. Her lips were trembling. "I don't know why you're bringing this up after we've had a nice holiday, but I won't have it. If what you're suggesting is what I think you're suggesting,

I won't hear it. No son of mine would do such a thing. Mother Mary may have had some plans for my boy but a sinner he was not."

"Mum, this isn't about sinning. It's about Aidan." She took hold of her mother's shoulders and held her squarely. "I'm just asking because hardly a day passes without my wondering whether there was something I should have done to help him. I'm looking for an answer."

Her mother shook her head and turned back to the sink. "I can't give you one. And you'd do well to leave your brother's memory alone and find a bit of peace nonetheless." As she passed Lucy the flatware, her hand shook. "I want this conversation to end. You're talking nonsense, gibberish. All your investigating isn't going to bring your brother back."

"I was gone. He was here with you. Did something happen? How did he seem?"

Mrs. O'Malley turned on the faucet. The sound of running water almost covered her words. "He was just fine is what he was. He had a part-time job at the Market Basket. He was making good money. He went to school. He even bought himself that new racing bike. It's still out in the garage, hardly ridden once," she said, as she choked back tears and then coughed to collect her composure. "Now who goes about wasting hard-earned money if there's no plan to use it? You tell me that. You're the detective."

Lucy dropped her dishrag on the counter, stepped behind her mother, and wrapped her arms around her mother's waist. "I'm sorry. I don't mean to hurt you or bring up a painful subject, but I'm not sorry to want to know. And I don't love him any less for asking," Lucy whispered in her ear.

"Sometimes ignorance is bliss, Lucy. You may never want to accept that, but it's the God-given truth. Some things are simply better off left well enough alone."

Lucy hugged her mother again. There was nothing else to say, and she didn't want to upset her more than she already had. But try as she might, she could never agree with her mother's philosophy. And it surprised her that in a family of law enforcement officers, she seemed to be the only one willing to revisit her brother's death.

10:09 p.m.

Archer stood on the threshold and pulled Lucy toward him. "If I'm relegated to the guest room, do I still get a kiss?" he asked. His eyes were bloodshot and she could smell cigar on his breath. "Are you at least allowed to sneak down the hall?"

Lucy didn't answer. Even at her age, her parents wouldn't hear of having an unmarried man and woman share a bed. But the O'Malley household wasn't designed to accommodate overnight guests so Archer would spend the night in Aidan's former room. Although his high school sports trophies, his collection of baseball cards, and the poster of Elle McPherson had long since been removed, the blue-and-brown-plaid spreads from Filene's still covered the twin beds. No matter how much Lucy wanted Archer, that she would spend the night in there was out of the question.

She kissed him, feeling the softness of his lips and the thickness of his tongue. Then she pulled away.

"I had a wonderful time. Thank you for inviting me here," Archer said.

Lucy forced a smile. The conversation she'd had with her mother still consumed her thoughts. She knew it had to be difficult, if not impossible, for a parent to accept that a child was depressed, miserable, unable to function, but the stonewalling had frustrated her for years. She'd even wondered whether her parents had been forced to ignore the problem because of the economic reality, the astronomical, largely uninsured cost of serious mental illness that they couldn't have begun to afford even on a commissioner's salary.

"Why'd you do it?" Archer asked. "Yes"—he nodded in answer to her perplexed look—"your dad and I could hear every word. The walls in this house don't hide much, and a screen door muffles even less," he said by way of explanation. "Your father tried to cover it up. I think he was upset for your mother, but all I could do was wonder what had gotten into you."

"Am I supposed to be quiet?" Lucy asked. "It was my brother after all."

"No. That's not what I'm saying."

"Then what are you saying?"

"I know you miss your brother, and I'm sure holidays are worse than other times. They have been for me. But you're incredibly lucky. Luckier perhaps than you realize."

"What do you mean?"

Archer steadied himself by holding on to the door-knob. When his spoke, his words were slightly slurred. "I wouldn't recognize my mother if she walked by me on the street. She never boiled me a vegetable or baked me a pie. She never made an Easter celebration. Hell, she never read a single bedtime story."

Lucy reached for his hand and squeezed his fingers.

"She might as well have been dead for all she was involved in my life, except that she wasn't, which made it worse. I wondered and fantasized about who she was and why she'd left. I wondered if my father had driven her away or if it was something I'd done. I raised the subject with him again and again over the years, but he never wanted to talk about it. He'd make oblique references to her or to 'problems.' That was it. In many ways he seemed as confused as I was. Then she has the gall after all this time to drop off a letter inviting me to lunch. She left it with Sapphire. The very idea that I could sit across the table from her and make conversation now after nearly thirty years of nothing is absurd. But that's not my point. My relationship with my mother doesn't matter. None of that matters now. I'm just telling you all this because sometimes I think we tend to take the people we love most for granted. Your mother loves you, and that's worth a lot. Don't hurt her."

The narrow hallway spun as Lucy listened to what he said.

"Your mother invited you to lunch after all these years? Why don't you go? Why don't you confront her and ask her all the questions you've been asking yourself?"

"It's too late. And, as I say, that's not my point. My point to you is to cherish the mother you've got. Maybe she can't take the truth about Aidan. But that doesn't make her a bad person."

Lucy felt a lump in her throat. She knew that much of

what Archer said was true. But at the same time, part of the closeness in her family came from candor, from confrontation. No O'Malley was subtle enough for innuendo.

"You make the choices you want. I respect that. But I'm not like you. I can't pretend everything's all right when it's not." She leaned toward him and kissed his cheek. "Now go to sleep. Good old Philly awaits us in the morning. If you think my mother is so great, perhaps you should give your own a second chance. You may find that they're not as different as you think."

7

Monday, April 14th
11:05 a.m.

$\mathcal{A}$ s she gazed out at the cobblestone courtyard, Faith Herbert pressed her knuckle into her bottom lip to stop it from trembling. She'd known since the moment Foster's memorial service had ended that this day was coming. The only question had been how soon. She'd lain in bed listening to Bill's footsteps as he made his way down the hall to the guest bedroom. She'd spoken to several of her closest friends about trying to find a job, part-time perhaps, at the cashmere shop or the fine stationers in Bryn Mawr. She'd applied for a credit card in her own name and made an appointment with an accountant. Yet despite the preparations and anticipation, as she stared out through the rain-streaked windowpane, she felt completely lost.

She'd tried to imagine how life would be different without Bill. She'd had plenty of time for reflection as she'd moved through room after room, color-coding and tagging furniture and objects—the bird's-eye maple chest of drawers in the guest room, the leather umbrella stand in the foyer, the pair of eland antlers in the library—but nothing had prepared her for the sight of the moving van pulling into the driveway shortly after eight that morning. She'd tightened her robe around her waist, sipped her coffee, and shivered as she stared at the blue and white truck boldly marked SAFE PASSAGE. Ironic. It was what she thought she was getting when she married William F. Herbert, Jr., twenty-two years before, but it was the last term in the world she'd use to describe the life she'd had with her soon-to-be *ex*-husband.

The horses had been sold already—Jumpstart pulled out of retirement to be a school horse and Fern carted off to a private stable in Devon for a family who employed its own trainer. This house—her home—would go on the market next week. The more-than-competent Realtor had prepared the color brochure, and a flurry of activity was expected with the official listing for the desirable Gladwyne property. Faith could imagine the couples who would wander through, commenting about the number of bathrooms, the built-in closets, the flow of the floor plan, and the need to repaint the barns. They would whisper about the tragedies that had beset the sellers: "They lost a son," the Realtor might explain to prospective buyers. Or, if she wanted to stress the urgency to sell, she might disclose, "It's a divorce situation."

Faith shuddered. Damn them. Damn him.

The turn of the lock startled her. The door opened, and Bill stepped into the library. Behind him in the foyer, she could see two leather suitcases. His hair was still wet from the last shower he would ever take in this house, and she couldn't bear the thought of seeing the steam on the mirror if she checked upstairs. He didn't need to take another step toward her; just imagining the scent of his sandalwood cologne was painful enough. His cheeks were drawn but he still looked handsome in his pin-striped suit. And although his yellow tie was slightly too pale for this time of year—it really was a summer pattern—she said nothing. She had to accept that it was no longer her role to comment or correct.

He checked his watch, the platinum one she'd given him for their fifteenth anniversary, with the back engraved with the date and both their initials. "I'm heading in to the office so as not to lose the whole day," he announced.

That's it? she thought. Why was it that she could hardly function, that each breath felt labored, while he waltzed off to his legal practice, engaged with his clients, and logged hours worth $400 each? Why did life go on for one person while the other fell apart?

"The movers are done but for a couple of book boxes. I've already tipped them so you don't have to worry about that," he continued, seemingly oblivious to the tears that she now felt on her cheeks.

She turned back to the window and wiped her eyes.

"Faith." She heard his voice but couldn't find the strength to reply. Then she felt the presence of his body behind her, the touch of his hand on her shoulder. "Are you all right?"

What a question! How could he even ask? She hadn't experienced anything close to normalcy in weeks. There hadn't been a day in the past hundred that she hadn't second-guessed everything she'd done, everything that had happened, all that had been destroyed. And now she was supposed to carry on when she had nothing left.

Still, every fiber in her body cried out to embrace him and never let go, to forget all the hurt and blame that had transpired between them, and to cherish the memories they had, but she couldn't. Even Avery, their daughter, the one person who might have kept them together, knew of his infidelity.

The so-called marriage counselor had rationalized Bill's conduct as Faith nodded in feigned understanding: "Especially in reaction to intense grief, one partner or the other often seeks solace in the arms of a stranger. Your husband needed a temporary distraction without the commitment. It was a way to forget." But the "stranger" turned out to be nothing of the kind. Rather than a barroom pickup, or the flight attendant on one of his many shuttle hops to Boston, she was an associate at his firm, a magna cum laude graduate of Yale Law School who also happened to have acquired a doctoral degree in molecular biology, a brilliant blond patent attorney nearly fifteen years his junior, who was destined to make partner. And there was nothing temporary about their relationship. They'd been involved for more than a year, months before Foster's death. Bill had the audacity to bring his wife to the firm retreat while he was sleeping with another woman, one whose room at the Greenbrier had been just down the hall.

It was too late. She and Bill couldn't stay together and stay here. And neither could imagine starting over in a new community.

"No," she replied. The sound of her voice was unfamiliar. "I'm not all right. But my well-being hasn't been front and center on your agenda recently, so there's no point in your getting involved with it now."

"That's unfair."

"Unfair? What can you possibly know about fairness?" She struggled to stop her voice from cracking. "Having my husband decide a few business-trip trysts are worth twenty-two years of marriage. Having some young woman seduce my husband. Everything I've built and made and loved is gone. So don't accuse me of being unfair."

Bill took a step back, surprised by her directness. "You wanted this. You asked me to leave. You didn't have to add to the damage I'd caused."

"And you were more than happy with that decision."

His silence confirmed the accuracy of her comment. For the sake of appearances, for the sake of their daughter, he would have been willing to stay under the same roof, to purport to be a family. But he'd wanted something more. He hadn't been satisfied. That's why he'd taken a room at the Apollo on Arch Street three different times over a period of five days and stayed well into the late night hours with Miss JD, Ph.D., who'd probably confessed to her friends that she relished the seediness of low-rent sex and the gymnastics of insatiable older men. Although Faith's friends never discussed such sordidness, she knew the younger generation shared no such inhibitions about their sexual encounters. Faith shuddered to imagine the two of them—she in the type of tawdry lingerie that even Nordstrom wouldn't carry, and her husband panting like some rabid dog in his Brooks Brothers briefs. That there wasn't a restaurant in the hotel added insult to injury. He couldn't even pretend they'd met for a drink.

So when she'd asked for a divorce, he'd been all too

willing to agree. Even if he'd stayed, she'd never have felt secure. She'd have been suspicious of every alleged business dinner, every last-minute change of plans that required his presence downtown. She'd have been fearful every time she left the house, and knew she'd have ended up sneaking back early from whatever she was supposed to be doing to see if there was an extra car in the drive. That was no way to live.

"How dare you try to blame me? I won't allow you to equate what's happening with my choice. Am I supposed to overlook the existence of this . . . this . . ." She couldn't bring herself to mention the other woman's name. "I may not have much left to be proud of, but my daughter is not going to witness her mother's further humiliation."

"If this is about Foster—"

"It's not about Foster. It is about *our* daughter, our daughter who is alive and well."

"You've been strong. You've always been stronger than me. I couldn't deal with that pain, with that loss."

Faith stared into the deep blue of his eyes. She knew he'd suffered. Foster's death—the discovery of his bloody body nearly eighteen hours after his own fatal shot had taken his life—had changed them all, forever. She'd thought it was the greatest trauma they would ever suffer. And in many ways it was. But she'd managed. She'd read book after book on dying and child loss and grieving and coping, how-to books on conversations that needed to be had with surviving siblings and neighbors and friends. She'd written letters to Avery at boarding school every day, and spent hours shopping for the perfect care packages. She'd even tried meditation. But after one yoga class where the instructor asked her to imagine her roots going into the earth—an impossible task given that the class was conducted on the third floor of a strip-mall building—she'd abandoned the effort at spiritual peace and focused her energy on what she knew: increasing participation in the Episcopal Church by joining the Flower Guild, volunteering at the Boys and Girls Club. This summer she planned to expand her exercise regimen by playing singles as well as doubles in the Ladies' League at the Merion Cricket Club.

Then when she'd discovered Bill's infidelity, she knew what it was to truly ache. And by that point, there was nothing left to add to her life for distraction.

This wasn't about pain or loss. Bill's actions had nothing to do with Foster. She wanted to throw the timeline in his face, but all she could manage in response was "I'm sorry." The words came out flat, devoid of any feeling. "I'm sorry for you." Sorrier for me, she didn't have to add.

Bill shrugged and gave her a look as if he wondered who she was, or perhaps who she had become. It was the same puzzled expression she gave herself most mornings when she arose, looked in the mirror, and found herself unrecognizable.

"You can reach me through the office. I'll let you know the number when my telephone gets installed. I spoke to the accounting department and half my draw will be wired into your account on the first and fifteenth. That should get you through until . . . until . . ."

She nodded.

"Okay then." As he leaned toward her and gave her a kiss on her cheek, his familiar sandalwood scent filled her nostrils. She couldn't move. He was leaving for good. She'd never be able to enter Crabtree & Evelyn without bursting into tears. Their lives were henceforth separate. Mrs. William Herbert no longer existed. In her wildest dreams of envisioning life at forty-three years of age, she'd never thought she'd need for there to be an extra man for her at a dinner party.

Faith watched as he walked past the moving truck to his sedan, which he'd parked on the grass to keep out of the way. Even with the weight of two suitcases and a briefcase, his stride was quick and strong. He lifted his bags into the trunk, slammed the door, and then folded his trench coat neatly on the passenger seat. Before settling into the driver's seat, he removed his suit coat and draped it in the back. No break in rituals. For a moment, she allowed herself to wonder when he might return from this next business trip. *Never* seemed impossible to fathom.

She walked out of the library and stood in the entrance foyer. On the side table a silver platter held the daily mail. Without thinking she flipped through the pile of bills, catalogs, an oversize charity invitation, a members' newsletter from the Union League. What was she hoping to find? An answer to her problems, to her prayers, a handwritten note from her husband telling her that he'd made up the whole sordid story? That Little Miss Wunderkind was a figment of his imagination? Was there even any collection of words that could possibly mend the gaping holes in her life?

Her mouth was parched and she was about to head into the kitchen for a glass of water when her eye caught a light blue envelope. She picked it up and felt the thick, high-quality stationery. "Mr. and Mrs. William Herbert" was written on the outside in navy felt-tip pen. The engraved return address—a street in Bryn Mawr—was unfamiliar. Without bothering to get her silver-handled letter opener, she tore one end of the envelope and pulled out the single sheet.

Although this letter will no doubt come as a surprise— or perhaps a shock—to you both, I hope that it can be read in the spirit in which it has been sent. I am the biological mother of your adopted twins. Faith felt weak in the knees; she collapsed into a chair and held on to one arm for extra support, while her eyes remained fixed on a single sentence. Nine words.

This couldn't be happening. This couldn't have happened. It had to be some horrible prank, a practical joke the humor of which she didn't see. She felt coldness in her hands and feet and a tingling sensation along her spine. Her breathing was labored. Despite the pounding behind her eyes, she forced her focus back to the neat script, the sentences following the inauspicious beginning.

Having learned of Foster's tragic death, I find myself unable to remain anonymous anymore. Although I imagine that as a family you are suffering through a difficult period of grief and mourning, I believe it is time to offer Avery information about myself. As a psychiatrist, I more than understand how hard this awakening will be, and if she rejects my overtures, I will respect that decision. But I want her to understand why I made the choices that I did.

My only concern is for her well-being. Sixteen years is a long time but not a lifetime.

The signature belonged to Morgan Reese.

Faith dropped the letter as if it were laced with anthrax and watched it flutter for a moment before falling to the floor. She knew the name.

She rose and ran through the dining room. She banged open the swinging pantry doors, continued through the kitchen, and stopped only when she came to the mudroom off the side of the house. It was a rectangular space with a slate floor, the only room in the house that rarely, if ever, got the housekeeper's attention. Boots of various sizes formed a haphazard line along one wall. Jackets and hats were piled high on hooks. A croquet set with the mallets askew in the stand, gardening tools stored in a bucket, three folding lawn chairs, several shopping bags filled with donations for the Salvation Army, and the recycling bin for newspapers were crowded into the small space. Her attention immediately turned to the bin, which she tore through, throwing newspapers aside in her search for one particular Sunday section. Had it been one week ago or two? Could it have been three?

Faith remembered reading a profile. Everyone who had the slightest interest in the development of the area was following the story of who would become the director of the Wilder Center. There had been stories over the past weeks of all the doctors who had made the short list. As she'd sipped her coffee with warm milk and eaten two slices of oatmeal bread with margarine and cinnamon, she'd thought it interesting that nowhere in the lengthy article that outlined all of Dr. Reese's accomplishments, publications, and prestigious research positions was there any mention of a husband or children. But she'd dismissed that anomaly as either the necessary sacrifice of success or the selfishness she'd seen generally in people without children. She'd never suspected the truth: that this stranger had solved Faith's infertility problem by making her a mother of her own twins.

Her hands were black with newsprint before she found it. The front page of the Health Section had several coffee rings on it and the pages had been improperly refolded. Nonetheless the face on the cover was unmistakable. MORGAN REESE—THE QUEEN OF MENTAL HEALTH, the headline read.

She was about Faith's age, attractive, and similarly slender. She examined the picture. Was Morgan wearing a Chanel suit? Faith had several of her own carefully tailored designer outfits arranged by season in her walk-in closet. She scanned the text that she'd read so innocently at the time. They were both from good families, Main Line stock, and had been presented to society within a few years of one another. They probably knew many of the same people. Were they interchangeable but for the pile of credentials possessed by one and not the other?

She'd never wanted to tell the children they were adopted in the first place. There was nothing to be gained. They were a family. But Bill had insisted, and she'd finally acquiesced. Then look what happened. Even though they'd had no name, no identity, no biological parent wanting to reconnect, it had still been the biggest mistake she'd ever made. And the costliest.

How could this woman waltz into Avery's life? Faith was her mother. How could anyone try to come between them, let alone someone who'd never rubbed Vaseline onto her diaper rash, sat in the backyard examining an earthworm for most of a Saturday afternoon, spent hours carpooling a group of girls between elementary school, ballet, and riding lessons, or sat on the edge of a bed until the early-morning hours wiping tears from her face? How dare this woman try to make up for that now? Avery's happiness, accomplishments, heartaches, celebrations, and disappointments were Faith's—and Faith's alone— to cherish.

She didn't have the strength to stand so knelt on the floor amid the thin layer of dirt and clutter. How would Avery respond? Would she, like her father, be drawn to the intellect, the achievement? What if the bond was instantaneous? Would Avery dismiss the sixteen years that Faith had spent nurturing her and her brother? Was having filled the role of mother worth anything?

As she'd struggled in the past months with the chaos exploding around her, she'd taken solace in imagining times with the only remaining constant, her daughter: shopping for a prom dress; celebrating Mother's Day with a weekend at a spa; summer dinners together at the club; decorating Avery's new room. She'd felt confident that having that companionship for three months once school ended would be enough of a buoy to float her through the upcoming fall. Were even these simple dreams about to be destroyed?

She stood up slowly, willing herself to find the strength despite her weakened, trembling limbs. Pull yourself together, she ordered. She may not have the credentials that Dr. Reese had. She may not have her husband at her side. But she was a mother and a fierce one at that. If Foster's death was a symbol, it was to mobilize her to protect her remaining child from such a painful revelation.

Another mother was out of the question.

that if Foster's death was a *hypnet*, it was to mobilize
her to protect her reputation and/or from such a point a
revelation.

Surfaced! Another nerve-racking question.

8

Saturday, May 17th
4:00 p.m.

"*H*ey there." Even over the
telephone, Archer's voice was distinctive, not too deep
with a slightly nasal quality and a melodic inflection. Just
hearing it made her warm inside. "Sorry I didn't get up
with you this morning," he said.

"That's okay." She smiled, remembering the sight of
his long muscular body, broad shoulders, and tight but-
tocks as he lay on her cast-iron bed. One leg dangled over
the side, and he'd managed to cover his face with a pillow to block the early-morning sun that streamed through
her window. She'd kissed his back and run her fingers
through the thick brown curls on the top of his head, but
he hadn't stirred.

"The reading was fantastic but I guess it wiped me
out," he said, referring to the marathon poetry fest he'd
hosted the previous night. Lucy hadn't heard his key turn
in her lock, but he'd crawled into her bed just after four
in the morning, snuggled up to her with his arms and legs
wrapped around her, and pulled her to him. In her semi-

sleep she remembered the softness of his skin and the faint bitter smell of Dinkel Acker beer. She'd been barely conscious of his presence when he'd whispered in her ear, "If I promised to make love to you for the next twenty-four hours would you give up a day of work?" Then he'd kissed her lobe, sending a tingle through her body.

A few hours later, she'd showered, dressed, and tended to her pet rabbit while Archer slept peacefully. Before heading out the door, she'd left his white cotton boxers folded on the chair beside her bed, coffee in a chrome carafe on the kitchen table with the newspaper beside it, and a note with a red heart drawn on it, realizing as she'd drawn it that she could get used to the idea of living with someone.

"It was the reading that tired you out, was it?" she now teased. "And here I took credit for being such a great lover."

"And that you are. A legend in your own mind." Archer laughed.

"How quickly the romance of last night disappears in the cold, harsh light of day and your words of passion deteriorate into sadistic humor that wouldn't amuse a toad," she said in her breathiest melodramatic voice.

"What are you talking about?"

"Never mind. What's the plan for tonight?"

"Dad's expecting us at seven. And he likes—"

"Punctuality," she interrupted. "You've told me. I won't be late."

"Are you sure this is all right? I mean with your work."

"Yeah. I already talked to my Lieutenant and Jack's agreed to cover me," she replied, minimizing the extent of the logistical hoops she'd jumped through to make herself available for dinner. Her shift was four to midnight and her rotation for a new case was up. That meant she was responsible for manning the telephones and waiting for the call from police dispatch informing the Homicide Unit of a new job. But she'd worked enough overtime in five months to earn her a little leeway with her boss, and Jack had volunteered to take her place by the telephone as the "up-guy." She was free to go so long as she brought her beeper.

"I'll pick you up at six-fifteen." He blew a kiss into the telephone.

As she hung up the receiver, she felt a mixture of agitation and excitement at the thought of her impending introduction to Archer's father. She knew it was odd that in more than two months she'd never been to his house. For privacy, she tried to convince herself. And convenience. Staying at her apartment avoided the drive along Highway 30 West or a ride on the Paoli local to Devon. "Why go all the way out just to turn around and come back?" was Archer's rationale. Still when he came home with a Brooks Brothers bag of new white oxford shirts because he'd run out of clothes, she'd wondered whether he lived with these obstacles because he wanted to keep her away.

Those thoughts would end this evening. She would meet Rodman Haverill, "Rod" to his friends. "Although be sure to wait for him to invite you to use that nickname," Archer had instructed her when he'd extended the dinner invitation.

"I know Emily Post, too," Lucy responded. "I won't make inappropriate overtures or be too casual."

Archer had apologized, hugged her, and then added,

"The one thing I love best about you is that you say what's on your mind."

"What else am I going to do with my thoughts?"

That line had gotten her a second embrace.

Now she closed her eyes, trying to imagine what to expect. Archer had provided little detail. Would his father pad around his home in leather bedroom slippers like her father did? Would he barbecue a thick steak or have ordered in Chinese food ahead of time? Unfortunately, she had no information to help her form a picture. Contrary to her nature, she'd have to quell her curiosity for two more hours. Oh well, she thought. If he were anything like Archer, she'd adore him.

7:04 p.m.

Archer drove in silence. Lucy stared out the window. This far west of the city the homes were more spread out. Each expansive residence of Pennsylvania fieldstone seemed to command several acres of lush fields. In some areas the grass was deep emerald, in others it was lighter and mixed with patches of brown; the effect was a quilt of varying tones. She rolled down her window to inhale the fresh air and slight smell of hay. In the distance a chestnut horse grazed.

They crossed a small stone bridge, and Lucy glanced down at the rocky stream and the elegant sycamore trees growing along the wet banks. Then Archer turned onto a winding road. The car seemed to stall, then lurched forward as they climbed the hill. On their left, open meadows gently sloped away from the road to a pond surrounded by tall grasses. On the right stretched a black spiked fence behind which grew tall beech and birch trees. When they came to two stone pillars in which SUMMER HOUSE was carved, he stopped the car, reached into the glove compartment, and pulled out a small box. As he pressed the center button, the ornate iron gate slowly opened, creaking along its metal trench. He shifted into second gear and pulled forward.

Lucy glanced down the long driveway framed by rows of apple trees to the building beyond: a sprawling stone structure with an expansive slate courtyard in front. "What is this place?" she asked. "A museum?"

Archer shook his head.

"*This* is your home?" She'd seen houses as grand before but somehow never thought that real lives took place behind the walls, let alone the life of the man with whom she was involved.

"I actually live over there," Archer replied, pointing in the direction of a smaller stone building with dark shutters, a covered entry portico, and a small veranda off one side. Pristine white mortar joints accentuated the stonework, and a row of low, trimmed boxwoods created a path to the entrance.

Rather than turning in the direction he'd indicated, though, he continued to drive toward the massive building Lucy had noticed first. Pointing to a row of windows just under the roofline, Archer explained, "That's where I was exiled when I was younger, or should I say when I was a troublemaker. Now I'm in the guesthouse—what Father refers to as the garden service shed. I'm not sure whether that means he thinks I've improved or that I'm simply incorrigible." He shrugged.

"Can I see it?"

"Later." He winked. "We're already eight minutes late."

As they pulled up to the turnaround, she saw Rodman Haverill standing out front. Well over six feet, he'd clad his thin frame in a blue-striped oxford shirt and bow tie, a navy blazer, and gray flannels. His tasseled mahogany loafers shone from polish. He pushed up his sleeve and glanced at his watch to send a very obvious message, and she heard a slightly exasperated sigh escape Archer's lips before he shifted into neutral and cut the ignition.

"Hello, Archer." He nodded to his son and extended a hand toward her. "Miss O'Malley, I presume."

"Yes. Lucy. Call me Lucy. It's a pleasure to meet you. I've heard so much about you," she lied.

"I wish I could say the same." His deep voice had either a trace of vibrato or a slight tremor. Several dark hairs protruded from his prominent nose, and his bushy eyebrows overshadowed wire-rimmed glasses. "I don't monitor my son's comings and goings, and he keeps his private life to himself. Then he makes a general pronouncement about his relationships and that's that."

"I'll try to differentiate myself from the mob," she replied, stepping past him into the impressive two-story entrance.

A chandelier hung down through the double staircase. An enormous Oriental rug covered most of the marble floor, and a rectangular mirror in a carved black frame dominated one wall. Aside from two Chippendale side chairs, the space was empty.

"Your home is very beautiful." She could hear an echo.

"Thank you. It belonged to my mother's family. When Archer's mother and I married, my parents gave it to us, as I will give it to Archer and his bride when—"

He paused to clear his throat, but Lucy didn't wait for him to finish the phrase she dreaded hearing—*when he marries*. Her mother would make precisely the same kind of awkward comment. "It looks very English," she said to change the subject. "I went to the Cotswolds once and it reminds me of there. Only the houses were smaller." She laughed.

"It was designed by the firm of Mellor and Meigs," he replied, apparently ignoring her attempt at humor. "Walter Mellor and Arthur Meigs were considered instrumental in bringing the English pastoral mode seen throughout the Cotswolds to American residences. So you're right. You have either wonderful intuition or a better knowledge of architecture than I would have presumed for a . . . police officer." He patted Archer on the back.

"Cops will surprise you with what they know," she said.

He gave her a look—furrowed eyebrows and a slight pucker in the mouth—that she couldn't read. Then, apparently dismissing her last remark, he continued, "I would offer to show you around but I wish to avoid the wrath of my son so early in the evening. He tells me I'm prone to driving people away by boring them. So I suggest a drink out on the terrace. It's a mild evening and you might enjoy seeing the gardens, although they are certainly not what they'll be in a month or two."

He opened a large door and led them into a comfortable sitting room filled with overstuffed burgundy furniture corded in sage green. The floor-length drapes opened smoothly as he pulled the rings along a dark wooden rod, revealing the slate terrace that ran nearly the whole length of the house. They stepped outside. On an iron table was a tray with crystal decanters, a silver wine cooler with a corked bottle protruding from it, several glasses, and a plate of peeled carrot sticks.

Archer offered to make drinks while Mr. Haverill began what must have been his standard speech for newcomers about the grounds, the landscape design, the various renovations that had transpired over the years since the house was built. Listening, Lucy wondered how many prior girlfriends had heard this spiel. She imagined the lineup of women with bangs and matching sweater sets, daughters of matrons who prided themselves on membership in the Colonial Dames, and volunteers at Pennsylvania Hospital. Her predecessors probably knew the rules of polo and the ingredients in a Pimms Cup.

"The house was a constant canvas to my grandmother," Archer interrupted, offering Lucy a glass of Sancerre. As she took it, he mouthed the words, "If the pace doesn't quicken, there's more where that came from."

"Archer's quite correct. My mother, Emma, had so hoped that my wife would love this home, too. But as I expect Archer has told you, that didn't come to pass." The reference to Morgan seemed to change his manner of speech. His voice softened, and the tremor disappeared.

"Dad's mother was a perfectionist and she insisted on certain details: that the privet be kept at seventy-five inches, that the birdbaths be cleaned the first Monday of the month, that all the varieties of roses be replaced with Jackson and Perkins's 'John F. Kennedy' after the President's assassination," Archer volunteered. "God help the gardener who didn't follow her instructions."

Mr. Haverill chuckled at his son's remark, swirled the gin in his glass, and then took a sip. The ice cubes rattled. "A little light on tonic," he said, handing his tumbler back to Archer.

For a moment the only sound was the quick fizz of carbonation as Archer opened another bottle of Schweppes. Mr. Haverill walked to the table and picked up a carrot stick along with his newly diluted drink. "In addition to being the lone Democrat in a Republican bastion, my mother was a painter. She spent hours in this garden with her easel even after her doctors told her to stop. Many hours on her feet exhausted her."

"What did she paint?" Lucy asked.

"Mostly still lifes, a few portraits. She was an artist along the lines of the Boston School—realism with an enhanced natural beauty. 'The world is ugly enough,' she used to say, quoting Renoir. You might enjoy seeing some of her work after dinner, although one of her best oils will fill your view from the dining room table."

"That sounds lovely."

"She absolutely was," he replied, apparently mishearing. "The loveliest lady in all of Philadelphia. You can't begin to know how many people shared that view. Her shoes were too hard to fill for the next Mrs. Haverill."

Just then a petite woman in a black uniform with a white apron appeared from behind the interior curtain to announce that dinner was served. Mr. Haverill led the way to the dining room—a rectangular space with an inlaid wood floor, a large fireplace with a marble surround and mantel, and a long mahogany table. He held Lucy's chair, then took his place at one end while Archer sat at the other.

As Lucy pulled herself slightly closer to her place setting, she wondered how to address the problem of having dinner companions at opposite ends of a ten-foot table. To speak to Mr. Haverill, who still hadn't told her to call him Rodman, she would have to turn away from Archer and vice versa. Or she could look at neither and stare instead at Emma Haverill's beautiful oil: a composition of hydrangeas in a cobalt pitcher beside a bowl of fruit and an apple cut in half on the brightly colored tablecloth. She'd obviously set a high standard of perfection.

The Haverills' maid came around to her left side with a white casserole dish filled with a light brown puree. "Celery root?" she offered, wedging the hot dish even closer. Lucy negotiated the serving with more ease than she would have imagined given that she had to twist her spine to avoid being burned and raise her left elbow to get a half-decent angle. The process was repeated for string beans, brussels sprouts, and roast pork. When her plate was full she felt a moment of triumph. Not a drop of grease, sauce, or anything else spoiled the white lace place mat.

Mr. Haverill raised his glass. "To God and country," he said before taking a sip.

As Lucy drank, she had a momentary urge to suggest they get television tables, take off their shoes, and go sit in a circle in the den. But such a room wouldn't exist here; nobody had gone barefoot for more than a decade, and the idea of a folding snack table was certainly blasphemous. She should have extended the invitation for him to come to her home and almost laughed aloud at the image of her pet rabbit hopping over to Mr. Haverill to chew on the tassels of his loafers.

There was silence but for the sound of silverware brushing against china. Then Mr. Haverill asked, "O'Malley is Irish, I presume. Is your family from Philadelphia?"

"No. My father's side has been in Somerville, Massachusetts, for generations. My mother's family is from County Cork."

"How did they meet?" Archer asked.

"My mother came to Boston as an au pair when she was fifteen. She met my father when the family she worked for was burgled. He was a young police officer who responded to the call and took a list of what was stolen. He never caught the crook but he had the telephone number so he asked her out instead. They were married six months later and have been ever since. Forty-one years."

"They're Catholic," Mr. Haverill proclaimed.

If his implication was that they were still together because the church forbade divorce, nothing could be farther from the truth. Her parents' happy marriage was a source of tremendous pride.

"Historical allies of the Quakers, at least here in Philadelphia." She shifted the conversation. "As I'm sure you know."

"And what do you mean by that?"

"The Religious Society of Friends came to the defense of Irish immigrants because they empathized with victims of religious persecution. I read one story of Quakers patrolling Saint Joseph's Cathedral to prevent an anti-Catholic mob from destroying it. So even though the two religions couldn't be farther apart, they found a common ground."

"Who knew you were a history teacher," Archer said.

Lucy took a sip of her wine. "I'm fascinated by people who protect others when there is no legal or even moral obligation to do anything. You hear about firemen all the time, and believe me I admire them too, but I'm talking about the white students who lost their lives in the Civil Rights movement, the ones who jeopardize their own comfort or well-being to act on their beliefs. They seem so much nobler than the rest of us. And the Quakers were that for the Catholics."

"Are they nobler because they hold such strong convictions to begin with or because they act on them?"

"I suppose both. It doesn't do much good to believe in justice or equality or freedom of expression or whatever it might be in the abstract."

"So is that why you're a police officer?" Mr. Haverill cut a piece of meat, transferred the fork to his right hand, took the bite, and then rested his fork on the side of his plate. "Part of a quest for justice?" he asked with obvious sarcasm.

"In part, I suppose, although given my family history, I didn't have a role model for any other career. But I'm hardly the Good Samaritan. I often chastise myself for not even stopping to help someone on the side of the road with a flat tire. No, if I'm to be that nobler type of person, it will have to be outside the realm of my work."

"So what is it that a detective is supposed to do?"

"I'm told that a homicide investigator's mission is to hear the dead speak from their graves. But I think if I ever get to the point where I'm responding to voices, it'll be time for a career change."

Mr. Haverill smiled and for the first time in the evening, Lucy felt herself relax. Just then her beeper vibrated on its clip at her waist. She glanced at her watch: 11:32. Jack Harper's cell phone number appeared on the screen.

"I'm very sorry, but I must excuse myself for a moment."

Perhaps thinking she needed a powder room, Mr. Haverill gestured in the direction of a closed door.

"Actually, I need to use a phone if you don't mind."

"You'll find one in the library. This way." He stood up and placed his napkin onto the seat of his chair.

"Here, I'll show you," Archer said. "Excuse us." He bowed his head slightly in the direction of his father.

Archer led her back into the burgundy sitting room that they'd been in earlier. She was glad he'd come with her. The telephone was tucked inside a small cabinet that she never would have discovered on her own. She quickly dialed Jack's number while Archer waited.

"Harper," he answered.

"It's Lucy. What's up?"

"We've got a body. Caucasian woman. Late forties, early fifties. Looks like a suicide."

"Where should I meet you?" she asked.

He gave her an address on Belmont Avenue. "Brace yourself. It's on a golf course by the eighth hole but you can spare me the birdie jokes. It's a brutal sight."

9

Sunday, May 18th
12:03 a.m.

$\mathcal{A}$rcher drove with the windshield wipers on to dispel the thick mist that filled the night air. Lucy listened to the sound of the wipers and watched the headlights illuminate the blackness outside.

"That must be it," she heard him say. "Just ahead."

Looking up, she could see a flurry of red and blue police lights and a cluster of official cars parked at odd angles, blocking off the intersection of Belmont Avenue and Christ Church Lane, the entrance to Fairmount Links, a public golf course. A floodlight illuminated an expanse of grass and two ambulances. Dozens of people moved in and out of the light in silhouette.

Archer pulled to the curb.

"Thanks for the ride," Lucy said reluctantly, as she got out of the car. She shut the passenger door behind her, blew him a kiss, and then listened to the distinctive sound of his BMW as he shifted into gear and drove away. For a moment she had to resist the urge to sprint after him. She wanted to be home in bed curled up next to him, to feel his sides rise and fall as his breath moved in and out of his lungs, to hear his snores, to wiggle her hand between his legs and hold on to him. But this was her job. She took a deep breath and turned around to face the site of the disaster.

A group of policemen congregated around a large white sign prominently displaying the golf club's logo. Several of them drank coffee from Styrofoam cups, one kept the few curiosity seekers at bay, and another spoke on a two-way radio. As she passed, she flashed her identification.

Yellow police tape held up by makeshift stakes marked off a giant square surrounding the eighth hole. The Medical Examiner's van was parked just outside the barrier with its back doors open. Homer Ladd, the assistant examiner, bent over the front seat of his vehicle organizing his bag of tools and checking his bag labels to make sure everything he needed for his fieldwork was in order. Despite the late hour, his night was just beginning.

Jack stood just inside the perimeter with a camera around his neck and a Dictaphone in one hand. Although he combed his hair over his ever-increasing bald spot, tonight the wisps seemed in disarray and shot at odd angles from his head. "Sorry to interrupt your dinner."

"Hard duty," she mumbled as she followed a few steps behind him toward the body. "What's going on here?"

A Mercedes sedan with a buckled front fender rested against a large maple tree. The driver's-side door was open and the airbags had been deployed. Glass from the shattered windshield and broken headlights littered the well-kept grass. The roof and trunk were dotted with dents and the taillights were shattered, too. Frank Grif-

fith, a Crime Scene technician, squatted by the passenger-
side door. He lifted a short hair from the leather seat with
tweezers and placed it in a Baggie.

"What is it?" she asked, leaning over his shoulder. A
faint floral aroma filled the interior of the car.

He shrugged. "My SWAG?"

His Scientific Wild-Ass Guess was not what she
wanted, but she'd have to wait until all the evidence had
been gathered and processed through the Crime Lab to
get a definitive answer.

"How'd a front-end accident manage to damage the
top and back?" she asked. "It looks to me like someone
bludgeoned this car."

"Why don't you give me a few moments to do my job
before you start demanding answers or speculating about
them yourself?" Frank asked without shifting his focus
away from the interior.

"Sorry," Lucy said in a less than heartfelt apology as
she took a few steps away. "Why are the criminalistics
guys here if this is a suicide?" she quietly asked Jack.

"Come on," he said, nodding in the direction of a sand
trap where a figure with a black tarp draped over it was
visible. "I'll show you."

A paramedic hovered, unwilling to accept the futility
of his presence despite the arrival of the Medical Examiner's wagon. Two cops wearing black Windbreakers
with CRIME SCENE written in white lettering stood a few
feet away. One was making several notations in a small
spiral notepad. The other, a young officer whom she recognized but did not know by name, smoked an unfiltered
cigarette.

When the two of them approached, the smoker ground

out his butt with one foot, reached into his pocket, and removed a rubber glove, which he pulled onto his hand
with a snapping noise. He moved to the tarp, took hold of
the top end, and pulled it back.

A woman lay on her back with her stiletto-heeled
shoes crossed at her ankles. Blood covered her chest,
arms, and hands. A black hole in her flesh and burnt fabric marked the bullet's entrance somewhere in close prox-
imity to her heart. Mascara had smeared onto her cheek
and blood was streaked across her chin. One eye was
open, the other shut. There was something familiar about
the face.

"Who is she?"

"Name's Morgan Reese. A doctor. License lists her address in Bryn Mawr."

Lucy covered her mouth with her hand to contain
her gasp.

"Do you know her?" Jack asked.

She shook her head, trying to organize her thoughts.
The mother of Archer, the lost love of Mr. Haverill, and
here Lucy was in the middle of the night to investigate her
horrible death. She couldn't hold out with her information for long, but she needed a chance to collect herself.
It was too early in her career in Homicide to fall apart
over a body while her seasoned partner watched.

Fortunately Jack didn't belabor the point. "The police
found a thirty-five caliber handgun just beside her body,"
he continued, pointing to where a white outline in the
shape of a pistol had been spray-painted onto the grass.

"Was death instantaneous?"

"She was dead by the time the EMTs arrived. We're
assuming a heart wound, which would mean pretty

quick—almost instantaneous depending upon where she hit—but we'll need an autopsy to tell us definitively. There's also a fairly nasty head injury—blunt-force trauma. When I told you we thought suicide, we hadn't seen that yet. Contact was on the left side toward the back of her head. Hard to imagine it was even physically possible for her to do that to herself."

"Who called the police?"

"A woman named Gertrude Barbadash. She heard the shot. She lives by herself over there," he replied, pointing behind them to a yellow clapboard house that Lucy hadn't noticed before. Nestled back from the road, it had a long covered porch in front and black shutters on all the windows. "The place is called the Rabbit Club. It's my understanding she runs it."

"The Rabbit?"

"It's a men's club. Bunch of guys meet a couple of times a month to cook. Old Philadelphia," Jack offered, as if that phrase somehow clarified the situation. "Barbadash is the house manager. The club provides her with living quarters upstairs."

Lucy glanced over at the building and noticed a small light in a window on the second floor. Not the most hospitable setting, but perhaps the pay was good. Although many of the houses along South Concourse Drive and Parkside Avenue had been rehabilitated, the neighborhood surrounding this section of Fairmount Park wasn't the best; she certainly wouldn't want to live alone in a seldom-used building in the middle of a seasonal golf club.

"Where is she now?"

"A paramedic took her to the ER. She complained of

dizziness," the officer explained. "She's an older lady and was visibly upset."

As anyone would be, Lucy thought. Age had nothing to do with it.

"What else did she say?"

"Not much. She was reading in her bedroom and heard a shot. She called the police but was too scared to look out the window."

"What about the car wreck?"

He pulled out a notepad and flipped through several pages. "She didn't mention it. Just said she heard a 'deafening bang' that was 'very close.' That's all she described."

It did seem odd that she'd missed the crash, the broken glass, perhaps even the sound of repeated banging, no more than three hundred feet away.

"Who found her?"

"Officer Callahan. He and Mike Regio responded to Barbadash's call. On the way up Christ Church Lane, they saw the car. They got out and started looking around. And here she was."

"What about the Mercedes?"

"It's registered to the deceased."

Lucy looked at Jack, who'd furrowed his brow. He seemed lost in thought. "So what happened?" A car accident, a head wound, and a bullet to the chest. Whatever demons Dr. Reese had tried to escape caught up with her tonight.

"Your guess is as good as mine. There's no apparent blood in the car. Looks like both head and chest injuries were inflicted after the crash."

"As I told Harper, we found this in her purse," the police officer said. With his gloved hand he held out a piece of light blue stationery with the initials *MAR* in the top right-hand corner. Across the sheet was scrawled in almost illegible black ink:

> *Dearest Avery,*
> *For all I've done, I'm sorry. I never meant to harm you or anyone. I hope that with time you will understand the choices I made and that you can find it in your heart to forgive me. We are all imperfect. Perhaps I was more imperfect than others, but you must never doubt my love for you.*

"And these." He handed her a ziplock bag containing an orange plastic canister. Lucy could see that it was a Klonopin prescription for Walter Reese. The antianxiety medication had been obtained from a pharmacy in Bryn Mawr. The prescribing physician was Morgan A. Reese.

"Who is Walter?"

"Don't know. Husband; maybe a relative."

"The other thing you probably noticed was this." The officer crouched down and pointed to a series of scars partially obscured by blood on Dr. Reese's limp wrists.

The three pinkish lines in her flesh, each no more than an inch long, ran perpendicular to her thin radius and ulna. The scars were revealing—but of a cry for help, not an intent to succeed. As a doctor, Morgan would have known that if she truly wanted to die, incisions along the forearm were more likely to sever high-pressure arteries. She could also have prescribed heparin or other drugs for herself to decrease her blood's ability to clot, making a parallel cut foolproof. That's not what she'd done—then or now—but whoever had bashed her in the back of the head wanted her death to appear self-inflicted. He might even have known about the failed earlier attempt and tried to capitalize on it.

Jack nodded to indicate they'd viewed the body long enough. As the tarp was replaced, Dr. Reese's haunting one-eyed gaze disappeared behind the blackness.

"Has her family been notified?"

"Family hasn't been identified. Her home telephone is unlisted."

Lucy paused before mustering the courage to speak the words that would reveal her personal involvement. It wasn't something she wished to share, but she had no choice. She took Jack's arm and pulled him away from the body. Suddenly she didn't feel professional at all. "Archer . . . my boyfriend . . . this is his mother," she stammered.

"You've got to be kidding."

She shook her head, wishing for a moment that she was.

Jack put his arm around her shoulders. The strength of his grip felt good. "Let me get you home. Lieutenant Sage can contact next of kin."

"Don't make me go. Not yet." She wanted to say the right words but knew her suddenly timid voice and tear-filled eyes revealed her struggle to maintain composure. "Let me finish here. Let me go back to the precinct and do the paperwork."

"O'Malley, you don't have to be a hero. The case can be reassigned. It's your boyfriend's mother."

"No," she blurted. "Don't do that. Please."

She didn't know Jack well enough to confess her true thoughts: that she was beginning to care deeply for

Archer and that she was going to learn everything she possibly could about his mother. She'd never known what actually happened with Aidan and it haunted her a decade later. Information—the truth—might help Archer and his father. And at the heart of what they would need to know was who murdered her. Although she had no doubt about her commitment to the task, for the first time in her law enforcement career, Lucy dreaded what she might discover.

"Please," she said again.

Jack paused before patting her shoulder gently. "I may be making a huge mistake here, O'Malley, but I'm not going to second-guess my partner's judgment about her own objectivity. You say you want this case; it's your call. Just promise you'll let me know if and when it gets to be too much."

"I promise."

He sighed. "Okay, then. We've got a ton of work to do. Let's get going."

8:12 a.m.

Lucy struggled to climb the narrow steps to her apartment. As she pulled herself up the banister, she felt as if her legs couldn't possibly carry the weight of the news she was about to deliver. Archer had dropped her off at the crime scene suspecting nothing. He'd kissed her good-night only a few hundred yards from the body of his dead mother. He'd no doubt returned to her apartment and slept peacefully, perhaps without even a dream to stir his slumber. How would he react now?

She stood on the landing and fished in her bag for her keys. It was only eight in the morning and she was surprised to hear the radio playing. The kettle whistled. Archer was awake already. She couldn't postpone the inevitable.

Lucy turned the lock and opened the door slowly. He stood beside the stove, stirring a tablespoon of honey into a steaming mug. Then he returned to the cast-iron frying pan in front of him and mixed the contents with a wooden spoon. As he cooked, he hummed along with the Beethoven concerto. From the threshold, she could see the line where his tan back met his very white bottom, a line revealed by the loose pajamas that hung low on his hips. The familiar smells of his breakfast—scrambled eggs, sausage, and fried apples—filled the small room. It was a Sunday morning ritual.

"Welcome home," he said, as he noticed her enter. "You must be wiped out."

She nodded, dropped her purse, took off her thin jacket and patent leather loafers, and sat in a chair. He'd lit a fire in the wood-burning stove. Several back issues of *Granta* were piled on the kitchen table. Without thinking, she picked one up and stared at the cover, an abstract arrangement of colors and faces.

"I didn't realize I'd have company for breakfast so I was going to do some reading. But this is much better." He smiled, and placed a mug in front of her. A mint smell emanated from it. "Are you hungry?"

The toaster popped. He removed the two slices of crisp wheat bread and put them unbuttered on a plate. Then he added two new ones. "What happened?" he asked, as he lifted the frying pan from the flame and scraped the scrambled eggs onto a platter.

She looked over at him. Her eyes welled with tears.

Archer came over to her and wrapped his arms around her neck. "In all honesty, I can't imagine how you do this job, face death day in and day out."

"It's not that. It's not the work . . . this is not the work. I'm not upset about . . . This has to do with you," she stammered.

He took a step back. "Why? What's wrong?" Then he shook his head. "I know you were surprised about my father, about the house. I probably should have given you some more information. Maybe it wasn't fair. I just didn't want it to take on significance that it doesn't hold for me."

She shook her head. "This has nothing to do with last night or dinner. Archer—" She reached out and clasped his hand in both of hers. "It was your mother. The victim was your mother. She's dead."

He sank down onto the floor and sat cross-legged with his head in his hands.

"I'm so sorry."

"What happened?" he asked without looking up.

Lucy described what she'd seen and what little she'd learned.

"So it wasn't suicide?"

"No, but we think her killer wanted it to look that way."

He pushed himself over to where she sat and rested his head in her lap. She ran her fingers through his hair. She could hear the sausage crackling in the pan and smell the apples starting to burn, but she didn't move. As a police officer, she felt frustrated to sit with the next of kin and know that there were no questions to ask. Archer hardly knew this woman except by name. He wouldn't be able to explain who Avery was, or why Dr. Reese might have been at Fairmount Links, or who might have had reason to kill her. She was more a mystery to him than to anyone. And because he hadn't accepted the invitation to lunch, hadn't responded to his mother's overture after nearly thirty years, he'd lost the opportunity to hear what she might have had to say. Lucy knew that he would be thinking of that more than anything else.

After several minutes, he stood, moved back to the stove, and turned off the flames. He leaned against the counter. "I can't miss her. I didn't love her. I didn't know her," he recited, as if he needed to remind himself. "And yet I still feel this emptiness." His voice cracked. "I only hope that Dad finds some relief. He's been waiting for her to walk back in the door ever since she walked out. Now at least he can abandon that hope and move on."

The sentence struck Lucy as callous, although it was a phrase she'd heard so many times before. *Moving on.* Confirmed information that a loved one was dead allowed the family to move on. Friends and relatives of a missing person were relieved when a body was discovered or when a defendant was convicted. She'd never understood why that was easier than living with uncertainty; uncertainty allowed for hope to be sustained. But she knew from everything she'd read and heard and seen that closure, even horrible closure, was universally welcomed. Maybe that's why Aidan's death still haunted her. There were too many open questions to move on.

"Are you going to investigate?" Archer asked.

She nodded. "Unless you don't want me to. The case

is assigned to me and Jack, but my Lieutenant would let me off if I asked."

"No," he replied. "I want you to do it. But I want you to make me a promise."

"Anything," she replied without thinking.

"Don't hide information from me. Don't try to protect me or my feelings or my family. I want to know ... everything."

She shuddered, realizing the predicament she was in. But she understood his sentiment completely. That had been all she'd asked for ten years ago and she hadn't gotten it. "I promise."

10

10:13 a.m.

$\mathcal{J}$ack Harper stood on the front steps of the Joseph W. Spelman Building, a drab, yellow brick structure with a few narrow, rectangular windows on one side that housed various divisions of the Department of Public Health, including the Medical Examiner's offices. He had his hands in his pockets. His Phillies baseball cap was pulled low over his eyes and he wore dark glasses. It was the belt-and-suspenders approach to keeping out the Sunday morning glare.

"Sorry I'm late," Lucy said, tucking her white shirt into her khaki pants. She still hadn't slept, and had barely managed to shower and change her clothes before heading to University Avenue. She'd stayed at the kitchen table with Archer until the last possible moment, reluctant to leave him with only Cyclops for company. Although she couldn't bring herself to tell him she was attending his mother's autopsy, he must have sensed where she was going because he didn't ask.

"Ladd will be in a bad mood whether we're prompt or not. No doubt he's none too pleased to have had his Saturday night ruined, and now his Sunday breakfast interrupted. Speaking of which—" he said, producing a crumpled paper bag from the pocket of his nylon jacket. "Have you eaten? I bought you a Boston cream just in case."

"Thanks. But I'm not sure even I could stomach that at this moment."

"A few more months on the job and you won't give it a second thought."

"Easy for you to say."

Lucy had never seen an autopsy before and would have been just as happy to keep it that way. Although she wasn't a squeamish person and had certainly dealt with enough violence and blood over the past eight years, watching Morgan Reese be cut open and have her vital organs removed and weighed was enough to turn her stomach several times over. She would have much preferred to get the report and photographs and meet with the Medical Examiner—as she'd done numerous times before—but Jack had insisted that they watch this one live. With a prominent Caucasian female victim, Lieutenant Sage was sure to be keeping close tabs on their investigation.

"And you never know what might come out verbally or visually that never makes it into the report," he'd said as she had left the station to break the news to Archer. "Not that I'm impugning the integrity of our ME's office. Never. But it's happened to me before that when I'm looking at something on a body, a mark, a bruise, who knows what, I learn something that no picture or typewritten word is ever going to teach me." He'd smiled and tweaked her cheek. "I've been at this job a lot longer than you. Just for a moment let me pretend to know something you don't. Indulge me."

"Bring it on then," she'd said, referring to the autopsy. But now that the moment had arrived, whatever bravado she'd mustered had disappeared.

"You're sure about this?" Jack asked, offering one more opportunity for her to beg off. She nodded. "Okay, tough guy. Here we go."

They registered at the front desk, showed their badges, signed a visitors' log, and were given clearance for their firearms from the security officer. Lucy followed Jack as he headed down a circular staircase to the basement. She appreciated that he knew his way around without having to ask. Even after five months in Homicide, she felt lost as soon as she stepped inside the Medical Examiner's office. Perhaps it was the overwhelming odor that disoriented her—the unique scent that Jack had described as a "sweet version of soured milk." Now that smell of death filled her nostrils.

"By the way," he said, as he pushed the door open. "Crime Scene recovered a bullet from the soil just beneath where her body was found. It was a thirty-five caliber. Thing appears to have gone straight through her."

Ladd stood by a stainless-steel sink scrubbing his forearms. Hearing them enter, he shut off the water, dried his hands, and removed a pair of latex gloves from a box by the sink.

"Let's get started," he muttered. "Ellie's already done the preliminaries."

The preliminaries referred to the collection of digital photographs of the corpse both clothed and undressed before the medical examination had begun. They documented patterns of blood splattering and tears and burns on fabric, as well as the external condition of the body, any bruising, cuts, or abrasions. From an investigative standpoint, these often yielded the most information.

Ellie Montgomery, a short, athletic woman, was the photographer for the Medical Examiner's office. She'd taken the job as a way to finance her artistic career, but after more than twenty years on the squad, any distinction between the two had disappeared. Her reputation for perfection and precision was well known throughout the police department. Although she frequently testified at trial if the defense didn't stipulate to the admission of her photographs, in one notable case the integrity of her picture had been challenged. It was that case that made her a legend. She'd been on the stand under heated cross-examination and, according to all accounts, hadn't been the least bit shaken. "My work is my art and I take my duties extremely seriously. My allegiance isn't to the judicial process. My loyalty is to these bodies," she'd explained. "Besides, there's no need to alter them. They're absolutely beautiful just the way they are." The defense attorney hadn't known what follow-up question to ask, and had slinked his way back to his seat.

Now Ellie stood in one corner, loading a cartridge into her digital camera.

A stainless-steel gurney—one of three in the large room—held the body of Morgan Reese. She was naked but for an identification tag attached to her big toe by a wire. Beside her was a narrow stand on wheels, the top of which was covered with metal instruments—scalpels, knives, ladles, spreaders, tweezers, and a saw—as well as a tape recorder and a clipboard. Her skin appeared to have a violet hue under the fluorescent lights, and her eyes stared vacantly at the ceiling. Exposed, with her pelvic bones and ribs protruding, she appeared even smaller than Lucy had remembered from the night before. Part of her left breast had been shot away by the bullet's trajectory; a large nipple and areola seemed to cover most of her tiny right breast. Her hair was matted against her head by blood, and her hands were encased in plastic bags.

Lucy took a step back, hoping no one would notice. She wished she had a chair to lean against, but there was nothing. "Think of it as character building," her mother always said about surviving difficult experiences. She wondered if an autopsy qualified.

Ladd pushed the "record" button and began his narration in a low voice. "Morgan Reese. Forty-six-year-old Caucasian female. Five-four, one hundred nine pounds." He turned the tag on her toe to read off her Social Security number, and then slowly walked a full circle around the table. "External examination reveals no skeletal deformities." He pressed his thumb into her thigh and released it. Lucy watched the skin grow paler with compression and then return to its violet hue. "Mild hypostasis noted."

"That's when blood pools in the lower body," Jack whispered.

Lucy forced a smile to indicate she appreciated the translation, but Jack mistook her grimace for nausea. Moving closer to her, he took hold of the back of her arm.

"You okay?"

She nodded even though she knew she couldn't look convincing.

"If anyone needs a bathroom, it's the door by the sink," Ladd said without looking at his audience. "At some level we all get used to this process, but at another we never do. These are human beings—lives that are now over. That puts us in a sacred position." He reached for Morgan's left wrist, and turned it over in his hand. "Perpendicular scarring, apparent self-inflicted lacerations. Given the coloration and condition of scar tissue, these wounds are old—somewhere between fifteen and twenty years."

He released the arm and repeated on the other side. "Lateral bruising on right forearm consistent with a defensive posture. Extensive bruising on left cheekbone and around left eye." Moving to the end of the table, he gently lifted Morgan's head and cradled it in his two hands. He turned it slightly to the right and then leaned forward to examine the area around her left ear. He closed his eyes and Lucy could see movement in his fingers as he felt along her skull. After a moment he pulled something from Morgan's hair, replaced her head on the table, and put the fragment in a small plastic dish. He then studied the blackened hole in her chest, which appeared almost star-shaped. Rolling her body onto her side, he examined the exit wound, which was substantially larger and had shredded tissue protruding from it.

Watching him manipulate this corpse, Lucy felt a wave of nausea, and her mouth filled with saliva. Pull yourself together, she thought. This is your job. You could have stayed in violent crimes and avoided death altogether, but you didn't. And witnessing the unthinkable is the price of being in Homicide. The image of Archer slumped over the breakfast table staring down at his untouched eggs and cold toast gave her courage. He needs these answers, she reminded herself.

Ladd made several notations on the clipboard, marking locations of the holes on a standardized form for females.

As he returned to the examining table, Lucy leaned in to see what he had done. From the diagram, it was clear that the bullet's trajectory had been almost a straight line, exactly what Jack had said given the location of the recovered bullet in the ground.

"Left anterior superior medial to left posterior inferior lateral at twenty degrees. Extensive stippling appears. You got this, Ellie?" he asked, pointing to the pattern of pinpoint hemorrhages.

"I did. And I got you the perfect star, too," she replied, anticipating his next question.

"Visible abrasions on right shoulder," he continued. He removed the paper bags from Morgan's hands. "Gunpowder residue appears on the left palm and fingers. None on the right hand."

Lucy glanced over at Jack. Whoever shot Morgan had done so at very close range. The star-shaped entrance wound was indicative of actual contact between the gun and the skin. The particular type of hemorrhage could be caused only by the discharge of burned gunpowder on her flesh. But what was the shoulder abrasion? Lucy took a step closer and peered around Ladd to get a closer look at what was a reddish rectangle, approximately two inches wide and four inches long. "Could that be from a seat belt?" she asked, remembering the car accident.

"Possibly."

She imitated the sweeping motion of pulling the strap diagonally across her body. "Meaning over the right shoulder and buckled at the left hip," she muttered.

Ladd glared at her. No doubt he didn't like to be interrupted during the examination. "That's right."

She turned to Jack. "That means she was a passenger. A driver's abrasion would be on the other side. Someone else drove her Mercedes into that tree."

"Now aren't you glad you're here?" he whispered.

Next, Ladd attempted to wiggle Morgan's jaw, which was immobile, and then moved her arms, hands, ankles, and feet. "Postmortem rigidity is incomplete, consistent with a time of death between nine P.M. and midnight." With that, he removed goggles from the pocket of his scrubs, adjusted them over his eyes, and reached for the saw. "Ellie, I'm ready."

With three strides, the photographer bounded across the room and positioned herself to photograph Morgan's head with its skull removed. Squatting, she looked through the viewfinder.

Lucy stepped away and closed her eyes. The mechanics she didn't need to see. She knew what was happening. With a scalpel, Ladd was making a careful incision around the skull, ear to ear behind the head, detaching the skin flap from the cranium and pulling it forward over her face. With a circular saw, he cut through the skull. She could hear the grating sound and almost sensed the dispersed white dust settling onto her skin. She shuddered again, and then decided it was better to watch. Her imagination was getting the best of her. At least the horror of reality would keep her grounded.

Morgan's face was completely covered by what appeared to be a burgundy bathing cap with sandy hair protruding. With a small chisel, Ladd opened the skull and removed the skullcap. With a few deft motions, Morgan's brain tumbled from her head into a sterilized bowl. Ellie's shutter started clicking.

"Subdural hematoma. Significant bruising and swelling." Ladd turned to his audience and sighed. "This woman suffered a head injury from a blunt force. With the bruising on her forearm, I'd say she attempted to deflect the first blow, but the second landed on the side of her head and knocked her out." He glanced back at the wood splinter in the plastic dish. Without a word, he picked it up, walked over to a cabinet against the far wall, and removed a microscope. He placed the splinter under the viewfinder. As he looked through, he said, "We'll examine this fragment in more detail, but I'd say you're looking for a baseball bat. The old-fashioned kind—a Louisville Slugger."

Lucy envisioned hours of combing through sales receipts from neighboring sporting goods stores and poring through local baseball team rosters, then cross-referencing those records with criminal offender information. As she was the junior member of this Homicide Unit, that endless task would inevitably fall to her. Unless, of course, they got enough real leads to fill her time.

"Why the gunshot? Couldn't the hematoma have killed her?" she asked.

"We're just getting started. I'll get you your answers, but you have to be patient with this process. We haven't even opened her up yet."

Apparently brain removal didn't count. It was going to be a long morning.

2:51 p.m.

Homer Ladd covered Morgan's corpse with the sheet, pulled off his gloves, and walked over to the sink to wash his hands. Her body now had a Y-shaped incision from both shoulders to the abdomen and down to her vagina. Her heart, lungs, kidneys, and other organs had been removed, weighed, analyzed, and replaced. Lucy had somehow expected the human body to be like a suitcase, so perfectly organized that everything fit on the way out but, by the end of the trip, couldn't be repacked. Instead, Ladd had managed to put everything back exactly where it belonged. In a few moments, Morgan would be wheeled out to the anteroom and sewn shut by a technician—suitable for an open-casket funeral if that's what her next of kin wanted.

Ellie collected her cartridges of film. "I should have prints ready in a couple of hours," she said, making a hasty exit.

Lucy and Jack followed Ladd out of the autopsy room, into the elevator, and up to his office on the second floor. The combination of a head injury and a bullet wound had made the autopsy longer and more complicated than most, and Ladd collapsed into a chair, obviously exhausted. They all were. But the investigation had just started. Now they were ready for some information.

"Cause of death was massive hemothorax and hemopericardium due to a gunshot wound to her chest."

"What about the blow to the side of her head?"

"People certainly can recover from subdural hematomas; the draining process is relatively straightforward. But she might have had memory loss, or even brain damage, depending upon what type of medical care she received and when. I can't predict the degree of permanent injury, but I can tell you it is highly unlikely she'd be dead. In any event, at this stage it's an unnecessary hypothetical. The point is that someone knocked her unconscious and only later—possibly as much as two hours later—was she killed by a gunshot wound."

Jack and Lucy exchanged glances. The situation was even more bizarre than they'd appreciated initially.

"In my opinion, the shot was a crude attempt to make it appear that the death was a suicide. The killer put the gun in her left hand after the fact—that's why we've got gunpowder residue on her left palm. Given the location of the bullet hole, Reese would have had to be a contortionist to get her wrist, hand, and chest aligned in that manner. And that's ignoring the fact that she was probably still unconscious when she was shot." He rubbed his eyes.

"Was she left-handed?" Lucy asked. "I mean, if you wanted the death to look like a suicide, wouldn't you put the gun in the hand you'd assume she'd use? Most people are right-handed. Unless you had specific knowledge to the contrary, you'd guess the right hand."

"Or the shooter was left-handed. If left-handedness were what you were conscious of, you might forget that you're in a minority," Jack added.

"Well, I can't help you on that scenario, but"—Ladd paused, and scanned his notes—"I can help on the first point. I'm almost certain that Dr. Reese was left-handed. There is a substantial callus on the inside of her left index finger from holding a pen or pencil."

Jack made a note to himself. Then he summarized. "So

she's in a car accident, gets out of her car, gets smashed in the head with a baseball bat, and then gets shot."

"That's correct in essence. But before she was dealt the blow to the head, remember there was some sort of struggle. We've got the bruising on her forearm. And we've got the yarn fibers under her fingernails."

"That's right," Lucy mumbled, remembering the scrapings he had taken from under Morgan's nails once the bags on her hands had been removed. He'd been able to ascertain that the material was wool, but he'd been unable to determine whether it was lambswool, cashmere, mohair, or something else. The minuscule amount would have to be analyzed.

"The victim may well have grabbed at her attacker's arm or torso and come away with a sweater sample."

"But she wasn't shot at that point," Jack interrupted.

"That's right. The bullet trajectory indicates the victim was prostrate and the shooter most likely knelt down beside her, put the gun against her chest, and pulled the trigger."

Lucy instantly regretted the promise she'd made to Archer.

"What about the drugs, the prescription medication found in her purse?"

"We'll have to wait for the toxicology report to come back to see if she ingested any of it herself."

"Who are we looking for?" Jack asked.

Ladd leaned back in his chair. "Given the angle of the bruising, the person is definitely taller than the victim. And the hematoma didn't come from a ninety-eight-pound weakling. Someone nailed her with considerable strength"

"A male then?" Jack asked.

"Aren't we stereotyping just a little bit?" Lucy responded. There were plenty of strong women in the world and the height threshold was only five feet four inches. Despite her own small stature, that requirement hardly ruled out the female population.

"Not necessarily," Ladd echoed.

"Since she was found wearing an expensive watch, I'm assuming robbery isn't a motive," Lucy added.

"I'd agree. But remember your killer isn't sophisticated in a criminal sense. This has the hallmarks of a crime of passion—not well planned and very hastily executed."

"Plus the killer had some familiarity with his victim," Jack added.

"What about the time lag, the time between the knock-out and the shot?"

"All I can tell you is that there was one. I don't know why there was an approximately two-hour lapse."

"And no one found her in the interim. That's the weirdest part. Where can you lie unnoticed, bleeding and unconscious, for up to two hours?" Jack asked incredulously.

"Apparently within the Philadelphia city limits," Ladd replied.

Lucy's mind raced with possibilities. What had caused the delay? Had the killer experienced second thoughts, panic, or remorse? Perhaps it was something as simple as that he or she wasn't sure the job was finished. Maybe the gun was sought in the interim to make certain. But couldn't the killer have known by checking Morgan's pulse? And once it had been established that she was still alive, why wouldn't more blows have been inflicted to end it then and there? Did the killer actually think the staged suicide would cover up the crime? Or . . . or . . . just maybe— "Could there have been two?"

"Two different killers?"

She nodded. "A baseball player and a shooter."

The Assistant Medical Examiner sighed. "I don't see why not."

She thought through the combination of scenarios. They needed a driver, a hitter, and a shooter. How many of the roles overlapped? Instead of narrowing the field, she'd expanded the possibilities.

"If there were two, I'd bet my pension they're connected. Otherwise you're talking about an almost apocryphal amount of coincidence."

"Perhaps," Lucy said. "It's also possible that the hitter may not have intended to kill. Maybe only the shooter intended to kill."

"What are you talking about?" Jack asked.

"Well, it's a possibility, that's all I'm thinking."

Ladd leaned forward and raised one eyebrow. "Let's leave that theory to defense counsel."

11

3:45 p.m.

A man in an argyle sweater rocked from side to side as he adjusted his cleats in the sand. Without making contact, he practiced his swing several times. Then he moved forward six inches, widened his stance, lowered his head, and hit the ball out of the trap. Sand flew as the ball was propelled up into the air and back onto the fairway. He watched until it had stopped rolling, replaced his iron in a blue leather bag, and got back behind the wheel of a golf cart with a green-and-white-striped awning. With a whir of the electric engine, he advanced twenty yards and stopped just a few feet from where his ball rested.

Lucy idled the engine of her government-issued Ford Explorer as she watched the careful choreography. "A good walk spoiled," Mark Twain had characterized the game. She tended to agree.

With the golfer safely away from the road, she continued along Christ Church Lane. Even from a distance, in the late-afternoon sun she could see vestiges of last night's crime: the bloodstained grass, an array of tiny squares of shatterproof glass, and yellow police tape that flapped in the breeze.

Approximately a hundred yards farther along stood the clubhouse for the second-oldest men's cooking club in Philadelphia. There was no sign, no ominous MEMBERS ONLY placard, just an uneven roofline and sagging porch to proclaim its historic significance.

As she pulled up to the building, she thought of Aidan's secret club—the beige tepee that he'd erected in the backyard with a circle of gravel around it and KEEP OUT marked in indelible ink on one of the plastic sides. Each day for several months she'd stared at the mysterious structure, watching him and Timmy Clarkson crawl in and out through the flap that served as a door. Despite her curiosity and unrelenting questions, her brother had offered no information on what transpired within, and despite her strident protests, neither of her parents had supported her claim of unfairness. "It's his tepee. The club is his idea. He can let in no one if he wants to be alone, or even all those who aren't sisters," her father had said when she'd appeared in tears, begging to be included. "That's what freedom is about. The freedom to choose."

Perhaps members of the Rabbit Club were simply men who had never outgrown the need for a fort.

There were no other cars in the small parking area. She shut off the engine and climbed out. A screen creaked. A narrow door was ajar. A woman with white hair, flawless brown skin, and walnut eyes stood on the threshold with her arms crossed in front of her chest.

"Detective O'Malley?" the woman asked. Her voice contained the slightest hint of a British accent.

"Yes," she replied, extending her hand.

"I'm Miss Barbadash, the house manager here. Won't you come in?"

Lucy walked past her into a large room. Against one wall was an open fireplace from which hung an oversize copper pot. On the table were several piles of white cards marked with "Please state your intentions," followed by boxes for "Accept" and "Regret."

"I was keeping myself busy," Miss Barbadash offered by way of explanation. "As you might imagine, I've been a bit distracted, but sorting through the responses is a relatively straightforward task. The caterer does like his head count as early as possible for planning purposes."

"Yes, yes of course," Lucy mumbled in confusion.

"May I offer you a cup of tea?"

"No thank you."

"Are you by yourself? I somehow expected there to be two of you."

"My partner's following up on some other information," she replied. Although normally no detective went anywhere alone, her Lieutenant had finally acquiesced to this single interview. Shortly after Morgan's murder, there had been a fatal stabbing in Chinatown, just blocks from the Roundhouse. Then at noon a call had come in on a suspicious prisoner suicide. The squad was overwhelmed. So Lucy had been authorized to talk to Miss Barbadash at the Rabbit Club—given the house manager's age and infirmities, even the Lieutenant was willing to let her skip a police interrogation room—while Jack tracked down the registration on the .35 caliber recovered from the scene. Unless there was a definite lead, he'd then head home. It had already been a long night. After this interview, she, too, planned to get some sleep.

"Please, this way. We'll be more comfortable speaking in the game room."

Lucy followed a few steps behind as they passed through an open kitchen centered around a cast-iron double stove with an array of spice jars on the top shelf. The single overhead light cast a yellowish glow on the discolored paint. On the walls hung brightly polished copper molds of rabbits.

"Members contribute all sorts of rabbit paraphernalia, as you can see," Miss Barbadash said in a tone that reflected her obvious pride. "We have quite a remarkable collection, I imagine one of the largest in the world. Although all in good fun, I believe it's become most competitive. Who can find the best rabbit? One member recently came here directly from his flight from South Africa. Imagine! Twenty-two hours on the plane—but he insisted on showing off the carved ivory rabbit head he'd found at an open-air market."

"Where did the mascot come from?" Lucy asked.

"You might be surprised to hear that it has nothing at all to do with the animal. Our original clubhouse was located on Rabbit Lane. Please watch your step," Miss Barbadash warned, pointing to the linoleum floor that had cracked and buckled in several places. "The members here don't welcome change particularly, so it's rather difficult to get repairs authorized. Of course, we all know where the hazards are by now so nobody trips. And there's much to be said for the older sort of charm." She nodded, seemingly to herself, as she stepped into a narrow hallway with a worn runner. The smell of stale liquor permeated the alcove. A black-and-white photograph of a Holland Lop eating a bowl of spaghetti, and group photographs of men in white shirts, identical ties, and aprons hung at slightly odd angles. There was hardly an inch of wall space left uncovered. "The closing-day pictures," she said, assuming that the quirky rituals were common knowledge.

Lucy stopped to examine one image. A face looked familiar and she stared closer at the typed list of members in the front row seated left to right. *Rodman F. Haverill*, it read.

"Do you know one of these gentlemen?" Miss Barbadash asked.

"I met Mr. Haverill for the first time last night," Lucy replied. "I'm a friend of his son's. I hadn't realized they were members."

"Practically our founding fathers," she said with an enthusiasm she'd not yet exhibited. "There have been Haverills here since the Civil War. Mr. Haverill Senior served two terms as our president, but the young Mr. Haverill has at least a few years before membership. The minimum age is forty although I'm quite sure we'll find a spot for him just as soon as he's eligible. May I ask you to step this way?" She gestured, and Lucy walked past her into the dining room.

The long rectangular table and thirty chairs upholstered in red leather filled the space. Under the window was a side table the top of which was covered in silver urns and candlesticks with rabbit-shaped pedestals and bowls and platters with rabbit engravings. Miss Barbadash opened one of the drawers. Packed inside were sterling silver forks, spoons, and knives, each engraved with a rabbit on the handle. "Bailey Banks and Biddle makes them for us. Each member buys a place setting when he's admitted. We've built up quite a collection over the years." Shutting the drawer, she made a sweeping gesture with her thin arm. "Just a bit farther along if you don't mind."

Lucy noticed racks of thinly spaced shelves built into the wall behind the stairwell. In some were folded white aprons. Miss Barbadash immediately explained, "That's where the members keep their cooking aprons. I wash them and return them to the appropriate cubbies after each meeting. Most were used yesterday, but a few members couldn't attend so theirs are still fresh. When a member passes on, his family receives the apron, stains and all. A kind of memento, I suppose you could say. Most appreciate it. In any event, here we are."

The game room was lighter and less cramped with several leather-topped square tables. Small porcelain rabbits in various sizes and colors filled a corner cabinet. Lucy took a seat and pulled a spiral notepad and pen from the pocket of her blazer. She scanned the room. What was the significance of this place? What, if any, connection did it have to Morgan Reese's murder?

As she settled across from Lucy, Miss Barbadash wrung her hands several times. "I've been the house manager here for twenty-eight years and the worst incident was a stolen ashtray. Members can rent the facilities for private functions and sometimes their guests want a souvenir. Those are generally when mishaps occur. Outsiders simply aren't as committed to preserving this place and its contents as we are. But nothing—nothing at all—

compares with last night. There's never been any kind of violence here."

"Can you tell me what you saw? Heard? Everything and anything you remember."

"I was cleaning the last of the supper dishes," she said, her voice trembling as she fought off an unwelcome display of emotion. She'd been able to maintain her composure so long as the conversation centered on a subject that had been her life and work for nearly three decades. But now that she faced a detective and was forced to recall details of a murder, maintaining composure was more of a challenge. "Mr. Burlingame was the caterer and he'd prepared quite a challenge of a meal as he's wont to do. Although the members do their own cooking, you can't expect them to clean up. I believe it's simply not part of their makeup. But be that as it may, I had cleared and scraped and was washing up when I heard a crash. Then I think I heard a horn and what sounded like breaking glass, although maybe not in that order. Maybe the glass shattering came first. I'm sorry to say I can't be certain."

"What time was this?"

"I'd taken off my watch because I had my hands in soapsuds, but I'd approximate the time at a few minutes before ten. Most of the members had left already, but there was still one foursome involved in a sniff match upstairs."

"Sniff?"

"It's comparable to dominoes. Rather a tradition here. The rules as to scoring are quite elaborate, and I'm not sure I can be much help. I'm a bridge player myself."

"I see," Lucy remarked. "Can you tell me who was still at the club?"

"Mr. Burlingame was here. His voice is on the more forceful side so I tend to know when he's present, and he'd brought a guest, a doctor. Our president, Mr. Nichols, was with him earlier, but it's possible he'd left. The others I can't be sure of. It's not my business to keep track of the gentlemen, but in retrospect, it's clear I should have. We do keep a book that records those in attendance at the meal as well as the food that was served, but there's no sign-out system. I'm sorry."

"That's okay," Lucy said, trying to sound reassuring. Miss Barbadash obviously wanted to help; her lack of definitiveness appeared to be a source of considerable stress. She could get first names from attendance records. "Did anyone else hear anything?"

"I don't believe so. If they did, they didn't mention it to me."

"After you heard the crash, what did you do?" Lucy prompted.

"I didn't want to disturb the men. I stood in the kitchen doorway, the one you came through, and I called out. No one responded. Then I thought I heard some banging, banging on metal, but I saw nothing. You know, my hearing is not what it once was and so I thought at the time that perhaps I was mistaken. I would have expected someone to cry out for help, or even come knock on the door if there was trouble. This morning as I've gone over in my head what happened, it did occur to me that my view was obscured by a row of birch trees. Plus it was very dark and we have no streetlights out here."

"What about car headlights?" Even low beams would have shone through the trees.

She shook her head.

"Then what happened?"

"I finished my work and went to my room."

"Had everyone left?"

"I'm afraid I couldn't say. The members come and go through the front entrance."

Lucy thought for a moment. If a foursome had remained in the club after the car accident, at least one of them should have reported it earlier. Was it possible that Miss Barbadash was confused and that the place was empty by ten? Or had one or more of the members chosen to ignore an accident just yards from their club? She thought of the question Jack had asked: Where can you lie unnoticed, bleeding and unconscious, for up to two hours?

"What can you tell me about the gunshot?"

Miss Barbadash gave her a perplexed look. She thought for a moment and then replied, "I was reading and I heard it. I looked out my bedroom window—my view is over the golf course—and I thought I saw two figures running off in the distance, but again I can't be certain. I wasn't wearing my spectacles and I'm afraid my vision is failing, especially in the dark and especially when I'm tired. Oh dear, I realize I'm not much help."

"That's not true at all," Lucy said, as she reached for her hand. Miss Barbadash was no different from hundreds of witnesses that law enforcement dealt with every day—the men and women, most of whom meant well, who couldn't recall, didn't hear, couldn't see, or didn't pay attention. It amazed her that any criminal was ever caught given the public's overall lack of observation.

"That's when I called the police," Miss Barbadash added.

At 11:03, according to the police log. That much Lucy knew. She'd already checked the confidential caller information, virtually the only information that could be obtained without a warrant.

"After I made the call, I did search the clubhouse with the hope that someone was still there. I was really quite fearful and wanted to leave, but I don't drive so I needed transportation. The building was empty. So I locked the doors and waited for the police up in my room."

After which point, Lucy knew the rest. She'd already confirmed Miss Barbadash's whereabouts for the rest of the night. She'd had an ambulance transport to the hospital; she'd been given a tranquilizer and admitted overnight to monitor her vital signs; hospital records had her discharged shortly before ten that morning. The discharge nurse had called a taxi to take her back to Christ Church Lane.

Lucy removed from her bag a picture of Morgan Reese taken from her recovered driver's license. The dead version was slightly older, but otherwise her looks hadn't changed much since the license was renewed four years before. "Do you recognize this woman?"

Miss Barbadash shook her head.

"Does the name Morgan Reese mean anything to you?"

The woman gasped and raised her hand to her mouth.

"What is it?" Lucy asked. She noticed that Miss Barbadash's hands trembled.

"Is that who it was—the lady in the accident? The police didn't give me a name last night."

"What can you tell me about her?" Lucy asked.

"Oh dear. I just . . . perhaps I should speak to our president."

"Please," Lucy asked. "Morgan was a very accomplished doctor, a psychiatrist at the University of Pennsylvania. Any information, anything at all you can tell us, is extremely important."

"I'm . . . I'm quite sure I have obligations to the membership. As I mentioned, we've never had any kind of trouble. No serious trouble at all. I don't want to speak up inappropriately."

"Well then, perhaps you should consider that she was the ex-wife of Mr. Haverill and the mother of his only child, Archer. You have a member and a potential member who are directly affected." Even as she spoke, she regretted disclosing the personal information.

Her eyes widened. "I didn't know." She looked down at the table, studied a ring on the leather surface, and rubbed the spot with one finger. "They always forget to use coasters," she said softly.

Lucy reached for her hand and covered the small fingers with her own palm. Miss Barbadash's skin was cold. "Morgan Reese is in a morgue and we don't even know what happened. I'm sure you don't need to be told of your civic duty, but if you can find the courage to share whatever you know, I'll be in your debt. The citizens of Philadelphia will be in your debt. Please."

The elderly woman glanced around the room as if to confirm that they were alone. "All right then. But you'll have to excuse me one moment," she said in a hushed tone as she rose and disappeared into the next room. Lucy thought she heard the scraping wood of a stuck drawer being opened, then shut. When Miss Barbadash returned, she carried an ivory-colored bond envelope. "I found it on the floor of the coat closet."

She handed it to Lucy. MORGAN REESE was typewritten on the front with a residential address in Bryn Mawr. Although there was a stamp, there was no postmark or other indication that it had been mailed.

"When? When did you find this?"

"A week or so ago. Sadly, I must confess that it could have been there for some time. I rarely get around to cleaning that closet. There are too many obvious messes that require my attention. The closet is thankfully out of sight." She wrung her hands. "I've been expecting a member to inquire about it, but no one has."

Lucy removed a pair of latex gloves from her pocket, as well as a small Swiss army knife. After covering her hands, she carefully sliced the envelope along one side and removed a single sheet of bond paper.

Check the account at BMTC in Avery's name. I expect you'll find the deposited sum sufficient to resolve this matter permanently. I trust that you'll tell her nothing—if you want what's in her best interest or know what's in yours.

Lucy looked up. Miss Barbadash was watching her read, no doubt anxious to find out for herself what the letter said. There was also the possibility that the author would remember where it had been misplaced and come looking for it. "Who knows about this letter?" she asked.

"No one. Members leave their personal belongings behind all the time. When I spoke to the police last night, I didn't realize its significance. I wasn't told the name of the . . . the . . . deceased."

"Who have you spoken with other than the police?"

"No one," she repeated. "I tried to reach Mr. Nichols this morning. Because he's our president, I thought I should apprise him of what happened and confirm that I had permission to allow you to enter the club, but his wife told me he was away on business and I couldn't reach him on the cellular number she gave me. Given the exigent circumstances, I thought it best to use my own judgment."

Lucy read the letter again, and then repeated the words aloud. "Do you have any idea what it's about?"

She shook her head.

"Is there anyone named Avery connected to this club or its members that you can recall?"

"I'm sorry. I haven't the slightest idea."

"You said you rented out this building for private functions. When was the last one of those?" she asked. Miss Barbadash seemed to assume that the letter came from a member, but, since it was unsigned and undated, it was possible she needed to cast a wider net.

"We had an engagement party here in February. That was the last."

"May I take a look at the log you mentioned? The record of who was here last night?"

"Of course," she replied, seemingly relieved to be able to provide something concrete as she got up to retrieve a rectangular leather journal that had been resting on a small desk under the window.

While Miss Barbadash was away from the table, Lucy removed an empty plastic evidence bag from her satchel, made a quick notation on the outside with a wax pencil, and placed the letter inside.

"Here you are," Miss Barbadash said as she handed her the book.

Lucy turned the pages. On the last one, someone had written in black felt-tip pen the menu for the gastronomic feast from the day before: oyster bisque, turban of sole mousseline, braised short ribs of beef, apple tapioca. The members were certainly ambitious. Underneath was a list of those in attendance, each man's name complete with first, middle initial, and surname; many even included a roman numeral or Jr. The list included the two members Miss Barbadash had mentioned—Dixon Burlingame II and H. Tripp Nichols—as well as more than a dozen others, including a single guest: David Ellery, M.D. It was an old-guard lineup straight out of *The Perennial Philadelphians*.

"May I borrow this?"

Miss Barbadash hesitated before agreeing. "You are the police after all."

Lucy tucked the journal into her satchel. One of these people not only had some connection to the victim, but also had some secret that he wanted preserved. Even if he hadn't shown up yesterday, his name no doubt would appear in the ledger for the prior week or weeks. Now it was her job to pick him out—and to figure out what, if anything, connected a Rabbit Club member, someone named Avery, and a body in the downtown morgue.

She stood up. "Thank you for all your help."

Miss Barbadash's face expressed obvious concern. And fear.

"We'll find out what happened," Lucy said, trying to

sound comforting. "We'll apprehend whoever did this to Dr. Reese."

"I do hope so. And I do hope all of this gets resolved quickly. It's rather difficult to be living out here alone knowing a prowler might be about."

"Can't you stay somewhere else? There must be a friend or relative who can put you up for a few nights."

She shook her head. "This place has been my home and my life. I really can't abandon my duties now after twenty-eight years. There's simply no one who could take over, especially on such short notice. If anything, it's appropriate that I . . . This is where I belong," she said, forcing a smile.

Propriety was hardly something Lucy would be considering if their situations were reversed. But everything about Miss Barbadash seemed unusual; her grace and elegance were part of another era. She'd elevated minuscule details to an art form, and correctly assumed that no one else, without careful training and guidance, could step in and understand the traditions she upheld. The members, whoever they were, were lucky to have her to hold down their fort. But if the letter were linked to Morgan's death, someone would be back to find it. And if Miss Barbadash wasn't about to abandon her duties, then only catching the killer—and doing it fast—could ensure her safety.

12

Monday, May 19th
7:33 a.m.

*L*ucy had barely slept. Twice in the night she'd arisen to look at the photocopy she'd made of the anonymous letter to Morgan. ". . . I trust that you'll tell her nothing—if you want what's in her best interest or know what's in yours." Was that a threat? The language seemed formal; "best interest" was a legal standard. Was the author a lawyer or had he consulted one? More important, who was the mysterious Avery? She'd thought to tell Archer about the note but decided to keep quiet until the Bryn Mawr Trust Company could provide some answers. Although she'd promised not to hide information, she hadn't promised to reveal every detail the moment she learned it.

She was meeting Jack at ten o'clock, but by seven thirty she'd already completed her morning run, showered, and dressed for work. As she sat on the edge of her bed and pulled on her socks, she wondered again whether Morgan's attempt to meet with Archer after all this time and her death just yards from her ex-husband's private club were pure coincidence. Had she been in trouble and feared the worst?

She went into the kitchen, poured herself a second cup of coffee, and ate a banana. Still hungry, she made a peanut butter sandwich on whole wheat bread—the only meal to guarantee she'd make it to lunch without a rumbling stomach. "A shot of vodka and a generous tablespoon of peanut butter is all you need for breakfast," her godfather had told her years ago as he'd dug his spoon into the jar of Skippy's. He was certainly the most energetic seventy-eight-year-old she knew, but at least this morning she'd take the protein and pass on the octane.

Fully clothed, Archer slept on the couch with the television tuned in to the early-morning news. He'd apparently been watching something on NBC when he fell asleep, and even the sounds of her emptying the dishwasher failed to arouse him. He was living proof that nothing but indigestion interfered with a man's sleep. Still, it was a relief that news of his estranged mother's death hadn't made him toss and turn. Trying to accept the information had to be painful enough without suffering from exhaustion on top of it.

The yellow wall clock ticked loudly, reminding her of every second that passed. She needed to get a subpoena issued to the BMTC for accounts opened for a beneficiary named Avery, but banking hours required her to wait until nine. She and Jack had planned to go through Morgan Reese's office later in the day, but she felt impatient, anxious to see who this woman was and how she operated. There was nothing more revealing than being in someone else's private space, sitting in a desk chair, lying on a bed, looking at the way the smallest items were arranged—a pen with a bent cap, a piece of Wheat Thin cracker on the floor, a pair of stockings in the garbage even though there was no run or tear in the nylon, a doodle made during the victim's last telephone call. Although Jack was by far the more experienced of the investigative pair, she wanted time and quiet. He'd laugh at her explanation, her reliance on female intuition, but she sensed there might well be clues to this case that weren't discoverable by taking samples, dusting for prints, or even analyzing financial records.

Lucy scribbled a note to Archer and slipped an additional carrot into Cyclops's cage. Then she left a voice mail on Jack's cell phone informing him of where she was going. Just in case.

There was little traffic and she made it to University City in less than twenty minutes. She parked in the lot for the Hospital of the University of Pennsylvania and made her way west on Spruce Street, past the enormous collection of red brick and white limestone buildings that formed the Quadrangle, until she arrived at her destination—a multistory structure that housed nothing but medical offices. The revolving door was already operational and she flashed her badge at the security guard by the entrance.

"I'm from Homicide. I need to take a look at Dr. Reese's office."

He nodded. "One of the other suitemates is already up there."

"Weren't you informed the place was to be secured?"

"Yeah. The precinct called yesterday and my boss gave me instructions. But we can't keep a tenant out who has a right to be in her own office."

He had a point. But Lucy didn't like it. She should have been called when someone else arrived.

"Third floor. Suite A."

The mirrored elevator opened onto a long, dimly lit corridor with well-worn brown and gold carpeting. An arrow on the wall pointed left for rooms A through F, and she quickly found the door, its frosted glass lettered in gold: David Ellery, M.D., Morgan Reese, M.D., Nancy Moore, R.N., IAAP. She paused, surprised to recognize the name of Saturday night's guest at the Rabbit Club, and then stepped inside.

The reception area was empty. A vase of wilted flowers in brackish water perched on the edge of a secretarial station. Colored ellipses swirled across a flat computer screen and a row of red lights on the telephone indicated that all incoming calls were still being forwarded to the service. Clear lines in the pile of the plush blue carpet evidenced thorough vacuuming, probably by the nighttime cleaning crew. A collection of well-worn magazines had been stuffed into a wall rack. Several were upside down.

There were three doors off of the reception room. One door was ajar and Lucy could see a heavyset woman with curly black hair squatting by her desk, seeming to sort through files on the floor at an almost frantic pace.

"I'm from the Homicide Unit of the Philadelphia Police Department." Lucy held out her badge.

Startled, the woman let out a cry. When she stood, her dress had twisted on her large frame and Lucy could see the navy blue knee-highs that encased her calves. The woman walked toward her.

"You must be Nancy Moore. I'm very sorry about your colleague."

Nancy adjusted her attire, pushed her hair behind her ears, and came out into the reception area. When Lucy extended a hand, she took it in both of hers and shook it vigorously. "I heard . . . I heard about Morgan and I just can't stand it," she said in a high-pitched voice with a Southern twang. For some reason, the sound was surprising. "It's all too much, too awful, too . . . I don't know what. I don't even work Mondays, but my husband agreed to help me out with the kids, get them off to school. I told him to take them to McDonald's for breakfast if he wanted to avoid problems. An Egg McMuffin and the kids don't make a peep, so that's the advice I gave him."

"Because you wanted to come to the office?" Lucy redirected.

"I just need to get in and out before David arrives, and he won't get here until noon or so because of rounds. He and I have problems enough and I just can't face him, not now, not after what happened. I've got to get out of this place. I've had it. First Calvin and then that gun and now this." The words spilled out of her.

"What gun?"

She stared at Lucy with a baffled expression. "You don't know? You're investigating Morgan's death and you don't know? David kept a gun in his office. A handgun, a pistol, I don't know brands, but I know it held bullets and fired. We all told him he was crazy, but he wouldn't listen. He said he knew what was best. Sure enough, just as I predicted, someone stole it about a month ago."

Lucy flipped to a new page and began to write. "Has it been recovered?"

"Of course not. The police thought it was one of Morgan's patients—this guy, Calvin. She already had a restraining order against him, as if those things are worth the paper they're written on. I'm not sure she thought it could protect her. That's when she started carrying a baseball bat. And sure enough, he wasn't arrested. You'd know better than me what kind of investigation the police did, if any. Why David even kept a firearm in the first place is beyond me."

"What can you tell me about this Calvin?"

"His name's Calvin Roth. He's crazy, and I don't say that lightly. I see a lot of problems in my line of work, a lot of strange people, bless their souls, but he was in another league. I couldn't tell you his diagnosis. Morgan was way too discreet and she took her obligations of privilege extremely seriously. But some screw in him was loose—or had come out, I should say. I almost lost a client over him one time because he wouldn't leave after his appointment. Even just sitting still in a chair, he was intimidating. My client said he drooled, and it didn't surprise me."

"Do you know when Morgan got the restraining order?"

"I'm not sure. But it was a while back, around Christmastime, I think it was."

"And she kept a bat with her?" It had to be the Louisville Slugger.

"Yes. I'd see her arrive with it in the mornings and leave with it in the evenings. Wouldn't surprise me if she slept with it under her pillow."

"But she continued to see Calvin as a patient?"

Nancy paused, apparently confused by the question.

"You'll have to excuse me. I really do need to get myself organized." She glanced at her watch, the band of which appeared embedded in the flesh of her wrist.

"Please. If I could have just a few more minutes of your time."

Suddenly Nancy's breathing quickened, and Lucy watched her chest rise and fall at a much too rapid pace. She was hyperventilating. "Do you want to sit down?" she asked. "Or can I get you some water?"

"No. I'm fine." Nancy leaned against the secretarial station for balance. She pursed her lips, exhaling loudly through her mouth. "What is it you want to know?"

"Was it just the three of you in this office suite?"

"We have a secretary, but she hardly ever shows, as you can see," she said, indicating the dead flowers with a sweep of her hand. "Some health complaint or another. You'd think between three mental health workers we'd be able to cure our own secretary of hypochondria."

"How long have you shared an office?"

"David and Morgan had been here for a while. I came in about two years ago. It's expensive space, being so close to the hospital, and David certainly wasn't going to give me a break on my share of the rent. He might have since I get half what he does for seeing patients and my office is smaller. But he told me it enhanced my reputation being associated with the two of them so I was actually getting something extra and I should be thankful. I don't know. It was a mistake. Not the space—other than the issue with Calvin, my patients like it just fine—but being around him. He's a very self-centered man. And arrogant as all get out, or whatever that expression is."

"What about Dr. Reese? Did you know her well?"

"Morgan? Nobody knew Morgan well. She worked so hard that there wasn't time to get to know her. But she was always polite to me." Nancy stopped abruptly. "Look, my husband's a lawyer so I know how this interview-with-the-police stuff works. If there's a place I can reach you, I'm willing to call. But I can't talk to you now." When she stopped speaking, her lips quivered. She struggled to keep back tears.

Why was she running away? What was this all about? Was she afraid of Dr. Ellery? Or was her fear of something else? How much did she know about the fate that Morgan had suffered? Although her conduct didn't make sense, it also didn't make sense to alienate a potential witness by forcing her to stay in a place where she was frightened. Lucy handed her a business card. "I won't keep you. But would you please call me so we can set up a time to meet? Your husband's welcome to come, too, if that would make you more comfortable."

Nancy nodded and took the card.

"And can you tell me which one is Dr. Reese's office?" she asked, looking at the two closed doors off of the reception area. She didn't want to have a run-in with Dr. Ellery for infringing on his privacy without a warrant. As long as she confined her search to Morgan's office, and Morgan's office alone, she could avoid any legal pitfalls.

"It's that one," Nancy said, pointing to the door farthest from the entrance. "If it's locked, there's a master key in the secretary's desk. Part of the problem around here. Security's not too tight."

A key was unnecessary. Lucy opened the door and

stepped into a large room, comfortably furnished with two upholstered armchairs facing each other and a desk with an ergonomic chair. Behind the desk, freestanding bookshelves were filled to capacity. Against the opposite wall, piles of books and files covered a credenza. A slight scent of rosemary was present in the air.

The carpeting in Reese's office also showed signs of recent vacuuming. Lucy removed her shoes so as not to track any dirt from outside into the room, and walked the perimeter, glancing out the single window into the alley below. This was her favorite part of being a detective. Unlike many of her colleagues who thrived on the adrenaline rush of pursuing a suspect or making an arrest, for her the thrill was deciphering what mattered. It was a careful process of selecting what was relevant to a crime from among the millions of external details that made up a life. In this process that was in part deductive, in part analytical, and in large measure intuitive, she needed to trust herself as she'd learned to trust herself in other types of investigations. Only now the stakes were higher. Missing a critical clue meant a killer might go free.

She stopped by the bookshelf and scanned its contents: a *Physicians' Desk Reference*, at least a dozen other volumes on medications, a DSM-IV-TR, a shelf dedicated to adolescent and childhood development, a section of Elisabeth Kübler-Ross volumes on strategies for coping with death, various psychiatric periodicals dating back years. Then her eyes stopped on two books down at the bottom, both of which had slips of colored paper protruding from their pages.

She removed the first one and stared at the black cover

and orange lettering of a current volume of the *Social Register*. Opening to the flagged page, she scanned the list of names—more than a dozen "Herberts," each with numerous seasonal addresses. Most hailed from New York City—if where one "wintered" could be considered the primary residence—with a Boston representative and two Philadelphia families included. She paused at the local names: *Mr. and Mrs. Jackson J. Herbert (Athena Preston)* wintered on Society Hill and summered on Mount Desert Island; *Mr. and Mrs. William Foster Herbert (Faith Aldrich)* resided in Gladwyne and Northeast Harbor. The long-established Pennsylvania–Maine connection at work. The next entry caught her eye. *Juniors: William Foster, Jr., and Avery Aldrich*. William and Faith Herbert had a daughter named Avery. Nothing revealed which particular listing had warranted Morgan's attention; although Avery was an unusual name, it was not so rare as to rule out other conclusions. A friend or even a patient could be anyone on this page. Nonetheless, she copied the Greaves Lane address in her notebook before replacing the volume on the shelf.

The second book was a trade paperback with the title *Motherless Daughters*. A blurb on the cover read ". . . a must read for the millions of women whose mothers have gone—but whose need for healing, mourning, and mothering remains." Lucy flipped through the well-worn pages, several of which had come loose from the binding. Blue pen underlined numerous passages. There were handwritten notations, brackets, and asterisks in the margins throughout. On the page marked by Morgan's piece of colored paper, the author wrote of surviving emotional abandonment through focus on positive memories and traits.

How many times had Morgan read this book? Was her interest personal or professional? As Lucy replaced the volume on the shelf, she remembered Archer's words. She was lucky to have a mother—a mother who cared, a mother who had devoted her life to her family, a mother who even after twenty-eight years was willing to discuss how best to iron a satin bow.

She walked back to the window. Staring at the nearby building with its still mostly dark windows, she remembered the trial of *Commonwealth v. Moses Walker* that she'd been involved with as a detective for the South Division. Moses had been fourteen at the time he coordinated and executed a series of home invasions around Jefferson Square. How a scrawny black kid had managed to return to South Philadelphia packed with two .38s, a .22, and a hunting knife and rampage for five straight weeks still baffled her. Despite a fairly good description and a collection of physical evidence, she and her partner had been unable to apprehend him. At one point, she'd even wondered if he literally disappeared into the underground water ducts after each horrible beating. Finally, it was a neighbor, hearing the desperate cries of a woman as she watched her husband being tied to a chair and beaten with the butt of a gun, who had waited below the fire escape and shot Moses in the thigh as he'd exited. The neighbor wasn't licensed to carry but the prosecutor was more than willing to overlook that technicality.

Then, amid much controversy, the juvenile judge had allowed Moses to be tried as an adult because of the heinous nature of his crimes. The press called him a victim, a product of poverty and the destruction of family values. It was the classic ghetto saga: He had no father. His mother, a crack addict, put macaroni and cheese on the table only by sleeping with a panoply of undesirable men willing to give her five bucks a shot, ten if they wanted to take a turn at her adolescent son afterward. Moses had scars on his face from being scalded; his leg had been broken twice before it received a bullet. By contrast, the prosecutor painted him as an animal. Rehabilitation was meaningless. He was incapable of following a moral code. He had blood lust. He'd confessed that the popping sound of breaking a bone or crushing a skull excited him. His parental situation was irrelevant because he wasn't human. This hadn't been about money—in five home invasions, he'd gotten less than $300. He sought the thrill.

Moses hadn't shed a tear or displayed any emotion during the three-week trial. He'd received multiple consecutive sentences that would put him away forever. And yet, more than the evidence, more than the passion of closing arguments, more than the defendant's eerie calm, what haunted Lucy most of all was that moment as the courtroom security guards escorted him to lockup. His wrists cuffed and his ankles shackled, he turned to the audience, scanned the crowd, and set his eyes on a woman who'd fallen asleep in the back row. Then in a voice that could have belonged to a member of a boys' choir, he'd called out repeatedly, "I love you, Mama. I love you, Mama." Even after he was out of sight, his plaintive words echoed in the corridor.

The bond between mother and child never broke.

Lucy returned to the desk and sat down in the black

nylon contraption that epitomized ergonomic design. What about Morgan? What was her story? Despite the thirty-six hours that had elapsed since the discovery of her body, her next of kin had still not been located. This woman apparently lacked a community of relatives. The only person who might be able to provide helpful information on her family was Mr. Haverill, but Lucy had held off on calling him until after Archer had had a chance to speak with him first. That opportunity couldn't occur soon enough.

The top of Morgan's desk held a fabric-covered blotter, a mug with the caduceus insignia of the medical profession filled with pencils and pens, and a stack of photocopied articles from various medical and psychiatric journals held down by a crystal paperweight from AmeriMed, the pharmaceutical company. A color photograph in a black frame showed Morgan beside a young woman with sandy-colored hair leaning against a split-rail fence. The pretty girl wore jodhpurs and held a riding crop. Behind them was a chestnut horse with a white star on its muzzle. Small digital numbers in the lower right-hand corner marked the date: April 27, less than a month before Morgan's death.

Lucy held the picture up to take a better look. There was something about the girl's features that resembled Morgan. Was it the eyes? Lucy removed an evidence bag from her satchel, labeled it, and inserted the framed picture.

Next, she slid the narrow center drawer open and gazed at its haphazardly arranged contents: two jars of Carmex, paper clips, rubber bands, a stapler and staples, dental floss, a small calculator with brightly colored numbers, pastel Post-it notes, a Mason Pearson hairbrush,

nothing more than the usual accoutrements of a professional woman. But tucked in the back was a second photograph, this one unframed, yellowed with age, and
curled at the edges. It had been torn and taped back together, making part of the background difficult to decipher. Lucy lifted it up to her eyes to get a closer look.
Although the photo had been taken decades earlier, the
figures in the middle were unmistakable. Wearing a pale
pink cardigan and white Capri pants, Morgan stood beside Rodman Haverill, with the iron gates of their mansion visible behind them. He stared straight into the
camera with his arm around her waist while she looked
away over her right shoulder. Her arms dangled by her
thin body, unwilling to return his affection.

Lucy flipped the picture over, hoping to find a date on
the back, but only "Kodak" was there. Then she put it in
her satchel. She might not be able to provide answers, but
perhaps Archer would appreciate the souvenir.

Surprisingly, the drawer on the left-hand side of the
desk held an answering machine. Its message light
blinked. Lucy got down on her hands and knees to look
underneath the desk. Sure enough, a telephone wire came
from the floor through a small hole in the bottom of the
drawer and connected inside. She hit the "play" button.

A computer voice announced, "You have four new
messages. First message. Friday. Three forty-three P.M."

"Hi, Dr. Reese. This is Natalie. I need to cancel my appointment. My SAT tutor has to come at the same time,
and my mother thinks college preparation is more important. Sorry. See you next week."

There was a bleep. "Message two. Friday. Four
twelve P.M."

"Hello. My name is Marsha Birnbaum and I'm an assistant claims coordinator at Journeymen," said the voice in the bland tone that seemed unique to health insurance personnel. "We're having a clearance problem with a prescription you wrote for a Walter Reese. Perhaps it's the diagnostic code. Please call me at your earliest convenience at extension three two six two. Thank you for using Journeymen. Have a good day."

Message three came at 4:31 P.M. from a male, who didn't identify himself. His voice was stern. "I've made a reservation for three at eight o'clock at Le Bec-Fin. I assume you remember where that is on Walnut Street. Believe me it wasn't easy on such short notice. I hope you're satisfied."

Le Bec-Fin was one of the most elegant formal restaurants in all of Philadelphia. Although Lucy had never eaten there—and probably never would given the prices and the fact that she didn't care for French food anyway—she knew of it by reputation. Meals no doubt consisted of several courses and lasted hours. If this man dined with Morgan on Saturday night, he had to have been one of the last people to see her alive—if not the very last.

The fourth message was a hang-up.

She rewound and listened again. "For three," he said. She'd heard the words the first time but their significance had escaped her. Who else had been included? Had the extra person come with Morgan or with the unknown caller? Although the chances were negligible of having voice-recognition software identify this man, she still popped the tape out of the machine and tucked it into her satchel.

The only drawer on the right-hand side of the desk contained a black day planner, printed stationery, blank invoices and index cards, and a Realtor's color brochure of an elegant home in Gladwyne. Flipping the brochure over, Lucy saw that it included small color photographs of the well-appointed living and dining rooms, the kitchen, entrance hall, and library, plus a lengthy description of this six-bedroom fieldstone mansion with every amenity, its horse barn, and landscaped acreage with mature plantings, all for an asking price of $3.9 million. Written in pencil in neat cursive was "Gail—cell phone: 610-533-4959." Gail Ripley, the listing broker, had included only an office number on the printed materials. Lucy kept the brochure, too.

Opening the day planner, she could see that every page had numerous entries—patients, meetings, lunches and dinners, even some personal appointments. Morgan's schedule was frantic, with times ranging from as early as six in the morning to well after nine at night seven days a week.

Lucy turned to the week-on-a-page layout for the dates that had just ended yesterday, the last week of Morgan's life. Monday through Friday morning was sufficiently filled, but the two patients listed on Friday afternoon had been crossed out, and Saturday and Sunday were completely blank. There was no reference to dinner out on any night. She flipped the page. As of this morning, Morgan's life was booked once again. So why had she scheduled nothing for the weekend she died?

It was almost nine thirty and she had to go meet Jack. Lucy stuffed the calendar into an evidence bag. This investigation was still in its infancy; it was too soon to make a judgment call. But she didn't like the nagging sensation she was experiencing: that Morgan had set about to change her life and somebody had successfully stopped her.

13

10:05 a.m.

$\mathcal{T}$he Reading Terminal Market was more crowded than Lucy would have expected for this time on a Monday morning. Businessmen, secretaries, cabdrivers, and probably more than a couple of police department personnel who had been at work since eight were on their coffee breaks; the Society Hill stay-at-home mothers, having finished their Pilates mat classes, came for fresh fish and cut flowers; plus, as usual, there was a steady stream of out-of-town visitors. Tourists in Philadelphia seemed constant; unlike Boston, where they tended to flock only in the summer, Lucy couldn't remember a season in the hub of Pennsylvania where she couldn't hear multiple languages and see groups of disoriented people with cameras and travel guides swarming the area's attractions. The converted railway station with its delicious food and market stalls was a mandatory stop.

Jack had suggested they meet here instead of the Roundhouse. The detectives of the Homicide Unit barely fit into their allotted space and she was just as happy to get away from the cramped office, bitter coffee, and end-lessly ringing telephones.

She wove her way down the long center aisle and found Jack already perched on a stool by the Amish bak-ery stall with a paper cup in his hand. His blue blazer was wrinkled and his shirttails hung over the top of his trousers. His eyes were red. Gulping his coffee, he stood as she approached.

"You look like you've been up all night."

"You got that right."

She felt a momentary pang of guilt. She'd gone home the night before, leaving further work into Morgan Reese's death for today and tomorrow and the day after that. Jack had explored investigative leads while she'd slept.

"Is everything okay?"

"Just the agony of being a parent." He took a swig of his coffee. "Sean had an emergency appendectomy at about three o'clock this morning," he explained, referring to the younger of his two sons.

Appendicitis was not that common in children and Sean was only twelve. "What happened?"

"By the time I got home yesterday, Sarah said he'd been complaining of pain in his abdomen all day. Nor-mally, I'd accuse him of making it up. He'll do anything to miss school, but staying in bed on a Sunday . . . never. Then about midnight his fever spiked way up, and Sarah was worried sick. Here I am trying to tell her not to get so worked up, that both boys are strong, that Sean is going to be fine, and meanwhile, I'm beside myself," he said, and then paused, scanning the crowd. "No matter how big he gets, he'll always be my baby. And I can tell you one thing. Your imagination plays horrible tricks on you. Anyway, I took him down to the emergency room. They did a CT scan and sure enough it was serious. The appendix was completely inflamed. The doctor admitted him then and there."

Jack often spoke with pride about his children, but she'd never heard him sound so vulnerable. Here was a seasoned cop, a veteran of the Homicide Unit, completely undone by a sick appendix. It amazed her how different the same person could be in his personal ánd professional lives. "But he's okay?"

"Yeah. Thank God we caught it, and the surgery went smoothly. He was in recovery when I left and Sarah is with him. I'm going to go back to spell her in a little while. I'm more concerned about her than him at this point. I don't want her driving tired and distracted."

"Please. Go whenever you want. Go now. There's nothing more important than your family. I can handle this investigation," Lucy said.

Jack smiled. "I never doubted that. But I'm just sorry about what you've had to go through the past twenty-four hours—attending the autopsy of your boyfriend's mother. Who would ever have expected that in the line of duty?" He took another sip of his coffee. "How's Archer holding up?"

"Okay, I guess."

When she didn't elaborate, he pulled his notepad from his jacket pocket. Flipping through several pages, he said, "Let me at least bring you up to date on what I got yesterday. I did manage to gather some information before calling it quits." He paused to read his almost illegible notes. "The gun's registered to David Ellery, the doctor Reese shared an office suite with."

"Who also happened to be having dinner at the Rabbit Club Saturday night."

Jack raised his eyebrows.

"Ellery called the police on April twenty-sixth and reported the gun stolen. There was a perfunctory investigation, mostly centered on one of Reese's patients."

"Calvin Roth," Lucy added.

Jack looked puzzled. "How did you know?"

Lucy quickly filled him in on the details of her conversation with Nancy Moore and her visit to Morgan's office.

When she was finished, he gave her an approving nod. "Good work, Detective."

"Thanks. I will say Nancy did seem genuinely panicked to get out of there."

"I don't doubt it." He pulled a piece of paper from his pocket, unfolded it, and handed it to her. "I got this from our files."

Lucy stared at the series of docket numbers at the top of the page followed by the caption "In re Calvin Roth" and then scanned the typewritten lines at the bottom. Dated December 30, it was a copy of Morgan's application for a restraining order against her patient.

Mr. Roth has been under my care for nearly a decade. In the past six months, however, he has repeatedly and incessantly called me at home and at my office and threatened violent behavior if I did not take his calls. He has shown up at my office and my residence without an appointment, and has followed me on several occasions. I am aware that he

has access to firearms. He has recently stated that
he will use one against me. I am in fear for my life.

It was signed under the pains and penalties of perjury.

"A stalker," Lucy said, imagining Morgan's terror. As
Roth's psychiatrist, she would know better than anyone
his deepest, darkest secrets, and the violence of which he
might be capable. "Nancy mentioned he wouldn't leave
after his appointments. But what happened with the
stolen gun investigation?"

"Nothing as far as I can tell. I checked with Jimmy
Bartlett, the investigating detective. He said nothing
really panned out. Roth had a solid alibi. He gets electroconvulsive therapy periodically, and he was hospitalized at
Friends Hospital over on Roosevelt Boulevard for a round
of shock treatment on the day Ellery filed the report."

The twenty-sixth had been a Saturday. "Did Ellery
know for sure that it was stolen on that day or was that the
day he discovered it missing?"

"Apparently both Ellery and Reese see patients on
weekends, so the office is open. I didn't grill Jimmy on
the particulars of the interview but I assume he didn't let
Roth off the hook without good cause."

"So that was it?"

"There were no other leads."

"No sign of a B and E, was there?" she asked. The
criminal population of those who would break in and
enter to steal a gun was quite different from the narrow
range of suspects who might have had access to the office
on the twenty-sixth.

"Technically, it's still an open investigation but Jimmy said nobody's doing anything on it."

No surprise, Lucy thought. There were hundreds of missing firearms in Philadelphia. Most were recovered as this one had been—when a corpse turned up, too. But whether Jack had been too tired to press Jimmy, or Jimmy had failed to ask key questions or explore important avenues, there was no point in debating the issues now. Jack had given her what he had. Dr. Ellery could supply the rest—assuming he was willing to talk.

"Morgan mentions in her affidavit that this psycho had access to firearms. Do we know whether he registered any or had a concealed carry permit?" she asked.

"I haven't had time to check," Jack replied, glancing at his watch. "But the gun that killed Reese belonged to Ellery. I don't see the relevance to this investigation if Roth has others."

"I was just trying to think of a plausible justification for a search of his home. Mental illness and propensity for violence are bases for revocation of any CCP. Seems to me we've got that," she said, waving the copy of the restraining order. "So we could use this court documentation in support of a warrant. It would get us inside." She paused, musing aloud and liking the strategy. Who knows what they might find while they were conducting a legitimate search for illegal weapons? "Do we even know where he lives?"

Jack checked his pad and read the address. "That's right by Fairmont Park and the Schuylkill River."

"Not far from where Reese was murdered," she added, finishing his thought.

He glanced at his watch again, and she could see the

anxiety on his face. No doubt he had calculated that
Sean's anesthesia had worn off and he would be waiting
for his father. There was a lot more information she
needed to share with him, including the bank account
lead, but now was not the time. "Go back to the hospital.
You're needed there more than here. I'll follow up on this
Calvin Roth stuff."

The lines in his forehead relaxed. Jack was obviously
relieved by her suggestion. "That'd be great. But don't do
anything stupid. Checking gun permit information is one
thing. Making a surprise visit to a psychopath is another.
Promise you'll wait for me."

She hesitated for a moment, wondering for the second
time in as many days whether she could honor her promise. But Jack was right. Calvin was dangerous enough
that Morgan had been genuinely afraid for her life. As
much as she wanted to be a heroine to Archer and quickly
come up with his mother's killer, she'd have to temper her
impatience. She nodded, agreeing with his terms. "Go be
a dad. I promise not to try a solo ambush."

10:52 a.m.

Across 12th Street, Lucy found a bench in the sun,
opened a square cardboard box, and took a bite of a still-
hot cinnamon bun. She had a weakness for the sticky
sweet dough, white sugar frosting, and melted butter that
seeped through the package. She'd call this treat an early
lunch. As she licked frosting from her fingers, she looked
again at the color brochure for the Gladwyne estate that

she'd found in Morgan's desk. "Old World elegance," it read. "A truly exceptional property."

She looked again at what she assumed was Morgan's handwriting, then flipped open her cell phone and dialed Gail Ripley.

"Hello? This is Gail." The woman who answered had a perky voice.

"Yes," Lucy said, suddenly wondering how someone interested in a $3.9 million residence was supposed to sound. Her experience in high-end real estate came from glancing at advertisements in the back of glossy magazines; she'd never even looked at a condominium as a potential purchaser. "I'm interested in one of your properties. I understand you're the listing agent."

"Which one is that?"

"In Gladwyne. A rather spacious stone house, or at least it appears that way from the brochure. And that's what I want."

"Oh yes." The woman sighed. "Greaves Lane, just off Conshohocken. It is a beautiful estate. But I'm sorry to say it's already under contract. I do have several comparable properties. Perhaps something else might interest you."

Lucy was startled. There couldn't be that many houses on such a short street. Was it coincidence? "When was it sold?"

There was a pause. "I'm really not at liberty to disclose. But as I said—"

"I'm not interested in something else," Lucy interrupted.

"I can take your name and number and get back to you if something changes."

"Yes. All right. That would be *lovely*." She gave her cell phone number.

"And your name again?"

She hesitated a moment before responding. "Lucille," she said. "Lucille Haverill." Somehow, for this one, "Detective O'Malley" didn't sound quite right.

11:43 a.m.

Gun control in the commonwealth of Pennsylvania was lax to say the least. Nobody needed a license or permit to purchase a handgun. Registration occurred only on subsequent transfers. Criminal background checks were done through the NICS—the National Instant Criminal Background Check System—a system that, because of its speed, often missed information. And, basically, police chiefs and local sheriffs could issue permits to carry concealed weapons to anyone. There was no safety training or other requirement of familiarity with safe storage or handling practices. Lucy had often wondered whether it would have affected her decision to go into law enforcement if she'd known beforehand how easy it was for the average or—a much scarier scenario—the unusual man on the street to get and carry a firearm.

Why spend so much money on a great police force ostensibly to keep citizens safe if virtually anyone had access to something that could inflict serious bodily harm or death in an instant? Statistically, many more people were killed with their own weapons—mishandlings, accidental shootings—than effectively defended themselves or others by brandishing their own weapon. She'd even seen a personal handgun used against its owner. Although she'd never pretend to understand either politicians or lobbyists, or to begin to fathom the power of the National Rifle Association, it was frustrating nonetheless. At least with the 1993 passage of the Brady bill, those with psychiatric histories were now denied permits to carry. Or at least they were supposed to be.

Now she was relying on this requirement to get access to Calvin Roth.

She quickened her pace toward the offices of the Inspector Headquarters Division, the department that kept all registration and concealed carry permit records. It was already close to noon and she didn't want to find the file room closed, its clerks on lunch break.

"Hey, Beth," she greeted the Head Clerk as she stepped inside.

Elizabeth Brogan had to be approaching seventy, but somehow she'd managed to avoid mandatory retirement. Lucy guessed that the various agencies overseeing her employment simply looked the other way. She had an almost photographic memory, the fastest filing fingers Lucy had ever seen, endless patience for even the dumbest of questions, and a smile that quite literally lit up the dingy, overcrowded space. Apparently she was the Gertrude Barbadash of gun permits. A successor would be virtually impossible to find.

"What brings you here today?" Beth asked. When she spoke, her mouth formed an O shape.

"I need whatever you can give me on Calvin Roth," she replied, reading his date of birth off the copy of the court documents.

Beth placed the spectacles around her neck onto her

nose and then typed information into her computer. "Let's see what we can find." Lucy couldn't see the monitor, but she watched the changing expressions on Beth's face; curiosity became concern when something apparently unexpected came up on the screen. "I should get the file," she said without providing any details. "I'll be right back."

As she punched in a code and disappeared through the locked door that led to the storage room, Lucy propped herself up on the counter, leaned over, and glanced at the screen. The angle at which she was standing obscured some of her view and made the light blue letters difficult to decipher. She flipped her legs over and jumped down on the other side.

Once she was standing in Beth's place, the information was crystal clear. Four registrations: a .22, a .35, and two .38s. The man had a small arsenal. And one CCP. Calvin Roth had a concealed carry permit for a .35 caliber, the same type of gun that killed Morgan.

Lucy jumped back over the counter and began to scribble an outline of information she could use to support a showing of probable cause. With any luck, she could have a draft of an affidavit in support of a warrant on the Assistant District Attorney's desk by the end of the day. She was still writing when Beth returned with a thick manila folder in her hand.

"This should give you what you need," Beth said, as she laid the file on the counter and opened it. Some of the pages were torn at the edges. One sheet of pink paper was folded over. Beth opened it. "I won't bother to repeat what you have already discovered," she said with a smile. "Yes, I did see you jump over our well-established barrier, so you know Mr. Roth is a gun owner. I suspect you were also clever enough to discern he has a permit to carry his thirty-five caliber."

Lucy nodded.

"Don't worry, I won't report you. This time . . ." she said, shaking a finger at her.

"Thanks."

She adjusted her spectacles again and read from another sheet of paper. "What I suspect you weren't able to glean from my screen was that this CCP application was originally denied. Mr. Roth apparently has a psychiatric history. But he appealed. They often do. Nobody likes to take no for an answer, especially in this arena. If I hear one more person go on about his constitutional right to bear arms, even I may throw up my hands and leave this dear job to someone else."

"So what happened on appeal?"

"His treating psychiatrist submitted a certification of mental stability—basically a report that he was of sound mind and judgment. According to the file, based on that submission, he was subsequently granted the permit. That was just about a year ago."

"Only a year? Who gave him the certification?"

She flipped through several pages, ran her index finger along one line, and then said, "A psychiatrist named Morgan Reese." Her expression softened with recognition. "Isn't that the poor woman who was found over at Faimount Links? Dear God, it never ends," she said, shaking her head as she turned the file so that Lucy could read for herself.

July 29th—just five months before Dr. Reese filed her own application for a restraining order because she felt threatened, because her patient was out of control. *Based on my experience as his treating psychiatrist, it is my opinion that he is mentally fit and emotionally stable enough to obtain a permit to carry a handgun.* Despite Lucy's disbelief, the words couldn't have been clearer.

How could this have happened? What did it even mean to be "stable enough"? It shouldn't be a question of relative degree. And how could the same person vouch for the sanity of someone she thought might kill her? More important, Roth's permit should have been revoked the moment Morgan appeared in court seeking protection. Another case falling through the bureaucratic cracks. More than ever, she felt as if being a homicide detective made her part of an enormous government clean-up crew, one assembled to deal with the mess left behind when other agencies didn't coordinate information. Or follow through on it.

"May I make a copy of that report?" she asked.

"Most certainly," Beth replied, pointing in the direction of a copying machine in the corner. "It may take a moment to warm up."

Lucy laid the single sheet of paper facedown on the glass top, inserted a dime, and listened to the outdated machine hum for several moments before a light crossed once over the document and snapped back to its original position. A second later, a warm piece of paper came out from the side. "Thanks," she said, returning the original.

"We aim to please, dear," Beth said. "Good luck."

14

6:02 p.m.

$\mathcal{L}$ ucy wandered along Belmont Avenue before turning east to the Schuylkill River. She loved this winding tributary that emptied into the Delaware. It seemed friendly, manageable; it was narrow enough to see what was happening on the opposite esplanade, so it offered a diversity of views. Early-evening joggers passed her and she watched them, wishing she could share in their carefree spirit, could go for a long run and enjoy the flow of the river's current, could forget events of the last two days. But instead, everything she learned increased her uneasiness.

Her affidavit in support of the search warrant was complete. Assistant District Attorney Nick Santoros would review it. Provided there was no problem with the establishment of probable cause, they could get a magistrate's signature and be authorized to go by early afternoon tomorrow. Now all she could do was wait. The law required patience. Plus she'd promised Jack.

Out on the river, several shells moved swiftly along the water's surface, and she paused to watch the unity of the oar strokes and to hear the call of the coxswain. She thought of Archer, his strong shoulders and his muscular thighs. He had the body of an athlete and could easily have rowed crew but sports held no interest to him. Or at least that's what he'd said on several occasions. Whether that was the truth, though, she now wondered.

Time had blurred since Saturday night and her dinner at the Haverill estate. With Morgan's murder, she hadn't taken a moment to process what she'd discovered that affected her personally—that Archer had hidden his heritage from her. She hated the nagging feeling of doubt that swelled inside her, a feeling she'd repressed by fixating on her investigation and the trauma he was experiencing. Before pulling into his elegant drive she'd had no reason to doubt the genuineness of a single thing he'd told her, but the pure and simple fact was that his omissions called everything into question. She wanted a person to be what he appeared. Life was too short, too precious for charades.

Questions to which she had no answers raced through her mind. Was it such a big deal that he was from an old-money family? Was their relationship any different simply because she'd learned he was rich? Was she suspicious of him or, if she were really honest, did she now doubt her own motives? *Had* she been overly impressed?

She envisioned Paul Doherty driving his Porsche onto the McGrath Highway. She'd stood in the parking lot of Dunkin' Donuts and watched him disappear up the ramp. Before that afternoon in early July, Paul had been her boyfriend for nearly three years, since tenth grade. His father had been the coach of the Somerville High School football team. During the winter of their senior year, Mr.

Doherty had been offered a job as head coach for Boston College. With his father's appointment, Paul could attend that institution on full scholarship, so Mr. Doherty gave his son the money he'd carefully put away over the years. "It was saved for his education and now I'm able to give him a better education than I could ever have paid for," he explained. Shortly before high school graduation, Paul spent the substantial sum on a royal blue sports car. He hadn't owned the vehicle for a month before he broke up with Lucy, just after he'd taken her for a ride and consumed a small box of Munchkins. "I just can't be tied down now. There's tremendous opportunity," he'd said, patting the steering wheel as if the leather interior would propel him into a life and world he'd always wanted. She'd managed to climb out of the bucket seat without saying a word and had watched him drive away, the tires screeching as he took a sharp right. Paul wanted the trappings of wealth and his father had been able to make that dream come true. Last she'd heard, he'd parlayed his $60,000 car into an engagement with a North Shore girl, apparently one easily impressed by four expensive tires and a piece of metal assembled abroad.

But it had never been something she craved.

Lucy wanted to discuss the reasons behind Archer's omissions—his deception—but there had been no opportunity. He hadn't been home when she returned from the Rabbit Club yesterday. That he'd gone to work seemed hard to imagine, but the last time she'd checked before falling asleep, the clock read 2:47. Then she'd left for Dr. Reese's office without so much as a perfunctory "Good morning." The only voice she'd heard before she departed belonged to the television newscaster reporting a traffic problem on Interstate 95.

Now she crossed the river and headed in the direction of Rittenhouse Square. Before she knew it, her ambling had led her to the front door of The Arch. She pushed open the heavy door and stepped inside.

The place was virtually empty. A lone patron sat at a table by the door with a newspaper and a beer. From his tousled hair, unshaven face, and dirty fingernails it was difficult to tell whether he was starting his bar activity early or whether he'd simply hung on from the night before. The smell of spilled liquor and stale cigarette smoke hung in the air. A collection of empty bottles and glasses covered one end of the long bar. A poster announced the night's reading event. Haiku. She'd pass.

Scanning the walls, she was surprised by the black-and-white photographs of downtown Philadelphia. Although the lighting and shadows created a noir effect, the subject matter was conventional: the bas relief panels depicting the zodiac signs above the ground-floor windows of the former Drexel and Company Building, the white steeple of the Old Swede's Church, the mansard roof of the Union League. She'd grown accustomed to Archer's eclectic taste and wouldn't have expected this work to appeal.

One image caught her eye and she moved closer to have a better look. It was a close-up of the carved panel of Gemini. Because of the angle of the sun, a ray of light shone through the middle of the photograph. Its effect was to divide the twins, severing their immortal connection.

Lucy remembered a pair of twins in her high school

class: Lana and Lori McDermott, identical girls. She'd spent countless homeroom hours staring at them, mesmerized by the very fact of their existence. What would it feel like to be half of a double? She couldn't imagine looking at her sibling and seeing her own face instead. She'd fantasized about being able to slip in and out of someone else's existence.

"Hey," said Sapphire, interrupting Lucy's thoughts.

Leaning against her broom, she paused in her task of sweeping butts and debris off the floor. Lucy could see the turquoise stud in her pierced navel flashing from the soft white skin of her belly.

"I'm looking for Archer," Lucy said.

Sapphire flicked her chin, indicating that he was in the back. "We missed you last night. I thought you'd be here, given that it was a party for the photographer."

Lucy stopped. That Sapphire wouldn't know what had transpired seemed extremely odd. Between her bookkeeping duties and her role as bartender, let alone her friendship with Archer, secrets were hard to keep. "I was at work late. I just went home and crashed." She didn't feel it was her place to explain.

"You've got confidence in him. I'll give you that." She shot Lucy a half smile. "I mean, to have him here working the crowd . . . alone. I was out of my mind jealous when we dated."

"What?" Another surprise about Archer's past was not what she needed, not now, not after Saturday night.

"I shouldn't have mentioned it. It was nothing." Sapphire looked worried. "In all honesty I've never seen him so enamored of anyone as he is of you. Really. And I've seen him with a lot—" She interrupted herself and covered her face with her hands. "I'm making a bad situation worse, aren't I? I'm sorry. I'm sure he'll be glad you're here," she added, glancing down the short hallway that led to Archer's office.

There was no point belaboring the conversation. "We'll see," Lucy said, trying hard not to sound too unfriendly as she headed in that direction.

"Come in," Archer instructed before she even knocked on the door. No doubt he'd heard her footsteps. Perhaps the brief conversation with Sapphire had penetrated the thin walls, too.

She stepped into the small, windowless room and shut the door behind her. Papers were stacked on top of a file cabinet in one corner. The coatrack resembled an upright grizzly bear given the mountain of coats, jackets, sweaters, and other outerwear piled onto its few wooden pegs. Manuscripts and portfolios covered most of the cushions of a sagging love seat.

He looked up from his desk. "How did it go today? Any news?"

She tried to read his expression, but couldn't. "We've got one lead. I'll know a lot more tomorrow." The last thing anyone needed was to generate a false hope that this investigation would be over quickly. Although the Calvin Roth angle had potential, it was a far cry from a closed case. "You look busy," she said, wanting to change the subject.

"And you seem surprised by that fact."

"I just know this can't be easy. Waiting. No answers. I worry about you."

"Don't," he replied dismissively. "*This*, this place is my life. She wasn't. Mourning the loss of her is no more painful now than it has been for years." He paused and shut the checkbook he'd had open in front of him. He dropped his pen and, with his elbows resting on the desk, put his head in his hands. "I heard your conversation with Sapphire." His voice was muffled. "I'm sorry I didn't tell you, but it was nearly two years ago. We spent some time together over a couple of weeks. I didn't even know you existed." Archer rose and walked around the desk to where Lucy stood. He reached for her arms, wrapped them around his waist, and then put his hands on her shoulders. Leaning forward, he kissed her, his lips moist and warm. "I'm flattered that you're jealous but you have no reason to be. Whatever happened between Sapphire and me has no bearing on us."

"Isn't it a little odd that she's still working here? I mean it's not like Philadelphia doesn't have a million other bars." Even as Lucy spoke, she hated that there was a whine in her voice. Everyone had a past—there was nothing to be done about it. Yet the thought of him and Sapphire together irritated her.

"She's good at what she does and she's honest. That's hard to find in this business. Besides, there was nothing between us."

"Does she still come on to you?"

"This is a totally irrational conversation. I was trying to find out information on your investigation and instead I end up in an inquisition on my sex life."

"Next thing you'll tell me is that I'm the first person you've slept with who doesn't belong to the Merion Cricket Club. Although I guess Sapphire holds that dubious honor, too," Lucy blurted out.

He gripped her shoulders and shook her lightly. "Stop! This is crazy. That's not who I am. You know that."

Maybe, Lucy thought. But she couldn't deny that she did feel more than slightly paranoid about this woman in her tight purple jeans that sat low on her hips. That Sapphire didn't wear a bra only added to the problem. She leaned into his chest. She knew her reaction had more to do with Saturday night than with a past lover; Sapphire was simply a catalyst for the more fundamental issue that tugged at her, the one that had led her to end up here in the first place when she had more than enough work to do elsewhere. Jack had an excuse to take time off from the investigation. Hers hardly qualified. "Then why didn't you tell me about your family?"

He sighed and cocked his head slightly, as if he wanted a different perspective. "You were the one who once said, 'Who we are can be different from who we might be destined to be.' I remember your words. We were sitting in front of your wood-burning stove staring at the flames and Cyclops had just taken a crap in my lap."

"He did?" She laughed. "You never told me that."

"Well, it was a romantic moment and I didn't want to spoil it over rabbit shit. But seriously, the moment you made that comment I realized I loved you more than I'd been willing to admit, even to myself. I knew you had a capacity to understand me—the *me* of me—in a way that no one had before."

She wasn't at all sure she was buying this story, but his face was so earnest that she decided not to interrupt.

"I feel so inarticulate a lot of the time, and now is definitely one of those moments. Maybe that's why I surround myself with artists and writers—the people I consider most expressive. I hope some of their talent wears off."

"Oh, please. I've come across plenty of creative types who can barely have a conversation or, if they do open their mouths, they're incomprehensible. Just say whatever you want."

"Thanks." He stepped away from her and leaned against the top of his desk. "How can I explain this?" He ran his hands through his thick hair. "My life was pre-programmed: St. Mark's, captain of the lacrosse team, summers in Bar Harbor, Yale, a slew of debutante cotillions where I escorted various girls I'd known forever down some presentation aisle, a summer on Wall Street as an intern at Merrill Lynch, graduation, a job at my father's company, dates with girls from the Cricket Club."

She must have given him an odd glance—she'd been right after all—because he added, "I can't tell you how many Bunnies and Marnies I wasted hours with, women who talked about marriage on the third date and didn't take their headbands off when they had sex. Think Papagallo shoes, Maidenform bras, plenty of martinis, and a complete absence of passion of any kind. One woman even had the audacity to ask me to watch out for her hairdo!"

"Thanks for sharing that," Lucy remarked. Although she didn't particularly want to dwell on the picture he painted, she could imagine it well. Instead of talk of bridesmaids' dresses and floral arrangements, her friends obsessed on greenback showers and registering at Home Depot; but the graduating class of Somerville High shared the same concerns as their Main Line peers: finding a mate, planning a wedding, decorating a home, settling down.

"I look at guys now—guys in their thirties with slight potbellies and smug expressions who chew on cigars and talk as if they're middle-aged—and I cringe. That was me in college. I even wore an ascot occasionally—some sort of weird Winston Churchill wannabe, who drank too much port and tried to talk like an intellectual. It worked in the investment banking arena, but I guarantee you wouldn't have been interested in me for a minute."

"I didn't know you worked for your father," she said, ignoring his last remark.

"Briefly. There was a huge sense of security that came with doing exactly what my father had done, and his father had done before him, and so on. The known, the familiar, even if it's not perfect, is better than the mysterious place of novelty, or something like that. But it wasn't me. The problem was that rather than quit I stayed in the job and quietly—or rather not so quietly—rebelled. I moved into a houseboat on the Delaware River and fell asleep at night listening to the scratching and patter of rats. My clothes stank of mildew. It was a pathetic effort at trying to be a bohemian when what I really needed was a different focus. After about eighteen months, I scrapped both a life in finance and the stupid boat. That was when I bought The Arch."

"How did your father take that?"

"He told me I was just like my mother."

They were both silent for several moments.

When Archer spoke again, his words came slowly, as if he were thinking about each one. "I love my father and I truly believe he loves me. It's taken us years to get to know each other, longer than most parent–child relation-ships. I think Dad finally understands that I'm not out to embarrass him; I'm just trying to find my own way. And I've accepted that he's not responsible for my mother's departure. That she may have felt stifled in her life isn't his fault. Perhaps they were looking for different things. He has a set of values that are basically decent. There's nothing wrong with the life he's chosen. I guess over the years we both realized we needed each other."

"Then why did it take you so long to tell me?"

He glanced down at the floor, and she wondered for a moment whether he was going to cry. But when he looked back up, his eyes were dry. "A noble reason and an ignoble one."

"Let's start with the good one."

"It's taken me a long time to get to this place. A place where I'm basically happy with myself and with the choices I've made. And I wanted to see if we could truly have a relationship without any reference to external trap-pings. Your apartment reminds me of childhood camping trips—warm and comfortable with everything we need but nothing extra. And look how great we've managed." He pulled her toward him.

She kissed his forehead.

"I suppose you're going to ask about my ignoble rea-son, too, so I might as well fess up," he said, his voice sounding lighter. "If the truth be told I don't think I com-pletely trusted you not to be enamored. Women have seen my house and it seems to change them. I didn't want that for us."

"If you think some overworked servant and a table that

could seat a cheerleading squad is the way to my heart, you're wrong. Though the meal was delicious." She smiled.

"Look, I'll be honest. I work hard because I want to, because I love The Arch, not because I need to pay the utility bills. And that gives me a great deal of freedom—much more than most people have. But I wanted to make sure that your feelings about me wouldn't change, that when you learned about my family you wouldn't try to convince me to go back and do what had been expected of me my whole life. I don't want to be a member of any board. I don't want to be courted by charities. If I'm philanthropic, I don't want anyone to know. I need to live my life my own way and I only hope that you'll think I'm a good person in what I choose. But I sold you short in ever thinking you'd care about any of this."

"You did."

"I'm sorry. Once I felt I really knew you and realized it wouldn't be an issue, it was too late. I didn't quite know how to announce myself. So I just thought it would be simpler if I took you home to meet Dad. I'd met your family."

She thought for a moment. Then she stared directly into his eyes and spoke matter-of-factly. "I don't want my appeal to be because I'm different. I don't like having my greatest asset be that I'm *not* from the Main Line. And I guess after last night, and then discovering about your other nonconformist girlfriend today, I'm wondering whether that's the case," she said, relieved to articulate how she felt.

"Don't be absurd. Nonconformity has nothing to do with your best assets. You're wonderful." He moved to the door and turned the lock. She heard the bolt click as it closed. "Now if you're very, very quiet . . ." he said with a smile as he pushed the pile of papers off the couch.

"What are you doing?" she asked, even though she knew she had no intention of offering the slightest resistance. There was still so much to do, so much to discover about Morgan's death, but for just a few minutes she wanted to forget, as she suspected he did, too. When she went back on duty, the status of the homicide investigation would be just where she'd left it.

"I could use some serious consoling," he said, apparently sensing her hesitation. "And you're the only one in the world who can do it," he added, reaching to undo the buttons on her blouse.

15

9:07 p.m.

$\mathcal{T}$he poet, an androgynous male with the incongruous name of Fred Smith, had just finished what had to be his hundredth haiku. There was unenthusiastic, scattered applause from the small crowd. As the noise subsided, one young man began clapping furiously. Fred smiled, walked over to where the man sat, gave him a prolonged kiss on the lips, and then slipped into the chair next to him. Sitting at the bar with a plate of lemon hummus and pita chips—the house specialty— and a glass of Chardonnay, Lucy felt relieved that he had at least one fan. Somebody for everyone. Archer thanked Fred, as well as the crowd. For the first time in nearly two days she felt peaceful.

"Praise the Lord that's over," Sapphire said as she uncorked a bottle and refilled Lucy's glass. "Sometimes I wish Archer would lighten up his act and get a real entertainer—a comedian or a master storyteller. But no," she said sarcastically. "We have to be subjected to Fred the homosexual haiku poet from Lancaster. Can you imagine? The guy's parents are Amish. Ask me, the world gets weirder every day. Plus he's managed to run up a one-hundred-and-forty-dollar bill that Archer will inevitably write off."

Lucy chuckled. A patron at the opposite end of the bar lifted a hand to get Sapphire's attention. "Do you have today's paper?" she asked quickly. She hadn't read it and wanted to see what, if anything, the press was saying about Dr. Reese's murder.

"Sure." Sapphire reached beneath the bar and produced a badly folded edition of the *Inquirer*. "It's yours."

It took Lucy a moment to refold the sections and find the front page. Foreign affairs, another article on the rising price of gasoline, a column on the Reese murder. Inside, one story caught her interest: DAVID ELLERY NAMED DIRECTOR OF WILDER CENTER, the headline read. "Appointment Follows Gruesome Death of Front-runner" was the subhead.

Lucy skimmed the article, pausing at a paragraph close to the end.

Ellery's longtime colleague and close friend Dr. Morgan Reese was the initial choice, one source close to the Board disclosed on the condition of anonymity. Following news of the psychiatrist's grisly murder, Ellery was notified yesterday that the job was his. "He accepted immediately," the source said. Calls to the police chief on the status of that investigation were not returned.

Only a few hours before, she had articulated her suspicions of Calvin Roth in an affidavit in order to search his residence. Now an alternative scenario seemed just as plausible, if not more compelling: Ellery reports his gun stolen. Focus is immediately on the psycho patient. A month later, that very weapon is used to shoot his competition for a prestigious and lucrative appointment to run a major new psychiatric hospital.

Had the theft been a ruse? Had Ellery been plotting Morgan's demise for weeks, a plot that included getting himself invited to the Rabbit Club? Means, motive, and opportunity—it seemed almost too easy. Besides, it made sense only if he knew for certain that he would get the appointment if she were eliminated, an assumption that discounted other candidates. For a position this desirable, there had to be plenty of qualified people.

Her mind was playing tricks on her. He was a successful professional—a psychiatrist no less. He wouldn't murder anyone.

The vibration of her cell phone interrupted her musings. "Detective O'Malley," she answered.

"This is Rodman Haverill, Archer's father."

"Are you . . . all right?" she stammered. That he'd even known her number was surprising, let alone that he'd called it. "I'm sorry. So sorry about your . . . about Dr. Reese."

"I very much need to discuss with you some details pertaining to her death," he said, apparently ignoring her expression of sympathy. "I'd like you to join me for lunch tomorrow at the Cricket Club. At noontime."

Tomorrow. She thought of the search warrant. Lunch would be over by two, three at the latest. There was still time in the day.

"Okay. I can meet you there," she replied.

"Very good. Please come alone."

She paused, thinking of what she might say to Jack.

He wouldn't approve. "All right." Even as she uttered the words, she had the strange sense that she was getting herself into trouble.

"I'll register you. Just drive right in. No announcement will be necessary."

"Fine."

"And Lucy, I would appreciate your discretion. With Archer, I mean."

This time she didn't respond. He could take her silence to be assent without a verbal commitment.

Across the room, Archer was engaged in animated conversation with Fred and his friend, oblivious to what had just transpired. What exactly was she doing? She sighed, wondering how the situation had become so complicated so fast.

10:15 p.m.

Gertrude draped her robe over the back of a chair, removed her slippers, and turned back the covers. Switching off the light, she settled against the pillow. The night was still; but for the sound of a few crickets through the open window, it was quiet. A sliver of a moon partly illuminated the room, so she secured her satin sleep mask and ushered in total darkness. She needed sleep.

Despite her exhaustion, peaceful slumber eluded her. As she lay in bed listening to the ticktock of her electric alarm clock, the events of the past two days raced through her mind. She couldn't bear that such sordidness, such violence, had left a stain on her club. In all her years of dutiful service, she'd never once had to escort a police officer inside the hallowed walls.

Creak. She heard a floorboard. The building was so old and drafty that even the slightest breeze rattled the windows or caused a door to slam. She was used to the idiosyncratic sounds and movements of the place.

A second creak was longer. Then she heard the sound of a door opening on its worn hinge. It must be a member, although what anyone was doing here at this hour escaped her. Unless . . . She thought of the letter she'd found and passed along to that nice young detective. Its author had known how to threaten.

She chastised herself. Nothing bad or untoward had ever sullied this club; its history was impeccable. She was letting her mind play tricks on her. But then again, it was possible. She'd obviously forgotten to lock the door, and times had changed. She'd read quite enough horrific stories in the newspaper to know that. Perhaps a homeless person had wandered in. Or a thief. But knowing she would never go to sleep until she'd set her mind at ease, she got up, took up her robe and slippers again, and unlocked her bedroom door.

The hallway was dark. So was the stairwell. She reached for the switch at the top of the stairs, but nothing happened. Changing that lightbulb was another task to add to her list, a list that had grown exponentially with the distractions of the past forty-eight hours. She listened but heard nothing. Gertrude, you're getting senile, she said to herself, refusing to accept that she just might be getting too old to be house manager.

There was an audible thump, and she paused in her descent. "Who is there?" she called out into the darkness.

For a moment she wondered whether she should call the police but decided against it. Her duty was to this club and its members. Part of her job was discretion, and part was to ensure that the fine gentlemen who belonged here could enjoy themselves in peace and quiet. She'd already exposed the club to intrusion and its reputation to possible damage by involving the police over the weekend. She would address this evening's problem herself.

Quietly she tiptoed down the stairs. A light was on in the game room and she heard rummaging sounds, the opening of drawers, the slamming of a chest as it closed. Since whoever was there made no effort to hide his presence, it had to be a member, and she felt relieved that she hadn't contacted law enforcement in haste. A needless incident might have cost her the job she loved. "May I help you?" she called.

Suddenly the light in the game room went out and she was plunged into darkness again. This behavior was very peculiar. Holding on to the banister, she felt her way down the stairs and through the short foyer. The building was quiet. Even the crickets had stopped. She stepped into the game room and flicked the wall switch, illuminating the room.

A man ran at her, knocking her aside as he made his way to the door. She stumbled backward, reaching for something—the wall—to try to maintain her balance, but her grasp came up empty and she fell against a wooden chair. The pain in her back was intense, and her head spun. His movement had been so swift and she was so startled that it was only after she'd heard a car drive off that she realized her intruder had been no intruder at all. If anything, he belonged here more than she did. Though why the club president had come by at this late hour and then made such a hasty exit eluded her. Mr. Nichols certainly could have asked for her help if he needed anything at all.

16

Tuesday, May 20th
Noon

The view from the street of the Merion Cricket Club didn't do justice to the sprawling red brick building with green shutters and trim that overlooked lawn-tennis courts. Perhaps that was the intent: Only members could appreciate the true elegance and majesty of the architecture. Ivy grew over much of the facade, giving the oldest parts of the historic clubhouse a bearded look. Mower lines were still evident in the grass. Lucy wondered for a moment how it felt to be part of the full-time maintenance crew, immigrants no doubt, who could hardly imagine when they arrived in Philadelphia that such a place existed for recreational sports.

Mr. Haverill had indeed registered her, and the preppy gate attendant waved her through with a sideways glance at her license plate. A series of arrows directed cars to a parking area by a newly constructed indoor-tennis bubble. She left her Explorer amid the array of dark-toned foreign imports and walked back toward the main building.

A few feet from the entrance she paused to watch several ladies' matches that were well under way despite the chill in the air. Lithe figures in short white skirts and warm-up jackets moved through the familiar choreography of doubles—serve, crosscourt return, down-the-line approach shot, lob, overhead winner. Standing quietly, she listened to the *ping* of balls volleying back and forth and the intermittent muffled sounds of polite banter or laughter. How different the game seemed in this environment, a far cry from the cracked Hard-Tru courts of Somerville High where local teenagers in basketball shorts and T-shirts smashed balls into torn nets or against chain link.

She climbed the steps leading to a covered rectangular porch. Not surprisingly, it was empty. The combination of ivy and the depth of the overhang kept the place dark and cool, no doubt more of an asset on steamy summer days than on one like today. Just inside a set of French doors was a spacious room divided into multiple seating areas by arrangements of wicker armchairs, love seats, coffee tables, and card tables. On two couches on either side of a stone fireplace lounged several women in velour tracksuits with pastel trim. Glasses of iced tea and a bowl of Goldfish crackers were arranged on a round tray on the table between them. On the opposite side of the room, three bejeweled elderly women played bridge with a single well-dressed, white-haired man.

"Lucy." She heard Mr. Haverill's voice behind her.

She turned to greet him. He wore a tweed blazer over a white polo shirt and pressed navy trousers.

"Follow me."

He led the way into a dining room surrounded on three sides by mullioned windows overlooking more tennis courts. Enormous crystal chandeliers added necessary light to the grim day. Despite the lunch hour, there were few other diners. The maître d' pulled back a chair, and Lucy somewhat awkwardly let him push her up to the table. A uniformed waiter immediately arrived with butter balls arranged in a pyramid on a porcelain dish. Using tongs, he then served each of them a round hard roll.

"I recommend the crab cakes. The tomato and basil soup is quite adequate, too," Mr. Haverill said, opening the menu.

"Sounds good," Lucy said, not bothering to look at hers. She had no strong food preferences and preferred to focus on the purpose of this meeting rather than ponder the lunch offerings. She unfolded her napkin and arranged it on her lap.

"Very well, then." He signaled to the waiter and ordered for both of them.

"I just have to ask you," she said when they were alone. "Why is this place called the *Merion* Cricket Club if we're in Haverford?"

He didn't appear to find any humor in the question. "It moved to this location at the turn of the century, but by that time it had established itself. The members wouldn't have been receptive to a name change."

"What about the cricket part then? Does anyone still play?"

"There's an annual game here to keep up tradition, but, sadly, cricket is not what it once was."

"Other than what I saw on a commercial for tourism in Bermuda, I know nothing about it."

"I wouldn't suppose you would. Boston was never much of a stronghold, but it used to be quite the sport of Philadelphia. In addition to interclub matches, there were international competitions, many of which took place right here, and our teams competed abroad with considerable success even against the Australians."

"Did you play?" Lucy asked.

"I did." He removed a stalk of celery from his glass and took a sip of his virgin Bloody Bull, a mixture of cold beef broth and tomato juice. "Many years ago when I was a student at Haverford College. It was a different world then. Cricket wasn't like sports today. Athletes came from the very best of families—not the public schools and the ghettos. The Newhalls dominated, and an impressive lot they were. But that all ended quite some time ago. The public didn't have the patience or the elegance required to maintain it as a major sport. Tennis has completely taken over."

She marveled at his arrogance. His class consciousness struck her as something out of *Masterpiece Theatre*. "You must enjoy tennis," she said, struggling for something to say as she looked out the window at the visual monolith of green.

"Not much. But I like the club when it isn't crowded. It can be overwhelming with the noise, the ball machines. Last week there was even a bit of a brouhaha in the taproom."

Revelry at a bar was a cardinal sin for sure. Although she'd been the one to broach the subject, the conversation was going nowhere, taxing both Lucy's patience and her curiosity. She had a million things to do in this murder investigation and discussing the moral decline of cricket wasn't one of them. "I'm very sorry about Dr. Reese."

At that moment, the waiter arrived with their soup. Mr. Haverill diverted his eyes from hers, studying the condensation that had formed on the water goblets. He took a taste, and rested his spoon on the edge of his bowl. "Morgan and I went our separate ways many years ago. Her untimely death is tragic, but I'd made my peace, as I believe my son has, too."

His sentiment echoed Archer's. Did he really feel nothing? Lucy didn't believe it for a second. Peace or no peace, she'd been his wife, the mother of his son. "Why did you want to speak with me about her death?"

He cleared his throat. "Excuse me if I seem taken aback. The women of my generation are not so . . . so direct."

"I've been accused of being blunt before," Lucy said, forcing a smile. "It's just, well, I'm sure you can imagine that this is somewhat difficult for me. To be here with you without Archer knowing."

"Are you suggesting he'd have a problem with that?"

"It probably depends upon what you have to say. But I wouldn't blame him for being surprised."

"There is little that surprises Archer, my dear. The sooner you realize that, the better off you'll be. But one of the reasons that I did invite you here was to protect him." He tore his roll in half, selected a butter ball, and pressed it into the center with his small knife. The bite he took was more butter than bread. "Morgan and I were married very briefly—less than five years. She made no effort to connect to Archer or to fulfill her role as his mother. She and I had been out of contact for decades, until—" He stopped, opting not to finish that thought. "It isn't fair to expose our family to whatever media attention may be generated by your inquiry into the circumstances surrounding her death. We're private and we want to maintain that privacy."

"I have no control over the press."

"Perhaps not formally."

"We have a separate publicity bureau that deals with the media."

"That may be. But reporters certainly call the precinct to obtain information. The department issues press releases on high-profile cases. That's what I'm trying to guard against: having our names mentioned in that setting. Morgan's involvement with the Haverill family has no bearing on what's happened and isn't relevant to your investigation." He leaned toward her. "Just so that I make myself clear, I'm willing to pay handsomely for discretion."

His arrogance aside, the idea that he'd actually lured her to his country club only to try to bribe her was insulting—even if what he wanted was beyond her power or control to provide. Apparently good breeding didn't guard against being an asshole. "I'm sorry I can't help you," she said. "My duty as a police officer is to conduct a thorough investigation. While there can and will be no gratuitous release of information—and our unit takes extra precautions to guard against leaks—I cannot agree to alter in any manner the way my partner and I will proceed because of my relationship with Archer or . . . for any other reason."

Mr. Haverill pursed his lips in an effort to contain his

irritation. Despite Morgan's departure from his life, and his son's decision not to proceed with a career in finance, Lucy suspected that in most areas Mr. Haverill's life had gone his way. He must have expected he could sway her or he would never have asked for this meeting.

"That said, if her personal life—or in this case prior life—played no part in her murder, you may get what you want. My department certainly understands the turmoil that can come from publicity. We're not out to hurt anyone. I will make every effort to be sure that information is disseminated only on a need-to-know basis."

It was the best she could offer, and he seemed to know it. They stared at each other for a moment but said nothing. Fortunately, the waiter, arriving with their crab cakes, provided a needed diversion. He set their plates in front of them and lifted off the silver covers that had kept lunch warm. "Enjoy," he said.

Mr. Haverill began to eat quickly, signaling that the conversation was over. Once the meal was over, too, they could go their separate ways.

Lucy leaned forward. "Since I'm here, may I ask you some questions?"

He looked up from his plate with obvious displeasure.

"Who is Walter Reese?"

"You mean 'was.' Walter was Morgan's father," he replied. "A wonderful man. He died shortly after our marriage."

Lucy tried to hide her surprise. Had Morgan illegally used his identity to get medication for herself? She remembered the message on the answering machine. No wonder the insurance company had questioned the prescription. But it still seemed odd that Morgan wouldn't have simply paid cash for the drugs and avoided the issue altogether. Why was she willing to risk her medical license to hide the fact that she wanted antianxiety medication? "Does Morgan have any surviving family?"

"Other than Archer?" He raised his eyebrows. "Not any of whom I'm aware."

"You mentioned, or almost mentioned before you caught yourself, that you'd had contact with Morgan. I assume recently. Is that right?"

He nodded but didn't verbalize a reply.

"Can you tell me why?"

He was silent.

"Look . . . sir, as I said, I'm going to do my best to help you. I'm trying to solve this crime as quickly as possible. At this point, we still know very little about Morgan's life, or why someone might have wanted her dead. If you have information that may be important and you don't disclose it, that leaves me with only one choice—a route I don't want to take."

"And what is that?"

"Have the Assistant District Attorney call you before a grand jury."

He coughed. "I beg your pardon."

"You and I actually want the same thing, which is to make this case go away. That's going to happen when we catch Morgan's killer. It'd be a lot easier if you tell me what you know right here, right now."

She should have forced him to come down to the precinct, to talk on her turf. But since she'd already made that mistake, she was determined to leave with something useful.

"You're tough," he said under his breath.

"That's my job."

He laid his knife and fork together on his plate. "She contacted me." He reached into his pocket and pulled out a piece of paper with a ragged edge. It appeared the note had been folded and refolded multiple times. Now he opened it yet again and glanced down, no doubt by force of habit; judging from the expression of concern on his face, he didn't need his memory refreshed. "She wrote to inform me that she had a substantial life insurance policy."

"How substantial?"

"For the sum of five million dollars."

"Why tell you?"

He hesitated briefly. "Because Archer is the beneficiary."

To buy a policy or even to pay premiums on an existing one of that size at her age was no small investment. Why would an estranged mother do that when she knew that the Haverill family was beyond affluent already? Morgan had to have known Archer never would want for anything. "When did she tell you this?"

"Two weeks ago. We spoke briefly. These are my notes on that conversation."

"Why did you take notes?"

"I'm not as young as you. I need reminders of events."

She couldn't tell from his tone of voice whether his comment was an attempt at levity. "Does Archer know?"

He shook his head.

"Why didn't she tell him herself? Why contact you? He's not a child anymore," she added. Then she remembered Morgan's luncheon invitation to Archer. Perhaps she'd intended to tell him, but he hadn't given her the opportunity. He'd never responded, not even to say he wouldn't come.

"Because she knew how I felt about inherited wealth."

She clasped her hands together and leaned toward him. "And how is that?"

He cleared his throat. "I doubt that what I'm about to say will make much sense to you, but I will say my piece nonetheless. As you well know, Archer is privileged. As a child, he had everything money could buy. He knows the house and all that I have will be his some day, perhaps not too long from now. And that luxury has allowed him to act irresponsibly. What he inherited, and what he will potentially inherit, has made him reckless."

Bar ownership didn't comport with Main Line expectations. That he'd created a lively meeting place for a diverse crowd apparently was lost on his father.

Mr. Haverill continued. "He gave up a meaningful profession. He provides a forum for artists who can't get a gallery and writers whom no one will publish, so-called creative types who don't even pay the bar bill."

"But he loves his job."

"It's self-indulgent. He's accomplished nothing except to make himself a big fish in a little pond of his own creating. He ignores even the most basic lessons that most of us learn about capitalism. He has no sense of social obligation."

She was shocked. She wanted to think of him as an old man who, because he had little to show for his life but money, was bitter that his son had chosen another path. That would be the most charitable view of his words. But, sadly, she didn't think that was the case. He didn't strike her as the type to question the choices he'd made. Self-reflection required openness that Mr. Haverill sorely lacked. His way was the right way, and Archer was the deviant.

"Morgan wanted to speak to me because she knew I would be upset about the policy. She'd found out about The Arch. I suppose she knew me well enough even after all this time to assume I disapproved."

"So then why tell you she was leaving more money to Archer?"

"What she said was, 'You won't have to think of your hard-earned wealth as being squandered. Leave your possessions to charity. Become the great philanthropist. Make yourself immortal. I'll take care of Archer.' She had the notion that she could step back into our lives and try to undo what she'd done. She didn't care if she undermined me."

Lucy remembered the conversation with Archer the night before: *He told me I was just like my mother.* Morgan would achieve in death what she hadn't in life: to give her son freedom from the Haverill legacy—freedom she herself had sought. This policy, her gesture, would ensure that he could do what he wanted, live the life he wanted, and be beholden to no one.

"Do you have a copy of the policy?" Lucy asked.

"My lawyer is in the process of obtaining it."

"I'd like to see it when he does," she replied. "When are you intending to break the news to Archer?"

"He'll be told when the time is appropriate," Mr. Haverill answered quickly.

"And when in your estimation might that be?" she asked, looking directly into his eyes.

"When I can have some assurance that this money

won't promote even more irresponsibility." He removed his napkin from his lap and laid it on the table. The meal was over.

"You're making a huge mistake, sir," she said, refusing to take the hint. "I know your son. He's smart. He's interested in the world around him. He recognizes talent, and he's interested in helping people. You grossly underestimate him if you mistake passion and commitment for irresponsibility."

"I asked you to come here for your help, not to lecture me. I think it's time we said good-bye."

She felt a surge of adrenaline fueled by anger. "You invited me here to see if I could assist you in getting what you want. I'm not sure exactly what that is, but I won't be bought and I can't be bribed. But I love your son and don't want to see him hurt more than he has been. So I'm offering my advice. Free," she announced, thinking for a moment of Lucy in the *Peanuts* comic strip, who dispensed psychiatric help from her makeshift stand only for the joy of hearing a nickel payment rattle in the jar. She leaned toward Mr. Haverill. "Tell him the truth. Tell him about what his mother did—then and now. It might help you both to get some secrets off your chest."

"This is not a game, Detective O'Malley."

"So don't try to beat your son."

He didn't respond. Instead, he signaled to the waiter and gave his house account number in lieu of payment.

As they stood, Lucy felt dizzy and realized her legs were trembling. She'd wanted to defend Archer and the choices he'd made, but her boldness came at a price. After all, this was the father—the only family—of the man she loved. In her effort to help mend Mr. Haverill's relationship with his son, she'd most certainly damaged any potential for one between her and him. She quickly reached for a chair to steady herself.

As she straightened up, she heard his voice.

"May I?" he asked, offering her an arm.

No doubt the gesture was designed to avoid the embarrassment of having his young, female lunch guest collapse on the way out of the dining room, but she welcomed the support nonetheless. Looping her elbow through his, she allowed him to escort her out.

"I'm relieved to see that you're apparently not as tough as you appear," he said, speaking out of the side of his mouth in a low whisper. He nodded to the maître d'. "For Archer's sake . . . and for my own."

17

2:15 p.m.

$\mathcal{L}$ ucy was relieved to see the familiar back entrance to the Roundhouse, so named because from an aerial view the building resembled a pair of giant handcuffs. There always were scattered cigarette butts leading from the front door to the street, and an orange cone marking a hole in the sidewalk pavement had been there for longer than she could remember. Pushing open the door, she smiled at the uniformed cop on duty at the reception desk. Even the stale smell of the air, the result of too many take-out meals and too little ventilation, soothed her spirits. This was where she belonged.

The Homicide and Special Investigations Units were packed. Given that there were multiple "live ones"—the unlikely euphemism for active investigations of dead bodies—many of the night shift had stayed on and the room was filled with noise: the clicking of dozens of computer keyboards, a litany of voices in varying degrees of pitch and volume, and telephones ringing so frequently that one interrupted another. There were many days when Lucy had to block out the sound because it was so overwhelming. But not today. At this moment she appreciated the chaos more than ever.

She wove her way through the tightly spaced desks toward her own, glancing at the various collections of personal mementos on each one. She didn't know the other detectives particularly well, and with little time for idle chatter, she liked these glimpses into their lives. She paused at the eight-by-ten glossy of a toddler dressed in a police uniform and propped against a fake sky background. "That's my boy," Ben DeForest remarked proudly. "Handsome fellow, don't you think?"

"He is," she replied.

"He sure loves the camera. Best of all is that the price for this picture included six wallet-size photos, too. Something for the in-laws."

Her own desk opposite Jack's was empty of any personal effects. She should bring in a picture of her parents, or maybe Cyclops. She'd wait a few more months on Archer, although he'd look the best in a silver-plated frame.

Jack was leaning back in his chair with his eyes closed. Much to her astonishment she'd witnessed the seasoned detectives napping whenever there was a moment of downtime. Years on the force must bring with it some of form of internal peace, something that certainly eluded her.

"Hi," she said softly as she approached, not wanting to startle him.

He opened his eyes and rubbed them with his knuckles as he sat forward in his chair.

"How's Sean?"

"The kid's tough as nails. He's already up and about." Jack smiled. "Thanks for asking."

"You'd do the same." Then she added, "Sorry I'm late. Has the warrant application been approved?"

"Santoros is reviewing it now. He paged me a few minutes ago and said we had to include the fact that Roth has no direct link to the gun recovered with the body. He doesn't want any claim that the application is misleading. But he told us to be on standby. Where've you been?" he asked.

"Morgan's ex-husband—Archer's dad—wanted to talk to me. I'm not sure it had much to do with the investigation, but one thing unusual came of it. Even though Morgan had nothing to do with her child—from what I understand they may well have been able to walk past each other without a hint of recognition—she had a five-million-dollar life insurance policy for his benefit."

"Five million?"

Lucy nodded, sharing his astonishment.

He paused, thinking. "Did Archer know?"

"No, and apparently still doesn't," she replied quickly. "Fortunately." She knew what had passed through Jack's mind and wanted to dispel his suspicions immediately. It was a lot of money, more than most of the world could fathom. A sum that large could easily have a corrupting effect, or at least most homicide detectives would think it could. But ignorance about his windfall wasn't the only thing protecting Archer; he'd been with her—and his father—at the time of the murder. His alibi was solid.

Jack moved to within a few inches of her and spoke softly. "There's a reason cops have partners and that has to do first and foremost with officer safety—and also with corroboration. We want to gather evidence in the most defense-proof way. I like you, Lucy, and I respect that you're tenacious. But let's not be renegades." He met her stare. "Okay?"

She felt a pain in her chest as she realized her mistake. Jack wasn't territorial; he just wanted everything done according to proper procedure. And she should want that, too. Her personal connections to the victim's family couldn't get in the way of how she'd been trained to perform an investigation. "I'm sorry," she said feebly.

"We've got a long time together and there will be apologies on both sides. I can assure you of that. But I can't say I'm not glad the first one came from you." He smiled.

At that moment, Frank Griffith approached the two detectives. Grabbing an empty chair, he turned it around, swung one leg over, and sat, straddling it backward. His curly blond hair partially covered his eyes, accentuating the disfiguring scar left by the surgical repair of a cleft palate.

"What can you tell us?" Jack asked.

"Not as much as I'm sure you'd like to hear," the technician responded. "The car was pretty badly damaged. Looks like someone took a baseball bat to it. No doubt the same one that whacked Reese, although we'd need to recover the bat to verify that. We got two good prints—one off the hood of the car and one off the interior armrest. No match came up in our system, but we'll send it over to the FBI. We also got a bunch of footprints: a woman's size seven and a half, something with a wedged heel; a man's ten and a half, probably a golf cleat; and another woman's size six with a stiletto heel."

"Wasn't Morgan wearing high heels?"

"Yeah, but given the imprint in the ground, I'd say it belonged to someone heavier. However, the ground was raked around the area where the body was discovered so none of these footprints were in the immediate vicinity. The killer obviously wanted to cover his—or her—tracks. Used a garden rake, nothing unusual, probably a metal one since we recovered no broken prongs."

"Anything else?" Lucy asked.

"Ballistics confirmed that the recovered bullet came from Ellery's gun. We've got a blood sample on the inside of the driver's-side door that doesn't match the victim. She was an AB. The sample's type A. The leather interior and steering wheel had been wiped clean with some kind of alcohol that the lab hasn't yet been able to identify. Stan's still working on it," he said, referring to Stanley Edmond, the chief chemist in the forensics laboratory. "Toxicology came back with trace amounts of Klonopin consistent with a prescribing dosage, nothing more, and a fairly low dose at that. But alcohol content was high. The gas chromatography–mass spectrometry test was positive for a blood alcohol level of point oh-seven. She was pretty pickled."

"Did you get anything from the fibers Ladd scraped from under her fingernails?"

"Only that they were navy blue cashmere. We don't have enough to try to identify a dye lot or a brand."

"What about the hair?"

"We did confirm that the recovered hair was not human. There were some food crumbs and a wrapper from one of those low-carbohydrate bars so it's possible an animal came to forage—a squirrel maybe, although the hair was pretty long—maybe a raccoon."

"Is that possible? A raccoon wouldn't crawl inside a car while people were still around, would it? Food or no food, it seems unlikely to me. And we responded right after Barbadash heard the gunshot."

"So what are you saying?"

"Just thinking aloud. I'm no veterinary specialist, but in my experience raccoons crawl around in the trash in a garage when everyone's asleep in the house. They're nocturnal and skittish. We had Morgan battling someone with a baseball bat, not the kind of quiet that promotes raccoon activity." She paused, thinking. "Is there any difference between a strand of fur from a coat and one from a live animal?"

"You think the driver wore a raccoon coat?"

"I'd speculate on animal behavior before I'd hypothesize about fashion, but it was just a thought."

Just then Jack's pager went off. He glanced down at the small BlackBerry to read the text message. "Time to head on out. We've got our approval. A magistrate's signature and good old Calvin Roth won't know what hit him."

18

3:45 p.m.

A darkened sky hovered over the small A-frame house. Set back from the street, it was surrounded by mesh and barbed-wire fence, a makeshift barricade. Sheets were drawn across each of the windows, blocking any view inside. Two flowerpots from which protruded an array of dead stalks, a pile of broken bricks, and an overturned wheelbarrow formed a heap to the left of the front door. To the right was what appeared to be an empty chicken coop. A lone bantam pecked at bits of dirt as it paraded back and forth, clucking quietly.

"Don't you need some sort of agricultural permit to keep those in the city?" Lucy whispered as she tightened the straps of her bulletproof vest around her waist and zippered her Gore-Tex Windbreaker over it.

"Why don't we let animal control tackle that problem? Just focus on the guns, O'Malley," Jack said.

She could see the tension in his face as he ran through his mental checklist. Executing a warrant could be hazardous duty, but it was especially dangerous when the property owner was a psychiatric patient with an arsenal of weapons.

They'd parked a block away and walked to the house with a backup team. The strategy was clear: Get as close to the front door as possible without detection, announce their arrival, and, if necessary, break their way in. But it didn't take long to realize that a clandestine approach was going to be difficult in this location. Shadows from an adjacent apartment building would provide some cover, and a row of thorny bushes along one side of the lot might help, too. But getting through the padlocked front gate was certain to blow their cover, unless Calvin was asleep or under the influence of some antipsychotic drug.

"Ready?" Jack asked.

Lucy gripped the handle of her Glock 9 mm. She could feel her heart beating in her chest. She had seventeen shots—sixteen in the mug and one in the chamber. She'd never before discharged an entire round, but today she had a nagging feeling of doubt mixed with a more than healthy dose of terror. *I am in fear for my life*, Morgan had attested. And look where she'd ended up. She adjusted her fingers ever so slightly, settling them in perfect alignment against the cold metal.

"You bet," she said, wanting to sound convincing. Ben DeForest and Elliott Langley, the backup team, nodded to indicate their readiness.

"Be careful, everyone." Jack crouched down, leading the way. He stayed in shadow along the perimeter until he was parallel to the padlocked gate. The three of them scurried behind him. He paused, glanced back in their direction, replaced his gun in its holster, and removed a pair of metal cutters. "Cover me," he directed Lucy.

As he crept toward the gate, Lucy scanned the windows of the house, searching for the slightest movement inside, the flutter of a sheet against a window. All was quiet. Was Roth there? If so, what was he doing? Although she could hear the sound of the lock being cut open, and the squeaking of the rusted gate as Jack made room for the detectives to pass, she stayed focused, refusing to be distracted even for a split second. She'd made one mistake in this investigation. She wasn't about to do it again. One glimpse, one turn of the head, was all it took to fail in the primary task of protecting her partner.

Before she knew it, Jack had returned to the protection of the shadows, tucked the cutters away in a bag that would be temporarily left behind, and pulled his weapon. He checked the chamber as if in his absence something might have changed. Then with a wave of his arm, he led them closer. They hurried through the open gate. While Ben and Elliott split left and right to surround the house, he and Lucy sprinted to the front.

Jack banged on the door. "Police! Open the door! We've got a search warrant!" he yelled, following perfect knock-and-announce procedure. He waited a second, then repeated his command. "Police! Open up!"

Lucy stood beside him with her eyes fixed on the doorknob. She knew it was a matter of seconds, but time seemed to have stopped. There was an eerie quiet, a silence that was palpable. Even the scratching of the chicken had stopped. *Come on, Calvin. Open the door.* This search had been her idea in the first place. Although Lieutenant Sage had agreed that it made sense, she knew she'd feel responsible if anything happened, especially if it happened to Jack. He was taking the lead because he was the senior detective. The man who was a beloved husband and the father of two put himself in harm's way before her. For a fleeting moment, she wondered whether she would ever have his courage or decency. He had qualities that even a lifetime on the force couldn't teach.

Give it up, Calvin. She wanted to beg. Even as she waited, hoping, she wondered how much time Jack was willing to give him to comply voluntarily before he broke down the door. That issue hadn't been discussed in advance. But knowing Jack, Calvin didn't have long.

A flicker caught her by surprise. Was the knob turning? Had the sunlight somehow caught the movement? Could the sun even reflect off tarnished brass? Just then she heard an explosion from within. Glass shattered. Instinctively she and Jack both ducked, and pressed themselves against the side of the house.

After a second, the quiet engulfed them once again. *Man down.* Every muscle in her body was tense as she waited for those fateful words through the walkie-talkie, but they didn't come. She squeezed the trigger on her Glock, but didn't pull. No trained police officer was about to shoot aimlessly into a building, and there was no target in sight.

She turned to Jack. His eyes remained fixed on the door, and he seemed to ignore her. Instead he stood and repeated his command for what she knew was the final time. "Police! Open up! We have you surrounded!"

Then he kicked the door, heel leading, a singular thrust using all the power in his leg. The wood splintered. He kicked again and the door fell forward off its hinges.

"Go! Go! Go!" she muttered to herself through a

clenched jaw. No matter how many times she'd stormed a home, it was never simple. Fear mingled with an acute sense of mortality. She was trained. She knew what she was doing, but it never got routine. She stepped inside, moving past Jack into the darkened entrance.

Her eyes took a moment to adjust to the sudden lack of light. The foyer was nearly empty but for an overturned bentwood rocker in one corner. Moving forward, spinning ever so slightly on the axis of her body with arms outstretched and gun raised, she made her way down a narrow corridor. She sensed Jack's presence behind her, but neither said a word. As they progressed she was acutely aware of a pungent odor, a stench that grew steadily stronger as she approached a doorway. The door was ajar and she hesitated for a moment, her instincts warning her against glancing inside. A ray of sunlight through the tiny window, the glass of which had been shot away, illuminated the overflowed toilet. Pieces of glass lay in a brown fluid that covered the floor. Blood stained the small pedestal sink, and a toothbrush floated in the clogged drain. What appeared to be human feces were smeared over a good portion of the walls, making a collage of brown and crimson on the peeling paisley wall-paper.

She gagged and coughed once to clear her throat.

Jack grimaced, then nodded, indicating that he would continue forward away from the stench and she should follow. Since someone—probably Calvin—had fired on a police officer from this bathroom, they could leave it to the Crime Scene team. Let them identify the bodily fluids and figure out what in hell's name had happened in a space no bigger than a closet.

They rounded the corner and stepped into a kitchen. It had a cracked linoleum floor, a stainless-steel sink, and a refrigerator with a door that hung slightly askew on a loose hinge. A small Formica table and two chairs, one of which had a tear in its plastic upholstery, were the only furnishings. On the table was a loaf of bread, a jar of peanut butter from which protruded the handle of a knife, and a tub of grape jelly. A meal interrupted undercut the seeming normalcy of the room.

An exposed lightbulb dangled from a cord. As it swayed slightly, it cast an odd shadow against the wall. Lucy surveyed the space, looking for signs of movement. It was then that she saw him. Tucked in one corner, hidden behind the shadow of a pantry door, was a person kneeling in a yogic child's pose, his head on the floor as if in a prayer position. Jack, too, stared ahead at the figure.

"Move slowly, keep your arms in front of you, and stand up," Jack directed.

Lucy could hear muffled sobs and saw movement as the man's chest rose and fell, but he still didn't look up. She took a step forward and spoke softly. "Calvin? Are you Calvin Roth?" Another step. She couldn't see his hands. "Just do as we say. We won't shoot. It's okay." She stopped. Her legs shook slightly and she felt perspiration run down her chest. Her bulletproof vest was too tight and her breathing was strained, but there was no time for adjustments.

Seconds passed as the three of them stayed immobile in their triangular configuration. Lucy could hear footsteps approaching but didn't turn around to look. No one said a word. Finally, she spoke again. "Are you hurt?"

She thought she saw his head turn, but couldn't interpret his response. "Calvin, we have a warrant to search your home. Your psychiatrist, Dr. Morgan Reese, was murdered. If you know anything about that, we need to talk to you."

His cry—a wolflike howl—made her spine tingle. The noise reverberated in the small space. He rolled onto his side and hugged his knees in a fetal position. With his bony thighs pressed into his slender chest she realized how thin and frail he was. Curled up in a ball, he seemed no bigger than a seven- or eight-year-old child. Could this possibly be their killer?

Seeing that his hands were empty, she stepped forward and grasped his wrist, which the fingers of even her own petite hand easily reached around. Despite his pathetic demeanor, in every state in the union his conduct was criminal. "You are under arrest for the discharge of a firearm within one hundred feet of a residential dwelling," she said, reciting the formal language of the statutory violation.

Knowing that Jack still had Calvin in his crosshairs, she reached for the handcuffs in her pocket, snapped the loops around Calvin's wrists, and squeezed them tighter. Then she pulled him to a standing position, and shoved him slightly to propel him forward toward the door.

"You have the right to remain silent," Jack began. "If you give up that right, anything you say can, and will, be used against you in a court of law."

Calvin displayed no sign that he was listening or understanding a word that was said, but Jack pressed on. "You have the right to an attorney. If you cannot afford one, one will be appointed. . . ."

The words blurred. Virtually every American knew the familiar series of warnings that police had developed following the Supreme Court's 1966 decision in *Miranda v. Arizona*. Pressure to talk in response to police interrogation would not be considered impermissible compulsion under the Fifth Amendment so long as a defendant was advised of his rights. Lucy remembered once arresting a drug dealer. A business card in his pocket contained his lawyer's address and phone number, and a printed summary of the rights he should invoke. But rote recitation by either the defendant or law enforcement didn't change reality. Cops said what they needed to say, and then did everything in their power to make defendants disregard those constitutional protections. As much as Jack or anyone else in the squad, she wanted Calvin to proceed without representation and confess to a murder. A lawyer would just get in the way.

As she steered Calvin from the room, Jack smiled, a silent signal that the warrant had been a good idea. They just might be able to close this case by the end of the day.

19

4:55 p.m.

$\mathcal{T}$he interrogation room was a little piece of hell on earth. Claustrophobically small and soundproof, with a single window that had been covered with industrial tape, it contained nothing but an unsteady table and two chairs. The paint had yellowed and peeled years before. The Homicide Unit had other priorities and allocating some of its precious budget to redo the interior was out of the question. Nonetheless, Lucy wondered whether the atmosphere was designed to be so uncomfortable, so stifling, that witnesses or defendants confessed simply in order to be taken elsewhere.

The adjacent room with its meager array of single-serving offerings—peanut butter crackers, Oreo cookies, cereal bars—doubled as the snack shop and audio and video room. Shelves along one wall held a dusty collection of recording devices. Lucy turned on the monitor. The camera, projecting from a corner behind the door, focused perfectly on Calvin. It was a grainy black-and-white image that, given the angle, distorted facial features somewhat, but not enough to cause identification concerns. Today featured a young Caucasian male, sitting erect in the chair, seemingly frozen, staring at nothing more than the discoloration on the wall.

She flicked the switch, and the monitor went black. According to standard procedure, no filming was to be done before a member of the Homicide Unit knew exactly what a suspected defendant was going to say.

Jack and Assistant District Attorney Nick Santoros waited just outside the interrogation room. They'd already decided on a strategy—Lucy would talk to Calvin first. He seemed scared, confused, but had responded to her initial display of compassion. Perhaps she could win his trust and get him to open up.

As they devised this plan, Lucy had raised what she feared would be a fateful question: Was Calvin so emotionally unstable that he was incompetent to waive his rights? If he confessed, or said anything at all that was incriminating, would a court later find that he lacked the understanding to have done so knowingly and voluntarily? How much was his psychiatric record going to serve as a shield to protect him? In other words, did they have to get a lawyer for him or risk forever jeopardizing their case?

"Crime Scene recovered part of a squirrel head clogging the drain." In her mind, evidence of animal mutilation didn't point toward mental stability. "I'm just concerned that we may not have covered our bases."

"People do eat squirrels," Jack had remarked. "You saw the condition of that place. He clearly can't afford filet mignon."

"But we were also hoping he owned a navy blue cashmere sweater," Lucy had replied, reminding him of the forensic evidence gathered the night of Reese's murder.

The items sought in the warrant to search Calvin's home had included any such quality apparel.

"Look, you two. We've got a mental certification that he's fine," Nick had reminded them. He'd clearly wanted the debate to end. "Nobody would doubt Reese's qualifications to have made that judgment, and Roth's already received the benefit of that medical opinion once. Now he just may have to suffer the detriment, too. If it was good enough for the Inspector Headquarters Division to issue a CCP, it's good enough for me."

Still, as Lucy turned the knob, stepped into the seemingly airless room, and saw Calvin start dramatically at the sound, she wondered whether he was entitled to a bit more protection than they were offering.

She pulled out the empty chair beside him, sat down, and rested her hand over his. His skin was cold and clammy. "I'm not going to hurt you. I'm just going to ask you some questions," Lucy began, keeping her voice deliberately soft. "I urge you to cooperate. The quicker you can tell us what you know, the sooner this will all be over."

He turned his head away, and she stared at his profile: a prominent cheekbone, pointed nose, full lower lip, and delicate chin. "You knew Dr. Reese, Morgan Reese, didn't you?" He didn't reply, just nodded ever so slightly and then repeated the gesture with more vigor. "She was your psychiatrist, isn't that right?"

Again he indicated his assent without uttering a word.

"How long had that been the case? How long had you known her?"

Calvin met her gaze, and she noticed for the first time the intense black of his eyes. His lip quivered for a moment. He seemed to speak to avoid bursting into tears. "She's been my doctor for as long as I can remember. Ten years maybe. Could be more. I've lost track."

She knew from computer information that Calvin was thirty-one years old, but his age was deceiving. A decade seemed closer to half his life.

"When was the last time you saw her?"

He cocked his head to one side. His pause seemed endless. "Last week," he finally said.

"And where was that?"

This time he didn't hesitate. "At her office. It was my appointment."

That Morgan continued to treat this man even after she'd obtained a restraining order meant that every time he'd appeared for his session, he'd been in violation of it, but there was nothing to indicate he'd ever been charged with that offense. Why would she simply disregard the protection she'd sought and obtained?

"How often did you see her?"

"Why do you care?" He set his jaw and, for a moment, she thought he might maintain his defiance, but then he slouched forward and mumbled under his breath, "Twice a week usually, sometimes more. It kind of depended."

"On how you were feeling?" she suggested. She wanted to appear to be sympathetic, which she was finding she was. It was a feeling she had to resist. This was a suspect in a murder, not some ne'er-do-well adolescent, who had ducked school, hocked a family heirloom, or run a red light in his father's sports car. But there was something about his posture—stooped shoulders, arms crossed as if for protection, a leg that jiggled nervously up and down—that was way too familiar. She struggled to con-

centrate even as images of Aidan—the same vacant stare,
rounded shoulders, and pallid skin—filled her mind.

The winter before her brother's fatal accident she'd
been home for break and offered to treat him to dinner as
a celebration of his early acceptance to Boston College.
Lucy had linked her arm through Aidan's as they sloshed
through the snow in Central Square, chattering about her
life as a college freshman, her part-time job at the campus bookstore, and the upcoming tryouts for women's
track. She hoped to run the 10,000 meters, but sports at
the university level were a far cry from Somerville High
School's competition, where several of her teammates
quit senior year because they were pregnant.

The Thai restaurant had been deserted. Most of the
Harvard students who normally packed the various eating
and drinking establishments around campus were home
on midwinter break, and Lucy and her brother had their
pick of tables. Lucy chose a spot by the window. Aidan
seemed indifferent toward the menu so she ordered for
both of them. But neither the cheery waitress nor the
heaping plates helped to draw him out. Although he piled
rice on his fork, he never took a bite.

Finally Lucy pushed several dishes and glasses aside
and took both his hands in hers. "What's going on?"

He didn't respond.

"Please talk to me," Lucy said, pushing the food out of
the way. "I'm your soul mate, remember?" That's what
he'd always called her, and now she needed to believe
him. "Besides, what could be so horribly wrong?"

He lowered his head. "I can't go on."

She could still remember the yellowish light casting a
warm glow against the red walls, the smell of spices em-

anating from the ramen noodles, the sounds of a swinging door scraping the threshold and dishes being stacked in the kitchen.

"I feel like all my senses are gone," he continued. "As if I'm sinking. Sometimes I punch out windows—the small panes between the mullions—and I can't stop. About a month ago, I ended up in the emergency room because my hand was so cut up. But pain is the only thing that distracts me, makes me feel alive. You can't possibly know what it's like to be breathing, aware, and yet dead at the same time. Unless you crawled inside my head, you can't possibly understand."

The rapid jiggling of Calvin's leg caught Lucy's attention and brought her back to the present. She forced herself to focus on the interview at hand. "Since you began seeing Dr. Reese, was there ever a time you stopped? I mean, was your therapy continuous?"

"Does that matter?" he asked, although this time he barely mustered the inflection in his voice to transform the comment into a question.

He had to have known about the restraining order. He'd been present, and no doubt been given an opportunity to be heard, at the court proceeding in which the temporary order had been made a permanent one. Had he forgotten? Was he being coy? He was impossible to read.

"Excuse me one moment," she said, rising abruptly to leave the room. She'd often found that breaking the rhythm of an interview was a way to make progress. Solitary time did things to people's minds, and she wanted Calvin to have a moment to reflect on what was happening to him. She also needed a few moments to compose herself. Mental distractions were inappropriate at best. They could also be dangerous.

Jack stepped forward as soon as she shut the door behind her. He'd been waiting outside while she conducted the interrogation in order to follow up immediately on issues that arose during the course of discussion.

"I think we should bring in Nancy Moore, the therapist who shared the office with Reese, to explain why Reese kept treating this guy. It doesn't make sense. And while we're at it, let's meet with Dr. Ellery, too," Lucy said.

"I'll see if I can reach them by telephone. As you know, I'm not about to leave this building." He eyed her warily. Lowering his voice, he added, "Are you okay in there?"

She hesitated a moment, reluctant to confess that she was having difficulties. She was the rookie on this team and she didn't want to let him down. Not for an instant. Not again. She reached for the door handle. "I'm doing my best," she said with forced confidence as she checked the safety latch on her 9 mm.

Back inside, she decided not to sit down. A change of tack, a different physical posture, it was part of the baiting and waiting game. "How did you meet Dr. Reese?"

Calvin looked up. "The clinic. You know, the one over by the stadium."

She nodded. Although she wasn't familiar with all the particulars of the Medical School—the University of Pennsylvania campus was large and she'd had little reason to trespass on the domain of the doctors-in-training— no doubt a free psychiatric clinic was part of it. The details could be ascertained later.

"I had a doctor. This ass. He thought he was, like, Mr.

Smart Man. He wanted to be 'friends,' whatever the fuck that meant. But he managed to impress my parents 'cause he had all kinds of credentials and wore nerdy glasses. I can't even remember his name. He took a vacation or did something, and Dr. Reese covered for him." He leaned toward her, more animated now. "But she seemed different. She really cared." He paused, and cocked his head. "I guess everyone says that about their shrink. But if you're me, it helps a lot to feel that someone's in your corner. As I said, it'd been a long time."

"And you've seen her ever since?"

"You asked me that before, and I didn't answer." Calvin smiled, exposing his chipped front tooth, its diagonal edge menacing. "You figure you'll ask your question another way. I get it."

"Guess you got me pegged," Lucy replied.

His tone changed. "What does that mean?"

"An expression, meaning you've figured me out, figured out where I'm going."

"And you can't say that for yourself, now can you?" he asked.

Lucy didn't respond. She didn't like when suspects tried to make an interrogation personal. It seemed to happen more to her than other cops, perhaps because of her unassuming physical demeanor, but it irritated her all the same. "Why don't you just answer my question?"

He ran his fingers through his hair and jutted out his jaw. "She tried to cut me off. Guess my health insurance ran out. Eighteen months. That was all the coverage I could get after I left my job. How's that for ironic? I leave because I'm sick and I can't do my job, and then I can't get better because I've got no insurance. Doctors are all about wanting to help, but when the dollars aren't there, the altruism disappears. I let her know that terminating my treatment was unacceptable. I relied on her."

"What do you mean?"

"I mean she wasn't just going to walk away. I wasn't going to let her." His eyes opened wider, and Lucy could see a prominent vein in his forehead. "She was the only person who made me feel that I had a fighting chance here. And I was doing what she said. I was taking my meds. She couldn't just shut her door and say good-bye." He banged his fist on the table. "I needed her."

She had an image of crazy people as something else entirely: nonlinear, unresponsive, and dirty. They were people who drooled. She'd seen his house, seen the state of his bathroom. She'd had multiple reminders that something about him was more than a little off. But listening to his answers, hearing his frustration, she thought he seemed coherent, even rational. "So what did you do?"

"I told the bitch she couldn't turn me away. Period. That was when she said I was frightening her."

"Did you threaten her?"

"I told her she was keeping me alive. That if she stopped helping me, I couldn't be responsible. If that's a threat, then yes, I threatened her."

"Did you ever tell her you would hurt her or kill her?"

"That's what she said in court. I remember. She gave some pathetic speech about how I was stalking her. All I wanted was help! All I wanted was for her not to walk away! Everyone else had. The judge appointed some scumbag to represent me, some guy who treated me like I was nuts. Wouldn't shake my hand. Like my problems were contagious." He laughed. "And my asshole attorney never even asked me that question, what you've just asked, what I'd done or not done. Nobody wanted to know my version of events. Who would believe my story anyway? Not over a doctor."

"What happened?"

"I was told to stay away, that I could be arrested if I showed up at either her office or her home. But she agreed to have telephone sessions. At least we could talk."

"How was that?"

"Hard. Try confessing to a telephone receiver. Try getting an ounce of compassion from a dial tone. But then she got me started on ECT." He scraped his fingernails along the top of the table, making a scratching sound. "You ever tried it?"

Lucy shook her head. She knew nothing of electroconvulsive therapy, except what she'd seen in *One Flew Over the Cuckoo's Nest*, but it had to be the treatment of last resort. She couldn't imagine subjecting herself or anyone she cared about to that procedure if there were alternatives.

"Well, let me tell you. Electrodes strapped to your skull sending electromagnetic waves into your brain. Being anesthetized again and again and again so that you lie perfectly still. Waking up with a dry mouth and pain at your temples wondering where the hell you are and what's happening. Realizing that days have passed and you have no idea what you've done, what you've eaten, whether you've taken a shit. Sounds fun, doesn't it?"

Again Lucy thought of Aidan. He'd received no professional care for his problems. By and large he'd suffered in silence. The O'Malleys had neither the

propensity nor the financial resources to explore alternatives or seek second opinions. The Somerville community's remedy was a good night's rest, a proper breakfast,
and a little exercise—or confession. Her neighbors
placed their problems in Father MacGregor's hands, turning to the Church as the ultimate cure-all. Might Aidan
have survived with the proper medical help?

"No, it doesn't," she replied. "I'm sorry you had to go
through it." Then, remembering her line of questions, she
asked, "So when did Dr. Reese begin seeing you in person again?"

"Couple of months ago. Maybe more. This past winter. I'm bad with dates."

"Why?"

"You'd have to ask her. She told me I could come
back. I didn't question the invitation. So I just showed up
when she told me, and she welcomed me back with a hug.
Held me so fucking tight I thought she was going to break
my ribs. Said she missed me. Told me she was really concerned, that she worried about *my* safety, not her own,
that she'd made a mistake to cut me off. That she'd
learned from her mistake."

"Did she elaborate?"

"No."

"What about payment?"

"She told me to forget it. She said that I shouldn't be
penalized because of some corporate insurance decision."

"And the restraining order?"

"She promised not to call the cops. She told me no
one needed to know. Frankly, I don't think she wanted
Ellery and what's-her-face, the fat lady shrink, to know I
was a patient. She asked me to wait downstairs until just

before my appointments so that I wouldn't loiter in the reception area. I got the feeling she was kind of trying to sneak me in."

"Did you ask why?"

"I wanted to see her. I needed her help. I didn't give a shit what her issues were."

So, after posing a "significant threat," he'd been literally embraced with no real explanation shortly before Dr. Ellery's gun was stolen, and while a restraining order was still in effect. Something clearly didn't make sense. Dr. Reese's motivation was the missing link. What had been her mistake, and what had she learned? "Where were you on Saturday night?"

His eyes grew larger, and his mouth drooped. In a series of awkward jolts his chin tilted side to side, back and forth. The movement reminded Lucy of a bird at a feeder, the quick, reflexive manner in which its head cocked at the slightest sound. She repeated her question.

"NONE OF YOUR FUCKING BUSINESS!" he screamed suddenly.

The change in volume was alarming, and she was relieved to have been standing against the wall. She wanted as much distance as possible in the tiny room. Work with his anger, she reminded herself. "I didn't mean to upset you. But I need to know." She spoke in almost a whisper to heighten the contrast.

"You couldn't care less how I feel. You and your pals wouldn't have come stalking me if you cared. Do you know how fucking scary it is to be trapped? What it feels like to be surrounded by hostile fire? Did the police academy make you go through that exercise so you'd know how it felt?" He collapsed back into his chair. "I'd guess not. You're all the same. Take, plunder, destroy, with nothing to give back. That's why Dr. Reese was so special." He got up, turned his back to her, and proceeded to try to pace the length of the room, but it was too small; in one stride, he'd crossed to the other side. Turning back around, he had a confused expression, as if he weren't sure what to do in such minuscule dimensions. "I don't remember anything about that night." He slumped back into the chair.

"Nothing at all?"

He glared at her. "No."

"That must be scary. I mean, not remembering a whole evening."

"What would you know?"

Was he working her over, playing her? Was her empathy—her memories of Aidan—getting in the way of productive detective work? Maybe she needed to take a different approach. "Where I come from, people don't 'forget' huge stretches of time. But whether you're scared to tell me what you know, or whether you're simply lying as long as you can, I haven't determined."

"I'm telling you the truth. I don't remember. I had ECT and I don't remember."

"You're not honestly going to try that one again, now are you?"

"What are you talking about?"

"Well, it worked once with the gun stolen from Dr. Reese's office suite. So why not use it again, especially since the stakes are a lot higher this time."

"You want me to tell you I killed her? You're fucking crazy."

She leaned over him. Her face was just inches from him. "I didn't just fall off the turnip truck."

He slouched forward and hung his head between his knees. Wanting to send a clear signal that she wasn't buying his act, she turned toward the door, dismissing him. Maybe she'd give him a chance to reflect a bit more. She'd get a drink of water and check in with Jack to see what progress he'd made.

Suddenly she felt a stabbing pain between her shoulder blades. She stumbled, falling forward and banging her face into the corner of the wall. Her vision blurred as stars filled her sight. What had happened? She tried to turn her head, but couldn't. Calvin had his hand around the back of her neck. He tightened his grip, squeezing his thumb into her artery. With one knee, he repeatedly jabbed her lower back. Each thrust sent a shooting pain up her spine.

Stay calm, she told herself. Don't do anything rash. Don't cry out. She immediately thought of her gun, but her arms were pinned, wedged between the walls under the monitor, out of sight. And then she remembered. She'd turned it off, anyway. Until Jack returned, she was on her own, trapped in a soundproof room.

"Just let me go, Calvin," she heard herself say, although the voice sounded strange, high-pitched and unfamiliar.

He leaned into her, and she could feel his heartbeat on her back. It was racing. Then she felt the cylindrical barrel against her spine. Her gun. Her Glock. She hadn't even realized he had it. Tears welled in her eyes, and she bit her lip. She'd let down her guard, turned her back on him, and violated the cardinal rule of law enforcement by underestimating her suspect.

He pressed harder.

"Don't make this worse for yourself. Just let me go. It'll be all right," Lucy said, struggling to keep the panic out of her voice.

"No, Detective. It won't. You hear people talk about a battle with cancer. The war on AIDS. All this false macho military talk. But this is real, like Iraq or Afghanistan. Even Vietnam eventually had a fucking end. Well, I went to fight and lost. You think anyone wants to feel like I do? But depression always wins! So now I get to be a loser as well as a mental case." He laughed, and she could feel the heat of his breath on her neck. "She's gone, and there's no help left. Despite what you might think, even I'm not crazy enough to slaughter the only person who helped me get through the day, who made my situation bearable. But you wouldn't know about that, would you?"

"I do."

"Mine is outside any realm of experience you've ever had," he continued, ignoring her. "You get up every day. You get dressed, eat breakfast, drive your fucking car to your fucking job, go flash your badge and catch some son of a bitch who hacked up some lowlife as part of a bad drug deal. You go home, throw a hot dog in the microwave, watch TV, maybe even get laid. That's called functioning. That's what people do. Try living where any one of those tasks becomes a monumental challenge, let alone getting through all of them in a twenty-four-hour period. Just try."

"There are other doctors, other professionals. She wasn't the only one."

"I've tried. Dr. Reese was different. She was there any time of the day or night when I was alone, when I got scared, when I couldn't make my mind be still. She never disappeared. No one has ever been like that to me, you know, stuck around. Especially the last couple of months, we got even closer."

Keep him engaged, Lucy thought. "Why? What changed recently?"

"Dr. Reese reached out to me," he replied with what she thought were tears in his voice. Still she couldn't turn her head. "She reached out to me, wanting to talk. She said she'd realized something, that I was helping her, too. Now she's dead, and I'm supposed to live with my nightmares. Maybe you do know about that? Everyone's got those, the voices in your head, the devil torturing your thoughts. If not, maybe I could give you some of mine because I sure as hell can't handle them all. No, I can't."

She heard the click as he unlatched the safety. Oddly, an image of Cyclops flashed in her mind, his wiggling nose, droopy ears, and velvety fur. Who would ever understand the rabbit's idiosyncrasies, that he liked his carrots peeled and his water mixed with fruit punch–flavored Gatorade? She'd envisioned her own end and had never expected it to be particularly dramatic. No life history flashing before her. She wouldn't call out to a higher being, or her parents, or someone else she loved. Now apparently she'd been a good futurist. If anyone knew that her last thoughts were of her pet rabbit they wouldn't even bother to show up for her funeral.

She heard a grinding noise, followed by a deafening explosion and the sound of breaking glass. The building seemed to tremble as the noise reverberated. She felt something wet and warm on her skin, a thick, viscous fluid behind her ears and on one cheek. Opening her eyes, she saw that the walls were covered with blood. Bits of skull. Pieces of brain. And they weren't hers.

Calvin lay in a heap with his arms crossed underneath his body and her government-issued 9 mm by his side. What remained of his face was awash in red.

"O'Malley . . ." She heard a familiar voice, but from what direction the sound came she couldn't discern. She tried to focus. Someone stood in the doorway, and now that someone was making his way toward her. "O'Malley," she heard again. It was Jack.

She let herself collapse to the floor. She had no energy. She couldn't speak. All she knew was that as she lay on her side hugging her knees to her chest, she was alive.

20

11:15 p.m.

L ucy sat cross-legged in front of the cast-iron stove. She'd lit a fire and, with the door left open, she now stared at the blue flame of the Duraflame log, the only firewood the 7-Eleven sold in May. Beside her, Cyclops nibbled on the piece of kale that she dangled in front of him. Despite the warm evening and the heat generated by the flame, she shivered beneath a bundle of clothes—Venezuelan knit toe-socks, flannel pajamas, and an oversize sweater with worn leather patches on the elbows.

The CD of Andrea Bocelli's arias concluded, and she glanced at the clock. It was nearly eleven. Archer wouldn't be back for more than an hour. She'd appreciated that he'd been unable to come to the phone when she'd called. There was something about a dispute with a beer distributor, although she hadn't asked for details. Leaving a message with Sapphire that she was on her way home was infinitely easier than hearing his voice, facing his question—"How are things going?"—and being unable to bring herself to answer. Fortunately, after their awkward exchange the day before, Sapphire was even more eager to end the conversation than she was, and so had promised to relay the message as soon as he was available.

The telephone rang. She wanted to disregard it, but it might be Jack, or Lieutenant Sage, or someone else from the squad, and she didn't want to make the situation any worse than it was. She needed to be fine. The last thing she wanted was to be placed on paid leave for post-traumatic stress disorder. She shuddered, thinking again of what might have happened.

"Hello," she said. Her voice sounded flat, disengaged.

"Lucy, this is your dad."

For an instant she wanted to hang up. Then, if he called back, she could pretend she wasn't home. He might think the first responder had been a wrong number. Why had he called tonight, of all nights, when she knew she wouldn't be able to make pleasantries and small talk to get him off the phone fast enough? He was the master of investigation. She couldn't fool him. And yet she couldn't bring herself to confess the truth, how stupid she'd been, how close he'd come to losing a second child.

"Your partner called me. He seems like a good man. Told me what happened today. I understand I'm a very lucky father."

She wondered how Jack had found him and how he'd then characterized the afternoon's debacle. He was far from an alarmist, but even the barest of recitations would be shocking.

"Look, we don't need to rehash what happened in that interrogation today. I'm thankful it was that man's life and not yours." His voice cracked. "Perhaps I don't say as much as I should, or tell you as often as I think it, but I love you very much. And I'm extremely proud of you."

She felt a burning in the back of her throat. *Don't be,* she wanted to say. Her father had been a decorated captain, and then Commissioner, a legend in the Somerville Police Department. "I was an idiot."

"No, Lucy," he replied matter-of-factly. "You were human. And you know as well as I do that to be human is to have faults. Some are costlier than others, I'll grant you that. But the important thing is that you learn from your mistakes and that you press on. Sounds trite, I know, but the best of us have had to follow that advice. Saying a couple of Hail Marys along the way wouldn't hurt either, although don't tell a soul I suggested that." He chuckled.

"I don't know how the squad can trust me or trust my judgment."

"Harper dismissed any second-guessing of your conduct. He told me that you'd done a great job apprehending the guy, and that you've done nothing but a stellar job since you signed on with the Homicide Unit. Apparently your superiors agree."

"I find that hard to believe."

"These guys have been around a long time. Your partner's a seasoned pro. What happened today is a fluke, maybe partly due to inexperience, maybe partly due to naïveté or even carelessness, but a fluke nonetheless."

She struggled to think of something to say. They were silent on the line, and she could hear the television set in the background. Several Christmases ago, her father had given her mother an enormous satellite dish, expanding exponentially the possibilities for home viewing. In order for them to get their money's worth, the television seemed to hum constantly. Judging from the clapping noise, she guessed that it was a rerun of *Wheel of Fortune*, and wondered whether her mother was part of this conversation, too. Mrs. O'Malley loved game shows.

"I haven't regretted a single day I served on the force. It has employed the best people I know—men and women both—and it's one of the finest callings anyone can have. The danger comes with doing a noble job and doing it well. When you enrolled in the police academy after college, your mother and I were both scared as hell and proud as any two parents could possibly be. You're our baby. We want you to be safe. We want you to be smart."

"Neither of which I was."

"And now you've learned about yourself, about interrogation strategies, about dealing with a difficult suspect, and, perhaps, about your own weaknesses. Few of us get to learn all of that and still survive to tell the tale."

"I was thinking of Aidan," she blurted out. "I lost my concentration because I was thinking of him. This guy, Calvin, was talking about depression, about fighting mental illness, and I got distracted. I empathized. It was as if I was listening to Aidan's torment instead of a suspect in a murder investigation." The words spilled from her lips, yet it felt good to admit the truth.

There was a long pause. "You'll meet a lot of people with a lot of problems—emotional, physical—victims of abuse and abusers—those who have overcome economic or social handicaps, as well as those who have succumbed to the basest temptations. But it's a rare day when you won't find some aspect of an individual that isn't sympathetic. Humans aren't monsters. Or at least the monsters are extremely rare. The world is full of tragedy, and oftentimes the explanations for even heinous crime sound pitiful, reasonable. My point is that you've got to learn. If what happened today was the result of a lack of focus, you learn to focus. Training. Discipline. You've got what it takes. I know that. Apparently your supervisors know that, too."

"But—"

"Just don't quit," he interrupted. "I know the feelings you're having right now—we've all had them—but don't run away. Whether you were a little too sure of yourself, or whether you let your guard down, it's over. You've got to get a good night's rest and start tomorrow ready to protect and defend, as they say. Hold your head up high and move on to the next witness, the next piece of evidence. You're an O'Malley, and that heritage will serve you well when things get tougher than they should be."

She sighed. "Thanks." The word sounded silly, but she couldn't think of something eloquent to say. "I appreciate the vote of confidence."

"I'm your father, Lucy. I exposed you to this profession. I realize you didn't ever see much choice."

"It's a good choice."

He chuckled again and then fell silent. She couldn't tell whether he wanted to say good-bye, or whether there was something else on his mind. After a short pause, he spoke again. "By the way, Lucy, we all think about Aidan every week, every day, sometimes every minute. But he would've hated for something to happen to you on account of him." He lowered his voice, perhaps so as not to be heard by anyone other than her. "Aidan's agony broke my heart. Every parent wants the best for their kids, and we didn't help him. We couldn't help him."

Few can. Lucy thought again of Calvin, of his desperation at the thought of living without Dr. Reese by his side.

"Don't give up. Don't give in to fear or self-doubt. Don't be ashamed of your mistakes."

Again there was a long silence. Then Lucy heard her mother in the background. "Tell her to put slices of onion on her chest. Thick slices. Use yellow onions, not Vidalia, and certainly not red ones. It'll soothe her nerves. And tell her to add just a touch of brandy to hot milk. Hot, though not boiling. If it curdles—"

"Will you please—" It sounded as though her father had his hand over the receiver, but the conversation came through nonetheless.

"And tell her we're all praying for her. And tell her that her mother loves her, make sure to tell her that."

The voice was back on the line. "Lucy, your mother wants me to tell you—"

"I heard it all," she interrupted.

"All right then. I've said my piece. Now you take care."

"Dad," she said, just before he hung up.

"Yeah?"

"Thanks. Thanks for everything. I needed this call more than you realized."

"Not more than I realized, Detective, but I'm glad. You're still my little girl. And I love you."

With that the line went dead.

21

Wednesday, May 21st
8:05 a.m.

*T*he moment Lucy pushed open the swinging door and stepped into the Homicide Unit, the applause rang out. Two rows of smiling faces, the detectives, public affairs personnel, and administrative assistants all clapped enthusiastically. Several people put their fingers in their mouths and made high-pierced whistles. Only when the noise subsided did Jack step forward from the line to shake her hand. "Am I sure glad to see you."

She made no attempt to hide the tears of relief that streamed down her cheeks. All the dread she'd been experiencing since she'd awoken that morning washed away. Her squad and her department were willing to stand by her, and she vowed never to let them down again. "Lucky I forgot my mascara this morning," she said, as she rubbed her eyes. "Seriously, though. Although I'm sure I'll be teased mercilessly for my display of emotion, I can't tell you what it means to have your encouragement. I didn't fully appreciate until yesterday that I've landed myself in the best squad in the country. I'm not sure I deserve to be here, but—"

"Stop fishing for compliments, O'Malley," Jack called out playfully.

She smiled. He'd even protected her from a public self-flagellation. "As for Harper, you're either the best friend a cop could have or the best cop a friend could have."

"How about both?" someone called out.

Jack waved his hand dismissively. He was obviously uncomfortable with the attention coming his way.

Janet, the administrative assistant, stepped forward and hugged her, too. "We're all glad to see you reporting for duty."

As the line fell out of formation, her colleagues patted her on the back or the shoulder. The distraction was over, and work beckoned.

Jack and Lucy walked together toward their desks.

"You know how careless I was," she whispered. "I wouldn't blame you for a moment if you want to request a change of partner."

He stopped. Turning, she looked up into his face and tried to read his expression even as she fought back more tears.

"If you think that each and every one of us here hasn't made a mistake or two, hasn't misjudged a situation or ignored procedure, you'd be terribly wrong. And from where I'm sitting, I'll take a partner from a family of cops any day of the week over someone who jumped aboard the police academy bus after watching too many *Law and Order* reruns. It's in your blood, O'Malley, and mine, too. We'll be just fine." He leaned back against his desk and crossed his arms in front of him. "Now, I be-lieve we still have a murder to solve," he said, smiling.

"So I guess that means there'll be no wallowing in my own self-pity and doubts?"

"Not on my shift, Detective."

They both laughed, in part from the humor of the ban-ter between them and in part from the recognition that they had survived intact as a team. She was thankful for the emotional release.

"What's the news on Calvin?" Lucy asked after a moment.

Jack cleared his throat and rubbed his eyes with his knuckles. "Other than the handguns, the search of his place came up empty. There's nothing at all to link him to Reese's murder, and his blood type doesn't match the sample either. He was type O."

"What about the ECT story?"

"He was hospitalized Friday for a second course of it, but was discharged Saturday afternoon shortly before four."

His short-term memory had been wiped out and he was back on the street.

"I told Dr. Bradley, the psychiatrist at Friends who treated Calvin, that we'd be by at ten. He'd conferred with Reese several times over Calvin's care—and dosage or wattage or whatever it's called in ECT jargon. He also met with Calvin before and after each treatment was administered."

Somehow it didn't feel right. If Calvin hadn't harmed Reese at all, why had he reacted the way he did? Had he felt cornered and lashed out in fear? She shook her head. The what ifs, how, and why, would have to be addressed at another time. Looking back was a luxury afforded other professions, not theirs.

"Let's head over to Ellery's office." He walked toward the door.

"Any news on the dinner at Le Bec-Fin?"

"Yeah. I checked with the maître d'. There were a number of reservations for three people at eight o'clock on Saturday night. When I showed him a photo of Morgan, he remembered her instantly. Told me she came for dinner with a younger woman and caused a bit of a problem."

"What happened?"

"She'd ordered some two-hundred-dollar bottle of Cabernet and when the waiter asked for proof of age from her companion, she got up and demanded to see the maître d'. As he tells it, she explained that it was a very special occasion and asked if he'd make an exception. He said no, that he could lose his license. She was insistent, did the 'Who's ever going to find out?' routine, but it sounds as though he'd heard that before and he held firm. So finally she returned to the table. After she left, the maître d' realized that she'd ordered a second bottle and he wondered what was going on. He did a little investigating on his own, and it turned out she'd offered her waiter an extra hundred in his tip to pour two glasses and be quiet about it. Poor guy was fired."

"When was that?"

Jack shrugged. "I know what you're thinking, but the waiter wasn't terminated until Tuesday."

Lucy thought for a moment. "But what about the third person? Wasn't the reservation for three?"

"Absolutely. But the third person didn't show up. The maître d' was pretty irritated. It had been a last-minute reservation, and he'd done a fair amount of rearranging to squeeze them in as it was."

"What was the name on the reservation?"

"Nichols." Although relatively common, Nichols happened to be the surname of the president of the Rabbit Club. Could it be coincidence? Lucy wondered. "Did you get a first name?"

"No," Jack replied. "And the name didn't ring any particular bells with the maître d'. The number for confirmation was a cell phone, registered to a pharmaceutical company in Radnor. I tried calling twice but got no answer."

"Voice mail?"

"We're doing a voice match now with the message from Reese's answering machine."

"What was your impression?"

"To the naked ear—or whatever the expression might be—it sounds the same."

8:46 a.m.

They were in the parking lot when the duty officer came running up, waving a manila envelope. Al was assigned to desk duty after he'd taken a bullet in his hip and never regained full mobility. The several hundred yards had winded him. "Hey, Lucy. This came for you." He handed her the package. The return address belonged to a prominent downtown law firm. "It just arrived by courier. I thought it might be important enough to try and catch you."

"Thanks," she said, immediately realizing what it was. The Haverill attorney had tracked down the insurance policy and made a copy for her as she'd requested. It was the document that confirmed Archer's $5 million inheritance.

"By the way, I'm really glad you're okay," Al added, looking at the pavement. He kicked a cigarette butt aside.

"She's better than okay," Jack said. "Although all this display of humanity is unnerving, at least to me. Who thought we had such a bunch of sentimentalists?" He winked. "Let's go, O'Malley."

She settled into the passenger seat of Jack's Taurus, fastened her seat belt, and then undid the clasp on the envelope. He started the engine, adjusted the radio station, and flipped the car into reverse as he hummed along to a Celine Dion ballad. How quickly life returned to normal.

She removed the multipage document and quickly skimmed the fine print. According to the signature line, the policy had been purchased a decade before. At that time, Archer had been designated sole beneficiary. She glanced through the next several paragraphs until something caught her eye. The original value was ten million, not the five that Rodman had said. Perhaps he'd misunderstood. She continued to read, then paused and read the last page again. It was an addendum dated March 31 and in it, the beneficiary had been changed. Instead of just Archer, a second person was named: Avery Herbert. Next to the name, someone had scribbled in the margin in pencil, "Social Security number and address to be provided by the insured." Apparently that hadn't happened.

Less than two months before her murder, Morgan had

cut Archer's inheritance in half so as to include someone else in her legacy.

Avery Herbert, Avery Herbert, she mulled the name in her mind. Then the significance registered. She'd seen that very name on the flagged page of the *Social Register* in Morgan's office. She flipped back the pages of her notepad to the earliest stage of this investigation. Avery Aldrich Herbert, the daughter of Mr. and Mrs. William Foster Herbert from Gladwyne. Her memory served her well. Who was this person? What was Morgan's connection to the daughter of this couple? And was this the Avery of the letter Gertrude Barbadash had given her? If so, apparently a lot of cash was coming her way.

Jack stopped at a light and station surfed, settling for a Moody Blues classic. Lucy summarized the information from the insurance policy.

"So what do you make of that?"

"Avery could be a godchild or a niece, I suppose," he replied. "Maybe given what had happened with her own family, she'd had a close relationship later on in life with another kid. Maybe that had provided some kind of solace for her earlier choice about her son."

"Neither Archer nor his father was in communication with this woman. Years had passed. They know nothing about what she was up to," Lucy said, thinking aloud. "She could have had another family, more children, anything, and they wouldn't have known. Avery could be a daughter. The Herberts could be adoptive parents."

"You think this woman abandoned one child and gave up another? What kind of parent would do that?"

Lucy was wondering the same thing, although she had no answer. Somebody desperate, somebody sick. Neither description seemed to apply to the successful, respected psychiatrist that Morgan appeared to have been. "Do we have any idea who is the beneficiary of her estate?"

"Not yet."

She scribbled a note to herself to follow up. "It just doesn't make sense to me. Why spend a fortune on premiums at her age for one child she doesn't know and another child who belongs to a different family? I assume Dr. Reese had assets. Why not leave those to Archer and this Avery Herbert and call it a day?"

"There's a big difference between 'assets' and ten million cash. Maybe she wanted to make a statement."

"Yeah," Lucy mumbled. She thought of her lunch with Rodman, his disdain for inherited wealth. Morgan had clearly disagreed with his philosophy. She wanted her money to liberate her son, to give him freedom to do what he wanted to do.

"Nancy Moore came by yesterday," Jack said, changing the subject. "With her husband. The guy was a jerk of the first order. He introduced himself three times as 'Attorney Moore.' I finally had to tell him that I wouldn't forget. I can't stand when lawyers do that. Why isn't he just plain old Mr. Moore?"

"Makes him sound more important, I guess. Everyone wants a title."

"Whatever. Anyway, you were en route to the ER when she showed up so Ben sat in with me."

Was that his way of reminding her yet again not to fly solo? He'd made his point. Or if he hadn't, Calvin had done it for him. "What did she have to say?"

"Not a whole lot more than what you learned. She wasn't surprised about Calvin. She'd thought he was certifiably nuts and had begged Morgan not to see him as a patient, but the doctor was pretty dismissive of her concerns. For a while he stopped coming around—consistent with what he told you about conducting his therapy over the phone—but then he returned. She said Morgan wouldn't discuss it and didn't want her approach to therapy to be second-guessed."

"What about Ellery?"

"Apparently he took a backseat. Let the women duke it out. Even after his gun was stolen, he didn't get involved. According to Moore, he's fiercely ambitious. He was working overtime to try to get the appointment to run the Wilder Center. Took on a bunch of new research projects. Scheduled a lot more speaking engagements. As she described it, he became quite the man about town, meeting with various important faculty members and trustees of the University of Pennsylvania, doing everything he could to gain the spotlight over his contenders, chief of whom was Morgan."

"How did Morgan respond to the nomination?"

"Apparently she kept it to herself. As you said, her schedule was pretty packed to begin with. There weren't many more hours in the day to fill." He turned into the parking lot adjacent to the Spruce Street office building. "Okay, here we are."

9:25 a.m.

"I'm sorry, but you've just missed him." Dr. Ellery's secretary seemed genuinely disappointed to be the bearer of bad news. A middle-aged woman, she wore her graying hair in a topknot, red Lucite glasses on a chain around her neck, and a pink and green dirndl that accentuated her substantial bosom. "He's giving a press conference today at the Union League. He had some personal matters to attend to before then, and had me cancel all his morning patients." She forced a smile. "Is there anything I can help you with?"

"Uh . . . yes. Miss . . . ?"

She produced a black plaque with a faux veneer base from her top drawer and put it out on the counter of the reception desk. BETTY GRAHAM was printed in gold letters. "Despite what the doctors say, I don't want just anyone to know who I am."

"How long have you worked for Dr. Ellery?" Jack asked.

"Fifteen years, if you can believe it, and for Dr. Reese for nearly a decade perhaps. I can't recall precisely when she joined this office suite. Ms. Moore was the most recent addition, but even that's been a while."

"What do you do for them?"

"Filing, billing, scheduling, negotiating rates with health insurers, a little bit of everything. Increasingly, Dr. Reese took over her own paperwork, but Dr. Ellery couldn't function without me. I'm not sure he could find a paper clip, not that all my years of service are getting me any thanks." She pushed the fragrant bouquet of lilacs—apparently a fresh delivery—slightly to the right to get a better view of both detectives. Her long fingernails had been painted a bright magenta.

"Will you be going with him to the Wilder Center?" Lucy asked.

"No. The announcement had hardly been made and he

snatched up some young thing from the Behavioral Therapy Unit. She can barely type and doesn't understand the concept of filing, let alone the practice, but I'm sure you've heard that before."

"Can you tell us what kind of relationship Dr. Ellery had with Dr. Reese?"

"How much time have you got?" She snorted. "Let's just say that what started out as friendly deteriorated fairly rapidly once they were both nominated for the directorship."

"Could you be any more specific than that, ma'am?" Jack asked.

"I believe they knew each other professionally before Dr. Reese agreed to join this office suite. When she first started here, they seemed pretty friendly. I recall that they left together after work on occasion. I assumed they were going out for drinks or dinner."

"Were they ever involved romantically?"

Betty shook her head. "I would doubt it. Dr. Ellery fancies himself a bit of a ladies' man, but Dr. Reese was too professional for that—and, frankly, too cold. I wouldn't be surprised if you found . . . Let's just say she seemed to be perfectly satisfied without any male companionship. Anyway, for years they had lunch once a week. It was primarily to discuss office matters—I know that because they came back with more than a few new tasks for me—but it seemed that they were friends, too. My guess is they shared some personal information on occasion, maybe sought advice from one another. They seemed jovial enough together."

"What changed?"

"Dr. Ellery became Mr. Hyde once the list of nominees was announced. He wanted that position, and it seemed to me he'd do anything to get it. The man became a monster—giving orders, canceling patients so he could dine with the powers that be, more concerned with his physical appearance and social calendar than his work. I thought it was very unprofessional."

"Why did he want it so badly?" Jack asked. "Looks like he's got a fairly good operation going here."

"Power. Money. Prestige. You're the Y chromosome here. You tell me. The man loves the limelight, and becoming the director of the Wilder Center offered plenty of that. But then—just about the time we all thought a decision would be made—he had a little problem."

"What was that?"

"The Herbert boy's suicide."

"The what?" Jack and Lucy exclaimed in unison.

Betty was taken aback. "Foster Herbert, a young boy, maybe sixteen or seventeen. He'd been a patient of Dr. Ellery's for a while. A sweet boy he was, very polite, attractive, but extremely troubled. I did the insurance forms. I'm not the doctor and even I knew his diagnosis was dismal: 296.3x, sometimes with catatonic, sometimes with melancholic, and oftentimes with atypical features."

"Can you tell us what that code means?" Jack asked.

"It is major depressive disorder, recurrent," Betty recited. "The 'x' designates that other features are present."

Lucy neither wanted nor needed further explanation. After Aidan's death, she'd combed the DSM searching for answers. This devastating illness was ingrained in her mind. "Recurrent" meant it didn't go away.

"In any event, this past winter—January, I think it was—he shot himself right out behind the family barn while his mother and father were out to dinner," Betty continued, seemingly pleased to have a captive audience. "The parents blamed Dr. Ellery. I don't know the particulars, but there was even some stuff in the paper that was critical of the psychiatric care the boy had received."

"Do you happen to recall the name of Foster's father?"

"Sure. Bill. William Herbert. The wife's name is Faith."

"Do they live in Gladwyne?"

Betty flipped through a Rolodex, apparently one she hadn't bothered to keep current. "Yes," she said, surprised. "The monthly statements were sent to Greaves Lane, although I know the father requested that the final bill be sent to his law office at Leedes, Collin, and Wilkes. How did you know?"

"I remember something in the newspaper," Lucy lied. Foster was dead; his sister stood to inherit five million from Morgan Reese. How they were all connected, though—and how Archer might fit into the picture—remained a mystery. She scribbled the name of Bill Herbert's law firm.

"Do you know what kind of law he practices?"

She shook her head. "Anyway, as I was saying, I wouldn't be surprised if the suicide knocked Dr. Ellery out of the running. Not exactly what a psychiatric hospital wants to advertise, if you know what I mean."

"Sure. I can see that," Jack remarked.

But then something changed dramatically, Lucy

thought. Apparently the nominating committee was willing to overlook Foster's death once Dr. Reese became unavailable. She glanced at her watch. The scheduled press conference was a little more than three hours away.

"Then last Sunday," Betty continued. "When I saw the look on Dr. Ellery's face—absolute delight—well, it made me sick. Dr. Reese's body was barely cold. No better than an ambulance chaser, he was more than happy to benefit from this tragedy. He actually had the gall to walk over and kiss me. I've a good mind to bring a lawsuit. People pay real money to settle sexual harassment claims."

"Do you often work on a Sunday?" Lucy asked, ignoring her diatribe.

"Try never. But he called me early that morning and told me he needed me in the office. It wasn't even seven o'clock. But he was emphatic. He said he had lots to do since he'd be 'moving on,' as he put it. He offered time and a half, but his threat was what got me in on a weekend. Little did I know I was wasting my time."

"What was his threat?"

"That I would be fired if I didn't show up. Not that it mattered. I'm out of a job anyway. Dr. Reese is dead, Nancy Moore's vacating the office space, and Dr. Ellery isn't taking me with him where he's going."

That may be a blessing, Lucy thought. Once they were finished with the esteemed psychiatrist, he might not make it to the Wilder Center. And an orange prison suit made even a dirndl look good.

Out on the street, Jack could barely contain himself. "Bill Herbert's a partner of Carson Leedes!"

Lucy held up her hand to shield her eyes from the strong sunlight. "Is that a name I should know?"

"He calls himself a family lawyer. Nothing about family in his line of work, except that there needs to be something to destroy. Leedes is the most famous divorce attorney between Washington and New York."

"You're the happily married man. How do you know about him?"

"He had a client about eight years ago, a guy named Michael Lucas Abernathy the third. Good-looking in a flashy, stripper kind of way—he'd grown up in Jersey. His father—a guy named Abramowitz—made a fortune in bucket manufacturing. Mike came here, changed his name because he didn't want the ethnic taint, and bought a big old house in Haverford. Then he decided to divorce his high school sweetheart after fifteen years of marriage, and he hired Leedes to represent him. The legal proceedings weren't going so well—the judge ordered him to pay alimony that was seriously cramping his style—so he took matters into his own hands. Murdered his wife and her sister, who had been living with her since he'd moved out. The evidence was overwhelming. The guy was an idiot—prints everywhere. But before we could find him, Mike took his kid—a little girl—and fled. We tracked him to Puerto Rico, but then he literally vanished. No trace. Anyway, I must have questioned Leedes a dozen times. He claimed to know nothing."

"You didn't believe him?"

"No. But there was nothing left to do. His partners were no help. It's a prominent firm—leather chairs in the conference room, plenty of fancy art, that kind of deal. I got the distinct impression that the other lawyers leave

him to his own devices—or vices, I should say. The
work's unsavory but he's a major profit center, so they
look the other way. Leedes struck me as the type who'd
do anything for a buck."

"Abernathy has never been found?"

"Nope. And we had nothing on Leedes. Couldn't even
charge him with obstruction. He's kept right on practicing. The guy is worth a fortune. I suspect his partner Bill
Herbert is, too."

"Not rich enough to save his own son."

22

10:15 a.m.

"This is extraordinarily difficult for all of us," Dr. John Bradley said. He ran his slender fingers through his thinning hair. His face was drawn and dark circles ringed his green eyes, making him appear older than Lucy guessed he was. His blue shirt and white coat were wrinkled. He didn't need to tell them that he'd been awake all night. "We're as shocked as I'm sure you were by what transpired. I'm very sorry you had to suffer through that experience," he said, directing the comment at Lucy. "One of the most difficult things about treating persons with certain kinds of mental illness is accurately predicting the level of violence. Apparently we misjudged on Calvin. Seriously."

Jack, Lucy, and Dr. Bradley sat at a round table in the basement cafeteria of Friends Hospital. The odor of scrambled eggs and greasy bacon, well past their prime, filled the institutional space. Aside from a few nurses and technicians taking a midmorning break, and a doctor doing some paperwork at a table by the far wall, the place was empty. Lucy drank directly from a bottle of water. The lukewarm temperature was undesirable, but she didn't want to miss a moment of the conversation to get a glass with ice. Jack and Dr. Bradley sipped weak coffee.

"As I told your partner yesterday, despite what happened at your headquarters, in my opinion there was simply no way that Calvin could have murdered anyone only hours after he was discharged from his latest round of ECT."

"He'd been discharged. Didn't that mean he was all right in your view?"

"Yes. But that's my point. The effect of ECT is to bring about almost immediate calm. Calvin was on a course of six treatments given roughly one month apart. This was his fifth. He was very subdued."

Not that subdued. He'd managed to pin Lucy in a corner, pull her own gun, and then unload its bullet into himself. Next time she wanted to relax, she'd try another antidote. "When we asked him what he'd done Saturday night, he had no recall."

"I can believe that. The general anesthesia given to administer ECT produces short-term memory loss, but it's usually recovered in one to two hours. Certainly by the time Calvin was released from our facility that memory had come back. The other kind of memory loss we see tends to occur after a patient has received numerous courses of treatment—usually four to six. The memories can often be retrieved later on, but at least for the time being are gone. Calvin had experienced some of that, but relatively little compared to most patients." He paused, and stared at his hands. "Look, most sharks are harmless, but ever since *Jaws*, they've gotten terrible press. It's the same for ECT. There's a lot of stigma. I've been at this a long time, and I've seen some of the most hopeless cases anywhere. In my view nothing is as effective in the immediate treatment of severe depression and mania. In Calvin's case, his response to the therapy was terrific."

"But the point is, he couldn't remember what happened to him Saturday and there's nobody here to account for his whereabouts," Jack said. He voice was firm. Lucy surmised that after everything Calvin had put her through, Jack wanted to be able to pin Dr. Reese's murder on him, too. At least she wouldn't have suffered for nothing.

"That's all true." Dr. Bradley looked beleaguered, and took another sip of his coffee. "But I'd been intimately involved with Calvin's care. Neither Dr. Reese nor I thought that he was a danger either to himself or others. He is—or rather was—a frightened child, truly stunted in his emotional development. He was very dependent on Morgan. I just can't imagine that he would harm her."

"Did you know she had a restraining order against him?"

Dr. Bradley set his jaw, but said nothing.

"She considered him a threat—at least to her."

This time he stared down at the floor. No doubt the conversation was extremely painful for him. Lucy wondered whether he blamed himself for what had happened. He'd been too confident in the shock treatments and had explained away Calvin's propensity to violence.

"What can you tell us about the relationship between Calvin and Dr. Reese?"

He shrugged. "She'd been his therapist for a number of years. She brought me in because she wanted someone to administer the ECT. We hadn't met, but she knew me by reputation, as I did her, and I was happy to offer our facility here at Friends."

"Did you and she discuss any aspects of Calvin's therapy?"

"Not much. She was very respectful of his privacy."

"Did you know that Calvin owned guns, or that Dr. Reese had helped him obtain a permit to carry?"

"I did." He pushed his chair back from the table and crossed his arms in front of his chest. "Dr. Reese assured me that he never loaded them, didn't own ammunition. He just liked to carry them around."

"For his fragile male ego?" Lucy asked. Psychiatrists apparently could rationalize any behavior. Listening to him speak, she was debating whether he or his patient had been more out of touch with reality.

"As I said, I wasn't privy to the details. However—" He stopped, seeming to wonder whether he should volunteer the information he was now contemplating.

"Please, Dr. Bradley. I apologize for my lapse in sympathy, but we really do need to know anything you can share." Dr. Lunatic was apparently still sensitive to tone of voice.

"I'm not sure this is relevant, or that I should be telling you." He rubbed his eyes. "Calvin told me recently that Morgan had begun to act in a maternal way. That she'd been very nurturing, even physical. Those were his words."

"Sexual?" Jack asked.

"I said 'maternal.' More like hand-holding and an occasional embrace. What Calvin repeated to me was that something had happened in her own life. It sounded to me to be some sort of countertransference."

"Could you explain that?" Jack asked.

"Transference is expected in treatment, or at least in the kind of Freudian psychoanalytic therapy that Morgan practiced. The patient comes to view the psychiatrist as something beyond a doctor. The psychiatrist takes on a more personal role in the patient's mind—as parent or boss or lover. It can actually be a very important part of the therapeutic process because it allows the patient to explore issues with respect to those relationships in a more immediate way. Anger, jealousy, betrayal, disappointment all come much closer to the surface. The problem arises when it works the other way, when the therapist starts to see the patient in another role—perhaps as child. Sometimes a sexual attraction develops. Professional distance serves an important goal. Countertransference obviously interferes with the necessary boundaries."

"Can you give us any particulars?"

"According to Calvin, Dr. Reese had made several great mistakes in her life. Because of her therapy with him, she had come to understand at least one of those mistakes better. Her hope was that it wasn't too late."

"For what?"

"You have to understand. My information was coming from Calvin. I didn't need to explore the veracity of her comments. My concern when he and I spoke was the effect her disclosures had on him. Oddly enough, whether she in fact had said any of this, or whether he simply believed that she had, made little difference in the impact he experienced."

Lucy felt confused. The disparate pieces didn't seem to lead logically to any conclusion. "Does a patient have to be picked up by somebody after his hospitalization?" she asked, deciding to give psychiatric mumbo jumbo a rest for the moment and focus on concrete details.

"Yes. Absolutely. The required stay is relatively brief—less than twenty-four hours after the shock is administered. We want to make sure each patient is brought home safely."

"Who picked up Calvin?"

Dr. Bradley paused. His eyes searched their faces. When he spoke, his voice was so soft that both Lucy and Jack had to lean toward him to hear. "Morgan. Morgan Reese. Another woman was with her, but I wasn't introduced."

"Isn't that unusual? I mean, for a doctor to take a patient home."

He nodded. "Part of what I was mentioning before. I suppose I should have said something. It's just, well . . . so much of this process is about trust, and Calvin didn't have a lot of it. From what I could discern, he felt very grateful to Morgan. But I see now that I made a huge mistake."

That was one way to classify it, although not the one Lucy would choose.

"Do you remember anything about this other woman?"

"She was young—a teenager or maybe in her early twenties. I didn't pay much attention. Calvin never mentioned a girlfriend. I got the impression she was with Morgan."

They were outside on the street when Lucy's cell phone rang. "O'Malley," she answered before she'd even looked at the caller identification.

"I beg your pardon. I must have the wrong number,"

the woman at the other end said. "I was looking for Mrs. Haverill."

"Ah . . . yes," Lucy stammered, realizing immediately who it was. "This is Mrs. Haverill." Out of her peripheral vision, she saw the bewildered expression on Jack's face.

"Oh, good. I must have misheard. This is Gail Ripley from Ripley Realty. I have some wonderful news for you."

"Really?"

"Yes. The property you were interested in on Greaves Lane. Well, it's back on the market."

"Why is that?"

"The original purchaser was murdered if you can believe it. Perhaps you saw the story in the paper about that female doctor found on the golf course. It's quite horrible, really, a tragedy. Makes a good case for moving out to the Main Line, if you ask me. The city has simply become too dangerous. In any event, she'd used a fictitious name originally, but the lawyer for her estate notified our office that he would not close on the property, citing some act-of-God clause. Based on what I read, I'm not sure I'd characterize the situation that way, but the sellers aren't interested in pursuing possible legal remedies against the estate. They'd rather put the house back on the market. Less tawdry. I'm sure you can understand."

"I see."

"And between you and me, they're very motivated." Her voice softened. "It's a divorce situation. So let's get you in to see it."

Without having met any of them, Lucy felt terrible sadness for the Herbert family. Tragedy had struck more than its fair share. "Why don't we say three thirty? I can meet you at your office," she suggested.

"They've required twenty-four hours' notice in advance of a showing, but perhaps they'll make an exception under the circumstances. If you don't hear back from me, consider it confirmed."

23

1:00 p.m.

*T*he Gettysburg Address was
carved into the curved ceiling of the Lincoln Memorial
Room just above a life-size sculpture of the famous president. Stained-glass windows and heavy drapes kept the
room dark, but Civil War memorabilia on display in two
glass alcoves were illuminated with recessed lights. The
photographs, uniforms, medals, and weapons were part
of an era long since forgotten except, perhaps, by histori-
ans and members of the Union League.

As she waited for the press conference to begin, Lucy
nibbled on some raw vegetables that had been arranged
in a fan pattern on a platter. That, a few lonely pigs in a
blanket under a warming lamp, and a tired wheel of Brie
with its center gouged out at odd angles were all that remained of what must have been a buffet offered to the
press. Although it seemed gracious to serve complimentary food, Lucy couldn't help but wonder why David
Ellery needed an enticement to draw a crowd. Following
the murder of the first-choice candidate, wasn't his sudden appointment to one of the most prestigious and lucrative positions in the medical arena enough?

On the wall opposite the displays, rectangular bronze plaques listed the names of all the men of Pennsylvania who had perished in the War of the Rebellion. She crossed the room and read the list as if somehow a name might be familiar even though in 1865 her relatives were still busy with an acre of potatoes and a handheld plow somewhere in Ireland. Behind her, she could hear snippets of conversation between two elderly men, who debated the relative merits of decaffeinated coffee.

"Dr. Ellery will be speaking momentarily," announced a petite woman with short black hair. She made a sweeping gesture with one arm, turned, and walked quickly down the hall.

Lucy finished the last of her carrot sticks and followed behind, wondering whether her hastily conceived idea would work. The powder room was hardly the place for strategic planning, but she couldn't resist the opportunity when she'd seen Amanda Baldwin washing her hands at the marble sink. The reporter was aggressive, she knew that much. That she was also attractive—at least from a distance—was also not lost on Lucy, as she hoped it wouldn't be on Dr. Ellery.

Bamboo chairs with gold leaf and white cushions filled the adjacent ballroom. Reporters, as well as a large group of older men in pin-striped suits, had settled in the front. Photographers with myriad cameras leaned against the back wall, waiting for the proceedings to begin, and Channel 4 News appeared to be carrying the event live.

Lucy glanced around the enormous room with its dark wood paneling, walls of formal portraits in gilded frames, and arched windows covered by opaque white curtains to keep the light out. A decidedly political—

Republican only—club, and one that hadn't accepted women as members until the 1980s, seemed a poor choice for the Wilder Center's press conference with its new director, but someone must have decided the grand red brick building filled with a rich tradition was an improvement over the generic hotels that provided function rooms.

She nosed her way through the throng until she found Jack. They had barely enough wall space to lean against, but she still preferred to stand. The room was stuffy.

"That was a hell of a long trip to the ladies' room," Jack grumbled.

"I ran into an acquaintance." Lucy smiled, not wanting to elaborate. She hardly knew Amanda but she'd seen her at The Arch on more than one occasion. Worst case, she'd be out the cost of the pitcher of kamikazes she'd offered in exchange for a small favor. But if her plan worked, the $24 would be well spent.

"Santoros just paged me. The Bryn Mawr Trust Company is sending over its documents in response to the subpoena. We should have an answer to that deposit question tomorrow. The voice on Morgan's answering machine was a match with the voice mail from the man with the reservation. I relayed your theory about the Rabbit Club guy and he's checking employment information on Tripp Nichols. Wouldn't it be nice if we can place him at a pharmaceutical company in Radnor?" Jack smiled. "I said I'd check back with him after the press conference."

"Sounds good," Lucy replied.

Quiet fell over the room as Dixon Burlingame, Chairman of AmeriMed and head of the Wilder Center's nominating committee, took the podium. He introduced David Ellery, who flashed a smile for the cameras as he stepped forward and adjusted the microphone. Wearing a deep tan that masked the lines in his face, and a double-breasted suit that hung perfectly off his broad shoulders, he was the poster boy for eternal youth. He had azure eyes and slight dimples. Lucy couldn't help but wonder how many of his patients had experienced some sort of transference talking to him about their troubles.

"It is my great privilege to accept this appointment," Ellery said in a voice that purred. "As I'm sure you realize—or, if I have my way, you will soon realize—the Wilder Center is the new frontier. It will be a leader in every respect: patient care, research, psychopharmacology, and interdisciplinary approaches. My team will be able to promise results where others have failed. That is my personal guarantee." He banged the podium with one finger for effect. "I will assume my responsibilities immediately. This is an exciting time for all of us in the mental health arena and I look forward to the many challenges that await me. Now I'd be more than happy to answer your questions."

Hands shot up, and Dr. Ellery nodded politely, answering questions about his background and qualifications, the transition process, and the services the Wilder Center would offer. Lucy listened patiently, impressed by how smooth and polished he appeared. No doubt he'd been rehearsing, probably in front of a mirror, mastering the gestures and facial expressions, and reworking the timing, emphasis, and phrasing of his answers.

The press conference seemed to be coming to a close when a woman with blond highlights and a red jacket stood up. A cameraman from her cable news station stepped forward and began to film.

"Yes, ma'am," Dr. Ellery said, smiling in her direction.

"Your partner Morgan Reese was murdered over the weekend, isn't that right?"

He seemed surprised at the mention of the name. "Dr. Reese was well respected by all of us and will be dearly missed. She was my colleague, but not my partner. We shared an office suite, not a psychiatric practice."

"Nonetheless, isn't it true she was offered the position as director before you were?"

"I'm not sure what you mean."

"She was the first choice. The Wilder Center wanted her. Can you honestly say you weren't aware of that?"

"I . . . I believe it's public knowledge," he began, his voice seeming to drop. "There's been so much coverage of this appointment by all of you in the media that you'd think it was a presidential election." He forced a laugh, which the crowd did not share.

The woman persisted. "So her death was rather fortuitous, wouldn't you agree?"

At this question, several reporters pulled out their pads. Additional camera lights came on.

Dr. Ellery's neck flushed. The red started to work its way up his face, turning his tan to dirty crimson. "I'm not sure where you're going with these questions, but I don't appreciate the insinuations. I was as shocked and horrified as I expect most Philadelphians were when I heard of her brutal death. I'm sure the police are working diligently to find whoever committed this heinous act."

"Are you cooperating with them?"

"I'm sure I will be."

Jack elbowed Lucy.

"Don't worry. I heard," she whispered. "I'm not dead from the waist up. Yet."

"Where were you Saturday night?" the reporter continued.

At that Dixon rose and said, "Thank you for your time. That's all for today." He pushed against Dr. Ellery's back, propelling him forward.

"Why are you avoiding my question?"

"As I said, that's it. Dr. Ellery has been very gracious with his time. He's a busy man. Even busier now."

Flashes started clicking. The woman stood her ground. "Why doesn't he just answer the question and end the doubts, then? I would think the Wilder Center would want to clear his name."

"I assure you, the search committee has the utmost confidence in Dr. Ellery." Although the words were forceful, Dixon seemed disoriented. He clearly hadn't expected such a turn of events.

"An anonymous source claims you and Dr. Reese were together at the Rabbit Club shortly before her body was discovered."

Ellery turned. The rage on his face was obvious. His temples bulged, his face flushed deeper, and one hand was clenched into a fist. For a moment, Lucy wondered whether he might explode.

"I don't know who you are or what your agenda is, but I'll tell you the truth. No doubt you'll pay someone for the information anyway. I was a guest at that club, a guest of my good friend, Mr. Burlingame. Dr. Reese's arrival was totally unexpected. I don't know what she did or where she went after I left."

"Can anyone corroborate that she was alive after you departed?"

There was no reply. Ellery disappeared out a side door followed by Dixon and the petite woman who had announced the commencement of the conference nearly forty-five minutes before. Shutters were still clicking as the crowd rose from their seats.

Jack leaned toward Lucy. "That gal's good."

"Yeah. We learned something." She averted her gaze, not wanting him to read her face.

"All right, O'Malley, how did you make that happen?" he asked.

She gave him a blank stare.

"Come on, fess up."

"Amanda Baldwin hangs out at The Arch between stories," she said, feeling sheepish. "If you suggest it was my idea, I'll deny it. But I heard tell that if you give a journalist a tip, they'll say or do just about anything. And we're running out of time. I thought it beat having him lawyer-up when we ask the questions. After all, for people like Ellery, public humiliation is a lot more powerful than anything a cop could threaten."

3:50 p.m.

Aside from the Haverill mansion, the house on Greaves Lane was the most beautiful one Lucy had ever seen. The facade was sandy-gray Pennsylvania fieldstone; the roof was made of darker gray slate tiles. Dozens of leaded-glass windows with white-painted trim sparkled as the afternoon sun glistened off the front of the three-story home. Huge trees sprang from the manicured lawn, each one surrounded by a well-edged circular bed of dark brown mulch. English Ivy climbed a portico off to the left.

As Lucy pulled into the cobblestone drive, Gail Ripley alighted from her parked Volvo sedan. She had a matronly figure, but was well groomed in a crisp navy suit with white piping, matching high-heeled mules, and a double strand of freshwater pearls. Oversize dark glasses covered a good portion of her face, and shell-shaped earrings dominated her hefty lobes. Newly applied bright pink lipstick had overstepped the bounds of her full lips. The effect was to make her mouth look square.

Lucy sighed. For a moment she wished she hadn't put on an act, that she'd explained that she was a homicide detective investigating the murder of a woman who had some mysterious connection to this family. Then she'd be able to explore the Herbert house for whatever clues it might yield. But, she surmised, people like Gail Ripley weren't in the business of helping the police, especially if it conflicted with her clients' interests. And in this case it just might. The Herberts were going to hand over a healthy commission when this property sold, and Gail wasn't likely to do anything to alienate them in the meantime.

She'd been late for this appointment after Ellery's press conference and called Gail to request that they meet directly at Greaves Lane. "We don't generally do that, but in your case I'll make an exception. Downtown traffic is intolerable," she added in a voice that appeared to swallow the "o" in the word. "That's why I try to stay out of the city whenever possible."

Then Lucy had hurried home to change into the most conservative outfit she could find—a white linen skirt and pale blue sweater set. She'd come up with some excuse for her beat-up car, but without a stitch of jewelry— and especially without a prominent engagement diamond and wedding band—she wasn't at all sure Gail would believe that she was in the market for a multimillion-dollar home.

Gail's mules flapped as she walked toward Lucy with arms extended. "Mrs. Haverill. Hello. I hope you were able to follow my directions." The Realtor had a huge smile. She removed her sunglasses as she extended a hand. "You aren't related to Rodman Haverill from Devon now, are you?"

Lucy didn't respond.

"My late husband used to play tennis with him at the Cricket Club, but that had to be years back," said Gail. "I don't think I've seen him in decades."

"Really," Lucy remarked.

Gail smiled again, unaware that a poppy seed was stuck between her front teeth. "You know, it's such a small world in this area. An associate in my office grew up with Roddy Junior, the son. She thought maybe you were his wife. Hard to imagine the little Roddy I knew is big enough to marry, but I guess I'm dating myself. Anyway, I said I'd ask."

"Well, I'm sorry to be a disappointment," Lucy replied, feeling as if it were only a partial lie. She could picture the associate—a younger, and perhaps thinner, version of Gail.

"They couldn't be a nicer family if you happen to run into them. The gal who works with me says the son was always the most eligible bachelor. Obviously she's kept in touch now, hasn't she? But then again, you've already got yourself a Haverill." She laughed again. "What does your husband do?"

Lucy felt a wave of nausea. She'd take an autopsy over this woman any day. "Uh . . . he's in the entertainment industry." She struggled for something to say only to wonder why this had been the first vocation that had come to mind. It was no doubt an unpopular one in this stretch of Route 30.

Gail appeared perplexed. She clicked the tortoiseshell arm of her sunglasses between her upper and lower teeth for a moment before putting them back on. "Why don't we get started? This is a divine property and one that I'm sure won't last." She handed Lucy a brochure identical to the one she'd found in Dr. Reese's desk. "And let me give you my cell phone number, too," she added, obviously forgetting that Lucy had used that number to contact her originally. "This only has the office line, but I want you to call me anytime if you have questions or just want to chat about the possibilities that this one-of-a-kind estate has to offer."

Lucy wrote down the number, replicating what must have transpired with Dr. Reese days, perhaps weeks, before. She could imagine the scene: the psychiatrist in the pink cardigan and Capri pants, the image she'd seen in the picture with Rodman Haverill, getting out of her pre-crash Mercedes, standing in exactly the same spot, hearing the same spiel from Gail Ripley of Ripley Realty. But she'd decided to go forward, to buy a house far grander than a single professional woman could possibly ever need. Lucy stared at the heavy oak door and brass pineapple knocker hoping that her tour would tell her why.

"We prefer the house to be empty for showings, and the owner left, but I understand the housekeeper is still here. I doubt she speaks English, so you needn't monitor yourself," Gail whispered. "Do you and your husband have help? There are ample staff quarters here." She fumbled in her purse for a key attached to a large ring. "I've never seen a death between the purchase and sale and the closing—let alone a murder—and I've been at this for thirty years. Let me tell you, I thought I'd seen everything!" She turned the latch and the door yawned open. "Voilà!" she said, gesturing for Lucy to enter.

The two women wandered from one expansive, perfectly appointed room to the next. Gail kept up a running commentary on architectural details and amenities, crown molding, period hardware, marble baths, and custom built-ins, while Lucy looked for some explanation, some key hidden in this mansion that explained Dr. Reese's decision. She could find nothing. Aside from several indentations in the carpeting where a cabinet or bureau had been removed, and an odd gap in the seating arrangement around the fireplace in the library, there wasn't even a glimmer of the Herberts' story.

The master bedroom with padded fabric-covered walls overlooked the beautiful garden below and the barn beyond. Lucy stepped onto the plush carpet and was greeted by a sweet floral aroma. She circled slowly in the middle of the room, breathing it in. "Is that an air freshener?" she asked.

"Jo Malone," Gail said. "The owner wears the perfume all the time. I hope you like it since I'm sure it's embedded in these walls." She pulled open a series of doors that ran along one wall of the room. "Just look at these closets! All California custom, I assure you." She pointed to several rows of thinly spaced shelves, each one just able to hold a single professionally laundered man's shirt. "I believe the husband's side accommodates fifty, but I'll let you do the counting." She laughed. "And there are his and hers cedar closets up in the attic, along with a climate-controlled closet for fur storage. You should see the owner's collection. Too bad it's not included in the asking price." With that she sat down on the chintz bedspread, her monologue completed.

Lucy focused instead on the bedside table. A black leather Bible was opened to 1 Kings, chapter 3. Beside it two images filled a silver double frame. On the left was a handsome boy in a loose red T-shirt and bathing trunks, standing in the sand with a boogie board resting against his leg. His eyes were dark, his stare slightly vacant, but he had a big smile of white teeth and windblown hair. The right side of the frame held a photograph of a girl with an athletic build. She wore jodhpurs, dark brown riding boots, and a white T-shirt. In one hand, she held a leather crop, and in the other, a black riding hat with the plush red satin lining facing the camera. Lucy couldn't resist picking up the silver frame to get a closer look. Engraved on the top were the words HAPPY MOTHER'S DAY!

Both faces looked familiar, although she could place only the girl. It was the same person she'd seen in the photograph with Dr. Reese. She stared at the boy, hoping to retrieve a match from her memory bank.

"Attractive children, aren't they? They were twins.

Fraternal, I guess you'd call it," Gail remarked. "The girl's lovely. The boy—oh, it's such a tragedy!"

"Why is that?"

"He committed suicide this past winter." She shifted slightly, recrossing her legs, and then lowered her voice to a conspiratorial tone. "When they first approached me about listing the house, I knew what had happened. It had been in the paper, you know. I convinced them to lower their asking price by nearly a quarter million. Frankly, this place is a bargain if you look at the comparables, but I explained to them you just can't charge full market if there's been a violent death on the property— self-inflicted or not. Many prospective buyers can't get beyond that."

She looked again at the picture of Foster, suddenly realizing the significance of this face: the portraits, the snowy December night, the moment she'd first met Archer.

Whatever his family secrets, he'd danced around them long enough.

24

6:43 p.m.

$\mathcal{L}$ ucy sat alone in the cubicle temporarily vacated by the sole member of a joint federal–state task force on gang violence. Except for Eddie Herskowitz on the fugitive squad and Ben DeForest, the Homicide Unit's up-guy, the precinct was relatively quiet; most everyone had gone over to the Ukrainian-American Society for a retirement party. Hal Woodberry had been an integral part of Special Investigations. Other than the wrath he'd incur for the hangovers tomorrow, he'd be dearly missed. But Lucy had to leave the revelry to her colleagues. There were too many unanswered questions surrounding Morgan's murder to think of anything else.

She took a sip of bottled water and leaned back in the chair. Other than a neurotic attachment and a restraining order, nothing linked Calvin Roth to Morgan's death. But the mystery of who had accompanied the psychiatrist to pick up her patient from Friends Hospital remained. A young, unidentified woman had escorted her on what had to be a dismal errand less than twelve hours before she died. Ellery remained the lead suspect, but until Santoros

returned from the party, she couldn't get his okay on a
search warrant for his home and office, and there was still
no physical evidence to link him to the crime. Plus, he
had no connection to the morass of personal mysteries
that surrounded Morgan's life.

Perhaps that didn't matter. Perhaps her personal
choices in life had no bearing on her death. But something still gnawed at Lucy.

Turning on the computer in front of her, she followed
a series of prompts to bring up the Department of Motor
Vehicles' driving-record history. She typed in William
Foster Herbert, Jr., and the only address she had for him
on Greaves Lane. The information she sought appeared
instantly. He'd been issued a learner's permit two days
after his sixteenth birthday. There was no indication that
Avery Aldrich Herbert had done the same. For all his
problems, he'd been a careful driver. He'd received no
tickets and no moving violations in the four months that
he drove. But the screen of innocuous information appeared unusual, and she studied it for several minutes before the relevance occurred to her.

His Social Security number began, like every other,
with three digits. But his were 525. A child born in the
commonwealth of Pennsylvania would not have been issued such a number; those digits belonged to the state of
New Mexico.

She glanced at her watch. With the two-hour difference, it wasn't yet five o'clock Rocky Mountain time.
Lucy quickly dialed information and waited for her call
to be patched through to the Department of Vital Statis-
tics in Albuquerque.

"Yahto Jones, here." A pleasant-sounding man with a

singsong voice answered after nearly a dozen rings. "Why, isn't this something?" he exclaimed after she introduced herself. "I can't remember the last time we had an iota of interest from an Easterner. Now what can I do for you today?"

She gave him the little information she had on twins born sixteen years before, at least one of whom had been issued his Social Security number in New Mexico. "If you've got a birth certificate, it could help a lot."

"I'm going to have to put you on hold," he said, speaking slowly.

"I'll wait."

"The long distance call's going to cost you," he added, laughing.

"I think our commonwealth can still pick up that tab," she replied to humor him.

With that, the line switched to music piped in from a local radio station. She listened as the commentator announced a two-for-one drinks special and upcoming ladies' night at a local watering hole, then an advertisement for a casino just fifteen short miles from the airport. After an interminable mix of easy listening, Yahto finally returned to the line.

"We do have a record of those births. Took place at Our Lady of Grace Hospital. That used to be outside Los Alamos, but it shut down a while back."

"Are the parents listed?" Lucy asked.

"Yes indeed. Or should I say one is. The mother is a gal named Morgan Reese. The father's unknown, although I have to tell you, that's pretty common around here." He paused to slurp his coffee. "Ended up with twins she did. Now that's a handful," Yahto continued, seemingly amazed.

But Lucy wasn't listening any longer. She'd been right. Morgan had gone halfway across the country to give birth for the second and third times.

9:45 p.m.

Lucy climbed the stairs to her apartment two at a time. At the landing, she paused to both listen and catch her breath. Driving back from Gladwyne, she'd called The Arch only to learn from Sapphire that Archer hadn't shown up.

Through the door she could hear the Kronos Quartet. Despite Archer's protestations that its members were the great modern musicians of the twenty-first century, she found the discordant sounds jarring, so he tended to listen to the CDs when she was away. She imagined him lying on the couch with his head cradled in his palms, lost in the music he loved, blocking out the rest of the world.

She took a deep breath. Relationships were about discovery, she told herself. He'd done his best to remain a mystery to her. Now his time had run out. She opened the door.

To her surprise, Archer sat at the kitchen table, his head in his hands, with papers scattered in front of him, next to which were a glass, a fifth of scotch that was nearly empty, and a half-filled ashtray. The small apartment was filled with smoke. She stepped inside, dropped her bag to the floor, and coughed.

Hearing her, he looked up. His eyes were red, his skin

pale. Although they'd seen each other just that morning, he looked strangely unfamiliar.

"You knew about this," he said, waving a piece of paper at her. "How could you not tell me?

"I just found out the details of the insurance policy myself," she said, recognizing the document even from a distance. "I was going to explain as soon as I knew what it meant. You have to understand. This is an active investigation. I can't disclose anything that might jeopardize—"

"Don't give me the party line, Detective. I don't want to hear it." He refilled his glass. "My mother's dead on a golf course, and I'm reading about her life in the newspaper. I see these pictures of her. I learn about all that she's accomplished, and yet nowhere does it mention she had a family. It was so long ago that it's not even part of the relevant past. Can you imagine what that feels like?" He waved his hand dismissively. "No, you can't. Not with the way your family operates. The close-knit O'Malley clan that loves one another even when they fight. How perfect. How fucking perfect," he said, mockingly.

Lucy didn't know how to respond. She wouldn't deny that the closeness of her family sustained her, or that she would ever want anything else. She'd take intimacy— even with the inevitable confrontation it brought—over silence and distance any day. But she could empathize with the onslaught of information that Archer had been forced to process, and the disorientation it had caused. Perhaps it was best to let him vent his rage, frustration, and hurt.

"Then I'm told something that, for a brief moment, makes me feel special, makes me feel that she actually thought about me before she died, thought about me to the tune of millions of dollars. No small sum. Not an insubstantial hurdle she must have overcome to purchase a policy that size. If how much trouble you go to and how much money you spend indicate how much you love somebody, hey, I've hit the jackpot. Dad's enraged. Thinks she's still being manipulative. She's come back from the grave to undermine his value system. Because of her, I can continue to be the renegade that I am. Ha! But you know what? I'll take posthumous care if I couldn't have it while she was alive."

He grabbed his pack of Camels, stood, and walked to the oven. Turning on the gas, he ignited a flame and then leaned in, lighting his cigarette. He straightened up and exhaled a thick plume of smoke.

"Just as I'm trying to get my head around this revelation, I'm told I haven't got it quite right. No, it's not time to feel special yet, or ever, because somebody else—some person I've never met and know nothing about—gets half. Some other person is as important as I am. Even after she's dead, she needs to remind me of that. I never was what mattered most. I never will be. So why did she bother at all?"

Lucy stood and moved toward him, her arms outstretched. "I'm so sorry."

He shook his head and raised his palms, indicating for her to stay back. "My father told you about this, and you didn't bother to tell me. You knew about Avery Herbert. Whose side are you on?"

"You can blame me, but I'm not your enemy. I didn't know about Avery until I saw the policy earlier today. Your father had told me all the proceeds had been left to you."

"Well, who is she?"

Lucy wanted to delay the disclosure. He was too angry, and perhaps too drunk. But she also knew he'd fixated on the answer and wouldn't be deterred for long. "Do you remember Foster Herbert? You showed his artwork around Christmas."

He gave her a quizzical look. "Foster? Yeah, why?"

"Did you know anything about him?"

Shows at The Arch ran for a week. Foster and Archer must have spent hours—days—together. Two women in the same enclosed space for seven consecutive days wouldn't have a secret left—with or without alcohol to fuel the conversation. Yet she knew that Archer would come up empty.

"Uh . . . I knew he lived somewhere on the Main Line, so he must have told me that much. And I think he had a girlfriend. Or maybe he said it was a sister. I can't recall. But I remember a girl coming in to see the work once or twice. What is the importance of this anyway?"

She reached into her bag and found the picture she'd taken from Dr. Reese's office. "Is this that girl?"

He studied the photograph, his eyes darting between the recent image of his mother and the girl beside her. "I'm not sure. But it could be. As I said, I only met her a couple of times." Then he put the picture facedown on the table. "Why is Morgan in this?"

"Did you ever ask Foster why he'd approached you to begin with?"

"No, I did not. I own the place. I can show anything I want. What does this have to do with Morgan?"

"Did any of his work sell?"

Archer glared at her. "Look, I don't know what you're

doing or what you want from me, but I'm sick of your inquisition. You're the one who's been withholding information, information that directly impacts me and my life." He picked up the papers and shook them at her again.

"Did you sell one of his drawings?"

"No, for your information, I did not. The only one that sold I bought myself because I felt bad."

"Where is it?"

There was a long pause. When he spoke again, his words were a barely audible mumble. "I don't have it anymore. I gave it away." When he looked up at her, his anger had dissolved, leaving exhaustion in its wake. "You're supposed to be investigating my mother's death. Foster and his work had nothing to do with that."

His defensiveness convinced her that her hunch had been right. "Your mother wanted one of Foster's self-portraits, didn't she?"

The room was so quiet she thought she could hear the sizzle of the rolling paper as his cigarette burned. Even Cyclops, lying by one end of the couch, didn't stir.

"How did you know?" His tone was flat.

Lucy sat opposite, reached for his hands, and clasped them between her palms. "Can you tell me what happened?" she asked, ignoring his question.

He freed his hands, raised his glass, and threw back his scotch in one swallow. Then he collapsed back into his chair. "What happened? I wish I knew. She came into the bar one afternoon a couple of weeks ago. I didn't recognize her, although after she introduced herself I realized she hadn't changed that much. I think it was the oddity of seeing her after so many years. She started off by making a big deal about the fact that I hadn't responded to her lunch invitation, the one she'd sent me in March. She asked if I was angry with her—a pretty stupid question in my view—but I said I wasn't. What else could I say? 'You raving bitch' didn't seem worth the effort. I can't be any angrier at this point. I also told her that I didn't want explanations, rationalizations. Why she'd done what she did was her business. If she needed to get something off her chest, that was her problem. I couldn't make it mine. And then she asked about Foster. She somehow knew of the show and wanted to purchase one of his drawings. I told her I didn't have his work anymore. He'd taken the stuff back. But I had his home address, and she could contact him directly. And then . . . then . . . ," Archer's voice quivered. "She started to cry. It was a kind of quiet weeping—not wailing or hysterical, just the saddest image of this woman—a stranger to me who shouldn't be. She begged me to get her a drawing. She said she couldn't contact him, but she would pay anything if I could track one down. None of it made sense."

"So what did you do?"

"The best that I could. I called the cell number I had for Foster, but it was out of service. Then I remembered my drawing. I had it in the closet, hadn't yet decided where to hang it, or even if I wanted to, so I figured I'd give it to . . . to . . . I just brought it out and handed it over to her. She stared at it, crying, wiping her eyes, and crying again. She offered to pay, as if I cared about that. By this point, I wanted her to leave."

Lucy wished for a moment she could turn back the clock and coach him through the meeting again. Why had he been so unwilling to hear what she'd wanted—or needed—to say? He may have maintained his composure, his control, but he'd lost his only opportunity.

"I had to ask her to go. The bar was filling up. Sapphire was pretty busy. That was when . . . when she asked if I'd reconsider about lunch. She wanted to talk. 'You know what it's like to be a Haverill. You've rebelled, too,' she said. I told her I'd think about it."

"Was that the last you heard from her?"

"No." Archer lit a second cigarette off the burning end of his first and then ground out the small butt on a plate. "She sent me an invitation." He reached into his back pocket and unfolded a worn ivory card trimmed in red. It had several smudges on it, as if it had been opened, read, and refolded dozens of times in the week that he'd had it in his possession.

Your mother requests the pleasure of your company on Sunday, May 18th, at eleven o'clock at the Liberty Bell. Regrets only.

"Regrets only?"

"I took the formality as a joke, you know, given what she'd said about being a Haverill. It's actually an arrogant social protocol if you ask me. The premise is that if you invite a big crowd and assume most people will come, you want to hear only from the ones who can't. It's more efficient that way for the host, but much more awkward for the guests. They have to call and explain why they aren't attending. When I got her invitation, I figured I'd play along. I didn't respond because by that point, after everything, I planned to meet her."

"When did you get this?"

"Thursday. The day before . . ." His voice trailed off. He picked up the card and tore it in half, then quarters, and then smaller pieces still. "Then she's killed." They sat for several moments in silence.

"Why an invitation?" Lucy asked. "Do you think anyone else got one?"

"I have no idea."

"You didn't *go* to the Liberty Bell on Sunday, did you?"

He shook his head. "With all that had happened the night before, I completely forgot about it, but even if I had remembered, what was the point? She wasn't going to be there." He paused, closing his eyes. "So who is Avery Herbert?"

Lucy swallowed hard. She knew what she was about to say would come as even more of a shock than anything he'd learned thus far. "I'm not sure how best to phrase this, and tact is not my forte, as you well know." She forced a smile, which he didn't return. "Your mother had other children. Twins. One was Foster, and the other is this person on the insurance policy: Avery Herbert."

There. The words were out and with them the truth. Archer had no visible reaction. She walked around behind him, and gently rubbed his shoulders, feeling the tense knots in his muscles as she massaged them.

The telephone rang, but neither of them moved, and she listened as the machine picked up. An automated voice informed her that she'd won a three-day vacation in Orlando with an exclusive opportunity to purchase a time-share in a brand-new gated community. All she had to do was call a 1-800 number, and her dreams could come true. She almost laughed at the simple solution.

"Are they my father's children, too?"

"I don't know. I don't know who the biological father is. I was hoping you could help me."

He shook his head. "Who are the Herberts?"

"He's a lawyer at a prominent downtown firm, Leedes, Collin, and Wilkes. They live in Gladwyne, although the house is for sale."

"I know that firm. Carson Leedes is a partner. He represented my mother in her divorce from Dad. Even the utterance of his name still makes Dad ballistic. Neither of my parents wanted anything protracted or ugly, but Leedes doesn't know the meaning of a negotiated settlement. As my father puts it, Leedes 'eats acrimony for breakfast.' When Dad found out Leedes's firm was handling Mom's estate, he told me about the divorce. Before this morning, I'd never heard anything about it."

"What else did he tell you?"

"Only that she had wanted it. She claimed emotional cruelty. Leedes got her a couple of million dollars—she may have wanted out of the marriage but apparently was no fool with respect to Dad's money—and my father got sole custody, which was very unusual. She was given liberal visitation rights, which she simply never exercised. I guess the battle for some bucks was stronger than for her child. And he wasn't about to take her back to court to force her to comply. How do you compel someone to be a mother?"

He was right. It was an impossible task. "Have you seen a copy of her will?"

Archer interlaced his fingers, stretched his arms overhead, and then rested his head in his palms. "No. And apparently I won't. She set up an irrevocable trust years ago. All of her assets have been left to Penn's Medical School."

That explained the insurance. It was a way of leaving something for her children. The plan made sense, especially since neither of her children had been to her home, or would have a sentimental attachment to any of her belongings. They would get a substantial inheritance and not have to deal with the administration of her estate.

"So the Herberts adopted her twins." He had a pained expression on his face, the lines around his mouth seeming deeper than usual.

"I assume so, given the surname. We're trying to get copies of probate records."

"Hmmm." He ran his fingers through his hair.

Lucy opened a cabinet and reached for the airtight jar of coffee beans. She filled the grinder, pressed the button, and listened to the crackle and whir. Then she emptied the rich powder into a filter, filled the coffeemaker with water, and switched on the machine. A moment later the drip began. They could both use strong coffee.

Archer got up from his chair, moved to the fridge, and opened the door. He stared inside but reached for nothing.

"Why didn't you tell me this before?" Lucy asked.

"I didn't think it had anything to do with her death. And . . . and because I hate myself for not meeting her the first time and for not listening to her that day at the bar. I knew you'd think I was cruel, hurtful. You told me as much when I mentioned the original letter. You thought I should forgive and forget. But I don't work like you. You get stuff off your chest and then it's gone. With me, my feelings, my anger, they fester because there's nobody to confront. How do you hash it out with a shadow, a memory? And now my punishment is that I don't get to know anything. It's too late."

Lucy couldn't disagree. She knew that the mystery would haunt him, probably forever. He might learn all the facts, but he'd never know the truth. She walked over to him, wrapped her arms around him, and kissed his cheek. "I wish I could give you that opportunity. I wish I could buy you a day or a week with her. But the answers I might find for you won't be the real answers you want. I'm sorry. I'm so very sorry."

As she moved away, he reached for her and held her close. "Don't leave."

She held him to her. He seemed to belong to a different species, some strange, dysfunctional gene pool, and for more than a moment she wished she were embracing one of her own kind. That and a Florida time-share and maybe all her problems would disappear.

He buried his head in her neck and she felt his body shake. "Don't leave me, too."

25

Thursday, May 22nd
6:15 a.m.

L ucy had been awake most
of the night. Seated on a pile of throw pillows in the
dormer alcove with a cup of hot water and lemon, she'd
reread chapter three from First Kings nearly a dozen
times. It had been years since she'd studied any biblical
text, but she remembered the famous parable of King
Solomon contained in that passage, the story of the two
prostitutes who gave birth on the same day in the same
house. One baby was alive, the other dead. Both women
claimed custody of the healthy one, and brought their
case before the wise king to resolve.

> And the king said, Bring me a sword. And they
> brought a sword before the king. And the king said,
> Divide the living child in two, and give half to the
> one and half to the other.

One woman urged the division. *Let the baby belong to no
one.* But the second woman begged the king to give the

child to the first so as to spare his life. And that was how King Solomon knew to whom the child rightfully belonged.

Lucy stared out the small window at the crescent moon still visible in the early-morning light. Then she picked up the portable telephone and dialed her parents' number. Mrs. O'Malley's internal alarm rarely let her sleep past five. No doubt she was sitting in the kitchen with a cup of tea, scanning the clipless coupons from the newspaper insert.

"Are you all right?" her mother asked, picking up before the first ring had finished.

"I'm fine. I just miss you."

"You pick a fine time to check in, Lucy. Nearly gave me a heart attack. A ring before eight in the morning or after nine at night, and it can only be an emergency."

"I knew you'd be up."

Her mother chuckled at the end of the line. "One of these days, I'm going to sleep until ten and everyone will think I'm dead. But it's a blessing to hear your voice anytime. Now tell me, how's that beau of yours?"

"He's all right." Archer wouldn't appreciate having any of his personal angst made public. She'd yet to tell her parents that she was investigating the murder of his mother. Plus, she couldn't bring herself to confess that he was asleep not ten yards away. She'd been caught once when he'd answered her telephone, but the part of her that would forever remain her parents' child played along with the virgin-innocence fantasy she knew her mother maintained. Without a wedding band, unmarried couples slept in separate apartments, or at least separate rooms. "I actually called with a Bible question," she said, needing to change the subject.

"Let me mark this date on the calendar. It is truly a miracle." Mrs. O'Malley laughed again at her own joke. She'd had the good sense to get over her daughter's lack of interest in religion years before, and now kept her evangelical ambitions quiet. In return, Lucy attended Mass at Christmas and Easter, and tried her best not to take the Lord's name in vain, at least not in Somerville.

"I need to know about a parable in First Kings. There are these two women and only one baby."

"Yes. The story of King Solomon's adjudication," her mother interrupted.

"That's it. What exactly is the point?"

"Oh my." Her mother sighed. Lucy could hear her take a sip of tea and swallow. "It showed the Israelites the workings of God. Solomon had prayed for wisdom. This story was evidence that it had been received."

"The real mother was willing to endure the pain of giving up her baby in order for him to survive even though it meant she might never see him again. She put his interests far in front of her own. What about that part of the story?" Lucy asked.

"You sound like one of these feminist scholars. What have I raised?" Mrs. O'Malley asked rhetorically. "The role of a mother doesn't get too much study in the Old Testament, or the New for that matter. Because who wouldn't make that same decision? Who wouldn't put her child's well-being first? It's a law of nature, one you'd understand if you'd get about having some tots of your own." She paused, and Lucy could hear her take another sip. "When your brother Michael was born, I remember feeling so anxious, wondering if my instincts would be right. You hear stories—a woman can lift a car to free a pinned baby, or can pilot a plane to a safe landing to protect her family—but I didn't know. It could be lore. What would I do? What could I do? And then once when Mike was a toddler, I was boiling some potatoes on the stove. A big pot. I lifted it toward a colander just as he bumped me. All I remember was thinking that he would be under the stream of the boiling water. In a split second, less than that, I lifted my thigh to block him, and the water fell on me. He was spared. Not a drop touched him. After that, I didn't worry. I had a permanent scar to remind me that I had done the right thing. Or at least I didn't worry when my children were with me."

Lucy was quiet. All her life she'd seen the rectangular red scar that covered most of her mother's right leg. Mrs. O'Malley hadn't worn a swimsuit because of it, but she'd never before shared what had happened.

"Why didn't you ever tell me that?"

"There was no reason. Parents shouldn't be thanked or applauded for doing what's right. I wasn't a hero. I'm a mother. I did what I needed to do to protect Michael."

"So then why was Solomon considered blessed with special wisdom if he was stating the obvious?"

"In order for the Israelites to understand his special gifts, he had to draw on a universal truth, a natural instinct, something with which no one would disagree. A mother's urge to safeguard her child is just that. But my dear, why is this keeping you up?" Then she gasped. When she spoke, her voice was animated and had risen more than an octave. "You're not . . . you're not calling to tell me. . . . Oh, Lucy, your father—"

"No! Mom. Stop," she called into the phone, recognizing immediately the false premise of her mother's excitement. "I'm not pregnant."

There was silence. "Oh."

"But when I am, I'll wait until after eight to call."

9:05 a.m.

Jack could barely hide his astonishment. As they drove through the winding roads of Radnor, through fields edged with stone walls and blooming forsythia, Lucy relayed her discovery of Dr. Reese's children.

"And you have no idea who the father is?"

"No. Santoros agreed to send an intern over to the Probate Court to see if we could find out anything, but it's a long shot. We don't even know if the man was from Pennsylvania."

Jack thought for a moment. "Why'd you pretend to be interested in the Herbert house? Why go undercover?"

"I wanted to get inside, I didn't think they'd volunteer to give me a tour, and we didn't have enough for a warrant. I couldn't think of any other way."

"Well, if you buy the place, can I be the gardener?"

They laughed. "You garden and I'll cook." She pointed a finger. "There it is."

The massive pink granite slab rose from the earth. The AmeriMed logo was chiseled on both sides so that it was visible to cars approaching in either direction: BRINGING PHARMACEUTICALS INTO THE NEXT MILLENNIUM. The early-morning sun sparkled off the letters.

"Let's hope corporate America has some answers for us."

They turned in, and saw a long paved drive ending in a semicircle of red brick buildings. They were forced to stop at the security gate, where the guard checked their identification and waved them through. Dixon Burlingame's secretary had registered their visit with the Chairman that morning. "It's building A—directly ahead. Visitor parking is to the left."

As they approached, Lucy could see a white marble fountain that spewed water nearly ten feet in the air. Around it, topiaries grew in a latticework arrangement with hot pink impatiens planted in between. They parked and walked quickly to the entrance of what they assumed was the main building in the complex. They were correct: A brass plaque by the door read AMERIMED. BUILDING A.

"Detectives," a cheery voice greeted them as they stepped inside.

Lucy turned to see a tall woman with an hourglass figure wearing a fitted red and white suit and red sandals. Her blond curls were pulled back from her round, freckled face, and her hazel eyes glowed. She had a big smile. "Welcome to AmeriMed. I'm Summer, Mr. Burlingame's assistant. Won't you follow me?"

Her hips swung noticeably as Lucy and Jack followed her down a long, carpeted corridor. The walls on both sides displayed posters advertising the latest products—everything from headache medicine and cough syrup to catheters and artificial lungs. "We moved into this complex about five years ago. Building A, where we are, houses most of the executive offices, the Human Resources Department, and our boardroom. Building B is for our legal counsel, as well as for the team of staff scientists who handle our patent applications. Buildings C and D are labs for research and development. D also holds an employee health club and a day-care center. So we really have everything we need right here. Mr. Burlingame wanted this headquarters to be completely self-contained."

"And the Wilder Center is opening less than a mile away."

Summer looked startled. "Why, yes. Are you familiar with it? AmeriMed actually donated most of the land for that facility. It's very exciting. But I'm sure Mr. Burlingame can provide whatever details you need."

She swung open a mahogany door. The square room held a circular table and six armchairs upholstered in a sage green print. A tray with a coffeepot, several mugs, and a pitcher of water served as a centerpiece. A row of large windows offered an expansive view. "It's a lot of countryside out here," she said, smiling. "Please make yourself at home. Mr. Burlingame will be with you momentarily."

She was right. Lucy and Jack had barely taken seats and poured coffee before the door swung open and in strode a large man with a reddish face whom they instantly recognized from Ellery's press conference at the Union League. He wore a navy suit, a pink-and-white-striped shirt with a white collar, and a dark tie secured with a prominent gold collar pin. His hands were big with thick fingers. "Now, what can I do for you?"

It was somewhat surprising that he'd come alone, that there wasn't a personal lawyer—or at least one of the company's attorneys—present. Apparently he wasn't too concerned about the nature of the questions or the information he knew even though he'd brought the chief suspect, Dr. David Ellery, as his guest to the site of the murder.

Dixon pulled a chair out from the table and sat. He seemed to synchronize his wristwatch with the clock on the wall. "Nobody wants to waste time. You want to know what I had to do with Dr. Reese. It's a bit more complicated than you might think, but hardly incriminating. You can believe me when I say the only person who wanted this murder investigation less than you two is me."

"Why don't you begin by explaining your involvement with the Wilder Center," Jack said. "How come you got to head up the selection process?"

Dixon quickly recited a brief history of AmeriMed. For the past ten years he'd been chairman and chief executive officer of this major pharmaceutical manufacturer with revenues of approximately $2 billion annually. It employed more than three hundred people, not including the specialized scientists who were brought in as needed. Because of its extensive research into psychopharmacological agents—antidepressant, antiseizure, and antianxiety medications—the Wilder Center visionaries had approached him early in the conceptual phase of the hospital. AmeriMed agreed to their proposal. His company donated the adjacent land—approximately sixty acres—for the site.

"That had to be a huge investment. What did you get in return?"

"You mean besides a substantial tax deduction?" He chuckled, and then leaned forward with his fingers steepled in front of him on the table. "It's about money, Detectives. Pure and simple. You have no idea the value of a new antidepressant. Look at Prozac. It's been a phenomenon. People who didn't even think they had troubles are getting prescriptions. Who doesn't want to feel good? And that's just the tip of the iceberg. We're talking tricyclics, MAOIs, norepinephrine blockers, SSRIs, neuroleptics, benzodiazepines—it's endless. We will be a major supplier to the hospital, and an exclusive supplier for everything we make that others do, too. But that's only the half of it." A wide grin spread over his face. "What matters most to us is that we will use the facility to run our human trials on new psych medications in development."

"Like a laboratory?"

"Pretty much. The last phase of FDA approval is the human trial. You can induce bliss and happiness in all the chimpanzees and beagles in the world but at some point you need the real thing. That's the critical component. And it can be very difficult for us to enlist doctors who will agree to enroll their patients. The paperwork alone is overwhelming. The government's been going after the kind of incentive programs we used to use. So the Wilder Center is perfect. In exchange for our financial help, we get a captive population. Kind of like shooting fish in a barrel." He laughed at his tasteless analogy. "It's a mutually beneficial arrangement because the Center gets a great marketing tool. Its patients will get the latest drugs, many of which are still in the developmental stage. They don't have to go to Mexico or Europe. They can stay right here in a luxurious room with over a hundred cable stations and be medicated up the wazoo." He paused, seeming to gauge the reaction of his audience. "The promise of hope. That's what this facility is all about. Dana-Farber, Sloan-Kettering, they offer that for cancer. We're just applying that model of excellence to mental illness."

"And David Ellery is going to run it?"

"David . . . David." He seemed to gargle the name. "Ellery and I go way back," he suggested as if that were an endorsement.

"You're the chairman of the nominating committee that selected him?"

"I am."

"But Dr. Reese was your first choice?"

He looked surprised, then stared down at his thick knuckles. "That's right. Morgan was our top pick. She is . . . she was an amazingly gifted doctor. What happened is a great tragedy."

"How well did you know her?"

"I hardly knew her except by reputation when she submitted her application. She was one of the first to throw her name in the ring. We—by that I mean members of my committee—interviewed her extensively. We interviewed her colleagues and personal references as well."

"Do you happen to remember who those were?"

"Hmmm." He pulled a small walkie-talkie from his pocket, pushed a button, and started to talk to his assistant. "Bring me the Wilder file on Reese. ASAP." Then he turned back to Lucy and Jack. "I talked to hundreds of people during this process. The file will refresh my recollection."

"And you were asked to be in charge of this selection because of the relationship between the Center and AmeriMed?"

He nodded. "That's right. This was a huge investment on our part. Even in the best scenarios, we won't see a return on that for a long time. My board thought the only prudent way to proceed was to make sure we had someone we could trust running the place. We can have all the legal contracts in the world, but without a committed director, it would all fall apart."

"Aside from Ellery and Reese, who else applied?" Lucy asked.

"Who didn't apply is the easier question. I think everyone who'd ever gone to medical school submitted an application. But we were pretty clear on what we wanted which streamlined the process considerably."

"What was that?"

"Prominence in both the medical and business communities. Good contacts at the FDA, plenty of research credentials, excellent social skills, a history of successful fund-raising, . . . and . . . and . . . How shall I put this?"

Lucy and Jack leaned forward simultaneously.

"Little personal life."

"What?"

Dixon looked uncomfortable. "This probably doesn't sound right, but starting a hospital is not a family-friendly occupation. There are long days, sometimes even overnight without a break, business dinners virtually seven times a week, extensive travel, plus all the stress of actually overseeing the treatment of severely ill patients. You can't have a spouse or children clamoring for time. You can't want to take out your sailboat or ride your horse. The person has to be one hundred twenty-five percent—no, make that two hundred percent—committed.

Our Center has to be the center of the universe or it isn't going to get off the ground."

Just then the door opened. Summer stepped inside. She laid a thick Redwell folder on the table in front of her boss. Without acknowledging her presence, Dixon opened it and thumbed through the labeled files within. He removed one, glanced at it, and raised his eyebrows. "Morgan's personal references, here we are: Betty Graham, Rodman Haverill, and William Herbert, Esquire. The woman is her secretary, Haverill's her ex, and Herbert's listed as a friend."

Lucy struggled to suppress her surprise. Why had Archer's father been on this list? "Did you speak to these references?"

"I've known Rod Haverill for decades. I figured she had to be a first-rate politician. The man's got a worse temper than my own. To get a divorce and be amicable rarely happens under the best of circumstances. To get a divorce and list your ex as a character reference—never." He flipped some additional pages. "Looks like there's a report of an interview with Graham. It indicates Morgan was a great person to work for, polite, efficient, not volatile, fair. We want that. This staff is being handpicked and we need someone who can work well with subordinates." He pulled out a single typewritten page and passed it across the table to the detectives. "And Herbert . . . Herbert . . . what did he say?" He looked up. "I don't see anything from him."

Lucy scribbled in her spiral notepad. Then she asked, "Why did you initially pick Morgan over David Ellery?"

He leaned back and rested his clasped hands on his chest. "Let me be blunt. The gal had everything. Her professional credentials couldn't be matched. She was a devoted therapist. She knew everyone in the government, everyone in academia. She had her pulse on research. Plus she was a master at working a crowd. Could get people eating out of the palm of her hand, so to speak. That she was a sight for sore eyes didn't hurt. And she was alone, past childbearing years, and unmarried. Plus there was an unfortunate occurrence toward the end of the process that we thought made Reese preferable to Ellery."

"Which was Foster Herbert's suicide?"

Dixon nodded, obviously not fazed by Jack's remark. "Bad press. Pure and simple."

"So why'd you decide that didn't matter after Reese's death?"

He turned, glancing outside to the fields beyond. "This may sound crude, but a dead kid from six months ago paled in comparison with the media frenzy over her murder. Nobody was going to spend a lot of time digging up dirt on Ellery. There wouldn't be the print space or the journalistic energy. We thought we could slip him through. It was a calculated risk."

"Jesus," Jack said in disgust.

Dixon whipped around to glare at Jack. "Do you have any idea what it's like to build a pharmaceutical company? The Wilder Center is AmeriMed's chance to join the leagues of the multibillion-dollar conglomerates. You and your partner, well, your salaries will keep coming, mediocre performance or not. You can thank the taxpayers of our great state for that. In my business, mistakes mean heads roll."

"Unfortunately, that's what brought us here," Jack said

facetiously as he got up from the table and walked over to the windows. "Were you aware that Reese attempted suicide?"

Dixon paused before answering. "I was. But she explained it was during her residency and that it had been an impulsive response to a personal matter. Since that time, she'd dealt with whatever problems she'd had. She assured us of that. Plus the gal always wore long sleeves around us so who was to know?"

"Why don't you share whatever scheme you and Ellery concocted last Saturday," Lucy pressed, pointing at Dixon's tie. "The Rabbit Club." He and every other member had worn the same tie in the group portraits that adorned the clubhouse walls.

Dixon instinctively reached for his throat and adjusted his collar pin.

"Dr. Ellery came as your guest?" she asked.

He shifted in his seat, leaning away from the table. "He knew almost everyone there, but I believe I did invite him as my guest—technically. He came in his own car."

"And you were one of the last to leave?"

His jaw moved ever so slightly back and forth as he ground his teeth. "A group of us stayed late, too late," he offered, chuckling nervously. "Ellery, myself, a guy named Tripp Nichols. He works here—a vice president in sales. Our sniff game ended when our fourth left, but we stayed. We were up in the game room on the second floor. I think the beverage of choice was Drambuie by that point. And then Reese showed up, if that's what you're wanting to talk about."

"The club doesn't allow women."

"We're not that bad, Detective. And from the looks of her that night, Reese wasn't about to be deterred by something as inconsequential as a gentlemen's rule."

"So what happened?"

Dixon took a deep breath and looked back and forth between the detectives. Watching him, Lucy assumed he was trying to buy time. For a confident man, appearing without counsel, he was increasingly reticent, deliberate in his answers. She wondered exactly what it was that he was hiding.

"So? Are you going to tell us about Saturday, or would you rather talk at the precinct?" Jack interrupted his memories.

Dixon cleared his throat. "Morgan did come to the club. She was upset, possibly inebriated, and needed to speak to Tripp about a personal matter. There seemed to be another women involved, if you know what I mean. They stepped outside. David and I decided to call it a night. Even we know when enough is enough."

"Was Tripp still at the club when you left?"

"Yes, or at least I assume so. His car was still in the parking lot, but there was no sign of him."

"Have you seen or spoken to Tripp since?"

He paused.

"I'm sure I don't need to remind you that we can get our answers from telephone logs."

"When I heard Reese was dead, I called him on Sunday night. He was pretty shaken up about the news. He'd seen it on television. He explained that they'd had a disagreement earlier in the week, but was pretty vague, which confirmed my suspicion that he'd had something going on with one of her friends. And that kind of information I don't care to know, especially about my employees. I'm a family man." He forced a smile.

"Have you any idea who that person might be—the one he might be involved with?"

"He mentioned a gal named Avery, but I can't give you more than that. As I said before, that's the kind of information that I don't need or want to know." He pushed his chair back from the table and stood.

"Did you see anything as you were leaving? A car accident?" Lucy asked.

"No. Nothing. I came straight home and fell into bed. End of story. You can check with my wife on that one."

"One last thing," she said, standing. "Is Tripp here at work today?"

"No. He has taken the week off. He said he needed to deal with some urgent family matters. Under the circumstances, I thought that was a good idea."

10:36 a.m.

Lucy's cell phone rang as she and Jack walked across the parking lot. It was Nick Santoros. "O'Malley, are you with Harper?"

"Yeah. He's right here."

"First tell him either his cell phone's off or the battery died. I couldn't get through."

"Well, you got me."

"We got the subpoenaed records from BMTC."

"And?"

"Tripp Nichols opened a trust account less than a week ago with two hundred fifty thousand dollars in it for the benefit of Avery Herbert. Deposited a cashier's check. He gave his business address on the account."

"The company is called AmeriMed. I'm at its office complex now," she replied. "Nichols is a senior VP." She quickly summarized their meeting with the company chairman. "An affair between an older married man and her underage daughter couldn't have been a mother's dream. Apparently he was willing to pay dearly to buy them both off."

"So what can we do with the connection between Nichols and Avery?"

"How about apply some pressure?" she responded. "And I'd say the best contender is a charge of statutory sexual assault."

26

3:00 p.m.

$\mathscr{L}$eedes, Collin, and Wilkes had a dedicated elevator bank. Stepping into one of six cars, Jack pushed the lighted button for the seventeenth floor, next to which was a tiny brass plaque engraved MAIN RECEPTION. He and Lucy stood side by side, hands crossed in front of them, staring at the row of numbers that lit up one by one above the elevator door. Neither said a word. The universal decorum. Lucy could still hear her third-grade teacher instructing her classmates, as they stood crowded together in the elevator at the Museum of Science. "Stand quiet and face front. No talking."

A "ding" signaled that they had arrived at their destination. Stepping out, they saw a Hispanic woman wearing a floral-print blouse seated behind a massive circular desk. Her black hair was braided into cornrows.

Lucy flashed her badge. "We're here to see William Herbert."

Long purple fingernails with silver stars on each tip dialed the extension. "Please advise Mr. Herbert that there are two policemen here to see him," she said into the speakerphone after a female voice answered the line.

"Did you say police?"

"I did."

"What next?" the woman replied, apparently to herself.

The receptionist looked up. "You can take a seat. He'll be with you in just a moment, I'm sure." She smiled without opening her mouth.

William Herbert approached from an internal circular staircase and walked briskly toward them. He was undeniably handsome with strong features, large walnut-brown eyes, and thick brown hair. A quick check of his driving record had revealed he was forty-nine, but he could pass for a collegian in his khaki suit, white shirt, and yellow tie. Several steps behind him came an older man with a shock of white hair, a black suit, black silk shirt, and black tie.

"I'm Bill Herbert." He extended a hand. "This is my partner Carson Leedes."

"We've met before," Jack said.

"What can we help you with?" Carson asked in a heavy Southern drawl.

"Not you, Leedes. We need to ask Bill here some questions about Dr. Morgan Reese. You don't mind if I call you Bill, now, do you?"

Leedes stepped between Jack and Bill, blocking either's view of the other. "I am the managing partner of this firm. If you do not explain the basis of your questions, I'll have Security see you out. Are you intending to advise Mr. Herbert of his rights?"

"Now why would you ever jump to that conclusion?" Jack replied. "This is hardly a custodial interrogation. He's not a suspect . . . yet."

"We were hoping he could answer some questions for us. It shouldn't take long," Lucy added. Her authority and jurisdiction exceeded that of any private security force, but she also didn't want to precipitate a confrontation. They'd yet to get a single piece of relevant information. Carson's stare remained fixed on Jack.

Turning to the receptionist, Bill asked, "Louise, can you see if conference room B is empty?"

She flipped open a black leather book. "Mr. Lyons has it reserved for an associates' committee meeting. But that doesn't start until four."

"Mark us down from now until then," Bill instructed. "I presume that will give us enough time."

"What client number should I use?" she asked.

"Uh . . . just charge it to firm business."

"Use zero five six six one," Leedes bellowed. "This is obviously a Reese matter."

Bill looked startled, no doubt by the thought of billing a murder victim's estate.

"Follow him," Leedes directed.

The attorney offices lined the right side of the long corridor. Secretarial stations filled the internal side opposite. Carson took up the rear as Bill led the way. Lucy glanced in at the masses of papers piled atop each desk, bookcases filled to overflowing with files and thick tomes, gym bags thrown in a corner, and personalized screen savers floating across computer monitors. Almost everyone was on the telephone. It reminded Lucy to turn her cell phone off. She didn't want to be interrupted.

"This is the real estate department. I'm a partner in corporate, but I thought I'd spare you the stairs." He held a door open.

"I didn't know we looked that feeble," Lucy said.

Carson stayed behind to use the telephone at an empty secretarial station. She, Jack, and Bill stepped into a room with two picture windows that looked directly out at the blue glass facade of One Liberty Place. The sixty-story mixed-use complex had forever changed the skyline of downtown Philadelphia, and virtually all of the Round-house employees who had known the city preconstruction had strong views on the Art Deco skyscraper and its slightly shorter twin.

Bill followed their stare. "It dwarfs the rest of us. But this department did a good part of the legal work, so the real estate guys view it as a trophy."

"Leave it to lawyers to violate a gentlemen's agreement," Jack remarked, referring to the fact that Liberty Place was the first building to exceed the height of the hat worn by William Penn in the statue atop City Hall. Prior to 1987, a tacit understanding limited new development to the height of that hat. Now, apparently, nobody cared.

"Somebody had to do it," Carson said, making his entrance. "And somebody had to get rich off it, too." He reached in the middle of the table for a black porcelain mug embossed with the firm's letterhead, and poured water from a stainless carafe. "I'm glad at least the second somebody was me." Then he pulled out a chair and sat with his back turned slightly away from the table.

"Well, how can I help?" Bill indicated for them to take seats, too. "I read about her murder in the paper, but other than that—"

"Why don't you tell us how you knew her?" Lucy asked, trying to ignore Carson's presence. Aside from his Darth Vader costume, there was something about him that appeared ominous, as if he were breathing more than his fair share of oxygen.

"I didn't . . . or I should say, I didn't know her well."

"You were one of only three personal references on an application she submitted for a job as director of a new psychiatric hospital. How do you explain that?"

The fabric of the upholstered chair itched through Bill's suit, and he felt hot. Anxiety seeped into his skin through osmosis. He looked at the eager faces of the detectives, then at Carson's scornful expression. He got up, walked over to the window, and looked down at the street seventeen stories below where ant-size people scurried along. He wanted to be one of them, hurrying anywhere away from here.

"Why would she have done that if you didn't know her *well*?" the male cop asked. Detective Harper. He'd try to remember the name.

Bill felt stinging in his eyes. The last thing he needed right now were tears, but it was hard to avoid emotion and explain that he would have done anything for this woman he'd never met. He put his palms together and rested his lips on his fingertips, concentrating on the slight pain he experienced as he pressed his nails against his mouth. When he spoke, he felt the words stick in his throat. "She . . . she gave me the only things that have ever mattered to me in my life."

The female detective seemed excited by his answer. "Foster and Avery?" she asked.

He nodded. She knew. "My wife and I adopted her twins at birth. And they are . . . were . . . are . . ." He couldn't bear to articulate Foster's fate.

"Foster died last January," Carson announced as though it was the latest traffic update.

"We're very sorry for your loss. It must have been devastating."

Her tone sounded sincere, and he wondered if she was about to come over to him. There was something empathetic in her demeanor, plus she was attractive, and for a moment his mind flashed, imagining a kiss. But she stayed in her seat.

"How did you come to adopt them?"

"That question may call for privileged communication," Carson offered.

"So what? Are you telling him not to answer?" Harper's voice was hostile. He perched on the edge of his seat, looking as if he might spring at any moment. Bill had never known all the details of the Abernathy murder investigation, but there was clearly no love lost between this member of the Homicide Unit and his managing partner. Now Carson's designer tie and the throat around which it knotted were in imminent danger.

"What are you hiding?" Lucy added.

"Young lady, I suggest—"

"'Detective' to you," she responded.

Carson's smile was devilish. "I like feistiness in a woman."

Bill didn't want a fight. In fact, part of him had the urge to tell the story of how he came to be a father, the one he'd never said aloud before, the events that had changed his life forever. "I'm sure we can provide you with what you want to know. Let's just work together to figure out what we can disclose consistent with our ethical obligations."

"I had represented Dr. Reese in the dissolution of her marriage in the midseventies," Carson said, clearly wanting to control the release of information. "She approached me again approximately seventeen years ago. She was still unmarried but had become pregnant with twins. She wanted to place the babies privately immediately after birth, and asked me to help."

"Who was the father?"

"She never said. She told me very little except that she'd arranged to take a leave from her medical studies, and planned to give birth at a hospital in New Mexico. She wanted the utmost discretion. She asked that I place her children with a good family."

"Weren't you legally required to give notification?"

Carson raised his eyebrows and scowled. Bill had seen that expression before—at depositions when Carson was just about to eviscerate a witness, at partners' meetings as a prelude to his diatribe on productivity, and at associate evaluations, just before an announcement that a fifth year was fired. "There are thousands of children born each year—hundreds in Philadelphia alone—whose fathers are never identified. In some cases the mother doesn't know who the man is, or it could be one of many; in others the gentlemen in question simply disappear or move on. The only unusual component of Morgan's case was that she was Caucasian and affluent. But it is absolutely legal to adopt a child—or children—without paternal consent if consent can't be obtained. Adequate legal notification and perfect paternal identification are two very different concepts."

"So you approached Bill?" she asked, shifting the conversation.

"Carson and I are old friends," Bill replied, although his voice sounded strange. Carson had hired him directly out of law school. He still remembered their interview at the Charles Hotel in Cambridge, the one at which all out-of-town firms took rooms when their partners came to recruit at Harvard Law School. He'd intended to do what Carson wanted, to go into domestic relations work, to accept a mentor relationship, and to be groomed as the heir apparent to Carson's substantial portfolio of billings. But it hadn't gone as planned. A corporate crisis was one thing—handling irate executives, lost stock value, heated mergers, and complex accounting issues—but the desolation and sorrow of divorce work were too much. He hadn't wanted to hear one more pitiful wife calling for help, or the details of one more husband's infidelities. When he'd changed departments, he'd never expected to deal with another matrimonial dissolution in his life. He'd certainly never expected to be a client himself.

"My wife and I wanted children. I'd talked to Carson before about adoption. He knew the law. He'd explained what our options were. We'd been exploring an overseas placement when he came to me with the idea of taking Morgan's twins. For my wife and me, it was the supreme gift."

He and Faith had flown into Albuquerque late on a Thursday night. Neither of them had slept a wink in the $39-a-night airport Hilton where the air-conditioning was on despite the cool temperature, and the paper-thin walls kept them apprised of a gambler's bad luck and worse temper on one side, and an adulterous affair on the other. Early the next morning, they'd started toward Los Alamos in a white rental car with two empty child seats in the back. It had been pitch-black, and Faith had fallen asleep with her head resting against the window. As he drove, a brilliant sunrise illuminated the huge sky and red earth. Gazing across miles of flatland sprinkled with cacti and low brush to mountains beyond, he'd known his life was about to be transformed.

"Did you have any contact with Morgan at that point?" Lucy's voice drew him back to the conference room.

"No. She didn't want to know the identity of the prospective parents," Carson answered.

"She trusted Carson. We never met her," Bill added.

They'd arrived four hours early—the designated time was three o'clock. He'd been startled when what appeared to be an adobe complex turned out to be a Catholic hospital: Our Lady of Grace Medical Center. Even the name seemed prescient. In a dubiously labeled "waiting room," they'd done just that. It was cold; there was little light. There were no back issues of *Parents* magazine or *People* or *Good Housekeeping* or even *Car and Driver* to keep them occupied. Faith had jumped up and down to stay warm, while he'd paced the room. They'd barely spoken and never touched.

He'd had a glimmer that afternoon that somehow their marriage wouldn't survive. He'd expected them to huddle together on the wooden bench, to talk about their future family. He'd been so excited that he would even have been content to hear about his wife's plans for decorating the nurseries. Instead they were silent, lost in their own thoughts and different dreams. But his apprehension disappeared when an elderly Native American nun appeared, a wizened woman in a black habit, and handed them each a bundle: Foster to him and Avery to Faith, the sweetest blue-eyed babies he'd ever seen.

He'd grabbed the folder of medical files, and they'd gotten back in the car as fast as they could.

Bill now turned to look at his audience. Detective O'-Malley seemed to be smiling, as if she'd read his mind and shared in his happy memory. "Although I had very much wanted to meet Morgan, the anonymity she requested appealed to my wife, too, so I kept my mouth shut," he forced himself to add. "Everything went along accordingly. If you know of Foster's death, you know it was difficult—challenging perhaps is a better word. And then she wrote to us. It was in April—this past April."

"Why?"

"She'd managed to piece together that Foster and Avery were the babies she'd given up in New Mexico."

"Do you know how?"

He shrugged at the hundred-thousand-dollar question. "I've wondered about that more times than you can imagine. The only thing I can come up with—really the only connection—is that David Ellery was Foster's treating psychiatrist at the time of his suicide, and I suspect Ellery gave her information she shouldn't have had. It had to come from somewhere."

"Violating patient confidentiality," Carson added.

That wasn't all that prick of a man had violated. Bill couldn't think about him without feeling his blood run hot. He'd given press conferences to cover his tracks before Foster's autopsy was even completed. He hadn't cared about Foster's memory; he'd been desperate to protect his reputation and professional judgment. Bill had been so filled with rage that he'd wanted to kill. But being angry with the psychiatrist helped him get through the pain of his enormous loss. It was easier to think of Ellery's evils than of life without Foster or of how he'd failed his son.

"Yes. I suppose that's right. But I guess I can't blame him," he said, wanting to sound rational, calm. "I can't blame anybody. We'd tried everything to help Foster. I'm not sure there was anything in the world anyone could do. What do they say—if someone really wants to kill himself, he will?"

"What happened when Morgan did contact you?"

Bill stared into her eyes, wishing the others would leave the room. "As I said, we got a letter. Morgan wanted to meet Avery. She wanted to explain herself." He poured himself some water and took a long sip. The cool liquid soothed his dry throat. "The adoption issue—or rather its disclosure—had been a source of bitter debate between my wife and me. She had been adamant that we not tell the children they were adopted, but I had eventually prevailed upon her to tell them the truth. I'd always thought secrecy was a mistake. I think she acquiesced in part because we had no information to give them about their biological parents. She felt protected by that. There would be no one for them to search for. So we'd told them at Christmastime. It was very difficult, more so than I'd expected, especially for Foster. In retrospect . . ." He couldn't bring himself to finish his sentence.

Since the afternoon he'd discovered Foster's body, he'd been asking himself why he'd been so persistent about telling his children that they weren't genetically his. What did it matter? They were a family. He adored them. But deep inside he'd known they were living a lie.

He'd convinced himself that revealing the truth would make no difference. And he'd prayed it would help his marriage. He and Marissa were seriously involved by then. Her active mind, her ambition, her youthful body had made him feel alive, and yet he'd felt desperate at the thought of losing his family. Maybe, just maybe, telling the kids the truth would draw them all closer, would activate some sort of spark with his wife in their shared ordeal. They would need to come together as a unit. Her apprehension, her fear, was his fault, or so he'd told himself. Her dreams had always been caught up in the children, even more so than his. He'd certainly never encouraged her to focus on anything else. But he'd been wrong about the value of the truth—horribly and irrevocably wrong. And Faith had thrown that in his face, blaming him every single day since.

By the time they'd received Morgan's letter, he'd wanted to hurt her as badly as he'd been hurt. If she felt threatened, so be it. He didn't care. He needed to lash out at someone, something. He'd lost his son. She should lose her daughter, too.

None of it was particularly rational or noble. Now that he'd made a fresh start, he knew that. Marissa had helped him realize that. Maybe someday Faith would forgive him as he'd forgiven himself.

"You have to understand that learning of Morgan's existence came at a particularly bad time for us, although I suppose no time would have been good. We . . . we . . . had decided to separate."

"Faith's mentally unbalanced," Carson announced, as if he were practicing how the phrase would sound to a judge.

"But still," Lucy said, "listing you as a reference on her job application preceded her letter to you about your children. I don't understand that." Her tone seemed genuinely baffled, not accusatory. He appreciated her mild manner.

Carson glared at her. "I know what you're thinking, Detective. It was I who gave Bill's name to Morgan and advised her to list him on her application." He swiveled his chair to face the table. "Morgan was a remarkable woman but she lacked ordinary friends. She was too busy, too driven. With all the tremendous work she was doing—much of which involved children—there wasn't time. She wanted this job and she was a perfect candidate. What difference did it make that she couldn't produce some ridiculous woman to claim she was a marvelous hostess, wore understated couture, and shot a round of golf below eighty on a bad day? This absurd notion of well-roundedness—I've never understood it. Did anyone fault Sir Isaac Newton for being single-minded? The dilettante will be the demise of our society, mark my words."

"Thanks for the social commentary, but you still haven't told us how Bill managed to be the reference," Harper interrupted.

"That's my point. You're not criticized for your quest. As a detective, you're allowed to 'Stick to the facts, Mac.' Nobody faults you for not also being able to roast a rosemary chicken. Dr. Reese wanted me to be her reference. I wasn't actively representing her. Our professional relationship had been courteous. She needed help, and I would have been honored to provide it. But even I can accept that some people aren't the best acquaintances to show off if you are seeking political office, and the directorship of the Wilder Center was just that. I was flattered, but she was naive about the liability I might be to her quest. I've caused my share of controversy. So I told her to list Bill instead. I could give him whatever information he'd need."

"How did you think you could get away with that?"

"How? We did! If the poor woman hadn't been murdered, she'd be taking the job. She had dozens of glowing professional references. I knew the nominating committee was unlikely to ever check personal ones. And if they did, I could have coached him. As he's just told you, she had given him his greatest gift. What higher accolade can a man have for a woman?"

"Did you ever tell Avery about Morgan?"

He'd been listening in a fog. He'd heard his name mentioned, but had felt as though he'd disappeared. Now the detective's question brought him back to the room. They wanted to know what his daughter knew about the situation.

"Yes. Yes, I did. We did," he stammered. "Although it was against my wife's wishes. But I felt it was the right thing to do. My daughter's a grown woman. She's nearly in college. I wanted her to have a choice."

He'd fully expected some sort of reaction from Avery when he'd disclosed Morgan's letter. Throughout her adolescence, she'd had her share of temper tantrums over issues of far less importance than the identity of her biological mother. But she'd listened calmly, almost without affect, and hadn't asked a single question, or at least not at first. He'd wondered whether she'd heard him correctly, and he'd even gone so far as to repeat himself.

"Do you know whether they were in contact?"

"I don't. I gave Avery the information we had and left the decision up to her. By that point Morgan's name had been all over the papers in connection with the Wilder Center. Information was easy to come by. I also told Avery that if there was anything she wanted or needed to discuss with me, I would try my best to answer. She hasn't raised the issue since. But I can't tell you what conversations she might have had with Faith."

"Are you aware that she's a beneficiary of Morgan's life insurance?"

"Life insurance?" He shook his head. "I was not. But I expect paperwork would have gone to our house in Gladwyne. I haven't been back. Faith forwards only the bills, and even those arrive late."

"Does your daughter have any history of mental illness?" Harper asked.

"How in hell's name is that relevant?" Leedes said before Bill could respond.

"I know what you're thinking, Detective, given Foster's . . . situation. But I can assure you that Avery is different. She's outspoken and strong-willed. She seems quite sure of herself and has never had a problem getting what she wants. I've never seen signs of anything like depression."

"Is she right- or left-handed?"

The question startled him. "Right-. Right-handed."

"And where is she now?"

"Avery is at an all-girls preparatory school in Maryland. A place called Garrison Forest. She's taking her final exams in the next several days. I imagine with all that has happened in the past six months, she'll be quite happy to be home for the summer."

"How can we reach her?"

"As I said, she'll be here in a week. I can arrange something with you once she's here."

"And Bill will be present at any interview. She is a minor," Carson instructed.

He shook his head. "I can be there if she wants me to be. It's up to her. As I said, I'm done treating her as a child."

"Do you know whether she's aware of Morgan's death?" This time, O'Malley asked the question. Her voice was a pleasant change from the aggressive tone Harper had taken to fire his barrage of inquiries.

"I haven't told her. But I suspect Faith will have by now, no doubt with some degree of relief. Nobody wants a tragedy to strike, but I'm sure my wife wasn't too disappointed to learn that the source of her fears had been destroyed."

Jack and Lucy were silent on the way down in the elevator. Bill's parting comments implied that Faith Herbert had joined the crowd of celebrators over Morgan's death, but it was no doubt a comment born of complicated emotions. The man was obviously distraught over the loss of his son, and no one ended a marriage feeling nothing.

A bell rang, the elevator stopped, and a fat woman carrying two full shopping bags waddled on at the fourth floor. She smiled as she awkwardly pushed her way in and struggled to turn around. Lucy moved closer to the wall and focused on the illuminated buttons to avoid staring at the several black hairs that protruded from a large mole on the woman's ear.

Her mind wandered as she thought of the destruction of the Herbert family and her sense that Bill had been passive throughout. She remembered an amateur boxing tournament she'd read about in Florida. A 280-pound mother of two had volunteered to compete, had actually paid to enter the ring against another untrained woman. But her opponent had been too fierce, pounding her repeatedly until she dropped dead on the mat. All the while her husband and children had been watching, cheering her on, rooting for her. By the time they'd realized she was in trouble, it was too late.

They'd later claimed there was nothing they could have done.

27

6:58 p.m.

$\mathcal{L}$ ucy and Archer both stood up as the massive double doors to the library opened. Elegantly dressed in a tweed jacket, a navy polo shirt, and dark slacks, Rodman entered, nodded to Archer, and extended a hand to Lucy. Despite the formality, he looked peaked with pallid skin, drawn cheeks, and dark circles under his eyes. It seemed hard to believe that her lunch with him at the Cricket Club had been only two days before.

"Do sit down," he said, as the tall clock chimed seven o'clock.

Lucy resettled on the striped love seat. Archer sat in a leather wing chair opposite.

Rodman walked past them to the butler's tray table that held a crystal decanter and several tumblers and poured a healthy drink. He turned in their direction. "Archer tells me you wanted to discuss your . . . investigation. I don't know that I can be of use to you, but proceed if you must."

Her whole body felt tense. She had the desperate urge to stand and stretch, to roll her head on her shoulders, anything to rid herself of the nervous stiffening that seemed to overtake her body. Approaching her boyfriend's father to inquire about his ex-wife was far more difficult than even she'd imagined. She glanced at her notepad. Although she knew exactly the areas she needed to cover, it helped to focus on her own scribbled handwriting. She spoke without glancing up. "I need to ask you about your divorce."

He answered quickly. "There's little to tell. We'd been married five years. Archer had just turned three. I returned from a weeklong business trip to New York, and Morgan announced that she'd rented an apartment in Center City and hired an attorney. She left that evening."

"Did she give you a reason?"

"Detective O'Malley, what transpires between a man and his wife is private. The failure of that marriage changes nothing."

"Call me Lucy," she replied. "And that may be so, but privacy often yields when one spouse winds up murdered."

"The fact that Morgan is dead has no bearing on this."

"I need help. This case is in its fifth day, and believe me, that's a long time in the spectrum of a homicide investigation."

He took a step back, banging into the tray table behind him. The stopper rattled against the decanter.

Archer sat with his legs crossed, his right ankle propped on his left knee. His elbows rested on the arms of his chair, and he chewed on a thumbnail. "Help Lucy out, Dad. It'd be the chivalrous thing to do after all. She's just doing her job," he muttered, sarcastically.

"I've had enough from you," Rodman said, pointing a

finger in his son's direction. "You may be perfectly content to air our dirty laundry about your mother, but I'm not."

Archer stood abruptly. "She left you. She left me. What are you protecting?"

He stared down into his tumbler and then shook it slightly, as if to rattle invisible ice cubes. Some of the brown liquor splashed out onto his lapel, but he didn't appear to notice.

"Did you know she had two more children?" Archer blurted out.

Rodman's eyes widened. He coughed. "What are you talking about? That's preposterous."

"The person on the insurance policy—Avery Herbert. That's Morgan's daughter. There was a boy, too. A set of twins. Lucy discovered that."

"I don't believe it for a moment. Morgan wouldn't have made the same mistake twice."

"Is that what I was? A mistake?" Archer shouted. "For her, or for you, too?"

Rodman appeared momentarily confused. "This is absurd. I gave my life to you, to raise you. I won't have you addressing me in that manner. You—" He turned to Lucy. "Was this your grand design? To turn the few surviving members of the Haverill family on each other and see what you could uncover? Where you come from that sort of feeding frenzy may be appropriate, but not here. Not in my house. I don't appreciate your meddling."

"She's trying to find my mother's killer. Don't be a fucking snob."

Rodman glared. "And don't you ever speak to me that way again."

"Stop!" Lucy held up her hand. "Calm down, both of you. Look, I know this is hard for everybody. Mr. Haverill, why don't you sit down? Archer, you too. I'm not trying to whip up anything. Hysteria in my line of work tends to be counterproductive, and believe it or not, I have no prurient interest in your family troubles, whatever they may be. I know from my own experience how difficult it is to deal with painful topics. There are plenty of times when I'd be just as happy to put my head in the sand. But I do need some basic answers that perhaps, Mr. Haverill, you can provide."

Much to her surprise, both father and son followed her instructions. Archer returned to the wing chair and Rodman sat in a Chippendale armchair from which he could still reach the drinks tray. With their stiff postures and extended chins, the resemblance was obvious.

"Now, why don't you tell me what happened between you and your ex-wife."

"And you have yet to explain how any of this is relevant to her death."

Lucy bit her lip. It was a valid condition, but not one to which she was accustomed. When faced with a detective, most people either volunteered information or asked for a lawyer. They didn't negotiate. "As part of a murder investigation, we often have to re-create the victim's life. Understanding the person who died—in this case Morgan—is part of figuring out who would have wanted to kill her. Frankly, the bits and pieces we've learned about her life thus far don't fit together, or at least not well."

"I'm not sure I understand. What about all your forensic people? Aren't they supposed to come up with the answers? Why are you asking me about what transpired decades ago?"

"Our criminalistics people examine the crime scene. They gather clues that tell us how a person died. They also tell us what the killer left behind. But they don't tell us why. And without a why, all the clues in the world don't always lead to a who. I told you last weekend when I was at your dining room table that part of my work is to hear the dead speak from the grave, but I'm realizing that's not possible. A victim needs the people who knew her to speak on her behalf."

"So you're not listening to voices after all?" he said. "I suppose that's a step in the right direction."

"I like my job too much to leave it," she said, remembering her feeble attempt at humor from that first dinner.

"Ah."

"So, will you help?"

He scanned the room, his eyes resting on the French doors, and the view beyond of the flagstone patio and gardens. "She . . . I . . . I knew she was unhappy. You have to understand that when we met, she was so young. Barely eighteen. Except for a trip with her grandmother to Paris, she'd seen nothing of the world."

"How did you meet?"

He paused, as if to drum up the memory. When he spoke, his voice was softer. "Although I was fifteen years her senior, I received an invitation to her debutante party. I'd known her parents, not well, but we were generally considered part of the same social set, attended the same Quaker meetinghouse. Her father and I had the same alma mater. I hardly think they considered me a candidate for their daughter's affections." He chuckled. "It was quite a lavish affair, really, hundreds of people under a big white tent with panels that opened to the sky. The band played until the early-morning hours. Morgan couldn't have been more radiant in a long white dress with tiny pearl buttons and white gloves that came up over her elbows. She was a lovely woman." He closed his eyes. "After dinner, I asked her to dance and . . . and we did, song after song. Other men tried to cut in, and she politely declined. That I would receive such attention . . ." His voice drifted off. When he spoke again, his tone was decidedly more matter-of-fact. "I should have known she was not a woman to pin down. At one point that evening, she whispered to me, 'I play along because this gala is my ticket out. A grand way to travel, don't you think?' I was so swept up in her presence that I didn't ask her to explain. I never asked her to explain anything. Two months later, I took her to Italy—Milan, Venice—and proposed to her in Portofino on a cliff overlooking the Mediterranean. But I should have known that first evening. She was restless. Morgan never wanted domesticity. She wanted to escape her own upbringing."

"So why marry you?" Lucy asked.

"I've asked myself that same question a hundred times and have never come up with a perfect answer. How ironic that analysis became her profession." Rodman stood, refilled his glass, and moved toward the love seat. He rested one hand on the upholstered back. "She mistook the difference in our age for something more than it was. She thought it made me different from the other men . . . the boys, really . . . whom she'd dated. And . . . and I think she misunderstood what I might offer."

"In what way?"

"I was president of my company by the time we met. She thought that because I was in charge of my own destiny it would bring her freedom, independence. She wouldn't have to help a husband establish himself as so many of her peers were doing. She tended to view the world quite simply."

"She didn't want to schmooze with the partners so she married the man at the top?"

"That's a rather vulgar way to put it, but probably not inaccurate."

"Then she got what she wanted. What was the problem?"

"She didn't know what she wanted. Rather like her son, I might add, although I expect he won't be flattered by the comparison."

Lucy glanced at Archer, but his blank expression revealed nothing, no doubt because he was numb to Rodman's persistent criticism.

"As far as I could tell," Rodman continued, "her only valid complaint was that I had discouraged employment, which I had indeed. She had a baby. She had a house to maintain and a staff to run."

"What did she want to do?"

"Your guess is as good as mine. She had no higher education. We married before she'd even completed the first of a two-year college program. I don't know what she could have done. The thought never occurred to me. She was my wife. That was supposed to be enough." He pursed his lips.

"Did you stay in touch with her after she moved out?"

"Initially, our communication was quite frequent.

There were matters pertaining to the divorce. And . . . and there was the issue of Archer."

"The *issue* of me, I'll remember that." Archer poured himself a drink, too. Holding the decanter, he extended his arm toward his father, offering a refill, but Rodman didn't appear to notice. Archer threw back his head and drained the tumbler in one gulp. Then he refilled the glass and repeated the process.

For a moment Lucy thought to intervene. Inebriation wouldn't help, of that she felt certain, but the power of his father's words wasn't lost on her. She could drive Archer back to Center City.

"Once the court proceeding ended, Morgan quickly faded away. She'd decided to go back to school. She told me she was even considering medical school. At the time, the suggestion was humorous. She hadn't spent a single day of her life gainfully employed. The hours alone would be staggering. But I also knew to keep my thoughts to myself. She'd never listened to me and she wasn't about to start now."

"And what about Archer?"

"Archer?" Rodman stared at his son, as if just now recognizing his presence. Archer stepped forward in anticipation of the answer. "This is a very difficult subject. I still don't see—"

"Just answer her question," Archer instructed.

"Oh my." He raised his hand to his mouth and covered his lips with a fist. "How shall I put this? It was difficult for her to let him go, don't misunderstand me, but difficult on an intellectual level. You see, she felt no emotional connection to him. She had no natural instincts. He was a stranger with whom she couldn't imagine how to deal. She kept saying, 'He's your child,' as if she'd had nothing to do with the process and I was solely to blame."

Lucy knew that Archer had never heard the truth before. This conversation contained a level of candor that the Haverills hadn't shared.

"What about the first years?" Archer asked. "When she was still here." He spoke softly, the prior hostility gone.

"I hired a series of nannies to help. I thought she needed some free time. She could go to the City or the club. Her schedule wouldn't be encumbered. But nothing changed measurably." He turned away from his son, and stared at a small oil painting over the butler's table. The image was a round vase of white peonies.

"One evening, I came home early and found her standing in the doorway of the playroom, watching as the nanny read to you. You were in her lap, quite an adorable little boy in your pajamas, listening intently to a book called *The Story of Ferdinand*. It was about a bull that wouldn't fight. He only wanted to sit and smell flowers. It was your favorite—not surprisingly." He laughed briefly. "From the threshold, Morgan stood, weeping, her whole body shaking. I thought someone must have died. She was not a particularly emotional woman, or should I say she kept her emotions extremely well controlled. When I asked what had happened, she turned to me and said, 'Why is it so difficult? You're paying someone ten dollars an hour to do what I can't. What's wrong with me?' She was tormented by guilt over her shortcomings. She knew her feelings were selfish, wrong, but she couldn't change them. Life had always been about her, and her alone. Less than a month after that night, she walked out, and I knew she was walking away from both of us. Forever."

The room filled with silence. Nobody stirred. After a moment, Lucy mustered the courage to continue. His explanation wasn't over. "When did you stop communicating?"

Rodman seemed to have forgotten Lucy's presence. Her follow-up question seemed to confuse him, and he took more than a few moments to reply. "I gave her what she wanted in the divorce because I wanted the process to end. It was extremely unproductive. After everything was finalized, she occasionally sent a brief note. I knew she was off to medical school. I heard when her mother passed away. She informed me that she'd decided to become a psychiatrist. And she sent a change of address when she purchased her home in Bryn Mawr. That's about all. Even those notes stopped coming ages ago."

"So she never mentioned other children?"

"No." He shook his head. "Nor a husband. As I said, when I did hear from her, it was only in the tersest way. I can't say I didn't wonder about her personal life, but she never asked after mine and I wasn't about to inquire into hers."

"And then out of the blue you got the call about the insurance?"

"That's right. As I relayed to you at . . . when we met previously."

"If your divorce was so acrimonious, why thirty years later were you her personal reference on her application for the position at the Wilder Center?"

"I didn't know I was," he said, sighing audibly. "It's not a surprise, though. I know several of the major investors, as well as the chairman of AmeriMed. Despite what my son thinks about me, I have a very good reputation in the business community. I am respected. No doubt she listed my name because she knew it would help her cause. As I said, I would never expect Morgan's selfishness—or should I say self-absorption—to disappear. In this case, I suspect her connection to me was perceived as an asset."

"But they never called you. From what we gathered, she was offered the job without any check of her personal references except for her secretary."

He shrugged. "I can't explain the conduct of the nominating committee. All I can say is that Morgan would have been confident that my reference would be complimentary."

"Why?" she asked, remembering Dixon's remarks about Rodman's temper.

"She knew me. She knew what I stand for. And I may have learned a bit along the way, but I haven't changed since the day we shared an aisle." He sat down next to her on the love seat. "You're young. But take my word—it's difficult to hold that much animus in your heart for any prolonged period. My anger gave way to grief, and the sadness eventually ended, too." He reached into his pocket and withdrew a handkerchief. Turning his head away, he dabbed his eyes. He seemed fragile, as if the conversation itself had aged him.

Archer had covered his face with his hands. Lucy watched his fingers press into his eyes.

"Can you think of anyone who would have wanted to hurt her? Anyone at all?" Lucy asked after a moment.

Rodman finished his drink. "I don't know the details of where her life took her, so I can't provide you with names, but I wouldn't be surprised if you discovered a queue. As I've told Archer more times than I can recount, when you live the type of reckless existence that she did, you make enemies along the way. She was a hurtful woman. No doubt she tried to put her heart in the right place, but she was a hurtful woman nonetheless." He met her stare. "If I had your task, I'd be looking for someone else she discarded along the way. Not everyone is as charitable as I am."

11:17 p.m.

In front of her wood-burning stove, Lucy sat with legs extended so that Archer, lying beside her, could rest his head in her lap. He rubbed her left foot as she gently caressed his forehead. The lines seemed more pronounced than she'd ever noticed before, and she could see a few gray hairs sprouting prematurely from his scalp. When he closed his eyes, the veins in his lids glowed in the light from the Duraflame.

"Are you sure I can't make you some dinner?" she asked, knowing his response.

He shook his head. "Having your body as a cushion is much more important to me at the moment than a full stomach," he said without opening his eyes.

"You need your strength."

"For what? Running a bar? Yeah," he added, sarcastically.

"Look, Archer, just because your father doesn't understand your work, or just because he'd choose something else, it doesn't mean it's not worthwhile."

Archer rolled over and pressed himself up with his hands. "Do you honestly believe that?"

"I do. And I don't think you should beat yourself up. You work hard. You enjoy what you do. There's nothing dishonorable about that. Not everyone can produce world peace or invent the toaster or find the cure for soft-tissue cancer. Sometimes I think all of us would be better off if we'd embrace reality instead of focusing on how we fall short of expectations."

"How'd you end up so sane?"

She smiled. "I didn't. But it's a good act. One I learned early on from my parents."

He sat back on his heels and leaned toward her. "Do you realize that if you hadn't confronted my father today, he might never have told me about my mother? All my life I've begged him for information, and you learned more in an afternoon than I did in thirty years."

"Sometimes it's easier when the probing comes from a relative stranger."

He didn't respond. Instead he kissed her, then reached his arms around her and pulled her toward him, kissing her again. She felt his tongue inside her mouth and tasted his saliva, still scented with the scotch he'd drunk hours before.

"Thank you, Lucy. I mean it. I might have died never knowing, not understanding. And it's because of you, your persistence, your inability to be bullshitted." He smiled. "I saw my father today. I listened to him. He actually seemed human. I've built up so much resistance to him, his intolerance, his arrogance, that maybe I've never tried to understand. It was easier to believe my mother left because she couldn't tolerate him the same way I couldn't. I've wanted to blame him." His eyes widened with animation and he shook his fist. "You know, he remembered the Ferdinand story. That bull was the best! When he said that, I realized, shit, he *is* my father. He may be a far cry from perfection but he was the only parent I had. And for that, for giving me that insight, I love you even more."

She leaned toward him and kissed his cheek. Playfully, she whispered in his ear, "So how will you show your gratitude?" Then, realizing how deeply serious he was, she added, "I love you, too. And I'd do anything I could to help you through this nightmare."

The telephone interrupted their discussion. Lucy stood, feeling a stab of stiffness in her knees as she straightened her legs. "I'll get it," she said, grabbing the receiver from its cradle on the kitchen table.

"Hey there," Jack said. "Ben and I interviewed Sherrill Nichols, the wife of Tripp. We'd hoped to find him, too, but apparently AmeriMed is having some emergency meeting so he's out. Sherrill says Tripp was away on business last weekend—something in Atlantic City. She couldn't tell us where he was staying because he'd only called from his cell phone. But he left Saturday morning, was supposed to come back Monday, but then showed up at home a day early."

"That can't be right. He was at the Rabbit Club Saturday night. He's a member. Why hide his attendance from his wife?"

"We asked if she knew he was a member of the Rabbit, and she said, 'Yes, of course.' Kind of like it was a source of pride. So get this. Ben and I then checked with the nicer downtown hotels. Turns out the Hyatt had him registered for two nights, although he didn't stay for the second. He made no phone calls and drank most of the minibar. Had a three-hundred-dollar bill for incidentals. He got one telephone message from someone named Avery on Saturday around five P.M."

"He would've been at the Rabbit Club by that time."

"Right. But listen, it gets weirder. An Avery *Nichols* had a confirmed reservation for Saturday night, too, but she never checked in. Tripp's credit card was billed for the room."

"So was this their tryst?"

"Maybe. But we can't prove that anyone stayed in his room with him."

"How about the notion that it's easier to run up a huge minibar bill if you're not alone?"

"Hey, if it works for you, it works for me," Jack said, chuckling. "It'll be interesting to hear what old Tripp has to say about all of this. I'll see you in the morning. Good night, O'Malley."

After replacing the receiver, she walked back to the stove. Archer had removed his clothes. He lay on the floor, staring at the ceiling. The flames from the fire cast shadows on his body.

"What are you doing?" she asked, leaning over him and raising her eyebrows.

He smiled. "You were the one who wanted me to show my gratitude."

"I didn't need that big a show." She knelt beside him, ran her hand along his leg, and then kissed his belly button.

"Try and live with it."

28

Friday, May 23rd
12:45 p.m.

The morning had been spent reviewing documents and reports of interviews in preparation for the confrontation with Tripp Nichols. Lucy was eager to go and felt restless as Jack pulled into a Mobil station to fuel up the car. While she waited, she wandered into the adjacent convenience store, bought a pack of Dentyne, and tucked the seven cents of change into the back pocket of her pants. Feeling her cell phone reminded her that she'd failed to turn it on that morning. But although the message envelope appeared in the window, she ignored it; the morning headline had caught her attention: ELLERY RESIGNS FROM PINNACLE POSITION; WILDER CENTER SEARCH FOR DIRECTOR CONTINUES.

She picked up a paper from the stack, dropped a dollar bill on the counter, and began to read. Despite the article's length, it provided little information on the momentous turn of events. Ellery had resigned for unspecified personal reasons, according to the press release. And the doctor couldn't be reached for comment. Most of the two-page spread recited the hospital's development and its search for leadership. Dixon Burlingame was quoted briefly: "We are saddened by Dr. Ellery's decision, but we know we can find a suitable replacement. The Center will open on schedule."

Lucy brought the paper out to the car and handed it to Jack just as her cell phone rang. Caller ID showed A. Baldwin.

"I thought cops always answered their phones," Amanda said. "I've been trying to reach you for more than an hour."

"Why? What's up?"

"If I tell you, I expect you'll let me know what further details you find out."

"Is that blackmail?"

"Just a quid pro quo—a favorable one for you since I don't see any men in blue monitoring Ellery's comings and goings."

"What are you talking about?"

"I was outside Ellery's house in Haverford trying to get a scoop on the resignation story. But nobody was talking or even answering the door. Then about an hour and a half ago, a Town Car pulled up. Ellery came out of the house with three large suitcases and a laptop, and got in. My cameraman and I wanted to follow him, but when we got back in our van, the tire was flat. Slashed, if you can believe it. So much for parking in a good neighborhood. Well, I could hardly ask Ellery to wait up. Who knows where he's headed, but it certainly appears he'll be gone for a while."

12:59 p.m.

Lucy avoided a glance at the speedometer as Jack steered through downtown Philadelphia toward I-76. With one hand, she braced herself against the dashboard. With the other, she struggled to dial Betty Graham. The small metallic flip phone helped her focus. She could ignore the mayhem outside, the cars screeching to a halt, the bicycle couriers frantically scrambling for the sidewalk, and the pedestrians jumping away from the curb. But the tiny numbers enclosed in their gel covering were almost impossible to hit given the momentum of the car.

It was only when Jack was forced to stop behind a delivery van that she quickly could dial. He banged his hands on the steering wheel. "What the fuck is wrong with these people? Don't they know how to get out of the way?"

"Doctors' office," a voice answered.

"This is Detective O'Malley, Philadelphia Homicide."

Jack hit the horn. Frustrated, he pulled the cord on the megaphone and began to instruct all vehicles to move to the side of the road.

"Is everything all right?" Betty asked.

"Is Dr. Ellery leaving town?"

She paused momentarily. "Oh, yes, absolutely. He informed me that he had a personal emergency. I was told to cancel all appointments for the rest of the month and to tell his patients he would be back in touch with them when he returned."

"Where's he going?"

"Puerto Vallarta. That's in Mexico."

"Do you know what airline?"

"American. The flight leaves in less than an hour. He's got an aisle seat and a vegetarian meal. I confirmed them myself."

If they could catch Ellery in time, he'd live to regret crossing his longtime employee.

Her attempts to locate the gate or to contact the gate attendant were less successful. Each time the car lurched, she'd hit a wrong button in the morass of automated prompts, and heard the saccharine voice apologizing, "I'm sorry. I do not recognize that number. Good-bye." The number for airport security rang unanswered, and the emergency number was busy.

Sadly, she realized that even if she got through to someone who could provide assistance, she wasn't sure what she could say to convince the authorities to do so. They didn't have an arrest warrant. Nor did they have probable cause to have him stopped. Dixon's story provided a strong alibi. The gun belonged to Ellery, but there were no prints to tie him to a weapon that he'd reported stolen weeks before. "Don't worry about the technicalities," Jack said. "If we can stop him, we'll come up with some justification for detaining him. I don't want him out of this state, let alone the country."

She agreed. There was something fundamentally wrong with his sudden resignation and departure.

They pulled up to the curb and jumped out, leaving the car in a tow-away zone.

Jack and Lucy sprinted through Terminal A at Philadelphia International Airport. Although the security officers were reluctant to let them through the metal detectors without valid boarding passes, they were granted permission after they deposited their guns, shoes, and badges in a bucket. They continued barefoot, rounding a corner, running down a corridor, past a bookstand, a pizza and brewery outpost, and an array of souvenir carts until they saw Gate 3.

There they stopped in their tracks. The boarding gate was shut. The waiting area was empty. And Dixon Burlingame was walking toward them.

"Detectives," he said with a smile. "Decided to take a vacation, did you? You travel light."

"Where's Ellery?" Lucy asked, although they all knew the answer.

"He'll be back, but no time soon. Mexico is beautiful in the summer—fewer tourists."

"How could you do that? How could you help him leave?" She had the overwhelming urge to sock the smug expression off his face.

"Miss O'Malley, my first and foremost obligation is to protect my company and the institutions it supports. I'm fully aware that you don't have enough to arrest David, or you would have done so by now. I also know he isn't a killer. I was with him at the Rabbit Club—a fact you've confirmed with Miss Barbadash. I am his alibi. And I didn't leave his side until long after Morgan had departed with Tripp. But after what happened at the Union League, and after our meeting, I realized the power of suggestion, the damage that mere innuendo can cause. The Wilder Center can't risk scandal of any kind. We passed over Ellery once before because of that fear. This work is too important. Morgan's murder brought with it an air of . . . suspicion. He had to resign, and he wanted to leave. Now, if you'll excuse me, I have a new director to find. We seem to be quickly running out of candidates."

They stared at his back and listened to the sound of his departure, the click of the heels of his dress shoes on the polished corridor. He turned the corner and disappeared from sight as the PA system announced a flight to Miami.

29

6:30 p.m.

*J*ack steered the car up the gravel drive and then skidded sideways to block anyone from departing, or at least anyone who refused to drive over the lavender beds that lined both sides of the driveway. In front of the massive Tudor home, a silver Infiniti sedan idled, but there was no sign of a driver.

As they approached, the front door swung open and out stepped a middle-aged woman with bleached blond hair and a wide forehead. Despite the gray light of early evening, dark glasses covered her eyes. She wore a black pantsuit and had a fuchsia, black, and green print shawl draped over one shoulder. In her ringed fingers, she held a quilted clutch. When she looked up and noticed their presence, she gasped and took a step back. "Who are you?"

Jack and Lucy both produced their badges. "Philadelphia Homicide Unit. Mrs. Nichols?"

She nodded, obviously stunned that Jack addressed her by name.

"I'm Jack Harper. We spoke last night. Is your husband available?"

"He . . . he'll be right—"

The arrival of Tripp Nichols made any further answer pointless. His navy blazer strained to cover his wide girth and his wire-rimmed glasses pinched the flesh around his temples. His black hair bristled atop his head, and he had pronounced rosacea on his nose. "Who is asking?"

"This man . . . these people are from the police."

"We need to ask you some questions," Lucy said.

"That's not possible right now. We're expected for cocktails, then dinner. We're late already. And I have nothing to say to you."

"It'll only take a minute."

"Miss," Sherrill said, glaring at Lucy. "You heard my husband. You'll have to leave."

"Just tell us why you planned to stay at the Hyatt last weekend with a high school junior, and we'll be on our way."

"There must be a mistake." Sherrill turned ninety degrees to stare at her husband. "What are they talking about? You were in Atlanta."

The red of Tripp's face was spreading down his neck and disappearing into the collar of his starched shirt. "How dare you come to my home with false accusations? Get off my property! Now!"

"Which part don't you want to explain? The room you reserved for Avery *Nichols*," she emphasized, "or the bank account you set up for her benefit? Where did that two hundred and fifty thousand come from?"

"Could someone please tell me what's going on?" Sherrill asked.

Tripp put his arm around his wife's shoulder, more to keep her upright than to comfort her. His dark eyes appeared black. "I have done absolutely nothing wrong, broken no law. You have no business here."

Sherrill began to cry. She didn't remove her dark glasses, but her sobs were audible. She shuddered to rid herself of Tripp's grasp, but he held on tighter, apparently determined to present a united front to the detectives who were threatening his familial existence. Undeterred, she swatted at his hand, then forced herself free and took several steps away. She stood by the hood of the car with her arms crossed in front of her chest. "I don't believe this. This truly can't be happening," she repeated.

"Can't you see you're upsetting my wife? Call my lawyer. I have nothing to say to you."

"No!" came Sherrill's wail. Without approaching, she called to him, "I want to know, too. You're not going to call any lawyer. You're not going to call anyone. You're going to tell me . . . tell them . . . now."

"There's nothing to explain. I . . . I wasn't . . . I'm not—" Tripp stammered. His face looked as if he might explode. "I'm not having an affair with anyone."

Lucy reached into her jacket and removed the envelope that Gertrude had given her nearly a week before. Carefully she unfolded the letter. Both Sherrill and Tripp were staring at her, transfixed. She looked at him and then down at the page. Slowly, she read each word aloud. When she was done, she stood with her arm extended, offering up the letter itself.

Nobody touched it.

"The girl you're asking about, Avery . . . She's just a child. She's . . . Avery is my daughter." He hung his head.

The clutch handbag hurled through the air and pounded into the side of his face. He flinched and stumbled backward. Sherrill was beside him instantly, looming over him with her hands on her hips. "What daughter?"

"It was . . . it was a long time ago."

"How long?"

Nobody answered.

"Tell me her age!"

The huge man seemed frightened. His mouth gaped open.

"Avery is sixteen," Jack volunteered.

Sherrill paused a moment, considering the math. She clenched her jaw and flared her nostrils. "How could you?" Then she looked around and waved her hands at Jack and Lucy. "In front of the police. This is how you share news of your adultery? I want you out of my house immediately."

"Sherrill. Please. I can explain."

"Oh yes," she said facetiously. "Why don't you do that? I'm sure you've got a very good reason for cheating on your wife and stealing her money, too."

Tripp produced a handkerchief and wiped beads of sweat from his brow. Then he collapsed on the brick steps, and hung his head between his knees.

"What can you tell us about Morgan Reese?" Jack asked. His voice was deadpan.

"Another one!" Then recognition swept across her face. "That's the famous psychiatrist! I saw you with her at the Flower Show. Right in front of my face! Now I remember. You both got all flustered when I came over. I should have known. I should never have trusted you. What was I ever thinking? My father always said, 'The apple doesn't fall far from the tree.' Why didn't I listen?"

"It's not what you think." He looked at Lucy and his eyes seemed to beg for mercy, or for her to simply back off. His life was falling apart around him, and he didn't know what to say or do to prevent total destruction. "I'll tell you what happened. I'm not a murderer if that's what you think."

"Ohhh!" Sherrill screamed. "Oh my God. Someone, anyone, get him the hell out of here."

"Just give me a moment to collect myself," he said, as he adjusted himself on the front steps and took a deep breath. "I deserve that, don't I?"

Nobody said a word.

As he sat slouched on the front step, Tripp couldn't collect himself. He remembered the very moment, the devastating moment, he'd learned of Avery's existence as if it were yesterday, or just an instant before. It had haunted him ever since. Over the course of the past two months, he'd dreamed up stories, concocted excuses. Although he'd tried desperately not to believe it, he'd known as soon as he'd seen the expression on Morgan's face that night in March that he'd never survive what he'd done seventeen years before.

"I didn't even know about Avery until recently. Morgan never told me. You have to believe that."

Sherrill looked as though she were about to spit on him.

"My involvement with her was very brief," he lied. The affair was bad enough. Sherrill didn't need to know it was anything more than a one-night stand. "It was a convention—the American Psychiatric Association, I think it was. Things got out of control. I couldn't believe I'd done that to my wife, my family. I knew I would never let it happen again." He reached for Sherrill's hand, but she took a step back. "You and the kids have always meant—and mean—everything to me. I was an absolute fool, way beyond stupid. I can't tell you how many times I've berated myself."

"Tell me where you were last weekend."

He closed his eyes as he wondered how to explain. He'd fully intended to end any further communication once he'd set up the trust account. The girl—whoever she was—would be protected, maybe not forever, but a quarter of a million dollars could still go a long way, even on the Main Line. He'd assumed from the very beginning that Morgan had told him of her identity to blackmail him. She knew full well he'd be willing to pay a lot to protect what he had.

But the money hadn't been what Morgan wanted at all. She'd been adamant that they meet. He should never have agreed. Just because she'd rekindled a relationship with her abandoned daughter, it didn't mean he could do the same. He wasn't Avery's father, and had no interest in becoming her father now. Morgan wanted to make up for mistakes of her past. He didn't. And yet somehow, some way, he'd been persuaded.

He should never have taken her calls. She was a Siren, and he hadn't the will of Odysseus to strap himself to the mast and resist her pleas. Hearing her voice, he'd been more than reminded of why he'd risked everything to have her before.

He'd been stupid, especially about the letter. He hadn't had the courage to mail it, but in retrospect he should at least have torn it up. When he'd lost it, he'd been sure it was somewhere at the Rabbit Club. He'd been sloppy not to retrieve it earlier, but nobody would've cared; it wasn't signed or dated. Nobody would have given it any significance whatsoever if the recipient hadn't turned up dead a few weeks later just yards away from the building.

And when he'd heard of Morgan's death, he'd panicked. Maybe it had his fingerprints. Now he knew why his search of the building a week ago had come up empty.

Momentarily distracted, he fumed. How dare she? Even with a glorified title, Barbadash was a servant after all. She had no business nosing around in the property of the members. He'd make sure she was terminated—unless of course he was voted out of the club first, an act that could be his social death knell. The very thought of that shame brought him back to the current situation—Sherrill, the police, the need for an explanation. Fast.

"I finally agreed to have dinner with them Saturday night to meet Avery. It had to be a weekend because Avery was at boarding school and couldn't leave during the week. And I agreed to get her a hotel room, too, so she'd have someplace to stay. I assumed she wouldn't be able to go home." He turned to face the two detectives. "I told my wife I was going to be away on business. As you can imagine, I had to account for my absence." She never bothered to check his itinerary. He could be anywhere. Besides, a weekend sounded more plausible than just a night. It could be a multiday convention, a business conference. Drug companies had them all the time. She never seemed to mind when he traveled.

"But then my boss, Dixon Burlingame, heard I was skipping the Rabbit and insisted I change my plans. He was bringing David Ellery, an old friend of his who had been passed over for the position as director of the Wilder

Center. It was an appeasement dinner, so to speak, and he wanted me to join them. I couldn't say no."

No doubt Dixon's mandate had been a blessing in disguise. Dixon had saved Tripp from himself, from his own weaknesses. "So I called Morgan on Saturday afternoon and told her I'd changed my mind," he lied. He hadn't had the courage to deal with another conversation. He'd simply stood them up.

"Where did you reach her on Saturday?" Harper asked.

Did these cops know more than they were letting on? He hated this whole charade. He felt perspiration on his back. The pima cotton of his custom shirt felt clammy. "Uh. Come to think of it, she called me."

They didn't need to know that she'd called from the restaurant, and only after he was more than an hour late. *Where are you? Avery and I are waiting.*

"That's when I said I wasn't coming, that a meeting wasn't possible. I had business demands."

Work pressures. She should have been able to understand that, he'd thought. Her whole life had been about her career. Virtually every choice she'd made had advanced it, right down to the Wilder Center plum. "Avery wasn't my problem to fix. And then . . ." He coughed to clear his throat. "She showed up unexpectedly at the Rabbit." He should never have admitted where he was.

He'd never forget looking across the game room and seeing her in the doorway. Judging from her stance, her slight sway as she perched atop her stiletto heels, she'd been at least slightly inebriated. But even at that late hour, even in her condition, she was beautiful, more beautiful than his wife could ever dream of being.

He hadn't wanted to admit even to himself that he'd booked the room at the Hyatt for two nights—planned to be away from home longer than necessary—before the dinner was canceled, but he'd hoped. He'd hoped that if she appreciated his gesture enough, his willingness to meet their daughter, he could persuade her to spend one more night, one more time, one more for the Gipper. Avery could return to boarding school, and she and he could escape reality for twenty-four hours. How wrong he'd been.

How dare you? How could you do this to her? He'd heard her words, yet all he could picture was the last time they'd made love seventeen years before. She'd had her legs wrapped around his hips. Lying against her, feeling her small breasts pressed into his chest, feeling himself inside her, the memory still excited him.

"What is going on?" Dixon had asked, the scorn on his face obvious at the sudden interruption of a convivial men's night at the Rabbit. Who could blame him? A scene between his handpicked director and a vice president of his company hadn't been on his agenda, and with Ellery present, there was no hope that what took place would stay confidential.

Tripp had known from the tone in Dixon's voice that he'd had to get Morgan out of there. He and Dixon went back a long way, but nobody at AmeriMed was indispensable.

"I asked her if we could speak outside, and she agreed," he explained now.

He'd tried to take her arm, but she'd pulled it away. They'd managed to get outside onto the porch before she'd spoken again, a conversation he'd never repeat to anyone.

"Avery's in the car," she'd told him. In the partial moonlight, he'd seen the Mercedes, its engine idling, and a female silhouette behind the wheel. "Can't you appreciate what we've done? Can't you understand how hard it is for our daughter? You couldn't even find it in your heart to return her phone call today. You're a coward."

Then Morgan had turned to face him with a hard stare. "It was her idea to come here, to see what you considered more important than meeting your daughter, and now she knows. She knows about your pretenses, your airs. She knows what kind of deceitful social climber of a man her father is, and she understands she'll have to fight her own biology for the rest of her life to avoid inheriting a single one of your traits."

"This was your idea, not mine," he'd muttered.

"She loves her parents—her adopted parents—and claims she needs neither of us. She says that none of the choices we made matter to her anymore. But you know what she did want to know? Whether we'd ever been in love." Morgan had laughed in disgust. "I was tempted to tell her the truth, but I didn't want her to hate you. How silly of me to think I could prevent that."

"This is really not the time or the place to have this discussion."

"Oh, Tripp, the consummate protocol man. Well, you needn't worry about hearing from her again. She'll stay out of your way. You've done your final damage. To both of us."

Remembering the scene—or rather the horror—he sniffled loudly, and then turned to the female detective.

All he wanted was an ounce of compassion. Didn't anyone understand how difficult all of this had been for him?
"Morgan explained that the idea of an introduction had
been a mistake. I completely understood. I'd thought the
whole plan was a disaster from the beginning. I got in my
car and drove straight to the Hyatt. She was still on the
porch of the club when I left. And very much alive, I
might add."

"What did you do when you got to the hotel?" Harper
asked.

"I had a drink and went to bed."

These cops didn't need to know any more; they didn't
need to know his night had been a living nightmare. He'd
bought a fifth of bourbon on the way to the hotel but still
drained the minibar. Then he'd crawled into bed and
pulled the covers over his head. That was how his night
had ended—with his anxiety blurred by alcohol to the
point where he felt nearly comatose. His sleep had been
fitful. He'd awoken sick, crawled to the bathroom to
vomit, and then watched an old World War II movie on
television at four in the morning.

"What happened on Sunday?"

He hadn't left his room, hadn't gotten out of bed. He'd
thought about calling Avery but decided against it. Speaking to the girl would only remind him of Morgan, a
woman he had to forget if he was going to keep his life
and sanity intact. "When I'd rested, I showered, packed,
and went home. I didn't learn of Morgan's death until I
saw it on the evening news. Dixon called me later that
evening and confirmed what I already knew."

Sherrill paced frantically back and forth in the driveway. Her high-heeled shoes wobbled in the gravel. He

watched her awkward movements and the pronounced panty line that showed through her trousers. Suddenly she turned. Her eyes had narrowed into slits.

"You pig!" she said in a voice that was low and controlled. "You're nothing without me."

"I'm sorry," was all Tripp could manage. He felt utterly and completely beleaguered. "I don't know what else I can say." Suddenly he yearned for a golf course community in South Carolina, where two-bedroom condos sold for under a hundred thousand and the sun shone three hundred days of the year. Anything to get away.

"How pathetic is that? I should have known when I saw that trailer park you called home." Her lips curled and she barely opened her mouth as she spoke. He'd never seen her so angry—or so absolutely hideous. "Your father couldn't give away a piece of property, let alone sell it. You didn't know what it was to have manners, to travel in the right circles. My family, my money, we gave you everything you needed. You wouldn't even have a job if it weren't for me. AmeriMed wouldn't hire white trash, but being my husband gave you cachet. Don't think anyone on the Main Line would disagree."

Her words droned on, but Tripp didn't listen. There was nothing she could say or do to make the situation any more or less palatable. He was ruined. At that moment, he wanted to be arrested. If the detectives took him away, jail would at least bring him relief from the wrath of his wife.

"And this is how I'm repaid? This is my thanks? You make me sick. I never want to see you again." She paused, presumably to catch her breath. Turning to Jack and Lucy, her tone softened. "Now if you'll excuse me, I

have to call with my regrets for this evening's engagements. Too late, but regrets nonetheless." She swung
open the front door and disappeared within.

The detectives headed toward their car. At some point
Tripp had to get up off the front step, go inside, and either
pack his bag or hash out his differences with his wife of
nearly twenty years. Either way, there was nothing left in
his life of interest to the police.

30

Saturday, May 24th
9:30 a.m.

*J*ack turned off Interstate 95 onto the Baltimore Beltway. Sitting beside him in the passenger seat, Lucy fingered the arrest warrant as she listened to him hum along to the Charlie Daniels Band. In their case, the devil hadn't made it all the way to Georgia; Owings Mills, Maryland, was south enough.

The sky was clear and the traffic minimal. Once they exited the Beltway, the scenery was bucolic—rolling pastures, split-rail fences, and grazing horses. Garrison Forest was in equestrian country, a beautiful setting for the well-bred daughters of genteel Southerners to be educated. *Esse quam videri*—to be rather than to seem—was the school's motto, according to its Web site. The rigorous curriculum taught independent thinking, the milieu fostered impeccable manners, and the campus resembled a country club. The all-female student body was offered every conceivable educational, athletic, and artistic advantage.

Somehow Avery fit into this population. Was it possible that this prefect-elect was actually involved in the vicious killing of her own mother? Murderers couldn't be stereotyped, yet this one seemed particularly wrong. The genetic product of intellectual and academic excellence and the environmental product of an affluent and devoted family, she'd been given every opportunity. If Avery was guilty, what had happened?

Lucy and Jack had decided not to inform the school's administration in advance of their arrival. Who knew what contributions the Herberts had made to the endowment fund, and a possible leak was too high a risk. Nonetheless, as they drove onto campus, it seemed as though every clear-complexioned, blond student striding along the path with a leather backpack knew precisely why they were there. The stares followed the Crown Victoria as it made its way along the narrow paved road that connected a multitude of buildings until they reached Meadowood Hall, the large brick dormitory that housed freshman, sophomores, and a handful of juniors and seniors. Jack cut the engine, and they headed toward the front door.

The black-painted door opened into a stairwell. Looking up, Lucy could see three stories. Judging from the number of front-facing windows, the building contained dozens of rooms. And there was no intercom or other way to discern where a particular occupant resided.

She shut the door behind her and squinted into the sun. Under a tree, a girl in a yellow Lacoste shirt and white piqué culottes was reading Edith Wharton, a pink highlighter in one hand and a menthol cigarette in the other. As Lucy approached, she quickly ground out her butt in the soil.

"Do you know where I can find Avery Herbert?" Lucy asked.

The girl looked past Lucy to the threshold of Meadowood Hall, where Jack stood on the step wearing his dark aviator glasses, more closely resembling a member of the president's security detail than a homicide detective out of his jurisdiction. She shrugged. "Avery left yesterday."

"She did?"

"Yeah."

"Was that a surprise?"

The girl shrugged. "School is done in less than a week. She skipped two finals and took all her stuff. I hear she's not even coming back next year."

"Who picked her up?"

"Her mother."

Lucy thought for a moment. "Did she have a roommate?"

"Yeah, Margot Tyler."

"Can you tell us anything about their relationship, or friendship?"

The girl paused. "They'd been best friends in the fall, inseparable really, but I guess rooming caught up with them. That happens a lot, especially with new girls. Come to think of it, my mother's advice about sharing a room is the one piece of useful advice she's ever given me: Be friendly, not friends. You want the distance. My roommate now—we've got nothing in common. But that suits me just fine." She smiled.

Lucy smiled back, trying to quell her frustration at the mental meanderings that constituted this conversation.

"Anyway, there was a family crisis in January. Her

brother shot himself." She grimaced. "Must've been pretty awful. After that the administration switched Avery to a single. She needed privacy."

"Do you know where Margot is now?"

The girl shrugged. "Either taking an exam or studying for one would be my guess. You could check the library."

Lucy glanced around the lawn with the hope that this roommate would miraculously appear, but they were out of luck. "Can you show us which room was hers?"

She shrugged again. "I guess. I doubt it's locked." She stood up, dropping her book on the grass.

Lucy and Jack followed her inside, up one flight of stairs, and halfway down a corridor. Then she stopped. Slightly ajar, the door was covered with yellow and blue happy-face stickers, and a bumper sticker that read, WHEN THE GOING GETS TOUGH, THE TOUGH GO SHOPPING.

"This is it," she said, pushing the door all the way open.

Lucy stepped past. The small rectangular room had three windows all facing the back of the building. A bed with a mattress and a lumpy pillow, a walnut dresser, a desk, and a chair were the meager furnishings. A picture hook over the bureau showed where a mirror must have hung. The walls were bare. Propped in one corner were a broom and a dustpan.

"She had all this great stuff—some cool paintings, tons of CDs and clothes. I'm surprised she made it out in a day."

The three of them stood quietly for a moment. Lucy walked to the middle window and looked out at the fire escape, an easy exit after curfew.

"What time does the building get locked?"

"Ten. Eleven on weekends."

"How often can someone leave campus?"

"Juniors and seniors can leave after classes up to three weekends a semester. Most of us tend to stick around, though. It's a hike unless you want to go into Baltimore, and that place gets old fast."

"You don't happen to remember if Avery stayed at school last weekend, do you?"

"Are you cops or something?" She wrinkled her nose as the thought dawned on her, and then giggled. "You don't look like a cop, although I guess he kind of does." She smiled at Jack. "Anyway, to answer your question, Avery went home." She glanced at her watch. "I got to go. My English exam is in forty minutes and I still have thirty pages to read. Unless of course you know how *The House of Mirth* ends." She smiled again, and flipped her ponytail as she turned to the door.

While Jack searched the desk, Lucy opened the bureau drawers. Aside from a single Thorlo sock and a safety pin, they were empty. The closet was next. She reached for the knob and turned it, but the door was locked. Avery had left school. Why not leave everything open for the cleaning crew that would no doubt scour the dormitories over the summer break?

"You haven't got a pick set, have you?" she asked, keeping her voice low.

Jack reached into his back pocket and produced a jack-knife version.

"The gadget guru," Lucy remarked.

Jack knelt before the lock, stared at the keyhole, and then selected the appropriate-size pick. She watched as he fiddled for a moment, applying pressure until the pins gave way. Then he pushed the door open. She gasped as she found herself staring at a makeshift shrine.

Propped against the back wall in a thin frame was Foster's self-portrait. The face was larger than she remembered and seemed to consume the space. Turned sideways, the sad, dark eyes cast a vacant stare. White pillar candles, each resting on a small glass dish, were arranged in a semicircle around a square card. In a familiar scroll was written:

> *Your mother requests the pleasure of your company on Sunday, May 18th, at eleven o'clock at the Liberty Bell. Regrets only.*

The very same invitation Archer had received.

Avery was supposed to meet her father on Saturday night and then her half-brother on Sunday. Neither family gathering had taken place. It made sense that she'd wanted to leave her mementos behind. Forgetting all that had happened would be hard enough without visible reminders.

Jack removed a small camera from his pocket and photographed the scene. Then Lucy put the invitation, candles, and dishes in plastic bags, which Jack labeled. Their work was mechanical. Neither had anything to say.

When they had finished their tasks, Jack's voice broke the silence. "Let's find Ms. Tyler. I want to hear about Avery's regrets."

Sunlight streamed through the huge arched windows into the main reading room. At long rectangular tables sat anxious students, frantically cramming whatever details

of Spanish, chemistry, American history, or British literature they could in the final preexam hours. As a whole,
the girls looked tired and unkempt. Most wore baggy
sweat pants and T-shirts, and several had taken off their
shoes and tucked their bare feet beneath them. Although
a prominent sign on the door instructed, FOOD AND BEV-
ERAGES PROHIBITED, bags of trail mix, candy wrappers,
cans of Diet Coke, and bottles of Gatorade cluttered the
tabletops.

Lucy had entered the library alone to attract less attention. She'd been given a minimal description—slightly
plump, black hair, good skin—but the building was bigger than she'd expected and she knew Jack would be impatient. Stopping at the front desk, she inquired of the
head librarian, who barely looked up in response. "She
should be sitting by one of the two emergency exits."

As Lucy scanned the rows, she had an eerie feeling of
déjà vu. How vividly she remembered her late nights and
long high school days of caffeine-fueled studies. The
only difference between her and these girls was that,
when she'd been distracted at the library or had needed to
exercise her stiffening neck muscles, she'd glanced out
the window at the trucks on Washington Street or above
to the water stains on the perforated library ceiling. No
rolling green fields, ivy-covered buildings, or crystal
chandeliers provided distractions.

A girl matching the description sat at the far left table.
Sure enough, red neon illuminated the exit sign just over
her head. The librarian's description had been exact. The
school must be exceptional—or perhaps simply too
small—if the faculty knew the idiosyncrasies of each stu-

dent's study habits. Then again, the parents no doubt paid heavily for just that kind of attention.

Slouched over the table, Margot was reading a well-worn copy of *Great Expectations* with her nose just inches from the spine. An opened composition book revealed her notes and a collection of doodles in the margins.

Lucy leaned over and quietly introduced herself.

Margot started but didn't rise from her seat. A look of sheer terror instantly covered her heart-shaped face.

"My partner and I just need a few minutes of your time. It won't take long. I promise," Lucy said.

Reluctantly, the girl dog-eared the page of her text and pushed back from the desk. She stood and tried to pull down her midriff shirt to meet the top of her blue jeans. When that failed, she grabbed the belt loops on either hip and attempted to hoist her pants up. Despite her efforts, the rolls of her milky white belly remained exposed. Without looking around, she followed Lucy back through the swinging doors of the reading room and into the entrance hallway.

To Lucy's surprise, Jack had come inside. He was stooped over a glass display case, examining the hand-written letters of a prominent abolitionist. Looking up as the swinging door opened, he approached them.

"What have I done?" Margot asked. They were in an area that permitted speech at a normal volume, but she still kept her voice low.

"You haven't done anything. We just need to ask you a few questions about your former roommate."

"Avery?"

Lucy nodded. "Have you spoken to her since she withdrew from school?"

Margot shook her head.

"Do you know why she left?"

"No."

"We understand you had some problems in your friendship. Is that why she moved into a single?"

Margot bit her lip and appeared to fight back tears. "I'm sure I was part of the problem."

"Why is that?" Lucy asked gently.

"When we got here, we did everything together, really hit it off. But as the fall went along I gained some weight, and she was pretty critical of me. You know, the 'freshman ten,' although in my case it was more like twenty and I wasn't a freshman." She wiped her nose. "I'm not sure why Avery was so bothered by it. Maybe she thought I reflected badly on her. She said it showed a lack of control. But getting fat isn't contagious."

"But you lived together throughout the fall and for the month of January."

"Yeah, that's right. Her parents requested her transfer after her brother's suicide, but it didn't happen until the beginning of February. There just weren't any rooms available. I suspect her parents paid somebody to get the one she was in."

"How did she seem to you after her brother died?"

"Avery and her brother were superclose. He called her all the time. It used to get on my nerves, to be truly honest, because we'd be planning to do something, listen to music, go riding, and then he'd call and she'd be on for hours. He always seemed to be having a problem. I guess he had a lot of them or . . . or . . . anyway, his death was really tough for her."

"Did she tell you anything about it?"

"Not really. But she did say he'd written her a letter kind of telling her why. By the time it arrived, she'd already heard from her dad."

"Did you see the letter?"

"No. She never showed it to me. She just cried a lot."

For a moment Lucy wondered why it, too, hadn't been included in the makeshift shrine Avery had constructed in her closet. Perhaps his parting words had been too important to leave behind. "Before her brother's death, did Avery have any particular emotional problems that you noticed—moodiness or depression or anything like that?"

Margot thought for a minute. "This is hard for me, you know, because Avery and I had been really good friends. So I kind of feel like I'm telling on her. I'm just not sure what she wouldn't want repeated."

"This could be extremely important information. And Avery herself could be in a lot of trouble. You can either talk to us here, or we can go down to the local police station and you can talk to them." Jack's voice was matter-of-fact.

Lucy could sense his impatience, but she feared that badgering Margot wouldn't help the situation. "Avery moved out on you. What do you owe her?" She still remembered the slights she'd experienced from her peers and knew revenge could be a powerful motivator.

Margot slouched slightly, jutted out her right hip, and twirled a lock of hair around one finger. "I guess you're right. Besides, she was hardly Miss Nice Girl, if you know what I mean. Don't get me wrong. She could turn on the charm when she felt like it. But when she got upset, she had a wicked temper. She could really fly off the handle."

"Can you give us an example?"

"Well, one time she threw a book out the window—a closed window—broke the glass and everything, and there was another time that she smashed a mirror with her hairbrush. It was pretty scary to watch."

"Do you remember what prompted those incidents? Was it anything in particular?"

"The thrown book had to do with a guy. It was just after Thanksgiving. She'd been late to meet him at a dance this school was hosting, but she'd been stuck on the telephone with Foster—he was her brother—and by the time she showed up at the gymnasium, the guy was slow-dancing with this other girl. I tried to tell her he wasn't worth it. She just said, 'What would you possibly know about guys?'" Margot hung her head. "I guess she was right about that."

Lucy resisted the urge to say something comforting or touch the poor girl's chubby arm. Who could forget the pains of adolescence? "And the mirror incident?"

"That was after her brother's death. I don't know the details, but I gather she and he had just learned over Christmas that they were adopted. I didn't believe it. I mean, what sixteen-year-old just learns out of the blue that she's been adopted? It didn't make sense, especially because Avery was superclose to her parents. Her mom sent her packages and letters all the time. Her dad even took a Wednesday off to come watch a cross-country race. She was really lucky."

"But she broke a mirror?"

"Oh yeah. I came back to the room and she was crying and kind of ranting about her mother abandoning her and how she should have had an abortion if she didn't want her kids. I didn't know what was going on. Avery was pacing back and forth in our room, which was a feat given all the stuff on the floor. Then suddenly she went over to the mirror and just stared at herself. Her eyes bulged and she leaned into the glass. Everything was quiet and then suddenly she screamed, 'I hate you. I hate you. I hate you.' She started bashing the mirror with her hairbrush. It shattered, and her hand was all bloody." Margot stopped speaking. Her clear blue eyes met Lucy's. She'd obviously been horrified at the time, a horror her recollection had brought back. "I wanted to take her to the infirmary, but she told me not to. Instead her mother showed up a couple of hours later. Mrs. Herbert bandaged her hand, cleaned the room, and even hung a new mirror—one that was a lot nicer than the one Avery had broken. When she was through, it was as if the whole thing hadn't happened," she added, as though the miraculous cleanup had been equally traumatic.

"That must have been very difficult to witness," Lucy said automatically. She needed to placate the girl but her own mind raced far from this Maryland campus as she remembered the conversation with Dr. Ladd following the autopsy. She'd offered a theory. Could there have been two? Dr. Ladd's words echoed: "If there were two, I'd bet my pension they're connected." The damaged car, the baseball bat, the details of the murder scene were beginning to make sense. It hadn't been an apocryphal amount of coincidence.

But could only one have intended to kill? Maybe she'd been right after all.

"Shortly after that, she got her own room," Margot mumbled, but Jack and Lucy were already turning for the door.

3:05 p.m.

"Your killer's definitely a woman." Frank confirmed what Lucy already knew. "We've analyzed that hair sample— it's a raccoon. There's no recoverable DNA at the root, which is what we'd expect to find if the animal had scavenged in the car and the hair had fallen out. More importantly, the hair's been dyed and at least the last time I checked, salons around here aren't yet booking beasts. A fur coat or jacket—could even be something with raccoon trim."

"Anything else?"

"The alcohol used on the steering wheel turns out to be cologne. The chemical composition matches something called Verbenas of Provence, made by a British company and sold at only a handful of places for around fifty dollars an ounce. Plus our killer wasted at least two hundred dollars of perfume wiping off fingerprints."

"Was that Jo Malone?"

"I didn't take you for the fancy-perfume type."

"I may surprise you." Lucy reached into her knapsack and removed the plastic bags of evidence she'd collected from Avery's closet at boarding school. She handed them to Frank.

"What are these?" he asked.

"I confiscated a shrine. Can you dust for prints?" She stood.

Frank nodded. "Right away. Where are you two headed?"

"Gladwyne," Lucy responded. Then, turning to Jack, she added, "And I think we'd better hurry."

The Herberts' maid looked terrified as she opened the door to Lucy, Jack, and the team of four police officers and technicians who had been dispatched to execute the search warrant on the Gladwyne property. "Missus no home," she kept repeating even as Jack flashed the paperwork and walked past her.

They gathered in the grand entrance, and Jack issued instructions. The navy blue Windbreakers scattered as Lucy stood beside the maid, waiting for the translator to arrive. The small woman was visibly shaken. "*Esta bien,*" Lucy said softly, struggling for an appropriate idiom from her high school Spanish.

"*No tiene remedio,*" the woman responded in despair.

Within moments Jack returned from the mudroom carrying a shopping bag marked GOODWILL. He reached in and pulled out a raccoon jacket. "I guess she didn't want it to go to waste." With that, he shoved the jacket into a clear plastic bag and marked it with an appropriate inventory control number.

A Hispanic police officer who doubled as a translator had just arrived when Ben DeForest reappeared in the entrance. He'd been initially dispatched to search the barn and surrounding fields. Although he had a three-way radio, they'd heard nothing from him in the thirty minutes they'd been at the Gladwyne property. Now back inside the main house, he leaned forward with his hands resting on his thighs. "You've got to see this," he said, his voice excited but slightly out of breath.

Jack and Lucy left the maid in the custody of the translator and followed quickly on Ben's heels. They crossed the driveway and cut left behind the house across a field-stone patio. The trimmed lawn ended abruptly at an open expanse of field.

The large barn was constructed of painted pine. The door was open, and they stepped into a cavernous space with a hayloft above them and three stalls along the right side. Each had a brass nameplate secured to its hinged gate. An open black trunk against one wall revealed an array of tack, two well-worn rope halters, several snaffle bits, a pair of saddles, and myriad brushes. The smell of horses—hay, oats, and manure—permeated the air despite the fact that there were no longer animals in residence.

"This way," Ben said. He slid open the door to the stall marked JUMPSTART. "There." He pointed to the ground where a pile of hay had been moved aside.

Lucy took a step closer, leaned forward, and then dropped to her knees. There lay a baseball bat. The black script along one side read LOUISVILLE SLUGGER. The end flickered with spots of burgundy metallic paint.

"We've taken prints. Good prints. I e-mailed the image to Frank back at the Roundhouse. And I probably don't need to tell you we've got an exact match to Avery."

Back inside the Herberts' home, Angelica, the maid, offered what little she could. She'd been given last Saturday night off. "Mrs. Herbert doesn't do as much entertaining as she used to, and hardly ever goes out. I spent the night at my sister's," she said in Spanish. "I did notice the car had been moved in the morning, but when I realized Avery was here, I thought she'd gone to pick—" Her words fell off, but her mouth remained open and her eyes bulged in fear.

Lucy turned around. Faith Herbert stood in the doorway to the kitchen. Avery was visible behind her. The girl was tall, thin, and more beautiful in person than she'd appeared in her photograph. "Would someone please tell me what is going on here?"

"Your daughter is under arrest." Reaching for the handcuffs in her pocket, Lucy moved past Faith and stood inches from Avery. Close-up, she thought she could see the mild flutter in Avery's T-shirt as her heartbeat quickened. Reaching for the girl's wrist, she felt Avery's frigid flesh. The locking mechanism of the handcuffs seemed to echo as she secured them, and began to recite her rights. "Avery Herbert, you are under arrest for the murder of Morgan Reese."

"There's been a mistake." She heard Faith's voice behind her. "You don't know what you're doing."

Avery was immobile. Other than a single tear running down her cheek, there was no indication that she had processed what was happening or listened to what Lucy had said. She wore a blank expression that gave her delicate features a ghoulish quality. Lucy turned her away from the kitchen, and directed her toward the door. She felt Jack beside her, but didn't look away from the slender back walking less than a foot in front of her. The huge house was shrouded in silence.

"I murdered Dr. Reese."

Although the words were loud and clear, Lucy wondered if she was dreaming. But Faith repeated her confession.

Avery turned back in the direction of the kitchen. "Mom, don't do this."

"I'm only telling the truth. My daughter is not responsible for this crime. I shot her in the chest—just exactly as my son had shot himself."

Her red eyes now rimmed with tears, Avery looked at Lucy. "You see what she's doing, don't you? Don't listen. Let her go."

"Quiet, Avery. I forbid you to say a single word more to the police," Faith instructed.

"Mom, stop. I need you. I need your help," Avery implored. "What are you doing?"

"I killed her." Faith began to open her purse, and Jack instantly drew his gun. "I have nothing here to harm anyone, Officer," she said politely, as she extended the bag for him to see. She reached in, and then opened her palm to show him two unspent bullets. "You'll find these are the same kind as the one I used on Dr. Reese."

"Mom, please!" Avery cried. She started to collapse, but one of the attending officers grabbed her and held her by her armpits. "You were only trying to help."

"Release my daughter. She's young. She's done nothing wrong. I'm the one you want."

She seemed strangely composed as Jack handcuffed her and advised her of her legal rights. Avery cried quietly, still half dangling from the officer's arms.

As Jack led Faith past Lucy and Avery, the mother smiled. "I love you, my darling girl. You're my joy, my only joy. I wouldn't want this any other way."

31

Saturday, August 9th

2:14 p.m.

$\mathcal{B}$ill Herbert settled beside his daughter on the satin-covered settee. He glanced around the room, seemingly unnerved by his surroundings—a two-bedroom apartment on Lawrence Court that he'd moved into the previous March. With its minimal furniture and bare walls, the space had a transient feeling. He'd clearly never expected that his teenage daughter would reside there, too.

He'd lost weight and his cheekbones protruded dramatically. His temples looked grayer than Lucy remembered from when she'd seen him in May, and his half-glasses perched precariously on his slim nose. On a coffee table in front of him were a pitcher of lemonade, several mismatched glasses, and a pile of what looked to be shortbread cookies placed haphazardly on a plate.

Lucy and Archer perched opposite on small armchairs with mahogany frames and tight upholstery. Archer shifted uncomfortably for several moments, turning his body slightly sideways and resting on one hip with his long legs extended outward and crossed at the ankles. They'd been there for nearly ten minutes, yet the conversation hadn't progressed beyond the barest of introductions.

Bill leaned forward and stirred the contents of the pitcher awkwardly, knocking against the glass sides repeatedly with a wooden spoon. "Lemonade?" he asked. Hospitality had been Faith Herbert's realm, and he seemed to be struggling to figure out what to do to accommodate his guests.

Archer shook his head, declining the offer, and Bill sat back with a dejected expression.

Lucy felt sorry for both of them. "No thank you," she added. "I had water just before we arrived." Given the difficulties of the situation, Archer couldn't be expected to comport himself with the best of manners. She reached over to rest her palm on top of his, wanting to demonstrate her support.

Archer had arranged this meeting with his half-sister on his own and unbeknownst to her. Only after it was scheduled did he ask Lucy to accompany him. "As my girlfriend, not in any official capacity," he'd implored. "The investigation's over."

She hadn't wanted to explain that an investigation is never fully over; there was always more information, more angles to explore. Out of necessity, cases had to be closed to move on to others. Trials happened and sentences were rendered. That was how the overburdened system managed to operate. But most detectives could recall the minute details of a case from a decade before, and would be more than willing to hear some new detail long after the defendant was serving time.

But that explanation was inappropriate. There were no professional problems standing in her way, and she'd agreed. Avery's criminal case had been quickly resolved once it was transferred to juvenile court, where she'd entered a guilty plea to one count of reckless endangerment, a second-degree misdemeanor. In wildly swinging a baseball bat at the hood and roof of the Mercedes, she'd placed Reese in danger of serious bodily injury. Although it was a relatively minor disposition, the prosecution's case for trial on a manslaughter charge had been extremely weak. Its own Medical Examiner would have had to testify that people recover from the type of subdural hematomas that Avery had inflicted, and he couldn't predict the degree of permanent injury, if any. Dealing lightly with Avery also served the ultimate goal: the murder trial of Faith Herbert. The government needed Avery as a key witness. In negotiating this outcome, her defense attorney had offered her testimony.

A court-appointed psychiatrist specializing in adolescent behavioral disorders testified on behalf of Avery at the sentencing hearing. Avery suffered from an acute anxiety disorder brought on by the death of her beloved brother, and aggravated by both the separation of her parents and the sudden discovery of her biological mother. Although she had suffered from certain anxiety issues prior to the events in question, the combination of extreme emotional pain, confusion, and alcohol had made her impulsive. Her aggression was temporary. She'd lashed out in fear, destroying the car. When Dr. Reese had tried to stop her—to calm her down—she'd been hit in the head. But Avery had never intended the resulting damage.

The judge, a sympathetic elderly man who had leaned down from his bench to offer Avery his handkerchief when her emotions got the better of her as she gave her personal statement, placed her on probation. His opinion emphasized the lonely struggles of a suddenly twinless twin whose life had been turned upside down in the space of only a few months. During her probation, she would live in an environment closely supervised by her father in coordination with her court-appointed psychiatrist and would perform 250 hours of community service; when she turned eighteen, presuming she had no further problems with the criminal justice system, she would be free to resume a normal life, however that might be defined under the circumstances.

Although her case formally had been resolved, Archer had negotiated with defense counsel for the meeting. Avery's lawyer had set strict parameters. Since Avery was still scheduled to testify in her mother's trial, there would be no discussion of the night of May 17 and no questions about Faith Herbert. Bill was to be present and would ensure that these conditions were met unequivocally.

Sitting less than a yard away from a brother she'd never met, Avery stared at Archer. Her thin lips quivered slightly, but she said nothing. Her father put his arm around her shoulder and pulled her slightly to him, a move she appeared to resist, so he removed his arm and rested his hands in his lap.

"I guess . . . I just . . ." Archer began. He paused for a moment and looked at the floor, collecting his thoughts. "I understand now that Morgan wanted us to meet. The

Sunday that . . . you know, the invitation she sent us both. The Liberty Bell."

Avery nodded, although the movement was almost imperceptible. "We're meeting now."

He shrugged. "Maybe this was silly, another one of my dumb ideas. It just seemed so inconceivable that you even existed, that I had a sister, that I felt . . . well, it's all been so disorienting."

"It has been for Avery, too," Bill added.

"Yes. Yes, I can imagine. And when I found out that Foster was your brother, my brother . . . I really loved his artwork. He had tremendous talent."

Avery's eyes filled with tears. "Nothing made him happier than that show, your show. I often wish it had never come down. Maybe everything would have turned out differently."

"I just wish I'd known then what I know now," Archer said.

"Me, too." For a moment the sides of her mouth curled up, and she smiled. It was a fleeting gesture but in that second her face was transformed. The blank slate of detachment disappeared. Unconsciously, she moved her bony fingers sequentially as if playing piano scales on her forearm.

"How's your mother?" Archer asked.

"We're not supposed to discuss her," Bill said.

"That's right," Lucy added, squeezing Archer's hand a little tighter.

"I'm sorry," he replied. "I forgot."

"It's okay, though," Avery said, looking nervously at her father. "I appreciate that you've asked. She's brave, braver than I'd ever be. She tells me she's okay, but that's just what she's always done: protecting me, not wanting me to worry even though I'm responsible."

Archer nodded.

"Her trial date is set for October." She leaned back on the settee.

Nobody spoke for several moments. The reference to Faith seemed to have stifled whatever progress the conversation was making. Lucy's glance fluctuated between Archer and Avery. There was an uncanny resemblance in their mannerisms, as well as their physical features. No one would doubt that Morgan had strong genes.

Suddenly Archer tucked his legs beneath him and leaned forward, agitated. "This is beyond awkward, and I'm sorry. It's incredibly stilted. Here we are sitting across from each other being monitored by your dad and the investigating cop who happens to be my girlfriend, and we're all here because of a woman who happened to be our mother but who neither of us knew. I'm not sure what I wanted to accomplish when I set this up. I somehow thought we should meet with . . . with everything that's happened."

"Or maybe you wanted to follow through on her wishes," Avery offered. "Morgan's, that is."

"As if what she wanted should matter." His tone was bitter.

Avery shrugged, stood, and walked to the window. Turning the handle, she tilted the lower pane open, letting in a peal of laughter and the sounds of two children talking and giggling. "Daddy, Daddy, catch me!"

"Ready or not, here I come!" The reply wafted up from the street.

"She wanted us to understand, you know; that's why

she wanted us to meet." Avery spoke with her back facing the room. "I think she thought if we were together, we'd somehow come to accept the choices she'd made. Kind of a 'Look, it's nothing personal. See? I abandoned all my kids.'"

"Safety in numbers," said Archer.

Archer's comment prompted Avery to turn back around. "Is there such a thing? But I do know that she didn't want us to think badly of her. She begged me several times not to hate her." She lowered her voice. "The problem is that I couldn't help it."

"Avery," Bill cautioned, fearing that she was about to tread into dangerous territory once again.

"It's okay, Dad. Nothing more can happen to me now," she said without a hint of defiance. Instead her tone was sad, resigned. "What mattered to me most, my family, has been destroyed. And I'm to blame."

"Foster's suicide, your mother's and my separation, those had nothing to do with you," Bill said, as if he'd recited that mantra a thousand times.

"And what about Marissa?"

Bill started at the mention of his lover.

"She moved out because I was moving in."

"It had nothing to do with you or anything that . . . had happened. It was only to make room," Bill said, unconvincingly. He turned to his guests. "This apartment is quite small, as you can see. But once the Gladwyne house sells, we'll consider something bigger for all of us."

Lucy wanted to ask whom "us" included, but she refrained. No doubt the answer was unknowable until Faith's trial concluded.

"Morgan told me she'd tried to kill herself once," Avery said, matter-of-factly, ignoring her father's attempt at comfort. "She showed me the scars on her wrist, as if I needed proof. I think it was her way of demonstrating that her choices had been difficult for her, or at least that they had had consequences. Then she wanted to talk about Foster, his depression, and whether I suffered from it, too. She claimed she'd been taking some psych medications herself. It was as though she wanted to identify with him, with me, with our problems. But all of it made me realize one thing. Being a mother isn't a job. It's either who you are or it's not. Does that make sense?"

Mrs. O'Malley's image flashed in Lucy's mind, their conversation about the parable of King Solomon and the story of Michael and the boiling water. *I wasn't a hero. I'm a mother.* Those had been her words.

"Look at what my mother's done—my real mother. Giving or not giving birth had nothing to do with the way she treats me or treated us. She'd give up her own life—literally—to help me. I know I am very lucky to have been given parents who wanted me, who would protect me, or at least try."

Lucy cringed inside. Given Archer's feelings toward his own father, she knew Avery's words jabbed. Bill and Faith Herbert had done everything in their power to overcome a biological reality, but she was not at all sure Archer would give Rodman that much credit; he'd done little if anything to compensate for an absent mother. Meanwhile, in many respects she'd taken her own parents for granted. She'd never considered other possibilities or how destructive they could be.

"I should have appreciated what I had," Avery said. "That was my problem. It sounds Pollyanna, but I feel that way now. I should never have sought more information. The little bit we'd been told destroyed my brother. I should have let Morgan make her overture. I didn't have to respond. She would have gone away, disappeared into the world she'd been in before. But I thought that knowing some biological truth was the key to unlocking the mystery of my brother and his mental illness. I was wrong. No discovery of some great truth about our bloodline was going to bring him back or make me whole."

The color had left Bill's face. He covered his mouth with his fist and looked at the floor.

Avery took a few steps toward the settee and rested her hands on its back. She leaned over the top toward Archer. "But I apologize to *you*. Because of what I did, she's gone, whether you would have wanted to know her or not. And for that I am really and truly sorry, more sorry than you can possibly know. You should have been able to make your own choice."

"I already had," Archer mumbled.

"But you planned to meet her—meet us—on Sunday, or at least she said you hadn't told her you wouldn't be there. I went to the Liberty Bell at eleven, wondering whether you'd show up or whether you already knew." She nodded slightly toward Lucy. "I took away your chance. That's what I have to live with."

Avery seemed to collapse beside her father, and she rested her head on his shoulder. Despite the maturity of her words, sitting tucked beneath his wing she appeared young, fragile, and lost.

Nobody spoke. After several moments, Archer reached forward and poured himself some lemonade. He took a long sip.

"Avery will pay her debt to society," Bill said halfheartedly. "She'll do community service. Lots of it."

"What did you work out with probation?" Lucy asked.

"I'm going to be helping kids—little kids—who have difficulty with mobility. They're on crutches or have braces. One adorable little girl is paralyzed. And I'll help them learn to horseback-ride."

"Will you use your own horse?"

"No. It's a stable where the animals have been trained very carefully. Mine is way too green. Or I should say, wild," she added to clarify. "These horses are amazing. They have a sixth sense for what the children need. They seem so happy to offer up the use of their own legs, their own movement."

"It sounds inspiring."

"I think it is—or will be. I want to be able to give them a sense of freedom and of security at the same time. And a sense of hope." Her eyes sparkled at the prospect.

"Maybe I should sign up," Archer said without looking up.

"Shouldn't we all," Lucy added.

Lucy and Archer ambled along Lawrence Court and turned east onto Pine Street. The mugginess had cleared, and the late-afternoon sun shone on their faces. The good-bye had been strained, with neither Avery nor Archer suggesting further communication. Archer had said nothing since they'd left Bill and Avery's apartment, but after several blocks, he reached his arm around Lucy and held her waist. His long legs against her shorter ones made their stride awkward, and she struggled to lengthen her step.

Although there wasn't a car in sight, at the crosswalk they stopped for a red light.

"Are you angry?" Lucy asked. It had been the question she'd wanted to ask since the day of Avery's arrest.

"What do you mean?"

"I was thinking about what Avery said, about depriving you of a choice to reconsider your relationship with your mother."

He shrugged. "I don't know what I feel. Her point was odd, at least to me. I never think of a child choosing a parent. Isn't it that what you're born with is what you get? Even in her case, it's not as though she got to interview the prospective candidates for adoption."

"There is that adage about picking your friends."

"And a lot of people do. More and more people I know have cast off their blood relatives because they're too complicated or too painful or just too awful. They get married and start again."

"Yeah. And their kids won't want anything to do with them," Lucy said, smiling. "It's a law of nature. It's called family."

Archer chuckled in agreement. The light turned green and they stepped into the street. He stared at the pavement ahead of him as he spoke. "For years, I was so filled with rage at what my mother had done to me—and my father, too—that I could almost imagine having done it myself. That kind of pain, the feelings of abandonment and betrayal, could make almost anyone violent."

"But there's a difference. You weren't. You aren't."

Archer shrugged dismissively. "And at the same time, yes, I am mad at Avery. I feel victimized by her crime. Whether she intended to kill or whatever the legalism is doesn't matter because the result is the same. Morgan's mistreatment of us doesn't justify what Avery did. Nothing could. Even I'm rational enough to grasp that concept. So I guess the answer to your question is that I'm waffling between understanding and anger. And at this point, I can't predict where I'll come out in the end."

"There may never be an end to how you feel. Or at least that's what I'm coming to learn. The best you can do is to live with the ambiguity. It's not in my nature, but I hope for your sake it's in yours." She clasped his hand in hers as they walked along, their arms swaying synchronously.

32

October

The courtroom was packed every day of the trial. Each morning Faith appeared at the defense table, impeccably groomed, the only sign of her anxiety the ever-darkening rings under her eyes. Each day she scanned the audience for her daughter, not realizing that Avery had spent most of the trial in a jail cell several stories below where she herself sat facing the judge. Avery had been held in contempt of court early on in this proceeding for failing to take the stand against her mother, an act that had made the prosecutor consider petitioning the court for the revocation of the plea agreement.

Ned Sparkman, the lead attorney on Faith's three-member defense team, hadn't told his client about the contempt. He feared it would compel her to testify in her daughter's defense, if not her own. But whether she sensed Avery's trouble or simply insisted on speaking to the jury, Faith had taken the witness stand, sworn an oath on the Bible, and told her story.

The afternoon after he'd heard her testimony, Judge Wickham dismissed the contempt proceeding and released Avery. At the hearing, he stated that he found the plea agreement reprehensible. "Despite its otherwise favorable terms, no competent member of the defense bar should have accepted a plea that required this girl to assist the government in the prosecution of her mother." Santoros wasn't about to file an appeal given the strong language of the court's decision. Avery's counsel left the courtroom without even so much as a handshake with her client.

Sitting in the front row, Lucy was mesmerized, listening to Faith's words hour after hour throughout the last day of trial. Faith's voice was sweet, and at times she appeared lost in thought, oblivious to the seven men and five women who sat in judgment. "A friend of mine once said how relieved she was that her son was back at school. She wanted him out of the house. She wanted the free time. And I remember thinking to myself, Is she insane or am I? Doesn't she understand that this miracle of childhood passes so quickly? There's nothing more precious." Faith wiped her eyes with a handkerchief. "And that was what Dr. Reese gave me. She'd given me motherhood. And then she wanted to take it away."

She described in detail all that had transpired. After receiving Morgan's letter, Bill Herbert had insisted that they share the information with Avery. At first their daughter seemed interested, curious perhaps, willing to listen to an explanation. Much to Faith's disappointment, Avery wanted to go into the city to see Morgan's office and to have lunch. Apparently it was on that day that she had told Morgan of her sorrow at leaving her childhood home. Her parents were divorcing; her mother couldn't afford to stay in the Gladwyne mansion. So Morgan set out to buy it through a secret trust.

"She wanted everything that was mine," Faith explained. "That included my home. It is hard for me to articulate what a scary feeling it was to see everything I cared about, but most especially my daughter, being taken away. I have no graduate education, no profession. No newspaper was writing of my accomplishments. My husband had already found success and ambition more attractive than shared experience, or caregiving. I feared that I couldn't compare in Avery's eyes, that I would fall short, that I would be the inferior mother."

After a few visits and telephone calls back and forth, Morgan promised Avery that she would produce her biological father, too. It was hard to imagine Avery's emotions at having her history unlocked. "She seemed excited, or at least intrigued. Who wouldn't be given the circumstances? Bill had set the relationship in motion, and I had to sit back and watch. It wouldn't have been fair of me to tell Avery how hurt I was."

But then Morgan offered a gift: the framed self-portrait of Foster, one of twelve charcoal images he'd drawn not long before his death. After that, Avery's response changed. It was then that she told Faith what had happened, the disclosures she'd made. She apologized for opening up to a stranger. "I never meant to betray you, Mommy," she said. That was all Faith needed to hear: *Mommy,* the magical word. And that was when Avery produced the letter.

My dearest Avery—

You've always understood me without my ever needing to explain, but I know this final act will be difficult and painful, if not incomprehensible. I've never felt I belonged, except with you. I can't ask you to stay home, to live with me, but you made life bearable, which made our inevitable separation unbearable. I don't belong in this family. My whole life I've had the sense of disorientation, disconnection maybe is a better word, but when Dad and Mom told us about the adoption, it reinforced that in me. I wasn't supposed to be here. I don't even know who I am.

I wanted to use my psychiatrist's gun. He has one in his office. He told me about it as if he were proud. You'd know who said that pride comes before the fall. You're the brains in our duo. I can't remember. But I did want it, that handgun. Maybe if I used it, he'd stop apologizing, stop making excuses for everyone. Maybe then he'd blame his stupid advice instead. But I never got the opportunity because he watched me like a hawk, as if he knew I might be considering the very act I was.

I had to do this. I didn't know how else to get rid of what I couldn't bear. Whoever that woman was— our real mother—she abandoned us, and I've been drifting ever since. I'd say she shouldn't have had us, except now the world is graced by you, but otherwise I hate her; I hate what she's done. If you ever meet her, if she ever comes looking for you, be sure to tell her how much pain she caused.

It was signed by her "loving brother Foster."

Faith didn't know her daughter had left boarding school that fateful weekend until she got a call around eleven o'clock. Avery was in trouble. She was almost incomprehensible in her hysteria.

Faith blamed Morgan. It was Morgan's fault, Morgan's insensitivity that put Avery in such a tumultuous situation. Morgan didn't know how to be a mother. She had let the girl drink wine when she'd taken her to dinner even though she was underage. She didn't realize that being a parent and being a friend were two separate roles. She let Avery drive her car even though she had no license and had yet to complete a driver's education course. It was irresponsible, more than irresponsible in light of the onslaught of emotions that charged the evening. She was more concerned with winning Avery over than maintaining appropriate boundaries.

After Tripp Nichols didn't show up at the restaurant, Avery asked to go to where he was—to see the club that was so important to him that he'd stood them up. Seeing him, seeing them both—it was all too much. Neither had ever really cared about this impressionable teenager.

The car accident hadn't been intended. Avery wasn't thinking clearly. She pushed the accelerator and crashed into a tree. But no one was hurt. The baseball bat was in the back of the car, and she'd used it to vent her rage. She was young, perhaps drunk, and destroyed by all that had happened, just as the court-appointed psychiatrist said. She'd lost her brother because of this woman. Her own family had fallen apart. Who could blame her for losing control? Hitting Morgan was an accident. She never meant to inflict harm. Morgan had put herself between a confused girl swinging wildly and a car. She may have been unconscious, but she was still breathing when Faith arrived. "She was absolutely alive," Faith stated without flinching.

It was Faith who fired the shot, who staged the suicide, who cleaned up the crime scene, who took her daughter home. "I needed to protect her. I wanted to protect her. I was watching my daughter be tortured. And I was tortured, too. I made it look like a suicide because . . . because that is a consequence I've seen. It's a death I know."

Throughout her hours of testimony, she never revealed how she'd had access to David Ellery's gun. The only possible explanation was that Avery, who'd known of its existence from Foster's letter, had taken it when visiting Reese's office and had it with her that night, intending to use it. But Faith would never admit to that degree of premeditation on the part of her daughter, and only repeated vaguely—and possibly perjuriously—that she'd had it for a while. Even on cross-examination, she conceded nothing, and Santoros didn't press. She had the matching bullets; she'd brought extra bullets in case the first didn't accomplish its goal. He had a fingerprint and a blood-type match. He had the coat. And she'd confessed. He'd demonstrated the requisite intent.

"Being a mother is everything to me. It's all I ever wanted. It's who I am. It's who I've been. Morgan Reese tried to take that from me twice. She succeeded once."

The jury was out and the court recessed. The court officer had ordered in sandwiches for the jurors to eat before they began deliberations. Faith had thrown herself at the mercy of twelve citizens, and all any of them could do was wait.

The gray sky hovered low over the courthouse steps. Lucy and Jack debated whether to return to the Roundhouse. Santoros would surely page them as soon as the court officer announced that the jury had reached a verdict. There was no doubt work to be done, another case to begin, or a lead from an existing file to follow. But it was hard to concentrate on anything else. Whether Faith's torment, whether her candor, would pay off in a reduction of the charge to second degree or even manslaughter was out of the prosecution's hands and in the jurors' hearts.

"Lucy."

The familiar voice startled her. Rodman Haverill stood at the bottom of the steps. He wore a trench coat and a canvas hat, and her immediate impression was that he'd attempted a flasher disguise. She almost laughed.

"May I have a word with you?" he called up.

Lucy looked at Jack. "I'll wait around here," he said, turning to head back inside. "Keep your pager on."

She hurried down the steps. "There's no verdict yet," she said, assuming that was the reason for his appearance. No doubt he'd read in the paper that today the jury would receive their instructions from Judge Wickham and begin their deliberations. The story in the *Inquirer* from the day before had included an almost verbatim recitation of the powerful closing arguments.

He shook his head. "That's not why I'm here."

Lucy said nothing, waiting for him to explain.

"I underestimated you, and I want to apologize. I appreciate all you've done."

She smiled. "It's my job, sir."

"Finding Morgan's killer might be your job. Dealing with destroyed families is something else entirely. Handling Archer and me is certainly beyond the call of duty. And you've done it more than gracefully. Perhaps I've waited a bit too long, but I've come to the realization nonetheless that the Haverill clan could use a bit of the O'Malley influence." His smile distorted his face, as if his features weren't familiar with the expression. "But the second reason I've come is on Archer's behalf. We've been at my lawyer's office this morning. He wanted to come to meet you himself, but there was some problem, some problem with the cooling system, that required his immediate attention. I tried to talk him out of it but . . . well, you surely appreciate that business better than I." He waved his hand, dismissing the problem. "So I've come in his place."

He removed his hat and stuffed it into his pocket. "I'll cut to the chase. Because of the Herbert girl's role in Morgan's death, she cannot be a beneficiary of the life insurance policy. Archer doesn't want the money—neither his allotted share nor the full amount that he now receives given the circumstances." He paused, and their eyes met. "Perhaps he spoke out of turn, but he told me of your brother—or rather of your sorrow over the loss of your brother. Archer wants to establish a commemorative foundation, a foundation that would cover the cost of psychiatric treatment and medication for adolescent males. It would be there to make sure that at least some of the millions of boys in trouble aren't denied access to care because of a lack of funds."

Lucy felt her heart pounding. Foster Herbert had had all the care money could buy, but others didn't. The interest on $10 million alone could help hundreds. Maybe it wouldn't change a single statistic, but she wanted to believe it could.

"Frankly, it's also consistent with something that would have pleased his mother. As you know, her estate was left to the Medical School. The money will be used for grants, grants to continue the pediatric research that she made her life—or I should say that she gave up so much of her life for." His voice softened. "Archer suggested his foundation be called the Aidan Foundation. He wanted to surprise you, but I thought that was improper. I thought it imperative that you have choice in the matter. Not every family is brave enough to expose its secrets."

A legacy in her brother's honor, one that her parents and their community couldn't begin to afford to do on their own, but one that would live on in an effort to spare others what the O'Malleys had suffered.

"It's a remarkable gesture," she said, feeling overwhelmed. "For once I'm not quite sure what to say. Aidan would be very pleased. I wish he could have met Archer, and you, too. Thank you, thank you both."

"No. It is we who must thank you."

He extended his arms, and she stepped forward into his embrace, feeling his stiff posture finally relax as she squeezed a little harder.

Please turn this page
for a preview of
Nancy Geary's new novel

BEING
MRS. ALCOTT

Now available
in hardcover.

$\mathcal{U}$ndergarments are like seasonal slipcovers; they need to be replaced every six months." Her mother, the late Eleanor Montgomery, had issued this directive so many times over the years it had become a mantra. And Grace remembered it perfectly now. "God forbid an accident befalls you, and someone you don't know should discover you or attempt a rescue." She'd even received the instruction on her wedding day almost forty years ago, just as she'd been arranging the thin diamond tiara amid her golden curls. That time her mother had leaned forward so that her own handsome face shared the mirror with her daughter's, opened her chestnut eyes wider than usual, and whispered, "Imagine if there were a stain!"

Every first of June and September Grace had heeded her mother's warning and purchased all new brassieres and underpants. She'd never had the courage to raise the obvious question. She'd simply accepted that worrying about impropriety after death was just as worthwhile as worrying about it ahead of time. And today of all days, she didn't feel like gambling that a corpse couldn't be embarrassed. Not after Dr. Preston's news.

Over the years, she'd always selected the same Swiss brand, the same cotton fabric, and the same colors. She bought three matching sets in white and three in nude. At one point just around her fiftieth birthday, she'd debated black, but ultimately rejected it as impractical. So her choices remained uninspired, but the lingerie was well made and feminine without being tawdry. When she'd moved from Boston to Cape Cod four years before, she'd found a small shop in Osterville that carried exactly what she'd been able to find at Neiman Marcus in Copley Place. And so the tradition continued uninterrupted, the new undergarments being folded neatly into the top drawer of her bureau along with a fresh lavender sachet, and the old being wrapped in a paper bag and discarded in the kitchen trash.

But this month she'd been distracted, preoccupied. As the engine of her taupe sedan idled at the exit to the covered parking lot at Massachusetts General Hospital, she'd suddenly realized that today was the fifth of June, and that the task hadn't been accomplished. Something in the parking attendant's face had reminded her even as her hand trembled reaching into her purse for change. Perhaps it was the girl's youth, the freshness about her smooth chocolate skin and neatly braided plaits that conjured a sense of optimism. Grace wouldn't be wasting money. Regardless of what might befall her, in whatever state she might be found, she wouldn't compromise now.

Although she made her resolution to adhere to her biannual ritual, she hadn't been able to face Mrs. Worthington, the proprietor of A Woman's Elegance: Discerning Lingerie for the Discerning Woman. White-haired Mrs. Worthington had a small, neat shop on Main Street with lace curtains in the storefront window, a powder-pink, upholstered slipper chair in the dressing room, and a large plaque proclaiming her membership in the AARP above the register. She'd offer to model some form-fitting, curvature-slenderizing, tuck-the-tummy lingerie, despite the fact that Grace had no hips or stomach to hide. Or she'd produce an absurdly suggestive nightgown they both knew Grace wouldn't consider. Each time this happened, Grace would smile politely and shake her head. Then Mrs. Worthington would return the garment on its quilted hanger back to the rack with a look of disappointment on her face. "It's never too late to add a little spice to your life."

Normally, Grace welcomed the familiarity, the camaraderie, but not today. She feared Mrs. Worthington might be able to read her face as clearly as if her forehead flashed a newsreel. She didn't want to be questioned. She didn't want to risk breaking down, bursting into tears, falling to her knees, losing control of herself. All she wanted was fresh underwear.

And so she'd ended up at the ghastly Cape Cod Mall, a place no sane person would ever want to visit, let alone patronize. But she'd wanted anonymity, and Filene's had a lingerie department.

The sprawling cement-block building was unmanageably huge, and as the automatic doors swung open, she wondered for a moment whether she could lose herself inside. Had she found an abyss off Exit 6 that would swallow her whole leaving nothing but her parked car outside as the only trace of her existence? The thought of poor Bain struggling in that circumstance almost made her laugh. She could not imagine her husband attempting to find her here. Elegant Bainbridge Forest Alcott, II, in his blue blazer, golf shirt, white trousers, and driving moccasins had rarely crossed the Bass River since he'd retired to Chatham. He'd stayed east of Exit 9, enjoying the peaceful off-seasons and the social summers, lowering his handicap from an eleven to an eight, admiring the harbor view, and swimming laps in his heated pool. Navigating this parking lot would be traumatic: a venture inside the mall to retrieve his wife would be hell, perhaps a worse hell for him than letting her disappear.

Filene's was nearly empty. At two o'clock on a Friday in early June, the lunchtime shoppers were gone and the summer hordes hadn't arrived. She read the store directory and navigated the escalator only to wander through tightly spaced racks and racks of leisure wear and weekend wear, designer sections filled with brands she'd never heard of. She stopped to examine the clothes: bright-colored business suits with faux pockets and handkerchiefs sewn in, coordinated tops with large bows at the neck, slacks that came with attached gold-buckled belts, loosely woven acrylic sweaters, and acid-washed jeans. It seemed a sea of colors and textures and labels, an array of merchandise priced at

$99.99 or $59.99 or two for $79.99. Finally, she spotted pajamas off in the distance and honed in on her destination. She knew then she was close.

Forty-five minutes later, Grace stared at the Formica counter where she'd piled her six packages of Jockey for Her. It was an odd choice, especially given her allergy to horses. She'd never worn underwear that came sealed in plastic, but she couldn't find her usual brand and the package said these were cotton, or at least mostly so, give or take a small percentage of spandex. Plus the model on the front with a towel around her neck and her bottom tilted toward the shopper looked alluring. Would that sex appeal rub off, hide her varicose veins and tighten the loose skin that draped from her backside? She wished she could envelop her whole body in a single transforming garment, a youth-producing unitard, anything to turn back the clock, even just to yesterday.

The checkout girl with an artificial stripe of red hair down the middle of her otherwise brown locks swiped her American Express card twice without success. "The magnetized strip must have gotten wet," Grace offered weakly, even as she sensed that there might be a more ominous explanation. And so the girl, whose badge identified her as Kim, called for authorization.

After reading off the account number, Kim seemed to be placed on hold. Several minutes transpired. To pass the time, the girl picked at something in her teeth with her long black fingernail and then stared at the underside of the nail in an effort to discern what the particle was. Finally, she said, "Yeah. Okay," as she glanced at Grace with a stern expression. Replacing the receiver, she opened a drawer under the counter, removed a large pair of black-handled scissors, and cut the plastic card in two.

"What are you doing?" Grace asked, even as she realized it was too late.

"You want the halves?" Kim extended a hand.

"I . . . I," she stammered.

"They told me to do it. AmEx isn't a credit card."

She felt dizzy. Bain dealt with all the bills. He'd always kept the checkbook, never delegating the task to a secretary or assistant even when he had one. He liked organization. He liked the control that came with knowing exactly what came in and what was spent. Although she knew there were problems—he'd explained as much in urging her to be careful with her personal expenditures—she never would have expected something so dire.

"I've been a member for decades," she pleaded, as if Kim held the power to change a corporation's mind. *Membership has its privileges.* What kind of a promise was that if it was revoked at the tiniest hint of difficulty?

"You've still got to pay on time."

Grace felt as though she might collapse. She looked around, wondering who else had witnessed her humiliation.

A heavyset black woman waiting patiently behind her with an armload of merchandise smiled knowingly. "You should think about a MasterCard."

"Yes. Yes. I'm sure you're right." She stared at the

two pieces of her credit card that Kim had placed on the counter in front of her. She remembered clearly the day Bain had given it to her just after they were married. It had been linked to his, two cards on the same account, the sort of permanent convenience a husband and wife should have. Now the scissor cut separated the *T*s from the rest of her last name, the name she'd taken from her husband along with the card.

Alco. It sounded like a cleaning service or a dog food.

She grabbed the halves and slid them into the interior pocket of her purse. "I'm sorry for the inconvenience," she managed to say. "It won't happen again."

The mall's interior was a mass of fluorescent and neon bulbs reflecting a glare onto the black floor tiles. Grace stared at the industrial strength planters, each potted with some species of palm willing to grow without a hint of natural light. The piped-in, overhead music mixed with a blare of sound from a nearby record store. Leaning against a planter for balance, she watched as a gum-chewing couple walked by, the girl seemingly oblivious to the fact that her boyfriend had his hand down the back of her pants.

"Noooo. No." She heard a high-pitched wail.

A mother dragged two crying children toward the exit. With a look of utter desperation, the woman in a shirt with a plunging V-neck and jeans that hugged her wide hips yanked on their small arms even as they both collapsed to the floor. "Just wait till I tell your daddy how bad you are," she snarled. "You'll be sorry then."

Her threat only made the little girl with light brown hair and dirty knees scream louder.

"I've a mind to spank you right here and now, you little brat."

The mother released the arm of her son and, with her free hand, slapped the girl on the side of her head. The small child looked up, momentarily silenced. Her cheeks were streaked with tears.

The girl sniffled several times, wiped her nose with her T-shirt, and then took her brother's hand. They shuffled just in front of their mother, who had lit a cigarette even though prominent signs throughout the mall proclaimed that smoking was prohibited. The mother swatted at the girl's head several more times as they slowly moved toward the exit.

Grace felt the sudden urge to sweep the crying girl and her sibling up in her arms and comfort them both. A daughter. A healthy little girl, who needed a bubble bath, a glass of warm milk, a bedtime story to make her sadness go away. Perhaps *The Lonely Doll* since she resembled its sweet heroine, Edith, and could think the book had been written about her. She could tuck her into the canopy bed with a feather duvet, adjust the little angel nightlight, and pull the pink-and-yellow-flowered drapes. Grace could share the nightly ritual she craved, the simple tasks of which she'd dreamed, with this little stranger.

Didn't this unkempt woman realize how lucky she was?

But instead Grace walked away. There was nothing she could possibly do to help, and no doubt publicly embarrassing the mother would only exacerbate the situation when they were behind the closed doors of their two-bedroom Cape.

She tried to distract herself by staring at the window displays of the variety of low-end shops. Athletic shoes. Plastic beach tumblers. Sun visors and caps. Fragranced candles in tub pots.

"We need more tests. It's too soon to tell anything conclusively. Why don't you take the weekend, talk to Bain, and call me on Monday? I've scheduled an appointment with a specialist, but it's not until Wednesday." Dr. Preston had a calm, collected tone, the sort that reminded Grace of voice-overs for investment commercials. There was a certain reassurance in such low male timbres. *Your retirement fund is safe. Your husband will take care of everything. You'll live to be a hundred.*

Staring at the series of X-rays on the light board that hung on the wall, she didn't believe a word.

Grace stepped through the entrance of Victoria's Secret and was consumed by the sweet-smelling perfumes, the bordello lighting, the salesladies with curled hair and black dresses. Tucked into alcoves along the pink-striped walls were nightgowns, shorties, pajamas, and bathrobes in all styles, colors, and sizes. Satin push-up bras and lace thongs hung from plastic hangers. Throughout the store, scantily clad dummies modeled styles that would make a Vegas dancer blush. She wondered whether this display was designed to appeal to the women who would wear such garments, to attract the men who wished they would, or to titillate the prurient browsers.

Round tables were piled high with panties. Size small was on top. Grace reached for a single pair of red underwear with lace covering the entire front.

She stepped up to the cashier and handed a twenty dollar bill to the attractive blonde with full lips.

"Will this be all?"

Grace did not reply.

"If you buy two, you get one free," she said in chirpy voice.

She stared again at the wisp of fabric. "No, thank you."

One was quite enough for her purpose.